"Splendid!" —*Newsweek*

"Stephen Becker stuns me. He just knocks me out . . . *THE BLUE-EYED SHAN* is . . . blue-blooded literature and bone-stirring entertainment!" —*Detroit News*

"As exciting as *Raiders of the Lost Ark*." —*Publishers Weekly*

"Reads like a cross between Joseph Conrad and James Clavell." —Houston *Chronicle*

"As entertaining as Robert Ludlum." —*Roanoke Times & World News*

"A kind of miracle . . . Becker handles everything . . . with consummate mastery." —Archibald MacLeish

(Continued on next page)

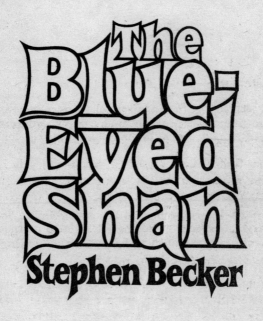

The Blue-Eyed Shan

Stephen Becker

TOR

A TOM DOHERTY ASSOCIATES BOOK

THE BLUE-EYED SHAN
Copyright©1982 by Stephen Becker
Map Copyright©1982 by Rafael D. Palacios
Reprinted by arrangement with Random House, Inc.

A Tor Book

Published by Tom Doherty Associates, 8-10 W. 36th St., New York, New York 10018

First printing, November 1983

ISBN: 0-812-58075-3
CAN. ED.: 0-812-58076-1

Printed in the United States of America

Distributed by Pinnacle Books, 1430 Broadway, New York, N. Y. 10018

FOR RON MYERS

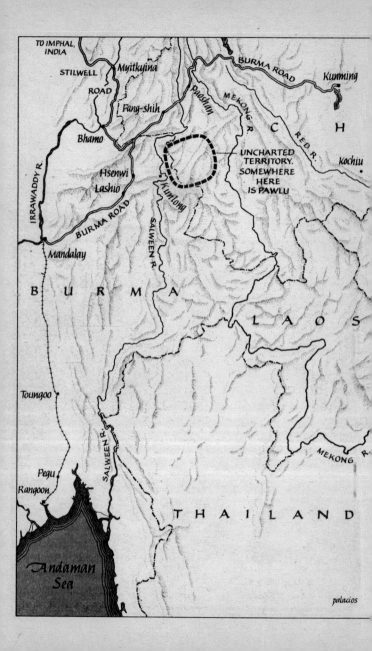

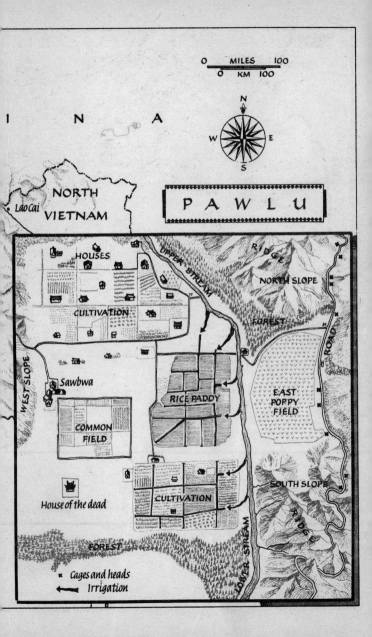

CHINA

North Vietnam

Lao Cai

PAWLU

HOUSES

UPPER STREAM

RIDGE

NORTH SLOPE

CULTIVATION

FOREST

WEST SLOPE

Sawbwa

RICE PADDY

EAST POPPY FIELD

ROAD

COMMON FIELD

House of the dead

CULTIVATION

SOUTH SLOPE

RIDGE

FOREST

LOWER STREAM

Cages and heads
Irrigation

Stephen Becker

The Blue-Eyed Shan

1

Ranga

The tame Wa are like pye-dogs, they will slink and snarl and grin for a bone. But the Wild Wa dwell high upon the mountain and smile for no man. Their villages are set in swales and dingles, tiny valleys off the ridges, and the entrances at either end are planted with dense thorny hedge, and the way in or out is crooked and winding. It was not always so. When the rifle came to these hills, men with swords, knives and even crossbows had to change their ways. No rifle can see through a Wild Wa hedge, and no bullet can wend the mazy way.

The Wild Wa are a small people and dark, and so feared by their neighbors. Their villages are scattered for two hundred miles along the China-Burma border, and they have no name for either country. Ancient legend call them sons and daughters of the southern islands. They are a religious people, and observe both rites of passage and planting ritual. A young man becomes a warrior by lopping an enemy head from an enemy body. An enemy is anyone who is not a Wild Wa, and it is customary to do this lopping after the monsoon, at the sowing of new seed. The heads do not immediately become skulls. The flesh is treated with preservatives known only to the elders of the tribe, the secret of which is passed along only when an elder dies and only to a mature male who has distinguished himself in headhunting. Upon treatment with these preservatives, a head will last many years.

After the entrance has been negotiated, the visitor or captive will notice the axis of the village, a long line or double line of trees. These trees are usually oak, which grows profusely above the line of occasional frost, and drinks less rain than the teak and pyinkado of the lower slopes and valleys. Into these trees niches have been cut; if the avenue is a double line of trees, the niches will face inward, and in these niches the heads are placed, so that a stroller along the avenue will walk between two rows of impassive faces, the flesh contracted, the eyes dulled. At the village of Ramoang, and also at Hsan Htung, there are avenues of two hundred heads.

At Ranga, which is not far from Pawlu, there are only fifty heads in a single row. Some are precious, and inspire greater awe than the others. The hair of one is yellow, its eyes blue. It has been embalmed and lacquered, and will last a while. At dusk the children of the village gather to contemplate it, and the headman explains that this was a wise man, who came from a far place, and whose virtues have passed to the village. It was Thuan-yi the warrior who took this head, in the War of the Bones, and many evenings he comes to stand idly by as the headman preaches, and the headman feigns not to see him, but finally does see him, and starts, and says, Ah yes, and here is Thuan-yi, who in single combat vanquished this blue-eyed Shan.

And then the headman turns to another precious relic.

2
The Lashio Road In

For and a half years after World War II, Greenwood remarked that he might never have entered China, there was no way to be sure, but that he had spent much of his life banging at the back door, along the Burma border.

"I could set you down on the spot," Gordon-Cumming said. "All I need is that half-mile of straight road."

"No, I won't go in blind," Greenwood said. He had encountered a few like this one, former proprietors of the world, lanky, sandy-haired, eyes like a loch in winter, and half the globe blushing pink with their conquests.

"Just as well, I suppose. The whole country's one great skirmish. The Union of Burma! Like the bloody Irish Free State. Irishmen of Asia, they say the Burmese are."

"The Kachin want their own nation. Shan sawbwas bow to no man."

"At least the Kachin were loyal. These Shan—" The Englishman shook his head. "We need more gin. Boy!"

The houseboy materialized.

"More gimlets. You make 'em fresh. No pitchers, mind."

Greenwood murmured in South Shan, "They're very good. They suit this sort of day."

The houseboy glanced up in surprise, and found light eyes smiling into his own.

"What was that all about?"

"Oiling the tongue," Greenwood said. "Got to warm up, you know. Even calling hogs. Had an uncle who did that. Used to warm up five, ten minutes."

"Strange folk, Americans. You're from one of those barbarous states, I suppose."

"Missouri," Greenwood said. "Pellagra, ringworm and fornication."

"Yet you speak Shan."

"We like to make friends."

"You won't make many here. The Karen are on the warpath too, you know."

"Down south."

"All the Burmese feeling their oats. Shoot a white man as soon as look at him. Shooting each other too. A hundred thousand bandits in those hills, and a half million weapons left over from the war, and every village a fortress. The bigger towns aren't so bad."

"You seem safe and comfortable."

"It's this little airport," Gordon-Cumming said. "Airport's like a foreign country. Pilot's like an ambassador."

From the verandah they contemplated the graveled runway, low shed, wind sock; the Fairchild Argus; and the forlorn, decrepit, cannibalized P-40, an old Flying Tiger fighter, the shark's teeth still sharp. In the shade of the shed t

Burmese squatted, smoking. Beyond the airstrip the plain simmered, gently now in the cooler dry season, and mountains rose hazy green in the distance.

"Burmese who work around airports would fight to the death for them," Gordon-Cumming said. "Elite group, esprit de corps and all that. Well, I'll find you some sort of lorry, but you're wasting time. Have you there in ninety minutes by air. Damn good ship, that Argus. Seven-cylinder Jacobs. Damn good engine."

"Seven cylinders? I used to fool around with cars. Cylinders came in pairs."

"Radial," Gordon-Cumming said.

"Just so it flies, and just so you fetch me," Greenwood said. "The money's enough?"

"The money's delightful." Gordon-Cumming grinned like a horse. "What the devil are you up to, anyway?"

"Just a tourist."

"Not likely."

"Visiting old friends."

"More than that. Bloody spy."

Greenwood was amused. "Want the truth?"

"Nothing against it in principle."

"I'm chasing some old bones."

"Old bones? Nonsense. Fossils? That sort of thing?"

"Ever hear of Peking Man?"

Gordon-Cumming frowned. "Some Chinese fellow, I suppose."

"Some Chinese fellow."

"You one of these paleo-wallahs?"

"Not quite. An anthropologist."

"Nonsense. You're a soldier. Sticks out a mile."

Greenwood said, "You're sure we're talking about the same stretch of road?"

"Must be. The only straight stretch for fifty miles. Eerie sort of place, Pawlu, if it *is* Pawlu. Not on the RAF chart, you know, but it's on mine. Nice valley, but those Wa in the hills . . ." Gordon-Cumming shuddered elaborately. "Barbarous. Everything out here's barbarous. Do you know in parts of Pakistan if a woman's raped she's cast out by her husband? Now, what's a marriage for if not times like that? And there's others slit a nostril for adultery! Wouldn't be a nose left in London! And on the other side, the Kachin won't marry a virgin! Muslims cutting off thieves' hands! Cambodia-side they keep slaves, d'you know that? Tibet too."

Greenwood asked, "Why do you stay?"

"Oh well. Where's the boy? Where the hell are those gimlets? Ah!"

Soundlessly the houseboy set out their refreshment, bowing fractionally to Greenwood.

"Fact is," Gordon-Cumming confided, "left an awful wife in London. You?"

"No wife."

"Wise man. No need, out here. Besides, I'm a flyer. And the weather's so good. Even the bad weather's good. Rest up in the monsoon, that's all."

"I had a fine little woman in Pawlu." Greenwood could not repress a proud smile. "I have a daughter, too. She'll be close to ten now. Brought her a present, I have."

"Ten? Almost a woman, out here." Gordon-Cumming gargled absently. "Tell you what, soldier. I wouldn't go in there at all if I were you, bones or no bones, daughter or no daughter. Burma's not what she used to be."

"Neither am I," said Greenwood. "This is good gin."

"Going to seed in the colonies." Gordon-Cumming suddenly sounded cheerful. "Family's a bit stuffy, you know. Wouldn't want me back, really."

"No colony now."

"That's right. Sun sets on Gordon-Cumming. Last a few years yet. Unless— Tell me, those Chinese Communists won't cross the border, will they?"

"Won't have to," Greenwood said. "Burma has fourteen political parties and they're all Marxist."

"Let's just drink," Gordon-Cumming decided. "No religion or politics in the mess, all right?"

"That's half of life," Greenwood objected. "Religion and politics, love and money, what else is there?"

"Well, there's war."

"That's right," Greenwood said. "I was forgetting."

And now the Lashio Road again, Hsipaw, Lashio, familiar but subdued, dustier, flattened, worn, the roadside too, wood and bamboo huts, all used, trafficked, weathered, and if the road held firm and they were not blown up by guerrillas—

The jeep bucked and sprang off a large rock.

Greenwood hung on. His driver said, "Huu. Damn bad road." Greenwood removed the sunglasses and glanced warily at the jerricans behind him. He was happier on foot, or aboard a pony, than jouncing along a public highway with rebels in the hills and inflammables in the back seat. He imagined a sheet of flame, the jeep incinerated. He resigned himself, and admired the morning. The January air was invigorating, and the mountains welcomed him like liveried servants, green and brown and humble, nothing like the Rockies or the Himalayas, and he had already spotted a blue-red-and-yellow parakeet and a pair of gyi, the tiny graceful barking deer that swarmed over Burma.

"Shan tattoo?" His driver blew smoke; sparks danced back over the jerricans.

Greenwood fingered his collar. The khaki shirt flapped open in the breeze, revealing intricate whorls of red and black among the curly golden hair of his chest. Greenwood was a man of agreeable and honest appearance, stocky, tall, thick in the neck, curly-haired, his eyes direct, expressive and warm, so that the Burmese, a trim and polite people whom in general he loved, often went wide-eyed themselves with pleasure, recovered, and giggled in embarrassment.

"Yes. Shan."

"You talk Shan talk?" The driver was lithe and carefree, in his early twenties, a great smiler, a steady smoker of beedies. His gentle brown eyes seemed to express all that Greenwood loved about Burma and the Burmese: patience, good cheer, manners, the equanimity of a people who walked hand in hand with the gods. Greenwood had also seen them murder and pillage; government by assassination had for a few years become customary.

"Yes."

"South Shan, North Shan?"

"South Shan mainly."

"In war." The young man, Aung, was certain.

"In war, yes. And before."

"Lashio Road, plenty good. Railway soon too. Plenty bandit meantime." Aung wore a lance corporal's shirt, British leavings.

"Quiet lately," Greenwood said.

Aung agreed. "Plenty quiet."

Greenwood plucked a beedy—a brown leaf of Burmese tobacco rolled and tucked to make a small tasty cigarette—from his own shirt pocket and set a match to it; he blew out the match and let it cool before he dropped it overboard. They were driving northeast and the sun was friendly.

"You kill plenty Japanese?"

"Nobody likes to kill," Greenwood lied drowsily.

"Guerrillas like to kill."

"Well, that's politics."

"Wa people like to kill. You know Wa people?"

"Well, that's religion."

"So," Aung said triumphantly, "plenty people like to kill."

"You're right," Greenwood said.

The victory seemed to please Aung. He subsided, savoring his own wisdom. Greenwood seized the moment and offered up a comprehensive thanksgiving, for good health, for the Burmese climate, for this glorious morning, for General Yang's mad odyssey, for the fate that had called him, Greenwood, back here to the one corner of the world he would fight forever to keep free and green and unchanged. He was thirty-five years old and sound. Not a pimple. All humors, winds, inner construction admirably in tune. God, if any, had been good.

A few miles on, Aung asked, "You go Burma side or China side?"

"Nobody's sure," Greenwood said. "You know how it is up in the hills."

Aung nodded. "Okay. Salween side or Mekong side?"

"Well, somewhere in between," Greenwood said.

"You need trail man," Aung informed him.

"I'll find a guide."

"I find you good one."

"I'll do it, thanks," Greenwood said. "You find yourself some passengers for the drive back."

After a moment Aung said, "Plenty trouble China side."

Greenwood said, "Want to know a secret?"

Aung caught his breath. "You tell me. I no tell any man."

Greenwood said, "Plenty trouble Burma side too."

Aung considered this nugget, then looked reproachfully at his passenger. "That is humor."

"That is humor. You watch the road, please."

Aung was laughing. "Plenty trouble *every* side."

"That's the first rule," Greenwood said. "Plenty trouble every side."

They crossed the river Myitnge over a rusting

iron bridge; far behind them, back by Mandalay, the Myitnge would spill into the great Irrawaddy; Greenwood had once stood on the bank and marveled at that rushing confluence. Now they rolled into Hsenwi, a metropolis sprawled over all of forty acres: a rash of huts, a rushchoked river, perhaps a couple of thousand souls, paddy and tobacco fields along the outskirts, and stands of oak and chestnut. Among the town's earthen buildings and wooden stalls, tin sheds and Quonset huts asserted war, the foreigner, intrusion, but even these outlandish structures had settled in like old residents, and the town was placid.

Greenwood warmed to the sight of blue-smocked children with shaven heads, who scampered toward the river waving bamboo fishing rods; he remembered his daughter, and a fish in a reed basket. Far off on the lake he thought he made out storks. Men, women and children of many tribes strolled the town's main street and many alleys. Some wore headbands; these were called gaungbaung, and he remembered what the Americans had made of that. He saw Shan with turbans and tattoos, and many women in mantles of silver tassels and disks. He saw men in longyi—the Burmese wraparound skirt—who were clearly Chinese. Outside the shops fish-shaped kites hung, as if hooked and dying, in the still air. For the moment he saw no Occidental. Usually in these towns there lived a deserter or two, a wandering ex-Nazi, a French adventurer, most often a leftover Briton like Gordon-Cumming, too human now and sensible to swap Maymyo for Windsor.

He did see a holy man, bearded, the eyes fixed on eternity, the beggar's bowl hung from a simple cloth sash cinching a simple cloth skirt. A temple too, and he remembered it, of stone, which was here an accomplishment, a devotion, an offering of sweat.

"You stop zayat?"

"Not yet," Greenwood said. A zayat, often merely a raised platform, was here a resthouse for weary travelers; its establishment was a good work, another offering, among these Little Wheel Buddhists. "Let's start you back first."

"Zayat, you leave luggage. Easier walking then."

"Luggage. Humor." Greenwood removed his dark glasses and examined this driver. Aung's gaze shifted. "I wondered about your English. It's better than you pretend."

Aung said, "It is when I want it to be."

"I won't leave my luggage anywhere," Greenwood said. "It wouldn't last ten minutes."

Aung made fierce teeth. "At a zayat? With a priest?"

"A priest isn't a watchman and you know it. He worries about the other world. It's only a field pack and a tommy gun, and if they turned up missing he'd look sorrowful and tell me to shed material illusion. He wouldn't even bother to tell me my driver came back for them. Now head for the market."

Aung smirked, then laughed aloud. Greenwood allowed a small smile. Aung drove on, by luck and by horn. Greenwood commenced sweating; on the open road their speed had made breeze, but now they were crawling. Pye-dogs loped and grinned, snarled and yapped. Monstrous crows picked at carrion and drew themselves up like martyr priests, indignant but resigned, before taking scornful wing.

Lowland Burman merchants in colorful longyi embellished their own stalls like stands of flowers. Conversation ceased, haggling died, and lambent brown eyes welcomed the foreigner— was he rich? a spy? an official? A former soldier, perhaps, on pilgrimage to a field of victory or defeat.

"Watch the chickens," Greenwood said. "No hurry."

Aung protested: "Chickens only one rupee."

"One rupee alive. Five rupees when a car kills them. Or a four-hour argument. And don't lean on the horn."

"No horn?" Aung was astonished.

"I dislike unnecessary noise. Exercise the priestly virtues."

"Chastity?"

"Patience, humility and silence. It's a lovely day; why foul it? Look at those brocades. Silverwork there. River fish. I'm hungry. No fruit at this season?"

"Silver from the mines at Bawdwin," Aung said. "And look there, plenty fruit, bananas. Also blinded paddy birds in bamboo cages. And there by the table—a Jew-man."

"A Jew? In Hsenwi?"

"Plenty Jew-man Rangoon side."

"Where did they come from?"

"India."

Greenwood was gazing at a swarthy, lugubrious merchant with a small hawkish nose and eyes at once cheerful, alert and ironic. He wore a blue longyi with a black aingyi—a single-breasted jacket—and a black skullcap. Before him, on a broad table covered with white cotton, lay row upon row, heap beside heap, of pliers, small wrenches, machine screws and wood screws, hammers and nails, nuts and bolts, braces and bits; all this Greenwood took in as they crept by, and he thought he recognized a stack of the little paperboard rectangles on which thumbtacks are sold by the hundred.

They chugged on. Greenwood pointed: a corral, donkeys and ponies. Aung pulled up. The horse-master was a Shan, so Aung kept silence and turned expectantly to Greenwood, who said, "Greetings and blessings."

"Blessings and greetings." The Shan was sturdy with a scraggly mustache and pointed beard, and unruly sideburns.

"A fine season," Greenwood said. "Has there been rain in the hills?" Villagers drifted toward them.

"Little, little." The Shan seemed to realize abruptly that he was speaking his own tongue with a true foreigner; he made rabbit teeth and stared hard at Greenwood's eyes, side arm, khakis. "This is not the stranger's first arrival here."

"That is true," Greenwood said amiably. He wondered how far coincidence could stretch, and almost asked this man for news of the village of Pawlu in the valley of the Little River Mon, but decided not to declare himself without need. "I come from Lashio, and not for the first time."

"Perhaps the stranger fought the Japanese."

Greenwood answered immediately, "Yes." Not all Burmese, not all Shan, had fought the Japanese. Their earlier quarrel was with their English masters, and the Japanese, men of Asia, had come to expel the English. Nevertheless, truth was respected here, and Greenwood did not hesitate.

"As did my village," said the horse-master, and Greenwood breathed easier. A child shouted "See the yellow man!" and the townspeople laughed.

"What village was that?"

"Kawsu, not far from Kengtung."

"Then you are a long way from home."

"One travels; one trades."

"We have nothing to trade," Greenwood said, and he raised his voice to sow rumor, "but my friend must return to Lashio with this vehicle, and anyone who brings him a paying passenger will share the proceeds."

The crowd murmured: "Good." "Aha." "Reasonably said."

Aung spoke now, and his Shan was not good. "Best wait here by horse, or go zayat? Travel man come what place?"

"Few travelers here," said the sturdy Shan. "Better to try the zayat."

"Good sense," Greenwood thanked him. "Blessings and greetings, Horse-master."

"Greetings and blessings, traveler."

Aung kicked the motor into life. Cautiously they wove among the pye-dogs, children, gossips and flirtatious women, with Greenwood waving little salutes. "I forgot to ask, where is the zayat," Aung said.

"Close by the temple."

And the temple was close by the market, and Aung and Greenwood simply sat for a time, allowing curiosity seekers to gather. Greenwood was properly courteous to the aged and properly reserved with the tittering women, and he made a joke or two with the children, who were always more forthright. He also advertised Aung's return journey, and in half an hour Aung had made preliminary contact with one obvious opium runner and one rotund, chirping peanut wholesaler, and after five minutes apiece of enthusiastic haggling they settled in among the jerricans, immediately lighting white cheroots.

Greenwood paid Aung liberally, fifty rupees, and they shook hands in the Western fashion. There was a pause, as between two men who in other times might have become friends. Greenwood wished him a safe journey.

"And you too," Aung said. "Thank you for not speaking wog English."

The zayat was a large one, of bamboo and timber, one room about thirty feet by thirty with a thatched roof, a cooking fire on a small hearth against the north wall, and an ancient monk in a saffron robe knotted over one shoulder. The monk was bald, serene, imperturbable. The sudden appearance of a huge fair-haired man bearing arms was only another of nature's accidents, another of the negligible obstacles on the road to Nirvana. Greenwood greeted him politely, and hoped that his weapons would not profane the house.

"A zayat can be profaned by bloodshed or concupiscence," said the monk, "not by things." He sat before a small prayer wheel with a bowl of cutch beside him, dipped a bristle brush into the yellow dye and proceeded to paint the wheel in slow strokes, humming on one note as he worked. Greenwood set his pack and weapon against the wall and sat cross-legged watching. After a time he asked, "Is there food? Drink?"

The monk said, "Bah! Only sleep."

After a time Greenwood asked, "Is there a tavern?"

"There is a wineshop," the monk conceded.

After a time Greenwood asked, "And where is this wineshop?"

"It is a few houses east." After a time the monk asked, "You are English?"

"American."

The monk shrugged at this pagan. "A kind of English."

After a time Greenwood asked, "Do you never eat?"

"As the gods provide."

Greenwood hoisted his traps and walked on to the wineshop.

All sound ceased as he entered. Calmly he nodded to the company, and conversation swelled again, murmuring along beneath the clack of tiles. This was a tavern of quality, with tables, benches and mahjongg. Greenwood sat by the wall. He ordered rice, fish and bananas, also rice wine of the lesser fermentation, more like rice beer. The room was gray with cheroot smoke, but the smell was soft, comfortable, like the taste of his food, the fish aromatic, the bananas sweet, even the red pepper not aggressive.

He bought beedies from the stout waiter and said, "I will take a hand at mah-jongg if needed."

"They play for money," the waiter said, "and consequently with skill."

"Nevertheless. The traveler alone must pay for his diversions."

"Of all sorts. A woman later?"

"No, thank you."

"No woman?"

"A vow."

"Then mah-jongg it is. More wine?"

"Yes. A cruet."

The waiter bowed, and Greenwood read his mind: here is a foreigner who is also a fool, who drinks and plays at one time.

Greenwood had drunk up half the cruet, and dusk had arrived, and lamps had been lit, before the invitation came. Men entered and left the tavern, some in longyi, some in robes, some in cotton trousers with the short mountain jacket. The same mix, Kachin and Shan and Chinese and the true Burman face from the lowlands far to the west. They smoked the white cheroots and the brown, and also beedies, and they bore arms, and they drank rice beer and tea.

"At the center table across the room there is a place," said the waiter.

A Shan, a Burman and a Chinese. Through the haze Greenwood recognized the horse-master.

He paid his tally, and tipped well, and set down yet more rupees. "When I leave I will take ten cakes of rice-in-leaves and five bananas."

The waiter approved. Here was prudence.

Greenwood saw knives, a kris, a kukri, few firearms; he felt conspicuous slinging his Thompson, lugging his pack. But other than monks and clerks there was not an unarmed man for hundreds of miles around; he sighed for peace. At the table he said again, "Greetings and blessings," and was bade welcome. "It is my superstition," he said, "to sit by the wall."

The three players consulted wordlessly; the Burman rose and bowed toward the seat, hands open.

"You are kind to a stranger."

"You are not a stranger," said Horse-master, "and it is no superstition. I like to keep an eye on the company myself. And the doors."

Greenwood said, "Help me finish this wine," and waited to hear their excuses; mah-jongg is played by four, but each for himself.

"A vow," said the Burman.

"A vow," aid the Chinese.

"I'll have a mouthful," said Horse-master.

The Burman wore a dark gray aingyi. Four white cheroots peeked from a pocket. He played with care, placing tiles precisely and quietly, grounding a flower or a season without obvious annoyance, exposing a ch'ao or a p'eng without obvious satisfaction. The Chinese played quickly and muttered. Horse-master played with a certain dash, an almost contemptuous flick of the tile, a nonchalance, an indifference to fate.

Greenwood played as a foreigner should; that is, like a beginner; that is, with care and deliberation though not so slowly as to be impolite. Losing required no great effort. These three were old hands.

Horse-master said, "Wu," and won big, with

four k'ang and a pair of red dragons; he was East Wind and collected double. Greenwood snarled at the loss, and Horse-master flashed a winner's grin. They shuffled the tiles. Horse-master asked, "Just passing through?"

"Yes," Greenwood grumbled. "It would obviously be too expensive to stay."

Horse-master laughed.

No one was cheating, though there might be a chipped or stained tile now and then that the others would recognize. Greenwood took his time. Games were played to appropriate rhythms and were not to be forced. The room itself was a haven, warm with the buzz of men at truce; anarchists, bandits, tribesmen, they were fighting the government in Rangoon and not the townsfolk of Hsenwi. Only to be left alone! That was all they asked. In their hills and villages, in their fields of poppy and tobacco. Even the Wild Wa wanted only serenity; it was unfortunate that their peace of mind depended on other men's heads.

In an hour he lost forty rupees.

Halfway through the second hour he won a limit hand, and he had his omen: he made Four Small Blessings hidden, and on the next tile the Chinese would have made Three Scholars.

The Chinese cursed; he was East Wind, and paid double.

Horse-master contemplated Greenwood. They saw each other more clearly. "On your way to where?"

"Kunlong," Greenwood said.

"Surely not to play mah-jongg."

"Surely not."

Horse-master smiled faintly, to show Greenwood that he liked a close-mouthed man. "Nor to piss into the Salween."

"No."

The smile persisted. A game within a game! The tiles were stacked. "Well then, you are with British intelligence," Horse-master said.

"I am not British."

"Some other tribe, then. But surely a spy. You will sit on a mountain above the Salween and spy on the Red Chinese with military glasses."

"Hiking out in six months to report on the number of donkeys, pye-dogs and silkworms. Forgive me, Horse-master, but if you were sending a spy among the Chinese—"

"True, true, by the gods! He would not have yellow hair and blue eyes! Who is East Wind here? Too much chitchat and not enough money-making."

Play continued. The Burman lit a cheroot, the Chinese accepted a beedy, Horse-master agreed to split another cruet of rice wine. They were old friends by now, the tiles warmed by four hands, no one winning or losing uncomfortably. The Burman was from Shwebo, a tobacco merchant, up for the harvest. Greenwood understood: tobacco was cut and cured in late summer, but opium was harvested in December and January. The Chinese was a buyer of tea. Of course. Horse-master grinned. "And what do you buy?"

"I sell."

The pause was gratifying but short. "A good sharp answer," said Horse-master. "So then. May one ask what you sell?"

"One may."

"By the gods, this is a talker! So then. What do you sell?"

"Peace of mind."

"Ah," said Horse-master, "a priest."

Greenwood called for a discarded 5-bamboo, and tuned up four overlapping ch'ao in bamboo with a pair of white dragons.

"That's pretty," the Chinese said.

"Like music," the Burman said.

"You carry plenty of luck," Horse-master said.

"I hope I don't use it all here."

"And how do you provide peace of mind?"

"I'm a prince's bowman." It was the old Shan phrase, and the Burmese image, for riding shot-gun.

"Finally we have it! Thus your tools, there."

"Thus my tools," Greenwood said. "The men of the hills come down with their harvest. The men of Kunlong bring it here. They return with silver. I am a lonely traveler and will work for the companionship."

"Honorable labor and the terms clearly stated," said the Chinese. "Stack tiles, now."

"You will not be long unemployed," Horse-master said. "Ox trains go up every few days at this season."

"I want to leave tomorrow," Greenwood said.

"Come to my horse yard at sunrise," Horse-master said, and they drank to it. Greenwood was careful not to win another game, and when they parted for the night he had lost just enough to pay for future favors.

His ten cakes of rice-in-leaves and his five

bananas were waiting in a flimsy reed basket. He bore them to the monk, who said, "What are you atoning for?"

The oxen were small and humped, the common Burmese beasts of burden. "These are honest Kachin and a couple of town Shan," Horse-master said. "The Kachin have sold some good jade and are heavy with silver." He hesitated, and his smile went lopsided. In harder tones he said, "If you walk crooked ways, it will be laid to me; and I will have every Shan in these hills after your head."

"If I walked crooked ways," Greenwood said, "the Small Blessings would not have come to me," and he opened his shirt.

"Bugger!" said Horse-master. "A Shan like me!" He tugged at his horse-jacket and revealed the edges of his own tattoos. "You had a Shan's luck last night. May it be upon you always."

"Thank you, elder brother."

"This is not to be believed," Horse-master said. "Wars make prodigies."

"They also make good men bad, and bad men good," Greenwood said.

"And which are you?"

"I cannot say. Perhaps my war is not over."

"Then you will need your Shan's luck."

"For sure I will," Greenwood said. "So I will not start by leaving you with half a lie. It is true that I was and am a prince's bowman, and sell peace of mind. But it is also true that I buy."

"And what do you buy?"

"Wisdom."

"Now, that is costly."

"I buy it bit by bit."

"Shrewdly said." But Horse-master was puzzled.

"I seek wisdom everywhere and at all times," Greenwood said, "and am a teacher."

Caution settled over Horse-master's features. "Then Your Reverence is after all a priest?"

"By the gods, no! Only a schoolmaster." Greenwood clapped him on the shoulder; to touch another Shan was to promise him truth. "At a great university where men and women have sought wisdom for three hundred years and more."

"Well, I am only a bad Buddhist," Horsemaster said, "but it seems to me that wisdom is, Do no harm."

"Or as the followers of Confucius say, 'Do not do unto others what you would not have them do unto you.' Yet you took my money with pleasure last night, you great thief."

Horse-master twinkled, and his answer was ready. "I told you: a bad Buddhist."

"Next time," said Greenwood, "I will strive to improve you."

The wagon train was on the road by midmorning, twelve oxen bearing little cargo: bolts of cotton cloth, bags of ax heads, a sack of knives like machetes, eight kegs of nails purchased perhaps from the itinerant Jew, and two cumbersome iron plowshares. The company was four Kachin, three carrying American M-1 rifles and one a carbine, all festooned with bandoliers; and two town Shan, one with a Lee-Enfield and one with a Springfield. East is East, Greenwood de-

cided, and West is West, and they sure as hell
have met. In the aftermath of war Burma was a
thirty-caliber society. His companions carried
sheath knives as well, and three of them canteens. The Shan were properly turbanned, but
the Kachin were turned out like veterans, with a
khaki shirt here and a cartridge belt there. They
were fine fighters and their women at home were
handsome, with much silver ornamentation and
bright-hued cotton trousers beneath their skirts;
but Greenwood was a Shan for better or for
worse.

The journey took two days and they never
trusted him a moment. They muttered "tommy,"
and he was not sure if it was an echo of the old
British army or a dark reference to his submachine gun. They spent the night at a country
inn, a hovel, one long room with a trestle frame-
work a couple of feet off the earthen floor and a
row of rotting straw mattresses an inch thick.
There would be rats, and a variety of insects in
the bedding. A Kachin would surely stand sentry.
They ate cold rice, cooked that morning, and
bananas again, and drank from their canteens.

Greenwood was a happy man, next day even
happier: they arrived at Kunlong and he saw the
Salween again. He was at six thousand feet, the
air cool and clear, the mountains vivid, the forest
etched. He saw the great union of the Salween
and the Little White Yi, as they called it here,
white water rushing, and he harked to the distant
thunder of it and blessed General Yang; General
Yang and his miracle, the bones of Peking Man;
and even if it was not a miracle but a tragicomic

mistake, God bless General Yang! The Salween again!

He strolled back to town and nosed about, and yes, there was one here who would guide him as far as Pawlu, a Wa but a Tame Wa. Greenwood only said, "If you're sure he's tame," at which the town Shan laughed. The Tame Wa's name was Jum-aw and he was about seventeen, perhaps a hundred and five pounds, but he had a merry eye and he knew the hills. Yes, he had traveled as far as Meng-ting, also Yuan-ting, and he had seen a flying fox, and was good at snaring hares. He had also seen the pyaung, which was a kind of bison, though he had never killed one; and he had brought down many gyi with his father's rifle.

Greenwood sensed that matters were running too smoothly, but he could think of no sane way to induce a little bad luck now so that good luck would follow when he required it. Jum-aw showed him to the local inn, at which a functioning shower had been contrived from oil drums and a waterwheel. The innkeeper suggested saing steak—wild cattle, they were—with sweet potatoes and rice, and hot wine, and then a nice local girl. Greenwood declined the nice local girl, a vow, he said, though he was also much aware of the endemic low-level syphilis in these cosmopolitan crossroad towns. He showered, and dined in state, chatting in Shan with the waiter, stretching his vocabulary and flexing his grammar; and he went to bed replete and exhausted.

In the morning he donned the cotton trousers, tunic and turban of a mountain Shan, and donated his khakis to a holy beggar. He wondered what would become of them, with his name tapes in the waistband and at the collar. He kept his combat boots. They were sturdy and comfortable, well broken in, and he had plenty of travel ahead of him.

He knew a Shan woman would not have waited four years, and for the thousandth time he wondered what his daughter looked like now, and whether she would remember her outlandish father, who must once have seemed a god.

3

Kunming

The two Chinese officers gazed down into a crate of particolored bits and pieces—medals!—then shared a glance of incredulity at this kaleidoscope of human foolishness. "The Order of the Tripod," General Yang intoned.

"Third class." Mayor Wei scooped out a handful and let them trickle.

"Ribbon and sunburst both."

"There must be a thousand of them."

The general made clown's teeth. His smile was a national joke and a national resource, sunny, benevolent, enthusiastic; mah-jongg players called him "Old Thirty-two Tiles." His eyes crinkled, his nostrils swelled, his ears winged out; it was the smile to which other smiles aspired. "How prudent! Apparently there is no genuine emergency for which the local authorities were not prepared. Motor fuel was of course a trivial consideration, as were rice and ammunition; but man's deeper and realer aspirations were not neglected. That reminds me"—he let fall the lid of the wooden box—"I want you to investigate the power plants."

"Sir?"

"Fuel, and possibly diesel trucks."

"I've detailed officers to forage and commandeer," Wei said.

"Commandeer. What we do best: conscript and commandeer. Just as well; no need to kill now. It's all over."

"Not while we hold the city." Major Wei, mountain-bred, once a textbook officer, now seemed disheveled and elephantine. He flopped into an armchair.

"But we do not hold the city," the general reminded him. "We have merely paused to regroup and supply—"

"We control all main avenues. We have the provincial governor under house arrest."

"—before fading into the west like the bandits of old. Really, you must not interrupt a general. It makes no sense to be a general if majors interrupt. In the old days you'd have been demoted for that, or even bastinadoed. As for the provincial governor—" Once more his smile illumined the room. "Poor old Lu Han. He can be an alderman for the Communists. A fate worse than death. All that paperwork." He stepped to the french windows—no mandarin's shuffle but a crisp military stride. His hair was short and bristly, his figure stocky and strong. "I wish we did hold the city. During the war—that other war—it was busy and optimistic and full of Americans. That was after Lashio, when we were chased out of Burma, a disgrace, I told you about that. I can even remember this hotel. The Yunnan Hotel, it was then. What is it now? Some monstrous name."

"The Grand Hotel of Kunming and of the Center of the Universe."

"That's it. Used to be full of diplomats and assorted air corps and infantry officers, and the customary contingent of amiable local ladies." The general allowed himself a bullish sigh. "There was a hotel near Les Invalides called de Kelly et de l'Univers. There was one in the Pyrenees, I was on leave with a Parisian belle, it was called de Lavelanet et des Quatre Coins du Monde, Lavelanet, that was the name of the town, Hotel of Lavelanet and of the Four Corners of the World. I remember eating a bowl of tiny fish there, heads and all, with warm bread and white wine, dozens of crisp tiny little fish, whitebait they were called, and the lady—"

The knock was thunderous. Major Wei's hand fell to his .45; his eyes requested orders.

The general wore a pistol but had drawn it less with each promotion. He ignored it now and merely nodded. Major Wei bawled, "Come in!"

The door seemed to implode: half a dozen soldiers and one prisoner. They lunged into the room like drunken pallbearers. General Yang saw a greenish flow of snot on a corporal's upper lip and turned away. His expression did not alter. From his breast pocket he extracted a chased-silver cigarette case. He saw, and approved of, Major Wei's anger.

"Sergeant!" Major Wei's bellow stilled the scuffle.

A burly middle-aged man dropped his burden and arched his back. "Sir!"

"Explain this schoolyard scrimmage."

While the major admonished and the sergeant stammered, General Yang inspected the prisoner, who was almost seated on the floor, hanging like a basket, sustained by a tangle of arms. The prisoner was bleeding. He wore cloth shoes, blue trousers, a blue horse-jacket and a cartridge belt. His hair fell well over the ears and eyes; General Yang saw, behind the fall of it, a bright gaze; the man was conscious and, from the set of his lips, possibly even contemptuous.

"A sniper," the sergeant was saying. "With the American M-one rifle."

A sniper? Why bring him here? But Major Wei was asking just that.

"He says he is a Red Bandit," the sergeant announced in portentous tones.

"Imagine," General Yang said. He went on in their silence: "Search him, Major."

Wei found nothing.

"Sergeant. You men. Release him."

The prisoner fell lumpishly. He tested his arms and legs and shortly sat up, wincing. The bleeding seemed to be from his right shoulder. "Who shot him?"

"I did, sir! Corporal Pao! Pao Wen-shih! Two-five—"

"A family history is not required. Wipe your nose. Major Wei."

"Sir."

"A medal for this man."

"Yes, sir. Which medal would the general recommend?"

General Yang devoted some seconds to this vexing question. "I think perhaps the Order of the Tripod," he said. "Third class."

"Fitting, sir. Noted."

Corporal Pao seemed to grow an inch.

"Sergeant."

"Sir!"

"Take this squad away now. Ask for Lieutenant An in the next suite and tell him General Yang orders a distribution of cigarettes and one beer each—what is that local stuff called?"

"Yunnan Dragon," said Major Wei.

"—for work well done."

"Yes, sir!"

But Yang saw that the sergeant was depressed and offended: no medal. "Sergeant."

"Sir!"

"You are—?"

"Chang, sir! One two two, sir! First battalion, second company, second platoon."

"Corporal Pao."

"Sir!"

"You heard the sergeant's answer?"

"I heard, sir!"

"That is how to make an officer remember you. Did you truly think a general wanted to know your given name and serial number?"

"First battalion—"

"Too late, Corporal. Thank you, Sergeant Chang. Outside, now."

General Yang at last lit his cigarette. It was an Antelope, acrid, a painful experience. For an instant he recalled fresh Virginia tobacco, and he decided that there should be a correlation, a ratio, between the cost of a good silver cigarette case and the quality of the cigarettes with which one furnished it. Turkish too would do. It had once been his habit (acquired in France after a harsh and unnecessary regime of army cigarettes, the mégot du poilu, the French doughboy's gasper, inconceivably vile and fabricated, the story went, in Algeria from camel dung) to smoke Balkan Sobranies. At the Chinese taxpayers' expense; but everything came back to that. God created the world and said, "The Chinese taxpayer will fund this project."

He made himself comfortable in an upholstered armchair behind an imposing desk. Before him a brass ashtray gleamed, a tiny glistening Buddha at each corner: a tourist knicknack. Beyond the french windows a pale winter sun westered. A long hard day. On the wall hung an almost expired calendar of 1949. And how did you pass Tuesday, 20 December 1949, General? Or in the Chinese fashion, twentieth day, twelfth month, thirty-eighth (and last) year of the Republic?

Well, in the morning I conquered a large city, the capital of Yunnan, a large and heterogeneous province in the extreme southwest of China. In the afternoon I governed it. I accomplished this with something under three hundred men, whose numbers will shortly be halved, and halved again, by desertion, opportunism, simple fatigue, a death or two. If I am lucky, my government will nevertheless send me the payroll for a full division. That is, if I have a government and if I can find it.

"So you admit that you are a Red Bandit."

With his left hand the sniper swept the hair from his eyes. His face was bruised and he needed a shave, but the eyes were steady and sullen. O gods, a hero, the general mused. A hero of the left. Well, very possibly. This one was old enough to be a veteran of the Long March. "I admit nothing," the man said. "I affirm it. I am a member of the Communist Party of China."

"And a brave one, I'm sure," said the general, "but a poor tactician. You gain nothing by sniping at my men, or even at me. We are only passing through, as you know very well. Liu Po-ch'eng, has Chungking and is slicing south. Lin Piao and the Fourth took Nanning on the sixth. You knew that? No? Then I bring you good news. Today is the twentieth and he will surely—"

"The twenty-first," said the sniper.

General Yang glanced again at the calendar, perplexed. "Wednesday? I seem to have lost a whole day."

"It comes of not sleeping," Wei said gently.

"So. At any rate"—he addressed the sniper—"we are of no real consequence."

"You arrested the governor," the sniper said. "He formally surrendered the province to the Communist armies ten days ago and you have arrested him."

General Yang grinned again, a pumpkin. "No. Lu Han surrendered to a delegation, and yielded his sword by telegraph. Never surrender to a delegation, Major Wei, or, for that matter, you, Master Sniper. What is your name?"

"My name is of no importance."

"True enough. I was only attempting to raise the level of discourse. Nothing is important but the march of the progressive and freedom-loving peoples of the world toward equality and self-determination. Have I got that right? Major, open those french windows."

Wei obeyed. The men observed a silence. They

could hear the creak and clatter of hand-drawn wagons; then a clop-clop, a donkey. "Look one look, Major Wei, and tell us what you see."

"I see strollers. I see a ricksha man cruising."

"Cruising a city without government, food, fuel or even useful money," the general said.

"I see a vendor of fritters. And a boy and a girl arm in arm."

"Enough," said General Yang. Even as he spoke they heard the vendor's cry, "Yuuuuu-ping!" and the squeak of a cart. "That is the calm of resignation, of acceptance," the general went on. "It is as if these people were saying, 'Han hastened, and was killed by a tiger; Lin loitered, and was killed by a tiger. Therefore we shall do what we would ordinarily do.' The bloodletting is over. In a day or two," he said to the sniper, "your comrades will march in the east gate as my shredded battalion toils out the west gate."

"Why not stay," asked the sniper, "and join the future?"

"I have my own future. It is in those two foot-lockers." He gestured. In a shadowed corner of the room the footlockers stood, one upon the other, gifts for Greenwood.

"Gold!" The sniper was scornful.

"Not gold. Gold is nothing, I agree. I have the past in those footlockers, and China's past is my future." If the message had reached Greenwood; if Greenwood had reached Pawlu.

"Works of art that belong to the people."

"Don't even try to guess," Yang said. "Do you know who I am?"

"I think you are Yang Yu-lin," said the round-faced, bushy-browed sniper.

"I am."

"Yang Yu-lin was a good man. Yang Yu-lin fought the Japanese hard, when his colleagues were too busy fighting us. You disappeared in the Huai-Hai battles." The sniper showed curiosity.

"Disguises," Yang said. "I was a woman, which was farcical, and a mule driver, which was at least honorable, and a Russian's servant, which was degrading. That reminds me—where is the colonel?"

Wei asked, "Colonel Ou?"

"We have only the one colonel," General Yang said patiently, "and I must ask you not to take that dry tone with me. He is a legitimate, decorated colonel in the army of the Republic of China, which he entered as a lieutenant and in which he has served for twenty years with gallantry and distinction."

"He has also served a myriad of Chinese women and he is a Russian."

"He is a Russian, *sir*," Yang said quite sharply.

"Sir," Wei said, and then, "I'm sorry, sir."

"Where is he?"

"Inspecting the guard at Lu Han's compound. Shall I send for him? The telephones work."

"The telephones always work except when you need reinforcements." Yang rose and strode to the sniper, who braced himself. The general reached for the cigarette case; the sniper flinched; the case flew open.

"No," said the sniper.

Yang sighed. "Don't be silly. These are Antelopes, made by the Chinese proletariat with Chinese tobacco, worse luck. Come now. Your sainted Mao Tse-tung wouldn't turn it down. You're not selling your soul; I fought the Japanese at Taierhchuang. Even a Communist may allow himself a moment of pleasure from time to time. Lenin was afraid of Beethoven, you know; it made him feel warm, and fraternal, and loving, and human, and reluctant to follow Marx and Engels in heaping contempt upon the gentle Kropotkins of his time. But a cigarette can scarcely be so potent."

"Much of that I do not understand," the sniper said. "What do you know of Lenin and Marx and Engels?"

This time the smile was glorious. "I was a Communist in nineteen eighteen," General Yang announced with extravagant pleasure, "before there *was* a Chinese Communist Party. I was"— he sighed richly—"a Parisian Communist. Même le drapeau rouge avait un certain chic francais. Even the red flag had its own French elegance." He paused to enjoy Major Wei's consternation.

The sniper pursed his lips, sniffed in a noisy breath and selected a cigarette. He then said, "Thank you," which gratified the general, who struck a match and offered fire.

"Just don't burn down the hotel," Yang said. "I have a deep, unreasoning fear of fires."

"Not unreasoning," the sniper said. "Footlockers are inflammable."

With great good nature the general said, "That must be it. But I was talking about the telephones, wasn't I. Let me tell you, last summer in Shanghai the gunfire across Soochow Creek, both ways, was murderous, with both sides pinned down for days, so somebody in a dress shop on the east bank would call the Marine Hotel on the west bank, or somebody in a waterfront godown on the west bank would call the East Side post office, and when the other fellow answered they'd shout, 'Red Bandit motherfucker!' or 'imperialist fascist motherfucker!' Something eerie and unpleasant in that: men kill and die, governments rise and fall, but wires and rails go on crossing all lines."

"What will you do with me?" asked the sniper. "What will you do with Lu Han?"

"Probably nothing. Lu Han did the correct thing. Yunnan is a large province, and there is no one left to defend it. He acted prematurely, that's all. Ten days ago there wasn't a Red battalion within a hundred miles of Kunming. There was, however, *us*. We stole a few marches." General Yang dimmed his smile by an obvious effort of modesty.

"It was brilliant," Wei assured him.

The sniper blew greasy smoke through an almost sympathetic smile. General Yang wondered what this young zealot saw: one obsolete fighting man, doomed to exile and oblivion because he took the wrong road to the shining city.

"It's tragic," Wei said, "fleeing like rats."

"No, it is not," Yang said firmly. "Tragedy is when we lose to our own deficiencies, not when the accidents of history defeat us."

"It is no accident," the sniper told him.

"Ah, of course!" General Yang was delighted. "How rare and reassuring is certainty! How I wish I knew as much about anything as you do—and I once did—about everything! Do remember me when the factions quarrel and you face a firing squad."

"I do not know what you will do with me," the sniper said, "or how much blood I can lose without dying, or how bad the pain will become. Or what to do with this cigarette, which is making me woozy."

Yang himself stepped across to take the cigarette, noting that the city's calm persisted, was even deepening, outside the windows. Kunming had seen armies before. When its name was Yunnanfu, it had seen its warlords, sieges, battles, massacres and famines.

And not only Kunming. In the last two decades alone half the cities in China had boiled over, and half the roads had disappeared beneath the flow of refugees, Yang among them from time to time with his footlockers. But then there had been at least someplace to go. This, now, was the end of the line, a few days more here, a few weeks more in the northwest, and then finie, la belle époque. There would be no corner of China that was not Communist, and this young sniper, bloody and streaked with filth, would become a righteous bureaucrat.

The general glanced once more at his footlockers, for comfort, and yielded suddenly to exhaustion. "Take him to An," he instructed Major Wei. "He is to be cleaned up, fed and watered, and the bullet removed if possible. No brutality. No revenge. Then I want a report on fuel, not omitting the power plants, and on rice. Then send the colonel to me."

Colonel Prince Nikolai Andreevich Olevskoy had entered China through the roof, so to speak, and was still angry. He had been angry for thirty-three years. A third of a century. Christ's lifetime. He had fought his way to the Amur and across into Manchuria in 1920, eighteen years old and a veteran of pitched battles, forced marches, murdered horses, rapes (active partner), frostbite, village massacres, train robberies and—he would never understand God's ways—a late attack of mumps that angered him more than all the rest, the piercing ache of his testicles and the fear, fortunately erroneous and unjustified, of impotence.

Now he swayed, resentful and indolent but sharp-eyed, in the back seat of an American jeep racketing down Yunnan Great Street toward Lu Han's compound in the heart of Kunming. He preferred the old name, Yunnanfu, perhaps instinctively, as he preferred St. Petersburg to Leningrad. He wore gleaming leather cavalry boots, whipcord jodhpurs, Chinese-officer's-issue battle jacket, white silk scarf and American helmet. In his cartridge belt were cartridges, cellophaned packs of Antelope cigarettes, a short bar of soft silver to be shaved or sliced for currency, and a capsule of cyanide against capture by the Red Bandits.

"Drive with the wheel as well as the horn," he admonished his second driver of the day, Hu, or Fu. He risked a glance behind: the second jeep trailed them at twenty meters, and he saw with minor satisfaction that his two marksmen were nested head to tail like pigeons, one scanning the avenue ahead, the other covering their rear.

The city was not ablaze and crackling, not panicky, not even normally noisy. Olevskoy gripped his carbine in anger, not fear; his first driver of the day, Fu, or Hu, had lounged at the curb in the parked jeep sucking smoke like any taxi driver, and been picked off by a sniper. Fool! Chinese scurried along the road, glancing up anxiously at this towering armed foreigner and dodging away like alley cats. Olevskoy noted them casually, barely distinguishing men from women, old from young; he would sense the enemy when necessary and was indifferent to the others. He recognized, acknowledged, his immediate subordinates and all who outranked him; the rest of Asia was a faceless throng that did not require his direct notice.

Above Kunming the sky seemed flat, gray and hostile, yet the city was warm even in December. Olevskoy preferred northern skies, clear, frosty, blue, wedges of geese and kettles of hawks. Here, in the south, skies hung heavy, often yellowish or greenish or muddy. It was a long way from Sobolyevo to Yunnanfu.

A long way from fifteen square kilometers comprising three villages and five hundred peasants, who his father assured him had been better off as serfs, healthier and harder-working, and at least the Olevskoy forebears had protected the vacant-eyed dolts and their well-marbled womenfolk.

A long way from the accommodating bosoms of Russian peasant girls to the slim Chinese maidens he fancied now.

A long way from his father's infinite river of rubles to the paper pay of a colonel in the Chinese army.

Shop signs and street signs streamed past his eye. Fish Alley, a market street. Fish, here? River fish, perhaps. Or saltwater fish up from Haiphong. He hoped the general intended to run south, to the Tonkin border, the French army, the Legion, French food, Frenchwomen. A temple: Buddhists here, many. A policeman, black uniform, blue sunburst, saluting. Olevskoy touched one finger to his helmet.

The jeep backfired. Olevskoy's grip clenched on the stock, then relaxed. He missed horses. Jeeps! Monsters.

And now this Lu Han. Another monster. Olevskoy was not impressed by provincial governors, most of them little better than warlords, enriched by squeeze, tax rake-offs, false army rolls, opium sales, a high turnover of war material. Olevskoy cared not a whit whether Lu Han lived or died, but General Yang's orders were explicit, and Olevskoy obeyed as he expected obedience. Before Lu's compound the jeep clattered and screeched to a halt, and Olevskoy took a major's salute. In 1939 Olevskoy had ordered an entire platoon, including its lieutenant, flogged for not rising when he entered their hut. Olevskoy's men now observed the niceties. "Armored cars, Major Ho?"

"Two, sir. In place."

"Light machine guns?"

"A squad at each of the four gates, sir."

"Infantry?"

"Road blocks twenty meters down each street

or alley. With permission, sir."

"What is it, Major?"

"Lu Han will not break out. The hare prefers a warren to a tiger in open country. We are guarding the exits when we should be defending the approaches. If the Red Bandits come in force—"

"We'll be long gone. Just keep them penned in for now."

"They lack food, sir."

"Good. Let them nourish themselves on a taste of things to come. They won't starve to death in forty-eight hours."

"So soon!"

"So soon. You'll want to pull the infantry back first. I'll give you the rendezvous when I know it, and the order of retreat. No need to shell the compound or burn it down; just clear out. Make your dispositions well ahead of time, and rehearse your officers. The object now is to survive."

"We are all tossed by the same flood," Major Ho said.

"The same flood. Waters rising many years now." Olevskoy liked this Major Ho: plumpish, with red cheeks, no hitch to his trot and a larcenous gleam in his shiny brown eyes. "Were you ever a sergeant?"

"For far too long, sir."

"Had you a nickname?"

Ho was visibly pleased by these attentions. " 'Finds-the-pig,' sir. My men never went hungry."

"I like that. And have I a nickname?"

Poor Ho froze. His eyes pleaded.

"Oh, come now," Olevskoy said.

"I dare not," Ho managed.

"It is a direct order," Olevskoy said lightly.

"Yes sir," Ho answered immediately. "The men call you 'Russian mink.' " He stood at rigid attention, eyes front, and swallowed once.

"Mais c'est bien gentil," Olevskoy murmured. "In Hopei they called me 'Knout.' Major Ho!"

"Sir!"

"Never fear to tell me the truth."

"No sir! I am—that is—"

"Speak, Major."

"I rather like women, myself, sir."

"Ah, you fornicator! Good for you, Major. Now stand at ease. The crisis is not over: I must inspect your dispositions."

Shortly he announced, "Good. You restore my faith, Major Ho. Have your men eaten?"

"A good breakfast, sir."

"Cold rice, no doubt."

"And tea, sir. We left a chit."

"Quite proper. The Generalissimo will certainly honor it when the Red Bandits have been driven out for good."

"As you say, Colonel."

Olevskoy clambered aboard his jeep. They were really too small for long men. "I'll send relief at eight. Lu Han won't stir. I wish we could hang the bastard. I despise turncoats."

Major Ho saluted; Olevskoy waved it off and prodded his driver. Behind them the convoy of jeeps barked to life. They growled away from Lu Han's yamen and swung wide onto an avenue. Olevskoy scanned the windows, the shadowed façades, and shrugged. Not much to be done, really, about snipers, agents, fifth columns.

Half a mile from Lu's compound he ordered his

driver to halt. Behind them their bodyguard skidded to a stop. Olevskoy vaulted out, felt a good surge of blood, a flow of muscle, the solid jolt as he landed. He rolled his neck and shoulders like an athlete, a wrestler, and tightened his buttocks. "Go home," he told his driver Fu, or Hu. "Go home. All of you. Now!"

At a beetle's pace, as if the vehicles themselves were struggling to comprehend this bizarre command, the jeeps crawled off. Olevskoy slung his carbine and took several vigorous strides, which accelerated to a trot and then a sprint. The thud of his heels, the jar to his spine, the stretch of his lungs brought joy to his soul. His blood pounded. A light sweat broke. When he spied a ricksha he cut across the avenue and hailed its somnolent puller. The scarecrow hopped to his feet; he wore rags and was barefoot. He gestured with both hands: In, in, good sir.

Olevskoy hopped aboard and said, "The best brothel." Again the man gaped. Olevskoy groaned. "A willowy lane." No response. "Night chickens, night chickens!"

A toothless smirk split the wrinkled face, a screech of laughter followed. The man hopped between the shafts. Olevskoy settled in, cradling the carbine. "The best," he said. The man might or might not understand. "None of your clapped-up crones."

"No clap!" the man shrieked. He leaned into his work.

"Clean women and young," Olevskoy said.

"Little sisters!"

Olevskoy remembered then that he had not set a price for this ride. Surely the man was joyful and would now overcharge him, prepared to create a noisy scene if Olevskoy resisted. He gave way to a sour smile. He had bought a roll of toilet paper on the black market in Kueiyang, and had calculated that thanks to inflation he had paid out more thousand-dollar bills than there were sheets in the roll. How princely—he could economize by wiping himself with thousand-dollar bills. He remembered Yuri Nikolayevich Malko lighting a Havana cigar—thirty-five years ago! —with a hundred-ruble note. Malko had nothing on Olevskoy.

Pedestrians stared at him. He waved amiably. Cities were bombarded, besieged, ignited, and hawkers went on hawking, weddings were solemnized, beggars solicited. He wondered if he would find a party in full swing at his destination.

The ricksha halted, the puller stepped aside. He named his figure. Olevskoy set his face in grim lines and stepped out, the carbine at port arms. The man shrank but stood his ground. Olevskoy had no notion of exchange rates these days, but the figures seemed to come to three or four cents American. "You robber!" He let his hands mask the money and counted angrily, stripping the bills away. "Thief, pirate, gangster!" He gave the man three times the amount asked and said, "Wait here, you turtle's egg, or I will have you hanged."

"I wait, I wait," the man cried. "I wait, my lord. A year if need be!"

Olevskoy shoved at a sagging wooden gate, entered a courtyard, skirted the spirit wall and barged into a deserted parlor. He recognized the

setting at once: armchairs, a stone bed, faded
wall-hangings, a winsome maiden in slit brocade
beckoning from a calendar advertising Yunnan
Dragon and December. Even blind he might have
been sure from the faint, oily scent, compounded
of tea, cheap perfumes, tobacco, perhaps opium,
and years of sexual effuvia male and female. He
pounded a table, calling, "Hey, the house!" Up-
stairs, footsteps, a scuttling. He watched the
wooden staircase and recognized the madam too,
about fifty, running to flab, with lipstick, weary
eyes and probably a gold tooth. She grimaced a
welcome. "You bring honor to my house." She
wore a plain green gown and black cloth shoes;
early in the day, nothing fancy. Early in the day
and late in the war.

"I bring money to your house and I am in a
hurry."

"Unseemly," she protested. "No haste, no
haste. Whisky? Yellow wine? At least be seated.
My house is yours, and pleasures should be
tasted slowly."

"Business, not pleasure. I come to buy, and I
cannot stay. With the world in ruins, you may
omit the elegant preambles."

"You come to buy and cannot stay? That
makes no sense."

"Listen now," he said. "In two days you will all
be Communists and not whores. Your girls will
be planting rice or weaving baksets or culti-
vating silkworms. Or they will be imprisoned
with others like them and taught to carry loads
of earth. Or they will be scrubbed clean and
issued one gown and required to memorize the
poetry of Mao Tse-tung. Or they will be executed

as playthings of the imperialist foreigners. Do you understand?"

"Of course I understand. But what is it you want?"

Olevskoy told her.

At the Grand Hotel of Kunming and of the Center of the Universe, no sentry dared even a snicker. Olevskoy ignored them anyway. With princely indifference Olevskoy went AWOL or, amid whole regiments, ejected two or three post-adolescents from his tent in the misty dawn, shortly emerging himself, natty, boots glassy and scarf snowy, to take the duty officer's report before salt fish and tea with his general. Now he said, "Corporal. There is a ladies' room on the first floor up. You will show this lady to that room and be sure she has soap, hot water and a towel. You will post a guard so that no man molests her. Is that clear?"

"Sir!"

The girl gazed timorously at her own feet. Olevskoy patted her head. "No one will harm you and you are for me alone." Of the three girls remaining to the old madam one had dyed her hair orange; Olevskoy rejected her out of hand. The second was an urchin who fled when he threatened slow death in revenge for venereal disease. This one was far the best: shy, good teeth, large and well-defined nipples, a deep navel, fine and downy between the legs. Fifteen, he had guessed. He and the madam had haggled, the madam had brought scales and Olevskoy had shaved silver. He had treated the old bitch to a valedictory vodka from the brothel's skimpy bar.

The corporal led her off, this young one. Olevskoy took the steps two at a time and strode into General Yang's suite, knocking for the sake of form as he flung the door open, tossing a salute as he reported, "Lu Han is under lock and key, General."

"Colonel. Nice to see you again," said General Yang. Major Wei sat in hostile silence.

"Passing through," Olevskoy said, in high spirits. "On my way to the cellars. Full of loot, these grand hotels."

"Go with my blessings," Yang said. "When you can spare a moment, we have work to do."

"I love my work. Won't be a moment," Olevskoy promised, and left them.

Yang heaved another sigh. "Sorry, Major; but would you be kind enough to close the door?"

Obliging, Wei said, "I cannot like him, sir."

Yang said, "It hardly matters. This is such a charade! And every chance that we shall all be eaten by savages within a month."

Major Wei was startled: "In Tonkin?"

"What remains of us," the general went on, ignoring the question. "Two months ago we had a full regiment and two colonels. Now a company and a half and two majors. I ought to promote you. The lowliest private should be at least a lieutenant."

"With the Order of the Tripod, third class."

"And sunburst. Those quitters on Taiwan will believe anything. Ah well," he said wearily, "we're all deserters now."

Later a knock interrupted their review of stores, fuel and ammunition. Again the major played his doorman's part. A private stood, approximating attention, straining under the weight of a wooden crate.

"But that's whisky," the general cried. "These princes have a nose for the commissary. I tell you, Major, if we'd had the colonel in charge instead of that—well, instead of the high command, we might have won this miserable war. From each according to his ability, to each according to his thirst. Over here, man. Set it down."

"Orders of Colonel Ou, sir," the private panted.

"Natürlich. Out, now."

The private snapped to, and saluted.

General Yang sighed. "You will salute only when covered."

Blankly the private repeated, "Covered."

"Only," the general explained carefully, "when wearing something on your head. A hat, for example. You know which part of you is your head?"

"Head," the private repeated, baffled.

"This part." General Yang patted his own gray hair. "You understand?"

"I understand, sir!"

"Good. Dismissed."

"Sir!" The private saluted.

"Drive him out of this room," the general groaned.

Major Wei gestured sharply. The private trotted away, leaving the door open. Before the major reached it, Olevskoy marched in. "Voilà du vrai," he said. "Johnnie Walker rouge. Crates of it in the basement."

The general flung his arms wide in hopeless admiration. "So now we have defeat and whisky. What more can the superior man ask?"

"What indeed?" Olevskoy exclaimed. "Step in, child, step in."

General Yang said, "O by the gods! Again?"

The girl wore a simple blue gown and was plainly frightened. "A consolation in time of retreat," Olevskoy maintained.

"We are not retreating," Yang said. "We are withdrawing in good order."

"An improvement," Olevskoy said. "Until now my whole life has been a retreat. Withdrawing in good order is like a victory." He rummaged in the crate. "Cups, we need cups."

"Will you excuse me, sir?" Major Wei was stiffly correct; Olevskoy scarcely noticed; Yang was amused. "There is that matter of fuel."

"Yes, dismissed," Yang said to the major, who left immediately. Yang turned to the girl. "Please be seated. There, yes, go ahead, no one will harm you. I am General Yang."

The girl sat like a doll.

"Poor Major Wei," Olevskoy said. "How he dislikes me! Well, General, what's new?"

"We're resupplying, using Lu Han's treasury. I'll give the men forty-eight hours for rape and pillage. We're all exhausted. If Lu Han had a bow and arrow we'd be in trouble."

"He hasn't. That Major Ho is a fine officer." Olevskoy sniffed at the open bottle. "The real thing. A few cases won't slow us up. The basement here is like a department store. I bashed in a door and there it was. American leftovers somebody forgot to sell off."

"No champagne, I suppose? A hamper of cold

chicken and a few bottles of Mumm's. A picnic at the border, while Lin Piao sulks because he wasn't invited."

"I always preferred Bollinger," Olevskoy said, "about five years old. Never trust a champagne over ten or twelve years old. Here we are. And one for the whore." To the girl he said, "Whisky. You know whisky?"

The girl's gaze darted from man to man. She nodded hesitantly and then astonished them: she giggled.

"To victory," Olevskoy said.

"Not funny."

"No." Olevskoy drank off the small cupful. "To defeat, then."

"To defeat."

"Funeral baked meats and Scotch whisky."

" 'Did coldly furnish forth the marriage table.' You remind me of Hamlet, you know. You look as I always imagined him."

"And why not? Am I not a prince? And my ancestors were Scandinavian." Olevskoy accepted a cigarette.

Yang's brow rose. "You never told me that last."

"The original Russians were a Swedish tribe. My line goes back to Ivan Kalita Moneybag—"

"You cannot be serious."

"I never joke about my family. You can look it up. And from Ivan back to Nevsky, Vsevolod, Igor and Rurik."

Yang said, "Mon Dieu."

"Good idea. We ought to stick to French now. March into Tonkin chattering away like Parisians."

The men replenished their cups. The girl sat like a child at a puppet show, only sipping from time to time. Olevskoy raised his cup and said, "Tonkin!"

General Yang raised his and said, "Pawlu!"

Olevskoy checked. "What the devil is that?"

"Not 'what,' " Yang said. " 'Where.' Pawlu is a place. It is a small, happy village either in China or in Burma, and it is where we are going, and for once in our lives we shall visit decent people and do no harm."

The argument lasted half an hour; the quarrel for the rest of their lives. Olevskoy stormed off with his juvenile concubine and appeased anger, lust and ennui at once by taking her in cold fury; she seemed to respond, which eased him, and when she breathed finally, "Ah! Foreign devil!" he chose to take the hackneyed compliment for truth. Calmer, he joined his fellow officers at the evening meal and made small talk correctly. A prisoner, he learned, had been taken, a sniper, and was under guard in the former laundry.

General Yang's kidney had commenced to twinge again.

The Red Bandits seemed to be regrouping; at any rate there were no reports of lightning dashes or encirclements.

Olevskoy rose when the general rose; the formal nod, replacing bows and salutes among this motley command, was offered; Olevskoy retired to nurse his grudges, helpless now short of outright mutiny, doomed to a mysterious and primitive village called Pawlu instead of the cosmopolitan Hanoi he longed for, the vin rouge and the poules de luxe and perhaps a commission in the Legion.

At the third dawn of this fleeting conquest the occupying troops assembled in the grand plaza before the governor's yamen. Rolls were called. One hundred and two men remained. Also thirteen vehicles of which seven were rachitic or tubercular. Arms and ammunition galore, another irony: they might never again fire a shot in anger. Olevskoy carried the carbine and the American .45, being fond of the latter. The Luger, he felt, was grossly overestimated. An American .45 stopped anything. This he proved before the caravan moved out.

General Yang received reports with satisfaction, saw personally to the safe stowage of fuel, and delivered a pithy lecture on smoking in the vicinity of same: he would personally execute any man found smoking within ten meters of the fuel carriers. "Discipline," he said to the ragged, wounded young sniper whom Major Wei had just delivered to him. "That much we have in common. You claim to be the fish, and the people are the sea; fish swim in schools. Have you watched fish in great shoals? Mysteriously hundreds of them will veer or leap at once."

"They survive," the wounded man said lightly.

Yang surveyed his line, his order of march. "Major Ho. Major Wei."

"Sir!"

"Your sections are ready to move out?"

"Sir!"

The general told the sniper, "Your famous Governor Lu Han is in there," and waved a swagger stick toward the compound. "Tell him for me he is a fool, but a lucky fool. Any other Nationalist general would have razed his little palace and hung him by the plums. Tell him that, and good luck to you."

"Well, good luck to you too," the sniper said, but General Yang, stately and erect—command presence a habit now, a necessity—was already taking his place in a presentable jeep, which promptly chugged across the plaza to the head of the line. Orders eddied in the morning light. Metal clattered and clanked. A motor hawked and spat.

"Who is this man?" Olevskoy asked.

"The enemy," said Major Ho. "A sniper."

"A genuine Red? The one who killed my driver?"

"The same, sir."

"The war is over, Colonel," said Major Wei.

"And my driver meant less to me than a Soo-chow whore. All the same, to kill him was an insult." Olevskoy and the young man performed a mutual inspection. Olevskoy saw a blunt but intelligent face, disheveled hair, tattered clothes and utter, ultimate defiance. He knew what the sniper saw: officer, breeches, boots, round eyes, big nose.

"You Americans are betting on the old stag," the sniper said. "You should have backed the young tiger."

"Not American," Olevskoy said. A cry echoed across the square, a tailgate slammed shut, another engine turned. "Russian. An old stag."

"Not Red."

"Not Red," said Olevskoy. "I am afraid you have made a mistake."

After a moment the sniper blew his nose through the fingers of his good left hand, and wiped the hand on his torn and stained trousers. "I have never seen a Russian, and I have been a Red for fifteen years."

The head of the column was moving out. A barrage of racing motors and clashing gears assaulted them, a drift of exhaust fumes washed over them.

"Long enough," Olevskoy said. "Out of my sight. Go to the bastard Lu Han and deliver your message." His voice was barely audible in the clamor.

The sniper frowned, as if this world were proving more complicated than he had been led to believe, and turned away, padding toward the compound, the knot of his sling bright white against the black of his jacket.

Olevskoy's hand went to his holster. Major Wei said, "Colonel!" but too late: swiftly Olevskoy drew the pistol and extended his arm, loudly he cried "Red Bandit!" The sniper halted, hesitated, finally looked back, scarcely stirring then, only his eyes widening a fraction, perhaps in fear, perhaps in a last impossible effort to glimpse the future, perhaps even in disgust. Olevskoy relished this second or two of shock, of finality, of a perplexity so deep and paralyzing that no one could speak, not even Wei, who had already spoken; and Olevskoy hoped, as he often had before, that when his own time came he would have notice, and could look death in the eye. He fired. The young man toppled. Olevskoy tucked away his pistol and turned to the majors.

"Just another Chinese," Wei said quietly.

"I've killed more Russians than I have Chinese," Olevskoy said, "and more Japanese than either."

"And the general's message to Lu Han?"

"On your way, gentlemen," Olevskoy said. "Keep your sections moving and remember we're just one long flank on both sides. Keep those flanks covered."

Major Ho said, "Sir!"

Deliberately, Major Wei turned his back.

4
Pawlu

The two mounted Kachin sat arguing beneath the suspended cage. They were half a kilometer from Naung, who lay on his belly in a pine grove uphill shading his binoculars and noting what he could: turbans, white blouses, black Kachin trousers, Yunnan ponies. One Kachin gestured fiercely at the cage, and for a moment the two appeared undecided. At this distance Naung could not identify their weapons. Rifles, surely, and the Kachin swords slung across their backs. He saw no pistols. A mercenary in the Japanese war, he had journeyed to Laos and Tonkin and had returned with his own weapons, the French M1935 pistol and M1938 submachine gun—mitraillette, as the French had taught him to call it—because they used the same cartridge. Well and good, but his mitraillette was not accurate beyond fifty meters.

He would take them close and take them sure.

The Kachin came to agreement. With a last glance at the cage they turned off the road and onto the mountain trail. The last Naung saw of them, before teak and pyinkado swallowed them,

they were peering about cautiously rifles at the
ready. Fools! Beginners! They rode bareback and
they rode well, with the knees.

Naung squawked twice, a parakeet.

A parakeet answered.

Naung took up his weapon and loped soundlessly through the forest. There was not time to
ask travelers' intentions. Traders came with oxen
or mules, and not bearing arms. Kachin were not
bad people but this was Naung's valley. It was
the Sawbwa's valley really, but Naung thought of
the Sawbwa as king, or fool-king, and himself as
commander in chief.

He skirted East Poppy Field, his blood running
hot and strong, the breath in his lungs like wine.
His valley and his people. Killing was common-
place and not difficult. But not all men had such
good reasons.

Unless they climbed to the ridge, the Kachin
would cross or round East Poppy Field, which
was precautionary terrain, for show and
maneuver; Pawlu proper began half a mile to the
west, through Red Bullock Pass. The pass was
the first line of Shan defense and the people of
Pawlu had never, so far, needed another.
Organization. Method. Naung was proud of himself. He was a born fighter.

Wan was waiting at the pass. Naung raced to
him. "Kin-tan?"

"North Slope. Mong, South Slope. Don't fret.
No one will outflank us. What is it this time?"
Wan was a bull of a man, powerful, over forty
monsoons and could lift a grown goat in the
crook of one elbow. He would surely have been
First Rifle if Naung had not acquired foreign

experience and then become a legend for his Long-Haul-with-Koko. Beside him Naung, who was thirty and wiry, felt a stripling.

"Two Kachin."

"A brave people. No help for it. Weapons?"

"Rifles." Above them a cat seemed to miaow. Naung scanned the sky. "There. A kite."

"Waiting for carrion. And there it is: your Kachin."

The two horsemen were bordering the field by the north path. Naung and Wan lay among sheep-stagger-bush on the south slope of the pass; the Kachin would ride directly toward them for half a minute or more.

"How shall we do it this time?"

"We just take them," Naung said. "No pranks and no haste. We can kill them a ten of times."

"Once is usually enough," Wan said. "I think we should stop talking."

Naung examined his weapon again and unfolded the trigger. This trigger simply folded forward out of the way—that was the ingenious safety; and for firing it had to be deliberately plucked down. Naung had thirty-two rounds in his magazine and hoped to use no more than two. Perhaps the pistol this time? Wan was sighting an old British rifle. Traders brought ammunition, two and three cartridges at a time, once a full box of fifty, and the pompous Indian wanted an ounce of silver for it. Wan had taken twenty for ten catties of rice. Wan now had half a magazine, but his was a bolt-action rifle and if he missed, or if his round of unknown origin misfired ... No. Naung would use the mitraillette, to be certain. He trusted his own ammunition. It was four years old and more, but the gods had blessed his Long-Haul-with-Koko and this ammunition was sacred.

They saw the Kachin at the same moment and there was no need to speak or signal. The two horsemen approached at a leisurely walk, squinting here and there, rifles still at the ready. They seemed to believe that because they were not singing and dancing no one would notice them. Now Naung could see bandoliers, a silver ornament in the turban; one of these Kachin was missing an eye and wore a bit of colored ribbon on his blouse, probably a British or American medal. The sun washed them in clear golden mountain light.

Naung and Wan fired simultaneously. No refinements: they aimed for the heart and fired. The Kachin were dead before they fell. The ponies bucked and shied, the Kachin slid to earth. Half a ten of Shan emerged from the bushes and trees and caught the ponies while Naung covered the Kachin and Wan confirmed their release from this life. One rifle was an M-1, the other an Arisaka 99. The bandoliers were almost full. A blessing. In small leather bags they found silver pieces. One carried opium and a pipe of inferior jade. In the cloth boots they found articles of carved superior jade, doubtless for trading. These two men carried no food, no spare clothing, no religious objects. They were far from their own shrines, and would cross to the long night without ritual.

Naung freed his magazine and counted cartridges. Good! Only two gone! The lightest touch of the finger! For the hundredth time he wondered why this mitraillette had been conceived without single-shot fire as well. But only two gone! He was pleased. "Take the heads," he called out. "Leave the bodies on the upper slope. Sentries, back to your posts. Kin-tan, take charge. I'm going home. Cages tomorrow."

The men groaned and cursed. Naung laughed. "You call yourselves Shan! Bandits, more like. Scared to death of honest labor."

"All we ask is honest labor," they protested. "Is paddy-work not work? And the tea harvest? And the poppies?"

"We are farmers, and not roadside carpenters," one said.

"Nor killers either," Naung said, "but when there is work to be done, we must do it."

"And we will," Wan said, "but complaining is half the pleasure."

They all chuckled, and the strapping Kin-tan deployed some of the men, and the rest filed through the pass, two on Yunnan ponies, all of them cheerful, homeward bound, their women and children waiting for them, and the Sawbwa. It was the Sawbwa's work to see that no harm came to his people, that they dealt justly with one another, that they committed no blasphemy and comported themselves with honor, that no bandit or guerrilla ever set foot in their valley, that the Wild Wa never took a Shan head.

"They never learn," said the Sawbwa, his cloudy eye rolling. "How many heads are up?"

"Nine," Naung said, "along both sides of the

road, and some are naked skulls, now."

"Barbarous. It makes me feel no more civilized than the Wild Wa."

"It is the only way," Naung insisted. "We count a hundred bandits each moon who see them, think twice and pass on by." Before the Sawbwa he made a tiny row of Kachin boots, pipes, jade. "The meager leavings of two lives."

"It is the end of order. The earth's underpinnings tremble and shift. The last lakh of years is passing." The Sawbwa's pale, greenish skin gleamed; his thinned hair was white, his good eye was a doe's eye, his nostrils were broad and noisy, his teeth jagged and brown. He had been known to speak with the dead. "Before the war we killed only Wild Wa, and only when they came headhunting. Now the hills crawl with bandits and every man is his own state with his own law."

The two were squatting before the Sawbwa's house, chatting across an aromatic fire in the clay-and-stone hearth. A small vat of potato soup bubbled promisingly. If you stood one hundred rows of one hundred men in a field, that would make a lakh of fingers. So many years were the Sawbwa's concern; Naung's concern was tomorrow.

"You did well." The Sawbwa sighed. "But these cages! We never used to do that. Over in Yunnan they did it." From his shirt he drew a bamboo pipe two spans long: he plucked a brand from the fire and blew tobacco smoke. "It is well. Go to your woman and child."

Naung sniffed at the soup. Always that inner twinge when they said, "Your child." He rose,

bowed briefly, slung the mitraillette and padded
down the road. The Sawbwa's house overlooked
most of the valley, and the evening report was to
Naung an excursion, a bracing stroll to West
Slope and then, at sunset, a grand view east over
poppy fields and potato patches, plum orchards
and terraced paddy; the poppies were plump
now. The wood-and-bamboo houses, forty-two of
them, were hospitable in the late light, contours
soft and shadowed, fires flickering, knots of
farmers gossiping and smoking. And according
to the season there were pleasant odors, in the
autumn drying fish, in early spring the heavy wet
aroma of muddy furrow (Naung had learned
during the war that when the rest of Burma was
dry as a bone the Shan States enjoyed mountain
rains, and he took this as evidence of the Lord
Buddha's favor), in summer from the slopes rich
billows of sheep-stagger-bush blossom and in the
valley harvest odors, potato and barley and peanut, and the smell of paddy. In fall Naung shot
gyi and pheasant, and once he had hacked to
death a somnolent python, which was tasty
boiled.

He entered his own leafy lane. His house sat
well back among bamboo, looking south; at this
time of year sunshine was a blessing early and
late. High on the ridges above the valley Naung
saw rime now and then, in December or January,
like a Kachin mantle of silver; it vanished in an
hour.

Loi-mae was pounding millet. Naung stood outside in the dusk sniffing at a warm, moist
northerly breeze. He heard a toktay croak, and
counted: six times. Here where he was born he

had meat, drink, warmth, shelter, an amiable woman of beauty to share his life, and a step-daughter of nine who brightened his house like a flock of rainbow swallows. True, the daughter was not his; true, the woman had been another's; never mind. Pawlu was all this and more: cool dry season, warm dry season, monsoon. The occasional wildcat, a flight of bats, good opium for relaxation. Pawlu was some two hundred souls who asked little of life yet had much.

Naung entered his house, feeling, as always when he crossed his own doorsill, a man of worth. "Blessings." Loi-mae came to embrace him. Lola skipped to them and tugged at his jacket. He let his cheek rest warmly against his wife's, and then he rubbed his daughter's head and drew her too into the embrace. His wife, Loi-mae, was a goodly woman and comely. He had wondered, for a time, whether Green Wood had found her beautiful as Western women were beautiful. To Naung she was the most beautiful of all, but not for size, or shape, or feature: for the soft voice, the hearth, the soup, the gentle hands, the constancy.

His daughter's beauty was unquestioned, and was still a source of wonder to the whole village, as was her bubbly disposition. She was a busy-body, welcome everywhere, an imp born of the sun and fated to laugh, skip, dance and make merry in the bright mountain light. When she passed by, plowmen paused to wave; when she transplanted, she cheered the whole paddy full of Shan. Even the other children liked her. Loi-mae had been more wary of the other children than of the grown men and women; these last, after all, knew hunger and death and were inclined to kindness. Loi-mae had not burdened Naung with her worries, but he sensed the narrow way this child had walked, and sensed too Loi-mae's relief, like a burden set down, that the child was a child of the village and not of a stranger.

He made a priest's face at his daughter. "Little golden one, what have you done with your day?" For some weeks after his return from Indochina, during his courtship of Loi-mae, he had been embarrassed by the child's tawny hair, by a golden glow that seemed to shine forth from her gleaming skin. And then Loi-mae had said, "Her father was a good man and she is a lovely child, and let us have no frowning or perplexities." Naung had answered, "She is a lovely golden child and all say so." Loi-mae had said, "Then let there be no fears and no forbidden words. She is a daughter of two worlds, and even her name is a name in both."

Lola was not merely nine now but nine and a half, and she spoke up sedately: "I ground millet. I found and fetched eggs. At Lower Stream I pounded garments. And Chung says I must learn soon to tap the poppies."

He feigned severity and said, "Well, that is not bad." Lola was a beautiful name, a beautiful word, musical and sweet. "I hope you found time to play." He lunged for her and hummed along her neck.

She squealed and giggled. "Not much time. Cha's wedding is only three days off and there is much to do."

"And what can a girl of nine do?" Naung scoffed. "What does a girl of nine know of weddings?"

"A girl of nine can polish the silver ornaments. Tui said I did well. And I am to dance."

Naung was proud that she had been chosen to dance, so did not mention it. "What do they use for polish in Tui's house?"

"Pig's grease and river sand."

"Too harsh," Naung said. "Pig's grease and paddy mud do better. That Tui was always a harsh woman."

"You lived with her long enough," Loi-mae said.

"Well, that was years ago before the war, when I was a boy, and you would not have me, and it was only a month or two. I don't envy Kin-tan."

"I am going to live with Weng-aw," Lola said.

"Not yet you aren't," Naung said, and nuzzled her again.

"When the time comes," Lola said firmly.

"You will live with more than one man," Loi-mae promised, "and when you become a wife it will be to a man you know and value."

Naung smiled at his wife, who returned the smile. There were moments in Naung's life so complete, so swollen, that he feared the gods' wrath, as if one day he might be made to pay a great price.

The moment dissolved. He sat on a reed mat and leaned back against the oak-and-bamboo wall, content. He felt for his pipe and tobacco, and lit up. "Beer would be good," he said, but Loi-mae was already scooping a cupful from the keg. Naung sipped and watched his woman work.

The beer danced in his belly. Millet cakes she was preparing, surely potatoes, maybe papaya. The venison was long gone. What more could a man ask? All this, and a floor of wide-planked teakwood too!

"Lazy man!" Loi-mae said. "Go bring us a fresh fish."

Naung groaned. "Why not ask before I light my pipe?"

"The pipe can be lit again. Or Lola will keep it burning."

Naung grumbled but was happy within. Loi-mae's face was round, her eyes bright, almost black, shiny with life, her lips full, her teeth only slightly stained; she smoked little and chewed betel less. Her body was strong but accommodating, and she loved him within her, or seemed to, and in this Naung was shy and uncertain; and she cried out encouragement and thanks. She was not stringy like Wan's woman, a scold.

He took a bamboo pole from its pegs on the rear wall, and a round wicker basket without a bottom, and a wicker creel which he slung on his back. "I'll go," he said, "but I'll be hungry afterward. And later—you know what fish does to a man."

"Big talk," she complained. "Who snored first last night?"

"Perhaps if my woman were less homely," he suggested, and she beat him out the door, pounding his back with the flat of her hands and laughing as she cried, "O! O! You rhinoceros!"

Light lingered over West Slope and the Sawbwa's house. Naung touched his pistol. The evening sounded normal, a calm voice here and a

laugh there, a pye-dog's yap. Naung hurried. He
would need more than starlight, and the moon
would be late tonight. The air of dusk was cool
and soothing on his face. He trotted toward the
upper paddies. They were submerged now, with
waterweeds growing that would later be
fertilizer. Each spring Pawlu dispatched a body
of armed men to follow the valley's deep stream
to the River Lae, a tributary of the great Salween.
These men made bundles of reeds and grasses,
and strung the bundles on bamboos, and laid
them down in shallow water, weighting them
with stones. Fat river fish came to the shallows
to spawn, and their eggs clung to the reeds and
grasses. At the proper time the men gathered
these reeds and grasses in great baskets and bore
them home, and scattered them in the paddies,
and soon the eggs hatched and later the fishing
was good.

At the edge of the paddy Naung removed his
cloth shoes and trousers. He waded out a few
paces; the water did not reach his knee. He swept
the surface with his bamboo pole. Nothing. He
went on sweeping. A silver flash broke the surface, but he could not see which way it fled. He
went on sweeping. Another flash, and he
pounced. Through a small hole in the top of the
round wicker basket he felt for his fish. He found
it, grasped the tail and hauled it up. Larger than
a man's hand. He dropped it into the creel, dried
his legs on his trousers, donned the trousers and
shoes, and marched home with his tackle and his
catch.

Lola laughed at the silvery creature and clapped her hands. While Loi-mae cleaned the fish

Naung hung up his gear, lit his pipe and swigged his beer. He sang to his daughter, who stole a mischievous sip of the beer. He sang about a little girl who strayed from the valley and was devoured by a leopard. Lola's eyes were enormous and her teeth gleamed in the firelight, and at the end she cried, "Her father should have rescued her!"

In the morning Mong fashioned bamboo cages while interested villagers murmured compliments. He drew a crowd always. He was an artist with bamboo, and their compliments were a way to say, "Mong, why should anyone else do this work when you do it so well? Therefore we will all smoke and gossip and be thankful." Mong cursed them with great good nature. He bound the bamboos with stout hemp twine; he slit, trimmed, lashed again, tested. When the cages were complete he cleaned his knife, and stretched. "I'm hungry," he said. His wife, Chung, was a famous stout woman, jolly in good times and even-tempered in bad; she was prepared for this announcement and came to him immediately with rice, cold chicken and tea. "Chung has not eaten it all!" a villager cried, and there was free and merry laughter, and Chung called out, "Let who will, sleep with sticks! Mong likes a good substantial woman!" Chung was aggressively round, and in the heavy heat before the monsoon, when the women often wore only the long skirt, her great breasts hung like ripe pumpkins. It was no surprise that she and Mong were raising a large family, seven healthy children, five of them boys, and in summer it was said jokingly that none were yet weaned and there was plenty for all.

Mong himself was a skinny bunch of dried sticks, short and bandy-legged, so the jokes included him, and some were by now village traditions: "Where is Mong today?" "Fallen in again." Or, "He slipped and was smothered." Chung would snort, hearing this, and her little brown eyes would flame in fun and pretended anger, and she would tell them, "Not one of you would last an hour, and Mong is still rutting like a hare after fifteen monsoons!"

The Sawbwa said that all women were meant to be like Chung. This was the highest of compliments, and it was generally agreed that Chung merited it. She bore herself proudly, even now, serving Mong his meal. While he ate, the villagers admired his work, squinted at the sun, smoked cheroots (small ones, the cheroots of mountain farmers and not the foot-long monstrosities that lazy low-landers had time to burn), poked their children in the ribs and told ancient stories of the miserly and barbarous Chinese. At the edge of the crowd Naung sat against the wall of a house and dozed.

When Mong had belched, and washed his hands in the dust, and smiled shy thanks at Chung, Naung rose casually and assembled his platoon. Mong would carry the cages, Kin-tan the heads. So many would stand guard, so many would dig, so many would carry posts and so many beams. Naung asked the Sawbwa, "Is it well?"

The Sawbwa was in good humor this morning. He blinked, and his filmy eye shone pale in the

tall sunlight, and he said, "All things have their
uses and their seasons, and this morning's work
is well done. It seems to me the hot weather will
come a day or two early."

The villagers murmured. The Sawbwa was
rarely wrong, and now that he had spoken, it
seemed to them that, yes, the teak leaves were
shriveling a day or two early, and perhaps the
goats had begun to shed, and down among the
pyinkado trees the monkeys were noisier and
more active than customary.

The Sawbwa tapped his turban as if saluting
and said, "Go then." Naung marched his men off,
the whole length of the village, from the
Sawbwa's house on West Slope down the dusty
road toward Red Bullock Pass, and when they
passed his own house Loi-mae and Lola waved
and the woman called, "Hurry home!" Naung's
men then exchanged the customary jokes about
those who spoiled women with excessive gallantry, and not merely gallantry but acrobatics,
and that was why the Shan never killed monkeys,
because the monkeys set high standards of
promiscuity, frequency and speed, standards for
men to live up to, but this Naung was embarrassing even the monkeys, perhaps because he was
over-educated by foreign travel.

They saw vultures on the upper slope, above
East Poppy Field. They crossed the field and
entered the grove in open order, a loose rank,
some bearing timber, some with weapons at the
ready, each man a scout. They only gathered
again at the road. From there they could scan the
hills thousands of feet above them, where the
Wild Wa lived. Naung glassed the hills carefully.

They marched north then, the bearers and Mong flanked by their guard, and two men like shadows in the groves to either side. They passed four poles, four beams, four cages, two of them down, the hemp slashed by impious travelers. On the road crows strutted, iridescent blue at the shoulder. Here the road was broad and straight, a true road, suitable for carts. The men kicked up reddish dust.

After some hundreds of paces Naung called a halt. The band of Shan conferred, and some dug at the earth here and there with their swords. They decided to place the cages one directly opposite the other, a double warning for travelers, who would thus pass between the staring Kachin heads.

The diggers worked with wooden spades fashioned from one timber and beveled. They would dig crotch-deep. Meantime the balance beams were fitted to the thick posts, and the wooden tholes greased with hog fat and driven. The sun was high now and the men worked slowly.

Mong took the heads from Kin-tan and sewed the flaps of neck skin to the bamboo slats. He then bound the cages shut. Naung ran hemp line through holes in one end of each balance beam and knotted it securely. These preparations took the time of one meal, or of a good bath in the stream, or of one cheroot.

When all was in readiness, Mong bound the cages to the inner ends of the balance beams. Two teams raised the posts and planted them deep in their pits; two teams shoveled dirt around them and tamped it firm.

When the posts were up, Naung hauled on his

hemp lines. The balance beams swung up, and the cages hung above the road, and the heads brooded down at them. Naung then tied the hemp lines through notches low on the posts. "No more digging for a while," he said. "No more construction. For a while we repair only. And replace heads as needed."

"Ten is a good number," Mong approved. "Five to the south and five to the north."

"But this is a double," said Ko-yang, "which makes eleven."

Mong scowled.

"Eleven is not a bad number," Naung said quickly. "One for each finger and one for the big finger."

Mong laughed, though Ko-yang seemed surly, and Naung breathed easier. "Now we make our visits." The men assembled and marched back along the road, and where the cages were down because fearful or defiant travelers had hacked through the hemp lines, Naung knotted or replaced the hemp. They continued south, beyond the teak grove and East Poppy Field, to repair the other five cages. Naung liked this road. He was a traveled man and knew a small thrill, an eagerness, at the flat dun glare of the road between the green groves, the straight run of it like the airstrip at Muong Sing. He liked it even better now, with his handiwork complete, six to the north and five to the south, eleven former highwaymen and brigands saying to all who approached, "Dawdlers, beware: see what befalls evil men here."

They trooped back to the village and lingered over a late noonday meal, each in his own house.

In the afternoon Naung made his rounds, inspecting all sentry posts, surprising a sleepy Shwe, taking him unawares by the throat and then delivering, for the twentieth time, a lecture on the functions of a sentry. Shwe was drooping, middle-aged, a smoker of much opium. Naung decided to retire him to farm work, with the Sawbwa's permission.

Naung took an hour off then, and played pigs-in-their-pens with Lola so that he could rejoice in her bright brown eyes, her wavy hair, her ivory skin, the warmth of her imp's grin, the tug of her fingers. She was almost ready now for women's clothes. Growing up!

In the evening he reported to the Sawbwa. The Sawbwa's breath whistled through the hairs of the Sawbwa's nose; the Sawbwa removed his turban to fluff the white hair and scratch the yellow scalp. "It is well done and still I do not like it," the Sawbwa said. "We are Shan and not Wild Wa. Our way should be the way of the Lord Buddha, and not the way of savages who worship stones and human heads."

"But if we must become like the Wild Wa to survive," Naung said reasonably, "then we must."

"If we become like the Wild Wa," said the Sawbwa, "then we have not survived."

The Sawbwa of Pawlu could distinguish faces at twice a man's length; at a hundred paces he could see, or at least perceive vaguely, the presence and motion of men and women on a hillside. His kidneys ached always; his urine was greenish yellow, but this did not alarm him because colors were to him muted and dull. He cleared his bowels perhaps once in three days. Sudden pains, sharp pangs in various joints and bones, were his way of life.

He knew that he was Chinese, and Yunnanese, but not Shan because the language of Pawlu had been gibberish when first he arrived there. Long before that, he remembered gnawing ravenously on acorns. He recalled a snarling, emaciated man admonishing him over and over, "Remember, you are fifteen! You are fifteen!" That was curious. He had celebrated his ninth birthday at the New Year, by burning a strip of red paper. The man was possibly his father and was urging him upon another man and insisting, "Not paper! Not copper cash! The silver piece!" Not paper, not copper cash, the silver piece.

This first man took the silver piece and plodded off. The second man set him in a wagon and handed him a lump of steamed dough and a bowl of hot water. To the boy it was meat and wine. He could not believe his luck. There were other boys in the wagon. There had been different boys and some girls too in a hut; once he had known their names; perhaps that had been home.

The wagon creaked and advanced. The spindly boys sat like caged larks, and after a time peered about. There were houses, birds, fields, farmers; the wagon was passing these, but it seemed that the world was passing the wagon. The sky was light and in the distance hazy mountains rose. The season was perhaps spring. The wagon was being pulled by a red mule.

They were very close to a pink mountain. The boy knew panic; how if they should take him up

so high? In his life he had never stood higher
than the bed of a wagon. This mountain was
carved. There were roads and flat spaces, and
queer squat houses. Now they passed red men
and red donkeys. Now they were closer still to
the mountain and he saw many red men and red
monkeys.

To the other side of the wagon he saw green
boys. Pleasure flooded his heart. Red donkeys
and green boys! Perhaps this was growing up.
Perhaps this was the true world, the world of
living people who had houses for shelter and
food each day.

The wagon halted beside one of the low buildings. "All out! All out!" The boys scrambled
down, milled and stared about. "Inside! Inside!"
Hastily the boys filed through a narrow doorway.
The door was of wood but the house was of stone.
Inside were many more boys and a few men. The
taller men could not stand erect, but stooped and
hunched beneath the low ceiling. The boy felt a
strong urge to relieve nature, the small convenience, but suppressed it.

For some minutes the boys huddled together in
the gloom. A man's voice called, "Sit down,
fools!" They sat down immediately. The boy saw
then that there were also donkeys in the house.
The house, like all the houses he had known, was
of one room, more spacious than his family hut.
As he grew accustomed to the dim light he
imagined that the men and boys who had preced-
ed him were also red and green. Odors here were
pungent.

His neighbor pressed against him; the boy
drew away, pressing against another. Bit by bit

all made room. It was possible to lie down, but
with no more than a hand's span of free space.
The boy's bladder pressed and he wondered if he
dared speak. Others were murmuring. He heard
a splash and splatter, and sat up in the gloom: a
donkey was staling. Almost immobilized by fear,
the boy sought anyone's eye.

A shadowy man finally looked at him. The boy
crawled two lengths and squatted before the
man. This man was surely red. There was a
narrow slit of a window, and through the slit
came a dusty ray of sunlight and it brightened
the red of this man's skin. "Small convenience,"
the boy finally whispered, trembling.

"Hey, hey, hey!" The man was mocking. The
boy cringed. "This one wants to piss!" Others
laughed. The boy hung his head. "Well, new boy,
I am going to be kind to you. Welcome to Kochiu.
For the conveniences one goes outside, or one is
beaten. If it is the small convenience, there is a
wall. If it is the great convenience, there is a
small patch of broken ground and your nose will
lead you to it." The boy was already squirming
through the mass. He scuttled out the doorway
and turned a corner of the house. There he
opened his trousers. Without result. He could no
longer make water. Fear grew in him.

"You there!" He jumped. "Hurry, now." This
seemed to be a green man, with glittering eyes.
The man came to him and said, "You are a new
boy?"

The boy nodded. He was still clutching his
member. The man patted his head. "Take your
time." At the kindly tone, the boy gushed tears
and piss at once. The man chuckled. "Both ends,

hey? How old are you?"

The boy was weak with relief; his water drained from him and left him content. He remembered: Fifteen."

Again the bright-eyed man chuckled. This was indeed a green man, with a large belly and fat shiny lips. The belly quivered as he laughed. "And your name?"

"Ming-tzu," the boy said.

"Well, Ming-tzu, my name is Shang, and I will help you when I can. Here in Kochiu we must help one another in all things. Do you understand?"

The boy nodded many times, full of love.

"You may loiter outside," Shang said, "but no more than a step or two from the house." And then he rubbed the boy's head and walked off.

If there was food here the boy saw none that night. At dawn he was awakened by coughing. Many of the men and boys were coughing. One man retched endlessly. The stench of manure and human waste was fierce. Outside someone was beating on a pan. Men and boys rose groaning and filed through the doorway. Ming-tzu hurried to join them. "New boys here!" They were marched to another building. In this building was a table, and behind the table on chairs sat three men who were neither green nor red but the color of men. Each was speaking to a boy. When Ming-tzu's turn came he quaked. "Your name?"

"Ming-tzu."

"Ming-tzu." The man held a small stick and pressed it against the table. "Your age?"

"Nine years."

"What?"

Ming-tzu covered his mouth; terror drove sleep from his head and hunger from his belly. "Fifteen!" he cried.

"Yes, better." The man pressed the stick again. He handed the boy a small rectangle of paper. "Listen to me, Ming-tzu. You are now a member of the Miners' Guild and this is your card. You will keep it with you at all times. Your number is two seven two seven nine, and you are registered in this book."

The boy did not know what a miner was, or a guild, or a card, though he had more than once seen a book. Now he knew what a book was for. He could count to ten, but a series of numbers was meaningless.

His lips trembled in a servile smile. He wondered where he should keep this new thing, this card. He clutched it and fell into line. Soon the line moved. Outside the low house that was his home, another green man, potbellied and bright-eyed, stood behind a steaming vat and bellowed, "Shrimp! Fried pork! Egg soup! Mandarin fish!" The boy was overcome and stumbled dizzily forward, snatching up, as the others did, a wooden bowl from a jumbled heap. The fat green man filled it, and the boy, glancing furtively about for enemies, hugged it to himself and scurried for the shelter of the wall, where others were squatting.

The shrimp, pork, egg and fish proved to be soggy millet in hot water. It was delectable. The rich savory taste of it brought tears of gratitude to the boy's eyes. He belched. Warmth invaded his chest and belly.

When the millet was gone and the bowls were collected, when men and boys had shat, when the sun broke above the rolling horizon, a stern wiry green man strutted down the path and addressed them. "New boys! You are now miners! Yours is a proud trade. Your contracts bind you for ten months, and your wages are three dollars each day, and if you work well you will be given a bonus."

What was a miner? A contract? A bonus? The boy had no idea. But three dollars a day! That he understood! Three Yunnanese dollars each day! That would buy a ball of steamed dough and cup of real tea!

The crowd of boys was trotted up the path, toward the hills. He found that he was still clutching his card. The hills were red, pitted and gouged. Some looked like squares of paddy, but all were red, some sandy red and some blood-red. Through these hills wound narrow lanes, and on the lanes were many red men with their red donkeys.

At length the boys were told to halt and rest, by a hole in the mountain. Ming-tzu looked back and caught his breath: behind him, far below, lay a vast valley. He had risen. He stared upward, being now so close to the heavens. He saw one fluffy cloud, no gods, no dragons. The stern wiry man, who had been all green but was now mottled pink, issued instructions. Ming-tzu understood very little. In the evening he would ask Shang to make all things clear.

The hole in the mountain was square and propped by timbers. "You will follow your captain," the stern wiry man said, and gestured.

A boy somewhat older than Ming-tzu, and wearing a shirt with pockets, rose and said, "Your cards." The boys filed before him; he collected the cards and slipped them into a pocket, which he carefully buttoned. This was like no button Ming-tzu had ever seen. It was flat and round and made of bone or stone or wood, and it slipped through a slit in the flap of the pocket. Ming-tzu considered this ingenious. He had seen buttons before, but they were knots of cloth that one forced through loops. "Now follow."

And to Ming-tzu's horror, the boy with pockets stooped and entered the hole in the mountain. This hole was less high than Ming-tzu. He struggled to shout, but fear took firm hold of his tongue. As the line of boys shuffled forward he shuffled with them. He passed into the hole, and into darkness; far ahead a spark flickered.

Now the boys descended, in single file. They descended by proceeding downward step by step, their feet seeking and gripping ledges to either side. Down the center of this descent hung a taut rope; to this rope the hands clung. After a time the space widened; this seemed to be a room; faint light again flickered. Ming-tzu stared wildly into the murk. He was quite warm now. He was even hot. Yet he shivered. Caverns were the haunt of phantoms, leopard spirits, ghosts, ancestors. In caverns were found bones and dead men. Had he died?

He was sweating when the troop was ordered to halt. Here a lantern hung on a spike driven into the wall. The boy saw men with picks attacking the walls. He saw stout cloth bags in stacks. These were homely objects and reassuring. He breathed easier: *work* was being done here. Work he understood. His father, if father that had been, was constantly seeking *work*. And Ming-tzu had found it!

Someone thrust a sack at him. He followed the boy before him and dragged the sack to a pile of earth that had been chopped from the walls by the men with picks. Bare-handed, Ming-tzu stuffed a sack. "Quickly, quickly!" cried a voice. Ming-tzu found that he could not carry the full sack. He scooped out a handful of rock and was flung violently forward by a lash as sharp as hunger. "Full sack!" the voice called.

The boy wailed. This he understood. One was whipped for impossibilities. "Cannot!" he cried. "Cannot, cannot!"

"Then do what you can," the voice said, echoing, and the boy understood: this was a lesson for the others as well. "And you will learn to do more each day, do you hear?"

"I hear! I hear!" Ming-tzu strained, heaved; his knees buckled.

"Not so, you fool!" Someone, perhaps the older boy, was wrenching at his arm. "So, and so, with the arms through the straps. Thus the legs bear the weight and the hands are free. Do you understand this, little pig?"

"Understand," Ming-tzu sobbed. "Understand."

"Then up you go to the sunlight."

Ming-tzu was streaming sweat. He stumbled blindly, crying, "Where, sir? And how, sir?" He found the hole and the ascending ledges and the anchored rope; he grasped the rope and forced his foot to fumble for a ledge.

He was knocked flat, and the breath whooshed out of him, and he lay wanting death.

"Not this one, turtle-egg! This one is for coming down. For going up, that one. You see there is first a slope, hey? You will go up that sloping shaft; you will come down the straight shaft."

The boy struggled to his feet. He had not before heard the term "shaft" but he knew it now. He lurched toward the sloping shaft and toiled forward. He stumbled. He rose. He toiled forward. He trembled in agony, the straps bit his shoulders like fire, in the dark demons lurked, bats, serpents, bloodsuckers, assassins. He proceeded by feel and by fear. How long this journey took he could not have said; but in the end he saw light. He stepped into daylight and fell flat. "A new boy." Someone laughed. The sack was removed from him. "Over there," someone said. Ming-tzu saw the hole in the mountain and recognized this spot. "Cannot," he said. The clout caught him on the nape and tumbled him hard. He lay gulping air. "Water," he gasped.

"Water! In the rainy season you will have water. For now you have the runoff at the concentrators. After work."

Ming-tzu understood "runoff." He would not try to understand more. Perhaps he would slip in his descent and come to a merciful end.

He did slip, but the body always wins these contests; he clutched the rope, found footing, proceeded downward, filled a sack, bore it to the surface. He repeated these actions for days. When at last he was told to rest, to return to the stone house, he asked how many days had passed.

"Not one day," someone said. "It is only afternoon."

Someone else said, "Cheer up, new boy. Only ten months to go, less one day," and there was a general chuckle.

Ming-tzu noticed that he was coated with a film of red dust.

Shang befriended him, and a grateful Ming-tzu performed painless sexual services in return. Shang was a wise man, so the boy asked him, "Why am I red?"

"It is the dust of the mines only," Shang said.

"And why are you green?"

"Because I do not go below, but tend the concentrators; in days gone by I went below, and the poison is in me."

Another day it occurred to the boy to ask, "What do we mine?"

"We mine tin."

And another day, "Then the tin is poison?"

Shang said, "No. The poison is called arsenic, and it lives with the tin as moss lives with a tree. It enters the skin, and it enters the lungs, and it makes the lips fat and shiny."

"What are lungs?"

So over the weeks Shang told him much. That there were perhaps one hundred thousand workers here at Kochiu. That the least legal age was fifteen but that half were younger. This tin was something like iron and was used for pots, wires, cups perhaps, knives and spoons perhaps, objects made of metal. Ming-tzu had seen the foreign foods in containers?

No. And who took this tin? Ming-tzu had seen the concentrators now, and had drunk the metallic water for many weeks; but where did the tin go then?

"Well, it goes to foreigners. Englishmen and Frenchmen."

"What are those?"

"Those are men from far places. The Big Noses."

"Then I do not like the Big Noses from far places."

"There are good men in far places. Russiamen are not bad men, I have heard. You remember that. Russiamen have warred on the rich."

"I will remember."

"And remember too that there are Chinese like us, Yunnanese like us, who also take this tin, and who sell it everywhere under heaven, and are very rich, and eat what they like, and never work."

"Never work! When they can if they want to?"

Shang was pleased with this boy. "You have rice every evening."

"It is so."

"And a scrap of meat once in ten days."

"It is so."

"And how if you could eat rice and pork and beef and lamb and fish and little pink shrimp three times every day without working?"

The boy found this bewildering.

Every morning and every evening he scraped

himself. Each boy carried a slat of bone in his belt, and with this he scraped away dung, simple dirt and whatever of the red dust, muddied by sweat, could be scoured away. When a boy died and his body was removed by the death-servants, his bone was kept in the house, and the flimsiest were bestowed upon new boys, so that a good strong thick bone was a sign of seniority, as was a sleeping space far from the donkeys.

What Ming-tzu learned, he remembered. He saw now that little boys were required because the shafts and tunnels were too small for grown men. This knowledge imparted a sense of worth, and of pride. When Squirrel—a truly little fellow, smaller even than Ming-tzu—commenced to vomit daily, Ming-tzu and some others joined to force upon him a few extra grains of rice, a few extra drops of water. Most of the boys suffered diarrhea. Ming-tzu suffered more from headache, and often dragged himself through a day when pain flickered and flashed like lightning.

Only the pipe relieved the pain. Yunnan was a province rich in opium. In some regions poppies rippled red to the horizon. Good black yen was cheap and plentiful, and that much the Englishmen and Frenchmen and their Chinese satraps would allow the miners: the bowl of millet, the bowl of rice, the strip of meat once a week or so, and pipes, stylets and yen in each house, for only pennies a day. Ming-tzu shoveled down his rice in late afternoon and awaited his turn at the pipe. Slowly peace replaced his pain. Often he and Shang shared a pipe, and then another, and drifted into sleep holding hands.

Most of the boys were soon bright-eyed like

Shang. Some trembled constantly and jerked convulsively in their sleep. Squirrel did not wake one morning, but lay staring at nothing; he was alive but uncertainly so, and died on the third day. As the weather changed, other boys died; Ming-tzu noticed that his household had altered. With the donkeys was now one water buffalo, and new boys had moved in to replace the dead.

One day he said to Shang, boasting, "I think I am green now too, beneath the red."

"Come along," said Shang, and they strolled to the concentrators. These were troughs in which the ore was cleansed by water. They first drank. Shang then took a square of cloth and rubbed at Ming-tzu's red skin. The red vanished; green sprang forth. With much mirth the boy and the man created a checkerboard of red and green.

"Are my eyes shiny too?"

"Yes," said Shang, "and your lips bloated. A real miner, you are."

"I was in the lower pit today," the boys said.

"Oh, that is hot!"

"I have never been so hot."

"Listen, boy: when you come up from the lower pit, rub yourself dry with your loincloth. You remember Two-teeth?"

"I remember him."

"He came up wet and the chill settled on his lungs."

"Shang," the boy asked fearfully, "how many die in one year?"

"About one in three," Shang said.

"Shang," the boy asked, "will I die?"

"It is for the gods to decide," Shang said.

The future Sawbwa did not die. He was in a middle-level tunnel one day, just down for another load, when a charge blew. He had not heard the shouted alarm, if indeed anyone had bothered to shout. The back collapsed. He knew that he was about to die and was sorry that he would not see Shang again. Only then did the searing pain stab through his left eye. He screamed. Feebly he strained against the rubble. He screamed again: "Shang!" Shang was nowhere near, but he could think of nothing else to shout. He heard voices: "Ai, so there was one in the tunnel." "I hear him." "Leave him." "But he lives." "The boss says to leave them. We pull them out and they are broken and useless and we must pay them off and turn them away. This way he saves a few coppers."

The boy inhaled a huge breath and shouted, "I am alive! I am well and can work!" This was or was not true. He could see nothing; his body was aflame with pain. Dimly he heard the scrape and scatter of rubble. Faintly he felt drifting air. His mind swam, and stars rose before him, spiraling into a black gulf, and then all was darkness.

He heard a gabble. This was answered by further gabble. He lay on his back still but was no longer in the mine. He was cool, and at peace. He could see nothing; a weight lay upon his eyes; he reached to pluck at it.

"Do not!" a voice commanded.

Terrified, he lay rigid.

The gabble continued. He longed for Shang. He understood now that two men were speaking a tongue not his. With horror he wondered if they were Englishmen or Frenchmen. He was immensely, wholly thirsty. His left eye throbbed as if a demon within were trying to emerge through the small hole in the center.

Now a voice spoke calmly in his own tongue. "You are safe here. The foreign doctor will make you well."

His horror doubled: "An Englishman? A Frenchman?"

"No. An American."

"What is that?"

"He is one who serves the Lord of all under Heaven by healing the sick."

The boy took this in. What was done for the Lord, or by the Lord, must be good and not evil. "I thirst," he said.

A hand propped him up; a cup was set to his lips. He gulped cool sweet water and fell asleep content.

It was perhaps the next day. Ming-tzu had slept and wakened, drunk more water and relieved nature. Now the voice said, "Lie still, and we shall look one look at your eye."

Ming-tzu held his breath, awaiting pain. The bandages fell away and there came a blinding dazzle of golden light. "Well, that is very good," said the voice. Ming-tzu squinted. He felt fingers on his face, his neck, his shoulder. Now he saw: this was a Chinese, in foreign costume. Or were there foreign Chinese? This had not occurred to him. If there were Chinese among these hated Englishmen, these hated Frenchmen? He had never seen an Englishman or a Frenchman to know what they resembled. "One eye is not good, and one eye is good," the voice said, and at that incantation Ming-tzu's vision cleared further. He saw a sad-faced Chinese, stocky and wearing eye-glasses. This man spoke again, almost jesting: "So then, you will not be cross-eyed; nor will the eyes be greater than the stomach."

Ming-tzu wondered if he was still red, if his eyes shone, if his fat lips protruded. How long had he lain here, out of the mine? The odor here was sharp, but not of men, animals or filth.

He could not think what to say, and so did not speak.

Later he stood in a pair of short trousers and a kind of shirt-without-sleeves before men and desks. He had eaten bits of meat twice each day for three days, with his rice. He knew now what these men did on their desks, with their brushes and their sticks. It was called writing, and was a way to send messages, like a shop sign or a poster.

"So you are the miner Ming-tzu."

The boy nodded.

"Let us see your card."

"There is no card."

"No card!" This man was stern of face, with a drooping mustache. "You were to carry that card at all times."

Ming-tzu said timidly, "The esteemed pit captain took it first day."

"And where is this pit captain?"

"He is dead."

"And the card?"

"This lowly one never saw the card again."

The mustache twitched; this well-fed man was smiling. "Then how can we know who you are?"

Ming-tzu stood silent.

"Or how old you are?"

"This lowly one is fifteen."

"Fifteen!" All three of these men laughed with enthusiasm. "Not a day over ten! So you lied about your age!"

The boy knew he was to be punished. He knew also that in the presence of the tiger no-speech is better than speech.

"So you will be paid at the children's rate," the man said angrily. "Not three dollars a day but one dollar."

Ming-tzu was wondering if he would be flogged, or go to prison.

"Well then, well then, how long have you worked?"

"This lowly one cannot know," he mumbled.

"Well then, what was the number of your card?"

"This lowly one—" But a memory sparked, other men like these, perhaps these very men; and his voice repeated the words before his memory had confirmed them: "Two seven two seven nine!"

They made owl eyes. "Why, this is a scholar!" one cried. The smallest shuffled papers. "That was the sixth month last year," he muttered, "and previously the twenty-seven thousands were used three years ago, so it cannot have been this same boy, and here we are at two ten thousands, and now the seven thousands," and peeking upward the boy saw the lips twitch and work like a mouse's, the man's finger gliding down the page as the others waited, amused, and the little man called out, "Ming-tzu! So it is! By the gods, I shall give him an extra dollar!"

"That is two hundred and seven dollars," the mustached man summed up gravely, "plus your contribution of one, makes two hundred and eight, less one hundred for opium, as stated here. No bonus. He has not completed his contract. So: one hundred and eight dollars for this retired miner."

One hundred and eight dollars!

"You will sign this."

"This lowly one cannot."

"Then make a mark here, so."

Clumsily Ming-tzu took the brush and stroked a mark.

The small man handed him a sheaf of limp bills. Ming-tzu's tremor overcame him at the sight of money; the bills slipped from his hand and fluttered to the floor. Swiftly he dropped to his knees, whimpering, swiftly he gleaned them. The men were entertained by this performance, and encouraged him with ribald suggestion.

He clutched to his breast his one hundred and eight dollars.

One of the men snorted. "His father got more than that for him."

Another said, "Go now. Hop the locomotive and go out the gate. You are no longer a miner."

"This lowly one must say farewell to Shang at the concentrator."

"You will hop the locomotive," said the mustached man, "and be gone from here."

Ming-tzu never again saw Shang. On the ore train a young man made as if to search him, but Ming-tzu snarled, and the young man drew back, raising one palm in peace. When Ming-tzu saw his left eye, reflected in a window in the town of Kochiu, he too was appalled and drew back.

He slept behind walls, in fields, in gutters and ditches. His one hundred and eight Yunnanese dollars bought him hot rice, hot field corn in street stalls, steamed dough and boiled water for almost ten days. He traveled west, toward the mountains, true mountains and not mine mountains. His back ached constantly. His knees and elbows were afire. His feet bled, but hardened on the road. He dreamed while awake, dreamed of flights of white cranes, of one-eyed locomotives, of fires that consumed whole provinces. In one village he told, haltingly, of the mine, and men and women pitied him and gave him one meal. This was a dry year. The meal was simple, millet and a strip of old chicken. That night he woke in agony. His back, his joints, his every bone stabbed; his body convulsed, he frothed at the mouth, he shrieked. In the morning clouds had gathered. A day more, and torrential rains all but dissolved the earthen huts.

The boy continued toward the setting sun. He hobbled, limped, starved. From time to time a wagoner pitied him. In a town called Mo-chiang he saw a foreigner, a man with a long sharp nose, pink skin and hazel eyes. This was perhaps an Englishman or a Frenchman; the boy scuttled away. That afternoon he saw an aircraft, and a street barber told him what it was; the third seen in these regions, though in foreign journals there had been pictures. It seemed to the boy that he had seen one before, perhaps through the twilight at Kochiu.

That night he was racked by fierce pains. In the morning the sky was leaden; by evening showers had cooled the land, and his pains had been eased.

Again and again unpredictable agonies exhausted him. Each time rain followed. He made, finally, the connection. It puzzled him. But thenceforth among his disjointed visions were apocalyptic downpours and epic floods. He also had a vision of the American, a fat kindly man with soft hands, who was a healer. He could hear again the outlandish, crooning tones of the American voice.

By now he was starving truly, and when he was overtaken by a trade caravan he made humble submission and asked for work. This request was greeted with hilarity. A stout, winy sort of fellow with the two upper front teeth missing, a man as bald as the moon, bellowed for an audience and cried, "See what we have here! This little green elf is unemployed!"

"One of those miners," a mule-skinner said, and spat a spumy gob. "What can you do, boy?"

Without thinking—there was little thought left in him, only pain and visions—the future Sawbwa said, "I can mine tin. I can see distant events. I can foretell rain. And"—remembering Shang—"I can play the woman's part."

They did not laugh. The boy's had not been an ordinary response. These men looked him over. The boy was one-eyed and a scarecrow. His hair was patchy and gray. He wore a loincloth. His complexion was not so green as the willow even in winter, but it was notably unhealthy.

"Furthermore I bring luck," the boy said, "like hunchbacks."

After some moments the stout bald man said, "Bugger! We'll take him to Lan-ts'ang and sell him there."

The boy saw that these men were uneasy. He fixed his good eye on each in turn.

"How old are you?" asked the mule-skinner.

"Fifteen,' said the boy, "or nine."

Then the men laughed lustily and were pleased that they had found him. "That is a considerable spread," said one. "We shall let him be nine when he eats and fifteen when he plays the woman."

At this a gust of laughter seemed to whip up dust all along the caravan.

The Sawbwa was on his way to Pawlu.

He saw himself in a good glass, and was allowed time to inspect his face carefully. The bad eye was unnerving, milky, with gray and brown swirls; it protruded slightly. His hair was indeed thin and gray. His pale yellow-green skin was finely wrinkled. His good eye no longer gleamed unnaturally, and his lips were no longer bloated.

He ran off at Lan-ts'ang before they could sell him, taking with him five copper cash, a wooden bowl and his loincloth. Westward he traveled, and upward, and once at sunset, when he had seen no other human being in a full day's travel, he stood on a high ridge and saw the sky before him aflame, and he could make out the sinking disk of the sun; and far below he saw a silver river.

He spoke to the gods then, calling from his ridge to the distant mountains, and the gods answered. He saw thousands of men on horseback, bearing banners. Again he saw the locomotive. He saw ships. He saw the dead pit captain. He fell to earth, and there he slept. He woke at dawn, freezing, and began what was to be the last leg of his journey, down and down to the silver river, and then up and up to the far ridge. Beyond that far ridge he would be safe from the mines, from caravans, from beggary, from man's evil. Beyond that far ridge lived the gods.

Beyond that far ridge he found a road, and he followed the road. It was early days, and there were not yet cages full of bandits' heads by East Poppy Field. The boy recognized poppies, and assumed dimly that they had been cultivated; here then were people, and here was the source of good black yen, and here was his destination.

He entered Pawlu and followed the narrow track north of East Poppy Field. He sniffed the air: food. He ambled openly, knowing no other way to travel. He stumbled often. He gazed vacantly at the sun, and laughed aloud. He did not know that he was watched, that word had already reached the village; so when he shambled down the slope and onto the large common field, and found a dense semicircle of villagers observing his progress and inspecting his person, his cloudy mind told him that the gods had prepared this welcome.

He advanced. He fell to his knees, set down his bowl and removed his loincloth. Naked, he pried the five copper cash from a knot in the loincloth and poured them into the bowl. He then kowtowed three times, touching his head reverently to the earth, and said, "Here is Heaven. I go no farther."

At first the villagers shrugged and tolerated him. He was a fool who raved and was clearly sick; it would not do to offend the gods by inhuman behavior. He had little to say for some time. He slept out of doors in all weather, seeming to suffer a horror of houses. He ate little, but more as time passed. He was like a wizened mouse who whisks his tail comically and destroys little grain.

But when he was stronger, he interrupted. That was offensive. To interrupt indicated low breeding and foreign manners. One would be saying, "If there is not rain soon—" and the child, or tiny old man, would interrupt: "Englishmen and Frenchmen must be destroyed." This was translated immediately; an interruption might, after all, indicate urgency. But the remarks seemed random and obscure, though not altogether unreasonable: no one in Pawlu objected to the destruction of the English, somewhere west of them, or of the French, somewhere south of them, or of anyone at all outside Pawlu.

Soon the interruptions came in Shan; the boy heard no other language, and was instructing his tongue. This, then, was the language of the gods. He listened and listened, and from time to time he interrupted. One would be saying again, "If there is not rain soon—" and the child would interrupt. "A locomotive is a one-eyed dragon," and this would necessitate conferences, first to translate "locomotive" from the Chinese, then to make sense of the whole phrase.

That was a dry year, and East Poppy Field showed rusty from the hillside. The sky was blue and clear, and when the boy, writhing, clenching, his good eyeball rolling, cried out, "The gods send rain! Tomorrow comes rain!" and fell unconscious, the old Sawbwa and the men about him were merely embarrassed. Two of the women carried the little fellow to the shelter of a wall, away from the blazing sun, and washed him down and tended him.

Next day a memorable downpour swelled the Little River Mon, and consequently Upper Stream in Pawlu, and consequently Lower Stream in Pawlu; it lasted all one day and half another, drowned the paddies, revived the vegetation, restored Pawlu's spirits and occasioned serious discussion of the boy. Most scoffed. But the old Sawbwa hated foreigners and had sensed in this boy a rare sweat of the same hate. It was decided to take the boy seriously for the time being. Perhaps he was inhabited, or visited, by a nat. Nats were forest spirits, some benign and helpful, others malign and baleful.

The boy confirmed his importance almost immediately. He fell into a foam-flecked trance one morning and spoke of the house that flies and roars like thunder. Two of Pawlu's men had seen aircraft, and knew what the boy was speaking of. But no such machine had ever droned through Pawlu's sky or racketed through Pawlu's peace—until three days later, when to the amazement of the entire village and the terror of half its people, a silver bird appeared from the west, crossed the valley buzzing like a bee and veered

off to the south. It possessed, they swore, four
wings, two on each side, and it emitted a modest
but steady stream of smoke. (When he heard the
tale years later, Greenwood surmised that a
French or British bomber, honorably surviving
World War I, had been achieving one of the first
primitive aerial reconnaissances Out East, probably making a zigzag run from Mandalay to
Hanoi and perhaps even taking photographs.)

After the third spectacular and successful
prediction of rain, the old Sawbwa adopted this
stunted, sickly, half-blind, discolored, demented
youth. Over the years the boy announced many
irrelevant visions, but he was never wrong about
rain.

So when the old Sawbwa died a few years later,
the village voted this grotesque the Sawbwa's
turban, wardrobe and bangles, being careful at
the same time to confirm Hu-chot (a polite
rendition of whose name would have been ''Tiger
Tamer'') as First Rifle with independent powers.
The Shan of Pawlu were religious, orderly,
traditional folk, but not to the risk of their land
and freedom.

And so this Sawbwa of Pawlu, spawned in the
hell of the Celestial Kingdom and banished by its
inhumanities, reigned for many years in his
mountain fastness, celibate, visionary, crippled,
shrewd and simple at once. White-haired where
he was not bald, wrinkled and squinting,
venerable and slow of speech, he was almost
precisely Greenwood's age.

5

The Bandits
in the Hills

Eight years before Greenwood's return to
Pawlu, Yang's flight from China, and the death of
the two Kachin, the Japanese had invaded
Burma. In January of 1942 they struck by land
from Siam and advanced with strategic caution
and tactical brio. Hastily the Allies—stodgy
Britain, stunned America (it was only a month
after Pearl Harbor) and feudal China—improvised a defense. This was necessarily a limited
defense. British generals believed in war but not
in combat. Americans were thin on the ground
and inexperienced. The Chinese (whom the
British, with perhaps justifiable reluctance,
finally deigned to admit to the "defense" of the
Shan States) believed that when you had trained
and equipped a good division you should not
erode it in battle. ("The Fifth Army," said a
Chinese general to a British general, "is our best
army because it is the only one which has any
field guns, and I cannot afford to risk those guns.
If I lose them the Fifth Army will no longer be
our best.")

At first the Allied line ran north-south, and the

Japanese thrust westward across Burma's southern panhandle. The Japanese then consolidated, struck for Rangoon and fanned northward; the Allied line pivoted to run east-west. By mid-April the Japanese had slashed their way to within two hundred fifty miles of Lashio, the western terminus of the Burma Road, strategically vital (every town, island, fort that fell in those first months were "strategically vital"), and the Lashio Road was defended by the famed Chinese 55th Division.

Famed ever after, that is. The battle lasted only a few hours. The 55th's General Chen (whom the theater commander, the most crusty, aggressive and frustrated of American generals, had proposed court-martialing a week before) deployed his troops in echelon along the road, unit after unit staggered back from an insanely narrow front. In effect this forced each company to deal with the whole Japanese advance in turn; and when Chen ordered his rear battalions forward, the Japanese swung wide, flanked, enveloped, isolated and annihilated. The 55th simply disappeared. It was never again listed on Chinese army rolls. The most crusty, aggressive and frustrated of American generals said next day to the most romantic, idealistic and melancholy of American correspondents, "There's not a trace of it. It's the god-damnedest thing I ever saw. Last night I had a division, and today there isn't any."

Two of the survivors were in apprentice American anthropologist named Greenwood and a Chinese major general named Yang. They survived because they never reached the battle.

Greenwood was then twenty-seven years old. He had spent his early adolescence hoping above all that his freckles would fade; also dismantling and reconstituting motor vehicles; and yearning after pudgy girls. He had spent his late adolescence at Harvard College, where motor vehicles were a means to an end—namely, women's colleges and their baffling inmates; and the two and a half years since his Master of Arts in 1939 absolutely without motor vehicles, fulfilling an anthropologist's dream: he had found an exotic people that no one had yet elucidated, and was living as one of them, in Shan trousers, Shan jacket, Shan turban, with a Shan beard (though golden), Shan tattoos, a Shan woman and by the grace of the nats a half-Shan daughter.

When he contrasted that life—Pawlu, Loi-mae, Lola, amethyst sunsets, blushing opal dawns—with his past (St. Louis, cars, proms, Cambridge, waistcoats, ritual sherry, sanctimonious and resentful women armored in layers of moral theory and underclothes), he wondered seriously if he should bother with a ticket home. But Shan life was family life, and he missed his own: each month he wrote a letter to his parents—pharmacy and notary public, soda fountain; Gray Lady and garden club—with a postscript to his younger sister, and after inscribing the magical foreign characters "Air Mail" and affixing a one-rupee stamp (he had purchased a hundred of those in Mandalay), he scouted the Nan-san road for a caravan. His postman was most often a ruffian, turbanned or skullcapped, ostentatiously armed. Greenwood informed these couriers that this was a message to his father, a great sawbwa across the water, and mother, a princess; he then proffered small silver and hoped for the best.

He had never been so happy and was intelligent enough to fear that he would never again be so happy. He heard in February of 1942 that the Japanese were invading Burma. Pawlu considered this irrelevant, at most insulting. Now and then bizarre tales prowled the mountains: the Dalai Lama was dead, Lung Yun had executed a Yunnan sawbwa, there was a road all the way from Lashio to Kunming littered with the corpses of foreign vehicles, opium was once more legal in China. (This last was exaggerated by Pawlu's natural desire for a favorable balance of trade. Opium was legal only in Japanese-occupied territory.)

Greenwood lit a cheroot and agreed that this was a degenerate age. He did not change his way of life. He made cooing sounds to his daughter and inexhaustible love to his little woman. In early April he parleyed with a Kachin amber merchant who mentioned the influx of Americans. Greenwood chuckled: a few diplomats and businessmen must indeed seem like a mob if they were American. Americans spoke loudly.

No, no. Soldiers.

The Kachin was only gossiping and had nothing to gain by lies. He was uncertain what a fleet consisted of, but reported that even before invading Burma the Japanese had, somewhere east of Shanghai, destroyed the entire American fleet—ferries, was it? gunboats? yes, yes—sending a ten, or perhaps ten tens, of aircraft to accomplish this with large bombs. The Kachin himself had spoken to Americans recently, down by Maymyo. All this was true, by the gods, and the great places of Asia were now Japanese. Singapore, which had once been English even as Burma was. Indochina. Siam. The Philippines. He believed the Siamese government had declared war on America; that was serious.

A rush of patriotism stunned Greenwood. Anger shook him, and he asked, "Have the Japanese set foot in America?"

The Kachin shrugged. "How can one know? Far places, far places."

Greenwood then forfeited all standing as an anthropologist by blurting, "Those buck-toothed bowlegged sons of bitches!"

The Kachin smiled. "They will free Burma. You watch."

Loi-mae knew immediately that the axis of Greenwood's world had tilted. He loomed in the doorway and explained. Loi-mae stepped to the cradle and took up their daughter. Greenwood said miserably, "We agreed I could not stay forever."

"All the same I am heartsick," she said.

Greenwood saw her fresh, not the native mistress but the wife and mother. He saw himself fresh, and he knew what treason was. "I too am heartsick," he said, and he had not seen much betrayal or death, rapine or destruction, so he wept openly before her.

And then Greenwood the father, Greenwood the Shan, no longer the gangling student but well fleshed and muscled, Greenwood who had toiled in the fields, stood sentry, tapped poppies, sat on the men's side at weddings, attended village meetings, shot game, been honored with tattoos, been mocked for pride when his little woman swelled and his firstborn was delivered, stood humbly before Pawlu and its Sawbwa and tried to say why he must leave. The men sat to one side and the women to another, and the sun westered low, the sky rosy. Yes, his woman was here. Yes, his daughter was here. Yes, the people of Pawlu were his people. Yes, his heart was a cracked bell.

But the land of his ancestors had been attacked. The graves of his ancestors had been desecrated. His father and mother had no other son. To fail them would be to insult the gods.

The Sawbwa understood these arguments.

How would Phe-win feel, or Wan or Mong or Kin-tan, if the Japanese came to Pawlu? If they took the women, the crops, the silver, if they quartered themselves upon the people?

The Sawbwa understood these arguments too.

Greenwood would leave his silver and his amber, and wanted only a pony, to take him to Kunlong and then Hsenwi.

The Japanese were attacking the English?

They were.

The Sawbwa himself detested the English.

Greenwood sat silent.

But it was not given to man to know the gods' intent. The Sawbwa would not oppose his departure.

Pawlu would weep for its loss but would send him on his way with blessings.

Loi-mae too understood but her anguish could not be contained; it spilled over in silent tears. Greenwood was unable to explain the ferocity of his reaction, the depth of his need to go; it was as if he were some primitive warrior who had never been blooded and could not bear the shame of it.

Next morning—ashamed, angry, sure that he was defying the gods, fate, luck, but unable to hang back—he bound his bedroll, strapped on the 1917 Smith & Wesson .45 revolver he had never fired in anger, touched every hand in Pawlu, embraced Loi-mae and hugged Lola tight, and started down the trail to Kunlong with Kintan for guide and escort the first day.

He pushed hard. In Kunlong he saw Chinese soldiers, on their caps white suns against blue, and this seemed incorrect; but he reminded himself that the Japanese would seem even less appropriate. He rode on to Hsenwi and was dazzled: Chinese troops and trucks jammed the roads. Rather, Chinese troops and American trucks. The noise deafened him. The trucks seemed to be headed for China. Why Chinese troops in Burma? Where were the Americans? The British? Somebody must be going south to Lashio!

He was hungry, he was tired, he was disoriented. Here in Hsenwi he was also hot, and the trucks raised dust. He wore cotton dungarees and a blue cotton work shirt and sweated himself muddy. "Where's the horse market?" he bawled. A scuttling Burman started in alarm and waved uncertainly. Greenwood waited for a break in traffic and urged his pony across the road, into an alley, toward the river. Vehicles rumbled, horns blared, the pony shied.

He sold the pony cheap, an ounce of silver, and felt worse, more treacherous and cowardly, be-

traying the beast than leaving Pawlu; it was as if
he had sold the pony for the cook-pot. He should-
ered his bedroll, checked his pistol and headed
for the Lashio Road. Trucks rumbled by, all on
their way to China. He crossed a bridge. On the
west bank of the river he sat on his bedroll and
waited.

An hour later, under hot cloudless skies, a
dusty automobile halted at his wave. "Lashio!"
he cried. The driver, a Burman, waved him
aboard impatiently. Greenwood never knew
what the man's errand was. They bucked and
twisted their way to Lashio, arriving at sunset.
"No more," said the driver. "English car. Stop
here."

"South," Greenwood said. "I want to find the
Americans."

"Lorry." The Burman pointed down a road.
"Much lorry."

Greenwood hopped out and trotted down the
road in the gray-green twilight. Lashio swarmed
with trucks; its very air was exhaust. He found a
truck depot (shortly he would learn to call it
motor pool) full of Chinese troops, and made
himself heard over the roar of engines:
"Americans! The American army! Where is the
war?" No one listened, no one understood. He
spotted what seemed to be a dispatcher's shed
and pushed through the doorway.

A number of Chinese officers were obviously in
full dispute. They fell silent and goggled at him.
"I want to go south to join the Americans," he
said quickly. "I want a truck headed south. Can
you help me?"

All but one Chinese showed incomprehension

or sullen resentment. The one exception, a ranking officer by the look of his shoulder boards, turned a round face to him and smiled a blinding smile. "Well! Company! I too swim against the tide. Can you drive a camion?"

"I can drive anything," Greenwood said. "All these trucks are headed the wrong way. Is the war over? Have the Japanese invaded the United States?"

"The war has only begun. No one has invaded the United States. I shall explain later. For the moment you are an American intelligence officer with vital information, and you must find the Chinese Fifty-fifth Division. Is that clear?"

"Absolutely. Speed is essential."

"I like you, laddie," said the Chinese. "Show me identification and behave imperiously."

Greenwood dug out his passport and glowered. He spoke forcefully. The Chinese officer translated. Other officers bestirred themselves reluctantly. In half an hour Greenwood was at the wheel of a six-ton truck—a Ford, of all things—blaring his way southward, his headlights boring through a thronged Lashio. "I haven't driven for two and a half years," he said. "Christ, they're all coming north! It's not a retreat; I don't see soldiers; what the hell is going on?"

"My English is rusty," said his companion. "By the way, I am Major General Yang Yu-lin."

"A major general! My name's Greenwood. I'm an anthropologist."

"And why have they sent an anthropologist here?"

"They haven't," Greenwood said, wondering if

he should add "sir." "I was in the Shan States for two years, more, two and a half. I just heard about the war a few days ago and I figured I better come out and be useful."

"Ah. An idealist. I feel much the same. It is not easy to be useful."

"Can you tell me what's happening? What's the situation?"

"The situation." Yang pondered. "You may not know that in nineteen forty the Germans swept through France and France simply collapsed. A few brave men stood their ground and died. Otherwise it was France repeating and paying for all her ancient sins, corruption, greed, cowardice, complacency, class. To a Chinese that sounds familiar. It was the end of the world, and during the retreat, somewhere along a hot dusty road crammed with refugees, crippled tanks, ambulances, horses and wagons, babes at the teat, fancy cars, deserters and trapped tourists, somewhere along that Via Dolorosa a journalist approached a wounded captain of French infantry, haggard and hobbling, and asked him for an appraisal of the situation. 'The situation,' said the captain, 'is desperate but not serious.' "

"Oh good God," Greenwood said. "I knew there was a war in Europe. What else have the Germans got?"

"Europe. They've invaded Russia."

"Holy Jesus," Greenwood said. "What about here and now?"

Yang recited a brief history of the war in Asia.

"Then why are these trucks rolling north?"

"Ah, well, you see, China needs supplies. It is now Chinese habit—" The general held his peace while Greenwood maneuvered past a file of dazzling headlights, skidding off the shoulder at one point but recovering quickly. "—Chinese habit to consider all battles lost but the war won. If you find this confusing, it is because you are limited intellectually, and do not possess a subtle Oriental mind."

The general was smiling again, teeth gleaming in the glare of oncoming headlights.

"We need supplies, you see." The general's tone was calm, amused, only faintly ironic. "We Chinese, that is. We need them in order to lose more battles but win the war. These trucks are of value in themselves; they also carry arms, fuel, spare parts, tires, personal effects, sealed chests of Burmese jade and silver, antiquities, and, I imagine, spools of electric wire, radio sets, boots, canteens and misdirected payrolls."

Greenwood groaned.

"Indeed. We have a general, you see, called Yü Fei-p'eng, who is in charge of transport. His mission is not to send a maximum of matériel to the front in a maximum of working trucks. That would be very Occidental and unsubtle. His mission is to withdraw as much matériel as possible from a lost battle so that we can win the war."

"Then Burma's lost?"

"No, but I fear it will be shortly. Then, you see, General Yü's wisdom will be validated; having salvaged great quantities of this and that, including some personal fortunes, surely including his own, he will be awarded a medal and promoted."

"And why are you the exception?" Greenwood

asked. "And why do you talk with a burr?"

"I was tutored once by a Scots lady," said General Yang. "I have been seconded to the Fifty-fifth Division and am merely obeying orders."

"Nobody else is obeying orders."

"On the contrary, everybody is. You forget: all battles are lost if they require combat. Patriotism demands that we withdraw in good order."

"Well, we'll find your Fifty-fifth," Greenwood said. "I wish I knew more about war."

"Never say that, laddie," General Yang admonished him. "Your wish may come true."

They struggled south for two long days against a swelling stream of northbound traffic, more and more of it on foot, more and more of it swathed in bloody rags. They discussed politics, the First World War, America, China, village life, the lost bones of Peking Man, unearthed outside that great city in the 1920s, and where were they now? "Ah yes, Sinanthropus pekinensis," said the general. "A cousin at several removes. A scapegrace. The family has not heard from him for ages." They discussed languages; Greenwood spoke English and Shan and read technical German; Yang's mother tongue was Mandarin, his French perfect if accented, his English burred and enthusiastic, his German military, his Japanese rudimentary. They enjoyed each other's company. Each was impressed, and saw in the other an exotic of distinction.

Twice they filled their tank from jerricans. Traffic thinned. They found a wounded lieutenant who reported in full. The 55th had vanished. Burma was surely lost.

"Drive me to Mandalay," said General Yang to Greenwood, with a loose wave at the wall of shadowed forest. "Turn right somewhere." Again that luminous, golden smile irradiated the Burmese twilight.

The lieutenant declined a lift, and proceeded northward.

In Maymyo the general and the anthropologist parted, firm friends, vowing reunion; they had, in the old phrase, made tea together and made water together. Yang attached himself to a Chinese unit retreating westward, and Greenwood haunted the small airport. He announced that he had just spent two years in the Shan States and had intelligence to deliver. By a combination of persistence, gall and tattoos he finagled himself aboard an RAF light bomber that barely lurched into the air from the short strip, and was flown, at the end of April and not a moment too soon, to Imphal in India.

For some days no one had time for him. The withdrawal had become a rout, and Imphal was crowded. He cabled his parents, after a battle with olive-drab bureaucrats; he wrote to them, and to his university. In mid-May he heard that the Japanese had swept north through Burma, entered southwest China along the Burma Road and reached the gorge of the Salween. Loi-mae! Lola!

A week later he stood at last before a sunburnt American colonel and asked to join the army.

The colonel said, "Let's see your draft card."

Greenwood said, "My what?"

The colonel said, "Your draft card."

Greenwood said, "What's that?"

The colonel said, "Boy, where you been the last two years?"

Greenwood told him.

The colonel was no fool. He enjoyed war, did his job well, and knew exactly where to put Greenwood, who raised his right hand the next day and swore various preposterous oaths. This recruit was then questioned intensively about the Shan States; was asked to converse with a Shan porter, who confirmed that he spoke the language well, that his tattoos were genuine, and that he seemed to know the territory; was set to work with an American sergeant who could field-strip any American weapon while you poured him a cuppa joe and reassemble it before the coffee was cool enough to drink; was interviewed by the aftermentioned General Stilwell, now exhausted, whose resemblance to a jungle cockatoo almost made him laugh; and was, to his enduring astonishment, commissioned a lieutenant of infantry within thirty days.

"Lieutenants have privileges," the colonel said, "and your first privilege is, you are going to learn to use a parachute."

"Now wait a minute," Greenwood said.

"Wait a minute *sir*," the colonel said.

In August of 1942 Greenwood was dropped into a poppy field half a day's ride from Loi Panglon. With him tumbled a radio so heavy as to be useless (it survived the fall but required its own donkey) and several crates of arms, ammunition and rations.

He was met mysteriously by a band of laughing

Kachin, who thought these methods of warfare a grand joke. Greenwood thought it a grand joke that, speaking South Shan fluently and sporting Shan tattoos, he should have been plumped down among Kachin, where Jinghpaw was the lingo and the Wild Wa were thick as fleas. But he was then a veteran of three months in the army and understood that there was a right way, a wrong way and an army way.

He enjoyed learning Jinghpaw. He enjoyed trotting about on a pony. He enjoyed shooting at Japanese. He enjoyed laying compass courses, sleeping in the open, sharing Kachin women and decorating his turban with finely worked bits of silver to commemorate successful skirmishes. He enjoyed glassing the hillsides and watching the Wild Wa watch him, little dark people who looked murderous, imps from hell, even at half a mile.

Most of all, he enjoyed working his way east and south, toward Pawlu; and trotting down the road by East Poppy Field, turban off and blond hair, shaggy, for a passport, to take the track along North Slope and make his way, watched, challenged, greeted with uproar, back to Loi-mae. He was in exuberant health and spirits. They coupled four times that night, a catalogue, a primer of pornography, and Greenwood made Pawlu his headquarters. Japanese were few in these hills but he roamed miles to fight his war, joining his Kachin warriors near Mong Paw or Mong Si or Mong Hawn, swooping about the border area like some flying battalion out of a boys' book, destroying whole Japanese patrols and the small fortified camps they used as field headquarters, firing at Japanese aircraft in sheer optimism, returning always, after days or weeks or months, to make certain of Pawlu's peace.

In 1943 he branched out: in addition to the occasional pilot off course, shot down, victim of mechanical failure, he had various British and American invasions and campaigns to keep track of, bits of fact and rumor racing through the jungle or across the plain. Greenwood's radio was long dead. He sent dispatches as best he could, suffered mild guilt as he fought his private war, fun, fun, he blew up a bridge, he raced north through Kachin territory to divert the Japanese from an operation called Galahad, he fought through the monsoon in the summer of 1944 because to the Americans war was not a seasonal occupation. Greenwood understood. Had he been told that the war was to last forever, his eye might have sparkled.

Late that year three separate but identical urgent messages rustled through the hills, one from his counterpart near Bhamo: A DC-3, crossing the Hump, had been posted missing with pilot, co-pilot and one passenger, a Chinese lieutenant general. Intensive search was obviously in order, not merely to rescue these fighting men but to add one more heroic verse to the guerrillas' unsung saga.

Greenwood sent men to all eight winds, and six days later, with a fired-up squad of mountain men who fought to the love of fighting, crossed the Salween north of Kunlong and penetrated a sparsely settled range of hills, along fifty miles of which not one village was large enough to be a dot on the Burmese map. There was a narrow river to cross. Greenwood was assured that a wooden bridge existed. Topping a ridge, he saw it, bathed in a clear autumnal noontime glow.

He also saw, seated, sprawled back against the railing at the east end, smoking a cigarette and *reading*, an oddly familiar, round-headed, uniformed figure. Even before he put a name to the man, he heard echoes of happy hilarity, saw the grin, recalled the old truck and the jouncing ride through Burma. He led his cutthroats downhill at reckless speed, valuted off his pony like a circus clown, and embraced the startled general with vigor. Recognition dawned; Yang smiled immoderately; the whole squad grinned in appreciation. "By God, laddie, I made it!" Yang cried.

Greenwood asked, "The pilots?"

Yang shook his head. "We all jumped. Into a gale. I never saw them again."

"They can't be far." Greenwood gave orders.

Yang told his story.

"You'll come back with me," Greenwood said. "We'll run you home by way of Yunnan."

"Ramghar," Yang said later. "Two years training with the Americans. We finally put together a Chinese army. Came down with the Five-three-oh-seventh and threw the monkeys out of Myitkyina. We'll blast our way into China yet, you watch. And you? Do you still pretend to be an anthropologist?"

"That was some time ago," Greenwood agreed. "My daughter is four years old."

"My son is dead," Yang said sadly, and they rode in silence.

Pawlu goggled at this apparition decked with insignia, and was properly impressed when his origins, rank and mode of transport were explained. Yang in turn was impressed when the Wild Wa were explained: they prowled the roads and trails at this season, and there might be skirmishes. "Then I can be a lieutenant again," Yang said wistfully, "if the knees allow, and the back pains." He offered the village a banquet in gratitude, solemnly conferring a gold piece on the Sawbwa. The Sawbwa was not so easily won; some primeval memory warned him off. The villagers saw this, and turned cool.

Yang maintained the courtesies and observed the Sawbwa, and after the banquet he asked if he might chat comfortably with him, through an interpreter. The Sawbwa condescended. Greenwood eavesdropped. Conversation lurched, stalled, flowed, ceased. The Sawbwa pressed a hand to his back and grimaced. "Ah, you too," Yang said with profound sympathy. The Sawbwa showed interest. Yang spoke mournfully. "Gravel. Had it for years. Kidney pains in the morning, kidney pains at night."

"By the gods, yes!" frothed the Sawbwa. "In the morning and at night."

"In the morning and at night," Yang affirmed, nodding lugubriously, and thus was born an alliance. Pawlu smothered Yang with affection when he overcome his back pains and sat a pony, charging with the rest to scatter the Wild Wa east of the village, using a bamboo stick for pointer and mapping tactics, smoking up cheroots and slugging down good mountain rum. Wan suggested a tattoo. Greenwood felt a pang of jealousy, which was allayed when Phewin, venerable now, declared the suggestion premature. Among the women there was a brief contention, as many strove to drag the general home; he remained aloof. Not two moons had passed before he was escorted to Nan-san bearing letters, messages, addresses, and united with Chinese irregulars who would see him safely to the interior; but they were two unforgettable months. Yang in a turban, pinching silver into its conical crown, Yang firing at Wild Wa from ponyback, Yang telling of his parachute jump, Yang drawing China in the dust and bringing the infinitely distant war home to Pawlu. His departure left Pawlu bereft, as if a whole vivacious family had rolled up its blankets and marched forever away.

The day came when Greenwood too departed. For six years he had not seen his native land, parents, jalopies, girdled women. When the war ended, homesickness, overpowered him. The cozy leathery smoky shelter of a paneled library; the shrewd infighting at conclaves of learned societies; tweed jackets and sherry; the advance of the human mind: his obligation now to pass along what life had taught him—all that tugged him back.

His farewells were melancholy but not too sad to be borne. Among the Shan too there was a sense of completion, time now to return to the old ways, to put war and foreigners out of mind and into legend. Greenwood, Loi-mae and Lola shed tears, but they were not the tears of despair; acceptance, rather, sorrowful resolution, the will of the gods.

He rode to Hsenwi by pony with Kin-tan for escort, to Lashio by jeep and to Mandalay by plane. He marched into headquarters—somebody's headquarters; who were these pale men in pressed shirts and shined shoes?—wearing his beard, cotton mountain clothes and well-silvered turban, carrying a submachine gun, feeling at once heartsore and immensely curious about the modern world. He discovered that he was a captain. He was given large amounts of money. He was placed aboard an aircraft and wafted to Hanoi, Manila, Guam, Wake, Hawaii and points east, emerging finally, huge and hairy, to horrify his tiny old parents and enrapture his little sister, now more than nubile. His mother shrieked, uncertain whether to enfold him or flee. His father quailed, but proudly, and slapped him tentatively on one shoulder. Merciless, Greenwood roared greetings, hugged and kissed, raised his little mother high, announced that she and his father were grandparents, wore his turban through the airport and all the way home, ate three sirloins for dinner and informed his adoring sister that incest was normal where he came from. "I had a letter from a *Chinese general*," his gray-haired mother boasted. "He said you were a *hero*."

"Yang will say anything," Greenwood told her, enormously pleased. "He's the best they have. I love that man," and he launched a few hero's tales. His parents' pride, his sister's admiration, tickled him; but in a matter of days deep depression gripped him. Greenwood was thirty-one years old and a hero in his own eyes and he was scared half to death of this clattering, frenzied new world.

In a month he had shaved his Wotan's beard and begun serving his life sentence. In a year he had typed his thesis on the Shan, sat for orals before a board of solemn owls who knew not one damn thing about the Shan, and become Dr. Greenwood. He celebrated his doctordom besieging, after a sumptuous dinner, a graduate student of noble proportions who, it transpired, was wearing a corset fabricated apparently of reinforced concrete and extending some four inches below the keep. The siege failed, the battering ram was withdrawn, Dr. Greenwood pitied American women and wept for Loi-mae. He encouraged a new beard. He taught. He drank rum. At a fusty tobacco shop he found beedies; he smoked them and became a character. Once each year he heard from Yang. He found a Thai restaurant redolent of familiar aromas. He knew that he would never be happy again, and actually considered returning to the armed forces.

He perked up when he received two copies of a strange letter, one forwarded by his proud mother, from Yang Yu-lin.

I can only say that I believe I know where they are, that they are the genuine article, and that I have a Japanese colonel who would prefer not to be hanged. If I send for you, come. Trust me. Say nothing. There is more at stake here than universities, armies, even countries. *Do as I ask*. There is none other I can trust.

No need to answer this; indeed, no way. I have spent eighteen interesting months in Peking but shall be on the move now. Man-

churia, I suppose, to hold out for a bit longer.
Can't imagine why; if you're a gambling
man . . . but I must not say that. Ici tout est
foutu comme l'as de pique. Victrix causa diis
placuit, sed victa Yango.

Greenwood rummaged in dictionaries: "Everything here is fucked up in spades," and something like "The gods favored the winners, but
Yang backed the losers." "If I send for you,
come!" The old romantic Greenwood rejoiced
and reminisced. That was the way to live: "If ever
I send for you, one mile or ten thousand, never
mind why, *do it*. Meet me at the Raffles in Singapore a week from Friday at noon: *do it*." As for
the bones, old Sinanthropus pekinensis, that was
at best dubious; someone had stumbled upon
plaster casts or clever fakes or "dragon's bones"
in some rural pharmacy.

But when in October of 1949 Greenwood received the first of three identical letters (this one
postmarked Hong Kong, the later two Macao and
Tokyo), he never hesitated. It took him a month,
and the influence of the president of the university (in the 1920s a secretary had informed a
caller, "The president is in Washington visiting
Mr. Coolidge"), to acquire a visa for Burma, and
another week to reach Rangoon; and he stepped
to the tarmac at Mingaladon blinded by his own
tears; but he was shortly in Maymyo discussing
air fares with Gordon-Cumming.

And now, a fortnight later, he was in Kunlong
on the road to Pawlu. He and the boy Jum-aw
washed at dawn and shared a breakfast of rice,

crushed sugarcane and tea. It was fu-erh tea, real
Shan tea, and the taste of it hummed in the
American's head like a hymn of welcome. The
two then saddled up—good heavy horse blankets
with a stout stitched loop for a sometime stirrup.

The ponies were Kachin ponies, longer in the
barrel and shaggier than Yunnan ponies, sandy
brown in color and vile of disposition, though
disciplined: a Kachin pony was unsalable until
its owner could put it through its paces—four
gaits—holding a full tumbler in one hand without spilling a drop.

Well, perhaps a drop. What was a drop or two
among mountain men? Greenwood was an hon-
orary Shan but continually crossed Kachin
trails, rubbed elbows with Kachin wanderers,
and could blurt his way through a campfire
negotiation, or lying session, in rude Jinghpaw.
He spoke it now to his pony, and Jum-aw trilled a
short laugh: " 'Every time we say good-bye to a
Shan, we say hello to a Kachin.' "

"Crazy country," Greenwood agreed. "And on
the ridges—"

"—the Wild Wa. And up north here—"

"some Lahu, and over by Bawdwin—"

"—some Palaung, and everywhere else—"

"—Karen and Burman."

"Is it so in your land?"

They were lashing bedrolls along the ponies'
necks, Kachin fashion, and not back on the crup-
per. "No, truly not," Greenwood said. "My own
land is a hundred days' ride from east to west—"

"Ah, ah," the boy warned him.

"That is no lie," Greenwood said firmly. "By
all the nats I swear this."

"One hundred days!"

"And fifty days from north to south," Greenwood said, "and in all that land one language will suffice, though the manner of it varies, as with southern Shan and northern Shan."

The boy was silent, absorbing this. Was it the silence of appreciation, or a gentle reluctance to express disbelief? Finally he said, "And are there birds?"

"There are birds, and bears, and goats, but not leopards or tigers or monkeys or elephants. I believe there are birds everywhere in the world, even on the mountaintops in Tibet, the deserts in Mongolia and the flat fetches of ice at the southern pole." Greenwood knew he had gone too far.

"Ice in the south?" Jum-aw smiled sympathetically.

Greenwood retrieved the moment: "Did I say south? Curse this poor tongue of mine. Naturally I meant north."

"Ah. Are we ready?"

"Food. Weapons. Ammunition. Fire. The rupee's worth of worldly goods. And you?"

"The same." Jum-aw cocked his head and allowed himself a diffident admonition: "Your turban is ill-wound."

"The habit is fallen away," Greenwood said with regret. "It will improve each day."

"Well then, let us begin. A safe journey."

"A safe journey."

They mounted, and took their ponies at a walk through Kunlong, the town coming to life in the early light, which was now golden and blue and green and no longer gray. For Greenwood it was like traversing, and then leaving, a metropolis. First the shops, temples, inns, the women at the wells or toiling up from the riverbank, men in vivid turbans and silver necklaces even now lighting cheroots and meeting in clumps to gossip and face east like sunflowers, the children squatting beside the road to pull apart the split seats of their knee-length pants. Then a thinning of the huts and houses, and a wider sweep of garden and farm, here and there even now a shell hole or bomb crater. Greenwood and Jum-aw rode side by side up the slope, out of town, out of the world, and then single file up the trail, bee-eaters and woodpeckers falling silent above them, toktays almost swarming on the broad-leaved shrubs at either hand, twice the crash and rustle of a wild pig or a startled hog deer invisible in the forest.

Too soon Jum-aw led them downhill to the main road again. Greenwood said, "Thank you. The forest was beautiful."

"Even Tame Wa dislike roads," Jum-aw said, slim and graceful astride his pony; his teeth flashed in a quick, self-deprecating smile. "Also the machines that travel them. But a rifle beats a bow for hunting, and the skill that braids rope is also the skill that hangs a man. No having the one without the other."

"And the same skill built this bridge," Greenwood agreed, as they paused by the abutment to contemplate this marvel of steel. "How did men cross the Salween before?"

"It was a day's march down to the water. Then at a double bend in the river—"

"Oxbow," Greenwood said in English.

Jum-aw was puzzled.

"That is my people's word for the rounded yoke that collars an ox."

"So." Jum-aw nodded emphatically. "Just so. There the waters run slower, and eddies may help. At the downstream curve the raft was poled and sailed across. It was then hauled all the way up to the top of the upstream curve, and from there it made the return crossing. And then there was a day's march up the far side of the gorge."

"The gorges are wonderous," Greenwood said. "Either from the lip or from the bowl a great river gorge is a sight to speed the blood."

"True. Then there are great rivers in your land also."

"In all lands."

"In the beginning God favored no one, or all alike."

Greenwood shut up for a moment, to savor this remark. He recalled other visions of it. We hold these truths to be self-evident, that all men are created equal. Man is born free and he is everywhere in chains. History is something that never happened, written by a man who wasn't there. Had life once truly been a siesta in the Garden of Eden? "Do the Wa believe that all was once peaceful and beautiful and bountiful?" They were on the bridge now, and the unshod hoofs clopped softly.

"The Wild Wa believe that all is still peaceful and beautiful and bountiful, as long as they take a few heads each spring."

Much of the time they rode in silence, the trail mainly rising but dipping at intervals to cross a

valley or round a ridge low down. For some
hours there was no intrusion of mankind. Greenwood saw cedars, pines and oaks, and in them
squirrels. He saw a hawk gliding, a white harrier
with black wing tips. His heart was at rest and he
seemed to feel his tattoos glowing lightly, as if
they too were a living part of this fertile landscape; but he kept his mind quick, and kept his
eyes roving. The Wild Wa would not prowl here
but others roamed, and these days no roamer
roamed in peace and innocence.

At noon they tethered the ponies well off the
trail, a quarter-mile into the forest, and cut slices
off the cold quarters of broiled saing, rolling
them around wild watercress, with bananas for
dessert and water from the canteens. They
debated a cheroot, and decided against it; a
Kachin or a Shan could, as the proverb had it,
sniff drifting smoke and tell you whether the
cheroot was white or brown.

On the trail again they proceeded in silence.
Jum-aw suggested a halt every half-hour or so for
serious listening. And yet when they saw their
first traveler it came as a surprise. Greenwood's
knees dug in; as his left hand snubbed the rein
his right grasped the tommy gun. Jum-aw's rifle
was unslung in the same moment. They were side
by side on a gentle downhill slope.

The man climbing toward them was old and
ragged. He bore a bulging round sack slung
crossways, and as he drew nearer they saw that
his face was northern, a web of fine wrinkles and
a parrot's nose. He wore no turban but a mangy
fur hat, and on his feet were leather slippers with
pointed toes.

Jum-aw voiced scorn: "A Tibetan beggar."

"A long way from home."

"They are everywhere."

Here where the trail was broad the sun beat down on these three; basking in it, the old man could not have been other than peaceful. But Greenwood said, "There may be others," and kept his grasp on the weapon.

Unperturbed, the old man approached, halted, placed his palms together and bowed. "Peace," he said in Jinghpaw.

In Shan Greenwood said, "Blessings and greetings. Have you traveled far?"

"I have traveled far."

"And how goes it?"

"As the Lord wishes."

"Then it goes well. And what have you there?"

"Ah." The old man's wrinkles deepened, his eyes glistened. "Here I have wonders."

Wonders. Greenwood noted the tattered purple toga, the tangles of gray hair fringing the fur hat; yet why should the gods not transmit their wonders through such as this? Need it be through priests and chieftains? "And you travel freely, safely?"

"I have seen no man today but you."

"Tell of these wonders, old friend."

"Tell! I shall do better. I shall show, and if you like, you will buy." With that he unslung his sack and set it in the road. Deftly he untied its mouth, dramatically he flung it wide and flat. His treasures lay heaped in the center. He sorted them with affection. "You see." He displayed a small stone cruet. "In this is bat's blood, for longevity and sexual prowess. And here"—he brandished a leather pouch—"are serpents' tongues in great variety, including one of the king cobra and one of the krait, each wrapped in a patch of cleaned and boiled sheep's intestine. These, of course, offer protection from snakebite but also from the priest's-cowl-poison of Kachin arrows."

"How time alters all things," Greenwood said sympathetically. "The Kachin have abandoned the crossbow for the rifle." Priest's-cowl-poison was aconite or wolfsbane, he knew.

"Well, as an honest trader," said the Tibetan, "I must confess that I have no defense against bullets. I have, however, this jade, and these, my prizes." He untied a small square of yellow cloth; the yellow was well-chosen, and made a bright background, showing a dozen small flawed rubies to advantage.

"You do this for two strangers," Greenwood said, "who could leave you by the side of the trail with your throat cut, and make off with these wonders."

"It is," the peddler explained, "as the Lord wishes."

"But I have no luck and little faith," Greenwood said sadly, "and no wish to buy such beauty when some bandit will doubtless take my head soon and all the rest."

"And where are these bandits? Which way do you travel?"

Greenwood waved vaguely. "Small east and big north. I confide this in a man of worth," he added. "You will kindly not gossip."

"Have I gossiped with you?"

"No indeed."

"Well then," the beggar said. "Still, I may tell you that all is at peace Salween side. I travel down from small west big north, and there is little news. East of the Mekong, wars and cataclysms."

"And by what road did you come?"

"Well, over many moons, Sumprabum and Myitkyina and Bhamo."

Greenwood knew the territory, and was disappointed; this was a well-traveled route, with rest houses and tea shops and occasional electricity now, and on the Irrawaddy north of Bhamo stout riverboats with stewards and teak fittings. He had hoped for more: high passes, monasteries, endless forest, the holy beggar passing unperceived among armies of hill bandits. Furthermore, it was of no damn use at all to know that Sumprabum and Myitkyina and Bhamo were calm; Greenwood had seen them all and was not headed that way now. "A long and arduous journey," he said. "And what place claims the honor of your birth?"

"Ah," said the beggar, "it is a small place and you will not know it, but a holy place. Gyatsa Dzong."

"But who does not know of Gyatsa Dzong?" Greenwood protested. "It lies in eastern Tibet on the holy northern river, the Tsangpo, which in Assam is the Dihang and then the Brahmaputra known and revered the world over."

The beggar rejoiced with his eyes, his hands, the very arch of his back. "Oh my lord traveler! You have gladdened this unworthy servant! Can it be that you have seen Gyatsa Dzong?"

"No, I have not," Greenwood lamented. "Only

heard, from those more fortunate."

The Tibetan bowed, acknowledging the compliment, and said, "And your own birthplace?"

"Saint Louis, on the river Mississippi, which is also holy, and the town is named for a bodhisattva."

"Surely a great city."

"No, no." Greenwood's downcast eyes made his apologies. "Only eight or ten huts in the mud and snow, and its citizens smear themselves with yak butter and stink all summer." He held forth the rubies, and the beggar took them casually, and bound them up. "We are heading into China and away from these peaceful hills," Greenwood said, "so will have little need of rubies. In Motai and Fang-shih—tell me, old friend, is there gossip of Motai and Fang-shih?"

"Well, Fang-shih is in China." Swiftly the beggar retied his sack. "So there is plenty of trouble to come. I heard nothing of Motai."

"Will you eat a bit? Or take a potato?"

"A Shan potato?" The beggar was overjoyed. Greenwood dug one out of his pack and and the man took it bobbing bows. "Peace and thanks."

"Strangers meet, and good is done," Greenwood said.

"So it should be always."

"Go with the Buddha, then."

"And you, lord traveler."

Greenwood and Jum-aw watched the old fellow trudge away, to the crest of the hill and out of sight.

"He carried a knife," Jum-aw said.

"Of course he did. To slice potatoes, to skin hares."

"No hares for that one. He is of those Buddhists who will not eat meat."

"I have never truly understood," Greenwood said. "There are Buddhists who will not eat meat, and there are Buddhists who live wholly off their herds, and I have known Burmese Buddhists to gorge themselves on chicken."

"And there are some who make fine soldiers," Jum-aw said. "But not that one. That was a wasted encounter."

"Cheer up," Greenwood said. "First, he was not a bandit. Second, all is well in Sumprabum, Myitkyina and Bhamo. Third, he will tell everyone he meets about the foreigner headed for Motai and Fang-shih."

Jum-aw liked the joke. "Which way is Fang-shih?"

"The other way."

"And how do you know so much of Gyatsa Dzong?"

"From maps and books," Greenwood said. "It is probably eight or ten huts in the mud and snow, and its citizens doubtless smear themselves with yak butter and stink all summer."

"Then you are a liar," Jum-aw said.

"Oh yes."

Jum-aw laughed uproariously, so that Greenwood had to shush him. What with nats and bandits it was best to proceed with decorum.

A fire was out of the question; late in the day they nosed up through pines and bracken, taking the ponies over heavy beds of pine needles to exasperate possible trackers. Jum-aw had spotted a clearing on a ridge; from the shelter of an

adjacent grove they could look out over half
China and half Burma, and take their rest in
peace. "Bears cross such clearings," Jum-aw
said, "but there are none hereabouts, I believe."

"Do they eat plants or animals?"

"They eat whatever is smaller than they are.
Best of all, they like grubs and honey." Jum-aw
was tethering his pony to a pine.

"Do your people ever hobble horses?"

"What is 'hobble'?"

Greenwood explained.

Jum-aw was emphatic. "A smart horse could
reach the sea overnight in hobbles."

"Not the sea!"

"It is a saying only. What will we eat? This
mountain life makes an appetite."

"You are a city boy," Greenwood scoffed. "Tonight we have cold barley instead of rice. Cold
saing if you like, or cold chicken. Tea would be
luxurious, but a fire is impossible."

"Fruit?"

"The little red prunes. And oh yes, peanuts.
Why do you ask? You helped me load. You know
what we have."

"I know what we have. I do not know in what
manner, or how quickly, you propose to consume
it. A fire would be a blessing," Jum-aw added
wistfully. "Nights are cold in these hills."

"Not as cold as death."

"True. Then we must eat great quantities. For
the inner fire."

They broke their bedrolls and shared the evening meal as the sun dimmed, filtering low
through the grove behind them. To the east night

gathered swiftly. "Plenty of Kachin in that night," Jum-aw said.

"Plenty of Shan too."

"A gentler people."

"Though fine warriors when the times demand it."

"And you too are a warrior?"

"I was a warrior when the times demanded it," Greenwood said.

"And now?"

Greenwood hesitated.

"If the question is less than polite," Jum-aw said with care, "remember that we may die in these hills. I am less formal than in the town."

"It was not that. I am thinking how to explain. It is not easy to explain even to my own people. I study the ways of man."

"That is a considerable study."

"It is an endless study." Night was rushing down upon them. An exhilaration close to fear, like chills and fever, coursed along his skin.

"Does the work have a name? Are you a magistrate?"

"The Shan have no word for it. I am a man of science, and my science is man. I am also a professor."

"I prefer to think of you as a warrior. Professors do not carry tamigans. What does this study teach you?"

"Sometimes it teaches me that men and women behave as they do because of the rules they set themselves. Sometimes it teaches me that they set those rules because of the way they behave."

Jum-aw mulled this. "Then it teaches you nothing."

"Like all attempts to learn everything." Greenwood was pleased when the boy laughed lightly.

"Let us listen to the night for a few moments," Jum-aw said, "and then you will tell me more."

They heard their ponies; that was a rustle. After a bit they heard a distant music, a faint chirping far below: peep-peep pupp*ee*! Ko-ki ko-*ki*! Tiktiktik! Jum-aw murmured, "Tree frogs in the valley." Nearer, only the ponies, until a bat whispered by. "There will be owls in the night."

"I remember. Among my people they bring luck."

The night was vast now, and empty; only Greenwood and Jum-aw.

After many minutes Jum-aw said, "What do you think about a cheroot?"

"What do you think?"

"We are on a hilltop. The smoke will rise."

"And the light?"

"Light is beneath a blanket, and cup a hand over the tip."

"Then we shall smoke a cheroot," Greenwood said.

When it was lighted, they complimented its fragrance, cloaked themselves in blankets, and passed it back and forth.

"So, what have you learned?" Jum-aw did not mock; he sought truth.

"Well, I have learned to ask you why you want to know."

"Ah. Then wisdom is questions and not answers."

"There is much truth in that."

"Well, I want to know because I am a boy from the hills, and I live now in a town, and each day I see new things. And I know that there are bigger towns, so there is much more to know, and the world is infinitely big—your own country is a hundred days' ride across—so there is an infinity of things to know. And you have seen more of the world, so I am to ask, and you are to answer."

"Good. Remember, though, that you know much that I do not know."

"That is true," Jum-aw said after a judicious pause. " 'The eye of the hawk is keen but the eye of the hog is close.' "

"That is a Shan proverb."

"It is. I saw your tattoos this morning. They are not extensive, but they are Shan tattoos."

"I am only a bit Shan," Greenwood said. "Here: let me ask a riddle. You know that until these last years, until the war, the Kachin would burst forth from a village every twenty years or so, and pack their silver and their goods, and half the village would go to a new place, many tens of warriors, and they would kill all the people there, every man, woman and child, and they would do this without ill feeling, and afterward they would make extravagant sacrifices to the ghosts of the slain."

"I know all that."

"And why did they do it?"

"Because they are a cruel and bloodthirsty people."

"Ah. You think it was because of what they were."

"I do."

"But there was no ill feeling."

"All the worse."

"Ah. But I think there was another reason, and that reason was the rule by which they lived, the rule by which they survived as Kachin and did not become some other people."

"And that rule was?"

"That when a man died, everything he owned—land, cattle, pigs, silver and wives too—passed to his youngest son. So with each generation there were multitudes of older sons with no land, cattle, pigs or silver, yet with their own wives and children to maintain. So they had no choice. To live by the rule, to remain Kachin, they had to go elsewhere, and make another place a Kachin place."

In the faintest starshine Jum-aw mediated, and there was silence. They listened, and heard only the night.

"Then it is reasonable to ask," Jum-aw said, "whether men do what they do because of what they are, or are what they are because of what they do."

"And that is the study of man," Greenwood said. "The beginning of wisdom is indeed questions."

After a while Jum-aw said, "Perhaps the Kachin are not so bad. The evil they do, they do to others. The Bghai Karen do evil to their own."

"In what way?"

"If a Bghai Karen marries out of his rank in life, he is strangled in a pit." The cheroot glowed.

"I never knew that," Greenwood said, truly pleased. "You see: for the moment I am your student, and you are my master. But the Kachin

too can be cruel to their own. They used to eat
their old ones, and some still do."

"Yes, yes," Jum-aw said with excitement.
"They set them on high wooden platforms and
poked them with long poles unti they fell off and
were killed."

"But again without malice. Only relatives and
intimate friends were invited to this convivial
ceremony, and afterward they made many sacrifices."

"Some did not eat their elders," Jum-aw said
with assurance. "Some buried their elders beneath the floor of the longhouse."

"That is true, and the spirits of the elders, now
at rest, brought luck and prosperity to the
village."

"So it is not simple," Jum-aw said.

"It is life, and life is not simple. A Kachin
woman must be faithful to her husband; but before marriage she may try any number of men, to
be sure she selects one she can be faithful to. The
Shan may take three wives, but a wife may
divorce her husband and keep her property."

"You had a wife?"

"Not quite. Because I am not a full Shan, but a
foreigner and adopted, I had a concubine to
whom I was faithful. The Shan call them 'little
woman.' "

"And now?"

"And now I am returning to Pawlu and I do not
know what I may find; as I no longer know the
way to Pawlu for sure, and have asked your
help."

"You have it," Jum-aw said firmly. "I have

known round-eyed men before and never have I liked one. I like you."

"My heart fills," Greenwood said. "I like you."

"Then ask me another riddle. Your riddle gave me great pleasure."

Greenwood considered. Again they listened, again they sensed no danger. Again the tree frogs' chorus drifted up from the valley. "Well, then," Greenwood said, "you know about malaria."

"I have seen men shiver and burn."

"It is borne by mosquitoes."

"I have been told that. It is not easy to believe."

"They take the bad blood from one, and their bite passes it to another. And you know that many Shan, most of the lowland Shan, suffer from malaria, and that it disappears sometimes for years and then returns."

"I know."

"But the monks—you are a Buddhist?"

"My people worship trees, thunder, tigers and certain hills."

"Once more I am your student." Again the cheroot reddened.

"About the monks," Jum-aw said.

"Yes. Among the monks there is very little malaria. Now, why is that?"

"Because they are men of the Lord," Jum-aw said promptly.

"But even virtuous men who are not monks fall sick, as do some very godly monks. Think and try again."

After a moment Jum-aw said, "Because they live in monasteries and do not mingle with the sick."

"And how if the mosquitoes mingle, what then?"

Jum-aw was now silent for some time. They sat motionless and hooded, ancient travelers in an eternal landscape. Jum-aw said, "I am your student. You must tell me."

"Well, you came close," Greenwood said. "I think, I am not sure but I think, that the mosquitoes are sickened by incense, and so avoid it, and here the monks burn incense day and night in praise of the Lord."

"Then it *is* because they are men of the Lord!"

"By all the gods, you are right!" Greenwood laughed with him. "And who is now the student? But it is not as simple as you first thought, is it?"

"No, it is not. Here, my friend. There is one good cloud left in this cheroot. And that is plenty of riddling for one night."

"It is." Greenwood drew in a lungful of sweet smoke, then snubbed the butt in the dry, crumbly earth. "We must listen awhile, and then sleep."

They listened awhile, and heard an owl. They observed the heavens, and saw the Hunter stride high. They lay quietly in their blankets, and the stars dimmed. They slept, and when they opened their eyes in the opal dawn, they saw six men in turbans seated upon the ground, calm, curious and lavishly armed.

6

The Burma
Road Out

General Yang's column straggled on. Communists were variously reported to the north, south and east, but always hot on the trail. When the tail of the column fell behind because Colonel Prince Nikolai Andreevich Olevskoy fell into a drunken stupor compounded by sexual exhaustion, General Yang was obliged to administer a polite but public rebuke.

Olevskoy was sufficiently bitter without that. He had spent much of his youth fleeing eastward, and much of his middle age fleeing westward, and now the trucks were backfiring false alarms, brake drums wearing through, spark plugs fouling, air filters clogging and mechanics deserting. He had no desire to walk to the Burmese border —indeed no desire to visit Burma at all—and his nostalgia for the cavalry was passionate: if he must flee west, how he would enjoy leading a squadron across Asia!

Furthermore, the skies were a shiny pewter-gray, with never the relief of a good rain.

Furthermore, the road was in terminal dis-

repair and road crews had vanished in the pre-
vailing chaos.

Furthermore, Hsiao-chi—in time he had asked
her name—was physically grimy.

And a bridge was out, its sheet-metal tracks
torn up for shacks or pots or crude plows; for
two days the battalion bivouacked and bickered
and reluctantly learned construction.

And bandits were reported to the west.

In five days the column had managed ninety
miles; Olevskoy could have doubled that with
horses. His headache was chronic; he announced
himself unfit for active duty and retired to his
vehicle.

He was at any rate traveling first-class, as
became a prince. He and his paramour were the
only passengers in a light canvas-covered truck;
they reclined on mattresses, were warm between
quilts and messed from the same cauldrons and
pans as the general staff, Yang, Wei and Ho.

Even this relative luxury he found insufficient.
True luxury, he decided, was a hot bath. In his
truck were Scotch whisky and American cigarettes, the practiced endearments of a mistress, and
the privacy due his rank and lineage; all he desired was a hot bath. Perhaps this Pawlu was a
famous hot spring. He would bathe twice a day.
Perhaps Pawlu was the capital of a utopian
Asiatic hot-bath culture, its secret jealously
guarded these many centuries, its borders
patrolled and approaches barred by a corps of
barbered and perfumed tribesmen in immaculate silk robes, the sensual refinements of its
spas administered by bevies of adolescent girls

in gauze trousers.

They would be infinitely preferable to his present rancid companion, who was, he conceded, considerably better than no body at all. He simply refrained from mouthing her, while allowing her to relieve him a variety of childish ways. He spent his days and nights lolling, drinking, smoking and remembering. He gave himself over to an orgy of recollection. The present was impossible. The future was opaque. In the distant past lay all that he loved.

His first memory was of his father weeping. Even now his heart and mind could almost relive the shock of that enormity, and of the sudden jabber that broke through the tears: his father, Prince Andrei Alexeevich Olevskoy, tall as a tree, broad as a barn, straight fair hair like a tumbled sheaf of wheat, weeping silently, tears gushing from Arctic eyes down ruddy cheeks like twin glaciers thawing over sandstone, and then, "Port Arthur! Mukden! Tsushima!" The god had crushed the boy in a wracking, clumsy embrace. Olevskoy was confused about the spate of words that followed but could recall, "Ce sont des animaux, mon fils, des animaux, ces Japonais!" And then a babble of warnings, admonitions, instructions, the gist of which was that these Japanese must—if not now, then in the boy's lifetime—be exterminated, or at least reduced to serfdom and slavery before they destroyed the Christian world.

The boy was appalled. He was four years old and his world was Sobolyevo, the Olevskoy estate, and beyond Sobolyevo were places like

Berezhov and St. Petersburg and ultimately a
vast and glorious land called Russia; and that
vast and glorious land had been invaded, overcome, perhaps overrun, by treacherous,
dwarfish creatures from some other world. "Remember! Remember!" the god had cried, and the
boy had stammered, "Oui, Papa! Oui!" All his life
"Tsushima!" had rung in his memory like a
curse.

Well, Olevskoy had not done badly. He had exterminated a few Japanese in his time. He had
also killed Russians, at least one Czech in a brawl
over a Siberian woman, innumerable Chinese for
unremembered reasons, and a variety of less
defined people in a variety of places and uniforms—Muslim Communists from the northwest,
Mongolians, assorted tribesmen, uncomprehend-
ing women and children trapped and annihilated
like insects by the fumigatory techniques of
modern war.

It was not precisely what his father had expected, but neither had his father expected to
lose Sobolyevo, and his peasants, and finally his
life. Olevskoy remembered Sobolyevo with a
fierce ache that thirty-three years had not
assuaged. There was a bridge crossing the brook
that fed the pond: "No carp," his father said,
"they're trash fish and eat the trout. Good only
for French kings, formal gardens and enclosed
fountains." Olevskoy fils, the little prince,
dashed across the bridge with old nurse Marya
screeching after him and her son Prohor, a year
older than Olevskoy, stocky and powerful, pig-
eyed already, light brown hair cropped to a centi-
meter, panting, "Go easy, boy. If you tumble and

bleed she catches hell," and a bit later it was not "boy" but "Nikolai Andreevich." It was Prohor he would always remember staggering into the great hall under towering armfuls of quartered logs, Prohor with whom, each spring, he had spurred a pony on that glorious day, the real hinge of the year, when it was permitted to ride after dinner; when the sun lingered; when mangy brown earth swelled through the falling snow; when roads became bogs; when flocks of kids and lambs, already weeks old, appeared as if by magic on greening hillsides.

Little Olevskoy also loved the barns on summer evenings. Once at dusk, when half the cattle in the west meadow were down for the night and the other half hesitantly ending their graze on the cool swatches of lush summer grass, Prohor had called him out to the horse barn. The two of them raced, nine years old, ten, and in the dreamy yellow lantern light of the high barn that smelled of sweet hay and rich manure his father and old Uncle Pyotr, Prohor's father—"uncle" the affectionate title—were standing vigil over a straining mare, down and sweaty. "It's the off forefoot," Uncle Pyotr said. Enormous shadows swayed on the walls, the stalls, the high beams.

Olevskoy pere asked, "Will you go in?"

"I must," said Uncle Pyotr. "Should the boy see?"

"He is old enough." And to the boy Andrei Alexeevich said, "The foal is badly presented. Come closer.

Olevskoy saw the mare's vulva, distended, a tiny muzzle and a tiny hoof peeping out. He saw blood and was momentarily queasy; slime. "At birth," his father was saying, "the forehoofs should be together, directly beneath the lower jaw. You've seen the lambs come. But one foreleg has gone awry. Do you understand?"

Olevskoy understood. He nodded over and over, unaware that he was nodding, eyes wide, one hand tight on Prohor's arm. His father gestured; Uncle Pyotr dipped both hands into a bucket, washed them and his forearms, and knelt. He inserted his right hand, groped, and entered further, to the elbow. The mare stirred, tried to heave, whickered once. Uncle Pyotr probed. Olevskoy was breathless. The foal's muzzle oozed, sticky, glistening. It will die, the boy told himself. It cannot breathe. It is already dead. Oh Lord God let it live.

Uncle Pyotr grunted and tugged. Bracing his left hand on the mare's rump, he tugged; "Ah," he said. Slowly his arm emerged, slick, dribbling. "Ah." A last quick tug, and beside the first hoof the boy saw a second, and suddenly the foal's head surged out, and two forelegs, and in another moment—Olevskoy could never be sure that he had not heard a sucking *pop*!—a tiny wet horse slithered to the straw. The mare's flanks heaved.

Olevskoy père knelt quickly. "A colt. Another son for Rurik."

Uncle Pyotr sloshed water between the mare's hind legs. "Now, if she doesn't take infection."

"Yes," murmured Olevskoy père. "Always that."

Uncle Pyotr glanced quickly at the prince and away. A few years later, when the boy understood that his mother had died of puerperal fever, he recalled that glance.

The men and boys stepped back. The mare struggled, half rose, collapsed beside the colt; wearily, patiently, she licked at her foal.

"We'll see how she cleans out," Olevskoy père said.

"The quicker the better," Uncle Pyotr said. "I'll plaster her then with comfrey."

Prohor too was entranced. Young Olevskoy was fascinated by this colt; he marveled at the blaze, like Rurik's. The colt wrinkled his muzzle; his ears quivered. Olevskoy fell in love. "Papa," he whispered.

"Yes, boy?"

"Will he be mine?"

The prince laid a tender hand on the boy's head. "Do you want him?"

"I love him," Olevskoy whispered.

"Then he shall be yours."

And he was; and that was a better night than winter nights with his tutor, Monsieur Grandin, who had a tic; when he corrected the boy a corner of his mouth quirked, as if in apology or fear. "A moins qu'il *nnn*'y ait une guerre! N'oubliez jamais ce *ne*! Avant qu'il *ne* pleuve!"

So Olevskoy never forgot that *ne*, and only ten years old read stories in both French and Russian, learning each language from the other, stories of war and of peace, one of them about Cossack country and raids and skirmishes, by a count and not merely a scribbler, and he remembered that count's death too. Olevskoy père, reading a letter in the shiny old leather-covered wooden chair, a throne beside the fire, reared back snorting and said, "So! Lev Nikolayevich is dead in Astapovo! Count Tolstoy! Some count! Mikhail Kirilovich says here the old man used to sit in the gardens at Yasnaya Polyana with flies wandering his face, and tell people, 'They are God's creatures as well as I and have the same right to a free and unfettered existence as I.' Mischa goes on. 'Fee, yes, but not on my face. What would it have cost him to give a small, kindly wave and simply make them fly somewhere else? It would have cost him being Tolstoy.' Well, God rest him. He was a fine buck in his youth, but I tell you, these last years he was not only a fool but a pain in the backside." (Five years later Olevskoy, fourteen and infatuated with Prince Bolkonsky, with Count Vronsky, with Anna and above all with Natasha, blushed to recall his father's words. And four years after that, wading an icy river with Semenov after a disastrous skirmish against a mob of Reds near Irkutsk, he had in midstream recalled that judgment, and thanked his father for it, and wished Tolstoy and all such sanctimonious populists in hell.)

The boy Olevskoy loved to watch the mowing too, and to sit with the peasants sharing their breakfast, their oatcakes and cold tea. And to sit with his father at dinner. Monsieur Grandin had no place at their table, and ate in solitary state, served in his own room by Prohor. At dinner Olevskoy's father saw to the boy's real education: czars and sabers and true geography, the borders of the Romanov empire, and what Kalmucks were, and Cossacks, and where Kamchatka was, and why an Olevskoy never beat an animal or a servant or— and the vehemence of this command persisted long after he had broken it—struck a woman.

Women came soon enough, but first love was
first love, and for Olevskoy it was the colt Kalita.
For three or four years, while women remained
only an odd species of soprano subordinate,
Olevskoy's nuzzles, kisses and gifts went to the
colt. Before boy or colt was grown they were become one. Olevskoy père was reluctant. "This is a
stallion of blood and not a gelding, nor a slug."

"He loves me," the boy said, and the man knew
he was right and shortly gave in. The boy overheard his father say to Monsieur Grandin, "The
colt is Bucephalus, and the boy Alexander," and
by then the boy knew what that meant, and was
proud. He and Prohor made the rounds of their
villages in all seasons, through snow and mud
and over dry, dusty summer roads, Olevskoy
breathing not air but the mingled essence of
forest and field and horse and youth, of sun and
wind and hay.

For a year or two of these rounds he was a shy
boy, haughty at first to mask his timidity before
these square, stolid peasants and their plump
daughters. Some of the peasants lived in wooden
shacks, others in mud huts that almost dissolved
away in spring. Afternoons, in the great house, he
was formally presented to counts, lawyers, rich
merchants, the provincial governor, district
councillors. Evenings he rode out, and the round
young women swarmed about him, and he grew
warm in the saddle; he was thirteen. Eventually,
after a frustrating English lesson with Monsieur
Grandin, whose English was that of Calais and
not London, he rode out with Prohor, wordlessly
bound for the village they had come, with reason,
to frequent, and at dusk, in the matted hay, the

girl Katya, blond and green-eyed, panted in his
face after he had flung up her skirts and found
his way, hot, direct and bursting, to the core of
her. He persuaded her then, with soft words and
a coin, to disrobe, and in the last light she stood
before him, breasts immense, thighs glowing,
eyes modest, her hands twitching with the need
to cover her golden triangle, to shield her bosom.

He took her again. He lay propped on his elbows ecstatic at this miracle, this moist heat, *he
was within her*! This was the mystery! His blood
roared. She squeezed, shifted, pulsed, and he
took his rhythm from her. The sheer rapture of it
took entire possession of him. He thought he
might swoon, faint away. The world ceased to
exist, only this warm flesh, the silky grip of hers
on his, the sweet odor of her and hay and heaven,
the gathering, scalding rush and the final
suicidal conquest of the woman, the field, all
Russia. All that he was, he gave freely in that
moment.

Prohor snickered and teased as they trotted
home. "By God," Nikolai Andreevich said like a
man, "there is nothing like it!" From that day
their rides were more than proprietary visits.
There were Katya and Varya and Masha and
more, and one night at table his father said
gently. "Go easy, boy. Monsieur Grandin tells me
you scarcely heed him. Women are well enough
in their way, but there is more to manhood than
that."

Olevskoy tried to answer but only blushed.

His father laughed fondly and proudly.
"You're a handsome young devil. You had better
let me tell you a bit about all this." And he did so,

as Olevskoy recovered from his confusion and returned to his beef, listening carefully, enthralled, nodding assent or comprehension, blushing slightly again at certain clauses of technical advice, and catching his father's serious tone and manner when the elder prince, this noble and titanic father, this personification of all northern kings, said, "Tumble all the village girls you like, my boy, but if you betray a lady, I'll flay you alive. I'll lash the skin off your back. Do you understand me? You are an Olevskoy."

"A prince," the boy said proudly.

"Anybody can be a prince," his father rebuked him. "Half Russia is princes and the other half counts. But you are an Olevskoy. And if you cannot pay proper tribute to God and Russia and your ancestors, then you are nothing. It is our fathers' fathers who made this land, and dedicated it to God, and all this"—with a wave encompassing table, great house, Sobolyevo—"we must deserve. Do you understand? We must earn it each day. And there is no such thing as a small betrayal. If you allow yourself once to be less than an Olevskoy, you will never again be an Olevskoy. Others may believe that you are, but you will know that you are not. And if you are not an Olevskoy, then you are nothing."

"I understand, Father," he said, but even that night he suffered doubt. His father worshipped only three things: God, family and Russia. And it seemed to Olevskoy that he too worshipped only three things, but that they were Russia, horses and fornication.

Russia, horses and fornication. And now there

was no more Russia and no more cavalry and he lay in a decrepit American truck with a soiled Chinese adolescent. The Russia he loved had vanished forever, and its princes drove taxis in Paris and boasted, "Jé parrle sans accieng parce que jé vieng dé Pétersbourgg." The horses he loved were now light, medium and heavy tanks, weapons carriers, armored cars and jeeps. The fornication he loved at least bore some resemblance to the original.

He crawled to the flap and peered out at gray-green China. Not even silvery-jade; only gray-green. A light rain. The road muddy but passable. Late afternoon. L'heure de l'apéritif. So many late afternoons. So many gray-green late afternoons.

He let fall the flap and crawled to his kits and crates. Life without ritual was chaos: he poured what he hoped was fifty cubic centimeters of Scotch whisky into his canteen cup, and added one hundred of water. "You. Hsiao-chi. Want a whisky?"

"Yes. Whisky." Her voice was frail but, thank God, pleasant. She seemed to be enjoying her excursion. Travel broadens one so. Cela change les idées. He mixed her a highball in a tin mug. "Long life and prosperity," he said.

She echoed him. It was perhaps optimistic. He sipped and grew benevolent. He was fond of alcohol, and his smile was unconscious, involuntary, ancient habit. He sat beside the reclining girl, his back to the driver's cab, and patted her without malice. Russia, horses and fornication, and the greatest of these is fornication. There would surely be women in Pawlu.

If Pawlu was only three bamboo huts by a mud flat, there would be women, and one would be the most desirable; if there were only two, one would be preferable to the other. Perhaps his little Hsiao-chi would be an exotic beauty in Pawlu.

"Where we will both be princes," Yang had said back in Kunming, in that hotel suite with hot water. For one insane moment, his mind outracing reality and creating possibilities, worlds, destinies, Olevskoy had made a fantasy of desertion, a dash south, one jeep, perhaps a squad, to the Tonkin border; but Lin Piao had Nanning and was halfway to Mengtzu and would surely head him off, and already he was curious about Pawlu, and how General Yang would achieve this promotion to prince, and his hand and cup had barely paused while these landscapes and flights unreeled, so he drank up and let suspicion and discontent darken his face. "Pawlu?"

"Trust me. Remember, I am Yang Yu-lin and I have given you Kunming and a hotel suite de grand luxe, and you even have a woman and a case of Johnnie Walker Red."

"You could be Yang Yu-lin in Tonkin too," Olevskoy said, and knew instantly how wrong he was.

"I'm afraid not," Yang had said. "You forget: I was scarcely permitted to be Yang Yu-lin in Paris, where at least I was a young and exotic specimen. Allow me to doubt that colonial officials in Hanoi will take this faded Oriental to their hearts. I can read your own desires: the French culture you know and love, the colonel of cavalry, the polyglot adventurer, soldier of fortune, prince—tu saurais un succès fou. But I would only be another damned Chink. You know what the French used to call masturbating?"

Olevskoy knew but shook his head.

" 'Polishing the Chinaman.' No, Nicky. Trust me. Pour us more whisky. And for this delightful creature as well. Ma chère Marquise! Tout va bien au château?"

Yang Yu-lin was born in Peking, the son of a treasury official and principal wife, and his earliest memory was of the crowded execution ground, and many stern men wearing queues, and pale severed heads goggling at him from the mud. A few years later he saw Boxers' bodies on the ramparts. One red-clad corpse clutched a crossbow; much of the head and right shoulder had been blown off by Western artillery, but the futile left hand clutched a crossbow. Yang Yu-lin also saw the Bengal Lancers enter Peking, after the Boxers had been put down with great carnage, and he resolved then that one day he would be a soldier and expel the foreigner from China. Being only eight years old, he also resolved to ask his father for a pony and a ma-fu, or groom, so that one day he might ride well enough to be a Bengal Lancer.

His father had other plans for him. The boy was bright, personable, even handsome with that round face, that joyous youthful smile. He was, furthermore, of a generous and outgoing disposition, the result perhaps of affectionate coddling by his mother, the second and third wives, the ma-fu and a household staff of fourteen considered—so exalted were treasury officials—superior to independent shopkeepers. His father had learned much in the treasury—for example, that money was good, that foreigners were powerful, and that you won a man's esteem, as you did the world's, by admiring his or its expressions of humble altruism while facilitating his or its murders, rapes and thefts. The necessary shifts and contrivances required an education of manifold and complex aspects.

Yang Yu-lin was consequently tutored by a motley faculty that slipped in and out of his life at confusing intervals: a seedy scholar who had failed the fifth-level Civil Service examinations, a musician who prepared for each lesson with a full hour of silent meditation, a Scottish lady as outlandish as a penguin, a French former sergeant given over to opium, an aged archer formerly of the Empress's guard, a calligrapher who fabricated his own brushes and ground his own ink.

And when the time came, Yang Yu-lin was enrolled in a foreign university in Peking, a Roman Catholic institution run by Frenchmen and their Chinese minions. Its Catholicism was incidental. Yang's father had no doctrinal prejudices; worshipping his own ancestors, conferring with Confucius and communing with Lao-tzu, being, in short, an ignorant and barbarous reactionary, he believed, like so many educated and civilized liberals, that the various forms of Christianity were so many childhood diseases—discommoding, itchy and to be suffered for no more than three weeks.

What he wanted for his son was entrée to the

European world. The authorities seemed to understand that, and even to sympathize; when Yang the elder explained to the headmaster, or Father Superior, that the Yangs were not Roman Catholic, nor even Christian, he was vouchsafed a haunting reply: "Oh, cạ va. Nous avons même un Anglais," which was translated, "Oh, never mind about that. We even have an English boy here." His perplexity was lifelong.

So at twenty-one Yang Yu-lin spoke, read and wrote Mandarin Chinese, a little Scots English, some Latin and much French, and had studied world history, physiology, government, economics (including the mysterious Marx) and French literature, not to mention the New Testament, Saint Augustine and papal history. He knew himself an upper bourgeois, a flunky trained to perpetuate an unjust world, and happily acknowledged the budding socialist deep within him—that was his dark secret, and for the moment, the time and place, Peking in 1913, he kept it locked away.

His father expected that ultimately he would become an ambassador, perhaps even president of a unified China—one Sun Yat-sen, a monomaniac and not a Pekinger, had established a republic, whatever that was, in remote Canton. Yang the elder had no faintest notion of what this republic's "Three People's Principles" might be (something to do with the worm people, in the old phrase, the ordinary people, the millions of coolies and peasants and beggars, people who did not even pay taxes). But whatever a republic was, whatever China might become, it was clear that his son, Yang Yu-lin, must play a major part in its history. Yang Yu-lin exemplified the Confucian ideal, the superior man, the prince; why, the boy was even expert with the bow and arrow!

At twenty-two Yang Yu-lin shocked his father almost into the grave by journeying to Canton and joining the army of the new China as a subaltern. At twenty-four Yang Yu-lin was promoted to first lieutenant and sent, at the head of a company of coolies, to France, where a mysterious war was in progress. The war was mysterious because it consisted principally of hundreds of thousands of men living in trenches, rising sporadically from those trenches to attack other men in other trenches, and dying by tens of thousands in their tracks. It was soon obvious to Yang that a whole generation of Europe's best, its most intelligent and compassionate, its most loyal and patriotic, those who cared most and therefore accepted their obligations, was simply being murdered, and with them was dying Europe's future.

Yang's coolies dug trenches, unloaded cargo from vessels and trains, were referred to as "labor battalions" and earned pennies a day. Their officers earned more, were often gratified by references to "our glorious Chinese allies," and became objets d'art, or at least knicknacks, in the salons of Paris. Yang himself knew an enormous success. He was taller than average, for one thing, and thus was never patted on the head by a hostess; he had begun to fill out and consequently to resemble a traditional warrior, unlike some of his fellow officers who were scrawny and jittery by nature, with marked tendencies to drop forks and duel steaks with fish knives.

Wrestling with tableware was Yang's most serious undertaking in World War I until he met Florence. She was the daughter of a steel magnate whose holdings, in northeastern France, should in logic have been leveled by a determined enemy but remained intact, positively humming, thanks to the highly civilized mutual courtesy that left also intact the German industrial works across the border, a refined arrangement that, in a reasonable world, would have proved definitively the superiority of commercial intelligence and morality over political or military. The paradox reinforced Yang's conviction that the flower of Europe was being—almost literally—ground into the earth by brutish politicians and generals. Believing that Asia was sure to predominate as a result, and in his own lifetime, he felt rather cheerful about this. Florence's father could only be an inhuman ogre; another paradox.

By then he was besotted. He had met her at dusk in the late fall of 1917. Paris was gray and drizzly, streetlights on early, an occasional quick waft of rummy fumes from a yellow doorway reminding homeward-bound pedestrians that cafes were oases. Yang went coatless deliberately because he enjoyed the attention his puzzling uniform drew from the bourgeoisie; more than once he was taken for Japanese or Indochinese. He was on leave and had been invited to a soirée at the apartment of a French colonel on the Avenue Ségur; the colonel was one of the few French

officers to whom Yang was required to report
directly, a just officer who had complimented the
young lieutenant and taken a serious, even
paternal, interest in this sprig of an alien culture.

Yang arrived cold, his uniform damp; spoke
gallantly to the astounded concierge, who actually pressed the light button for him so that he
could march up three flights without groping;
and entered a crowded flat, sensing immediately
that he was among sophisticated and cosmopolitan friends because conversation did not extin-
guish itself at his entrance, only fell for the
briefest moment from fortissimo to mezzo forte.
The colonel's wife came to shake hands, then
took his left hand in her right, smiling virtuously
as she demonstrated that holding hands with
Oriental gentlemen was all in a day's— No. Yang
rebuked himself for cynicism. She was doing
what any hostess would do. Furthermore, she
was a colonel's lady; to hear he was not a Chinese
but a lieutenant.

Then she presented him to Florence. "Mad-
emoiselle de Morvan, Lieutenant Yang de
l'armée chinoise." Florence de Morvan was
young, small and short-haired, with happy
greenish eyes and a mobile, quirky face. Yang
was half in love even before her first words: "I
never met a Chinese before, but I've always
wanted to *be* Chinese." They were shaking hands.
Yang, highly educated, well-traveled, man of the
world, crack shot, linguist, connoisseur, wanted
only to gape and dote yet summoned inner forces
to ask, "But why? In China a woman as beautiful
as you would have been betrothed at twelve and
probably married at fifteen to some aging ty-

coon." Actually he had said "gros industriel d'un certain âge," relieved that he had managed to speak at all and pleased by the aptness and fluency of his remark, and he was full of joy until she said, "Mais mon père est un gros industriel d'un certain âge!"

He fumbled for apologies, but she was laughing sweetly, laughing in merry delight, hooking her arm through his and saying, "Now you must let me find you an apéritif, and promise not to leave without me. You're the catch of the evening, you know. Vermouth? Whisky?" He said, "Pernod, thank you," and she said, "How vulgar! Where is your Oriental delicacy?" And he said, "I never knew what delicatesse was until this moment."

It was the coup de foudre, the lightning bolt of love. He was lost forever. He sipped his milky Pernod. About him the buzzing chorus of French, the frequent peal of laughter, warmed the room. Florence spoke of Lao-tzu, he of Victor Hugo; challenged, he improvised a translation into Mandarian of Hugo's famous quatrain about flame in the eyes of youth and light in the eyes of age. The incomprehensible syllables charmed her. She spoke of philosophy, serenity, order, art; he of war, destruction, revolution, death. "I suppose we must circulate now," she said. "Meet me at the door at seven."

They dined, they set a rendezvous for tomorrow, they prowled a flea market, they drove through the Bois in a horse-drawn carriage, a day passed, two, a night passed, two, and he could not say if he suffered more in her absence or gloried more in her presence; and then it was

evening and they were in her father's flat—that
gentleman was in Metz—and it was all amazingly
simple. Despite his limited experience, he was
versed in theory; classical pornography was high
art in China and he rejoiced her avid soul with
the Chinese names for this and that: the fish with
two backs, horse upon horse, the two snakes,
bamboo syrup, bird's-nest soup. "Oh that's *nice!*"
she announced with a moue of pleasure, a gleeful
frisson. He was slightly bewildered; whores
feigning ecstasy had whimpered, arched their
backs, screamed and moaned, but his little
Florence warbled and twittered. She was indeed
his bird of paradise. When she did pant, did cry
quickly, "Ah oui ah oui ah oui," he rejoiced; but
he was never sure when, or whether, or how
hotly, the true ecstasy came upon her. Perhaps it
was none of his business. How puzzling and
difficult to be a gentleman of the West!

His own ecstasy was, nevertheless, constant.
He was permanently intoxicated, perhaps insane.
He no longer lived on earth but in some starry
realm, lovers' heaven, gods' madhouse. In sober
moments, when at work or writing dutifully to
his father, he feared retribution. With her in
public places, he could barely breathe for joy,
pride, immortality. In private he knew impulses
to weep, rage aloud, hang himself—it was all too
much for one poor heart to withstand. He was
not sure always that it was *she*, precisely;
perhaps it was the loving and not its object that
he loved. He knew so little. He learned so much.
Winter passed. Toward Easter he took a furlough, and they traveled in the Pyrenees, less
ecstatic now and more occupied with tickets,

reservations, bathrooms, more aware of the sullen disapproval in Gascon glances, more oppressed by a small-town waiter's condescending stare. He gobbled his whitebait, mopped the bowl with good French bread, tossed off the last of a local white wine and said, "Let's go back to Paris."

Her relief was almost palpable, so he exacted a price: he wanted to meet her father. She agreed, giggling in mischievous expectation, and one day late in spring they made a date with Monsieur de Morvan. They were to dine at one of Paris's internationally beloved culinary landmarks where, in the words of Yang's by now good friend the colonel, "the doorman dresses like a field marshal and the gourmets unfold napkins three feet square, tuck them into their braces at the collarbone, and perform, for two hours, a gastronomic Götterdämmerung."

Yang bathed, shaved and dressed with care and elegance. He powdered his joints. His leather gleamed. His ribbons—both of them, one for being in Europe at all and the other for a visit to the front during which he and his party were, by only a moderate stretch of the imagination, shelled—proclaimed valor. He flagged a cab. En route he made a desperate effort to calm himself. This man, he mused, is rich because others are poor or dead. You love his daughter, who is only twenty-two and may or may not love you. You will be courteous and cautious until your moment comes. You will not, however, cringe, lie or prostitute your toothy smile. Entudu, mon lieutenant?

His imagination raced ahead: Florence, tear-

stained, was forced to choose, decay with her
father and bourgeois capitalism or build a new
world with Yang Yu-lin. Hands crossed on her
heaving breast, she— But the thought of her
breast distracted him. Would her father be kind
enough to leave early? The apartment was surely
out of bounds but there were comfortable hotels.
Only to be with her. Moonlight rippling on he
Seine. By the time he reached the restaurant he
was almost frisky. He overtipped the taxi driver
and strode briskly toward his fate.

Morvan greeted the lieutenant heartily; Yang
recognized the dinnertime camaraderie of the
international businessman. The mâitre d' bowed,
addressed Morvan by name, led them to the royal
table, secluded in a windowed corner, the
windows curtailed now, Paris by night blacked
out. They ordered. Conversation proceeded along
amicable and conventional lines: the war, the fall
of the Romanov dynasty, the possible Bolshe-
vization of Europe, the future of America. Yang
would never forget the grilled trout, the Macon
'II, the tournedos, the Richebourg '06, or his own
voice saying, out of nowhere, someone else im-
personating him, some fool, some clown, "Monsieur de Morvan, I am in love with your daughter
and would like to marry her."

He knew instantly that he had failed to slay the
dragon and was doomed to bitter exile, wandering the earth without his beloved. He looked
disaster in the face and reminded himself that he
was an officer and gentleman.

Morvan was simply incredulous, finding voice
finally and blurting, "My dear sir! You're

Chinese! It's not even a real army! You're only the head coolie!"

Florence's face had blotched red and white. "I didn't *mean* that!" she pleaded with Yang. "I never *thought* of marriage!"

Yang rose and dashed the remains of his wine in Morvan's face. He spoke to Florence: "Then think of it now. Let us leave this place hand in hand!"

Morvan was a cartoon of Gallic exasperation; Yang wondered—idly, it was amazing how much time one seemed to have in these moments of comic melodrama, these flashes of eternal verity—if he was about to thunder, "My dear sir! *That was a Richebourg of nine-teen-oh-six*!" But Morvan snarled, "Independent! Modern! 'Papa, I'm a grown woman!' This is what comes of it, you foolish girl! Shame and humiliation, for us and for him!"

"I'm sorry," she said helplessly to Yang, and tears started. "I'm so infinitely sorry."

Yang shrugged. He said, "Adieu, Florence." He bowed coldly to her father. He strode away. The last words he ever heard her say, and he heard the tears too, were, "Papa! Papa! He was very nice and he was my first Chinaman, and you hurt his feelings!"

Hurt his feelings! By the gods! Whether tears sprang first to his eyes or nervous laughter to his lips he could never remember, but he remembered the iron entering his soul. He collected his cap and gloves, leaving no tip, and marched stiffly down the red carpet and out the door; in his distraction he saluted the field marshal.

He walked all the way to the Avenue Ségur and craved audience of the colonel. By then his small, miraculous reserve of icy control had melted away; almost gasping, knotted in pain, he broke every code he knew, Oriental's, officer's, gentleman's, lover's, and sought the truth. He had judged his man well, a fighting colonel and not a desk colonel, a lover of God, country and wife and not merely a Sunday Catholic, wartime patriot, or lunchtime husband. The colonel was gentle. With his own hands he poured cognac for Yang. "There are so many like her now," he said softly, understandingly, forgivingly. "The war excites them, you see. They are young and rich and full of hot blood. Yes: her first Chinaman. After her first Frenchman and her first Belgian and her first Englishman and her first American and probably her first German, Italian, Senegalese, Algerian, legionnaire, spahi, aviator. I am sorry. If you love her, none of that matters, I know. Believe me. I know. 'Love is not love which alters when it alteration finds.' You know the verse? All you can do now is suffer."

Yang returned to the front next morning and applied for immediate repatriation. His application was denied. On his next furlough in Paris he joined what was in effect the East Asian Section of the French Communist Party.

He did not do that "because of Florence." Had she loved him, he might have remained in France, persisted in his suit, married her, advanced himself en bon bourgeois; or carried her back to Peking in a grand gesture of private revolution. Betrayed by love, he rebounded not to another woman or to idiocies like whoring and drink, but to thinkers and writers that French Catholics, and later French cafés, had taught him to love: La Bruyère, Saint-Simon, Tom Paine, Marx, Michelet—even, with a pang, Victor Hugo. He rebounded to a world of men and egalitarians. He attended meetings in public halls and private rooms on the sixth floor without water. He debated with French professors who stank of cheap tobacco and with wiry young Orientals who sniped butts from the gutter. One of these he liked extremely, a skinny Annamite barely older than himself who had changed his name from Nguyen Tat Tan to Nguyen Ai Quoc, lithe and quick, as confused about methods as any of them but surer of his goals: self-rule for Asia and equality for all men and women. "They argue, which must come first," Nguyen Ai Quoc scoffed. "I tell you, both come first. With the left hand we level wealth, income, wages, land holdings; with the right we level privilege and power. And if it proves impossible, or too slow, then we shall use both hands at once and in them will be weapons. Your Sun Yat-sen is a great man but he is no soldier."

"But you want power yourself," Yang protested. "You want to make a privileged class of revolutionaries."

"I want to destroy power! What man has a right to power over another? And as for a privileged class of revolutionaries, their privileges are poverty and exile and jail and torture and firing squads!" Then the Indochinese said more reasonably, "Someone must lead. Someone must make a society run. The question is, What is it to be run for? Those who are most selfless must lead; those who demand nothing for themselves, only justice for others. Their reward will be pain and sorrow and, in the end, freedom."

Pain and sorrow and, in the end, freedom. Yang did return to China, in 1919. There was no sign of serious socialism in North China, only a few professors, a debating society. There were adventurers, ignorant and barbarous, who became footnotes to history before his eyes, or warlords who lasted many years and were fascinated by certain aspects of the Occident, like flashlights and motorcars; not adventurers but true warlords, with roots in the region and limited territorial ambitions, but nevertheless ignorant and barbarous, they too.

Yang pursued his studies and conferred with his father. This pleased both men, the elder naturally flattered and the younger happy to give evidence of filial devotion and to receive what proved extraordinarily often to be wisdom. Yang's father was neither surprised nor angered by his son's political perplexity, and was gently relieved that the boy—nudging thirty now, but still his boy—was having second thoughts: could the political theory of nineteenth-century industrial Europe have any bearing on, or use in, a divided country—a divided colony of Europe and America, really—of four hundred million peasants, an ossified Confucian bureaucracy and generals and admirals from a comic opera? If there were universal principles governing all societies, then China must help to discover or confirm. If each society developed in its own manner, depending on the land, population, flora, fauna, history, means of production and distribution and communication available in successive periods, then could China learn at all from the Occident?

Debating these matters over tea and cigarettes, father and son decided that the young officer had advanced, and not prejudiced, his career by running off to Canton and then France; that China might indeed be unified in his lifetime and that he might play a hero's role in that process; and that perhaps Sun Yat-sen, who seemed to be making headway, represented a synthesis of East and West that might survive.

In 1921 Yang bade a dignified, highly emotional and correctly formal farewell to his father, boarded a train for Tientsin, and took passage on a coaster for Canton via Shanghai and Hong Kong. In Canton he rejoined Sun Yat-sen, who remembered him, complimented him on his service and decorations (Yang had added a Victory Medal and a Good Conduct Medal), questioned him shrewdly about North China, and commissioned him a captain.

Yang remained a military man in search of a government he could conscientiously serve. Sun died in 1925; faction reigned, and Yang faced a grim choice, not his first, not his last: join a beleaguered Communist minority directed almost contemptuously by Russians and Germans and an occasional Frenchman, or join an ignorant and humorless thug called Chiang Kai-shek who had laid out a detailed and feasible campaign to unify China. He joined Chiang. This unfortunately required him to butcher unarmed Communists in the larger cities of the Yangtze valley. He had never before killed, or caused to be killed, his countrymen, and it came hard. He had joined Chiang, after all, because the man was Chinese.

And now it was December of 1949, and the descendants, real or political, of those slaughtered Communists were chasing Captain Yang, now a full general, into permanent exile from a finally unified China. He sat in the gloom of a canvas-roofed American truck, on one of his precious footlockers, using the other as a desk on which, with the aid of a Coleman lantern, he perused detailed maps of Yunnan and Burma. Cities and towns, rivers and railroads, yes, even villages and major roads; but outposts, fords, ambushes, country lanes and mountain trails, no. "Major Wei!"

The sleepy major poked his head over the tailgate. "General."

"Fetch me the colonel, please."

"He won't come, sir."

"Try him. Oblige me. Remember, I am venerable."

Major Wei's head withdrew.

Amazing how whole cities ignored this convoy. Yung-p'ing had turned its back as one man. Tomorrow Pao-shan. A bad season for forage but soon they would be in game country; shooting parties might stock the larder with deer, hare, wildfowl. A few miles only, and it was taking weeks! Thank God for Virginia tobacco and Nicky's nose. A scrounger, as the Americans said, a born scrounger. These hills would be grim, an arduous march. Well, if Mao could cross half China with his thousands, I can cross a ridge with my verminous company.

Less than a company now. Fewer mouths to feed. Eventually, of course, they would all be wiped out, but by then he himself would be in Mandalay with—

"The colonel begs to report himself ailing, and asks to be excused."

General Yang sighed musically, richly. "Major, go back and tell him I need him. Tell him he's been sick long enough and I wish him a speedy recovery. Tell him if he isn't here in three minutes, decently dressed and disinclined to insolence, I'll have him shot immediately."

"Oh, he won't like that." Major Wei was delighted.

"His likes and dislikes are not my concern. Go now."

"Sir."

Insolence. If Nicky was drunk? He heard the voice of a round middle-aged Scottish dame: "flown with insolence and wine." Flawn and wain, she said. Render into Mandarin, please. Well, Olevskoy had better not be flawn. The colonel was shortly to become superfluous. That was a bad thing for a man to be in pinched times. Though there was still a good day's work for him.

"Was the invitation really so elegant, or did the major exaggerate?"

Yang favored Olevskoy with a grand grin. "He did not exaggerate. Il y a du boulot. I don't care what you do or don't do in your private whorehouse, but when there's work to be done you're a colonel again. Hop in here and take a look."

Olevskoy swung aboard and came to stand at Yang's side, leaning over his left shoulder to examine the maps.

"You smell awful," Yang said. He suppressed an ancient, persistent folk prejudice that foreigners tended to stink, or at least to radiate alien aromas. Vaguely he recalled garlicky cubicles in France. Greenwood, who spoke freely about most human vagaries, had once informed him that Chinese breath often smelled of ginger and red pepper.

"I want a hot bath," Olevskoy explained.

"You want half a dozen. Sponge yourself before you come into my presence again, my dear Prince."

"Yes, yes, pride," Olevskoy said, "all right, my apologies. Where the devil are we?"

Yang dotted the map once. "Here, between Yung-p'ing and Pao-shan. I don't want to draw the route, but follow the tip of my pencil. You see here, about seventy-five miles past Pao-shan, this is Fang-shih. It's a Chinese Shan State, quite civilized. There's a sawbwa and some Europeans, or used to be, and maybe even a hot bath."

"Rest and rehabilitation?"

"No time. Lin has Meng-tzu and he's still moving, and there's an army driving southwest from Ch'eng-tu."

"We'll beat them to the border, I hope."

"Yes."

"Any aircraft at Lo-wing? Or fuel?"

"We shall not even approach Loi-wing."

Olevskoy refrained from insolence, only asking in a flat and therefore ambiguous tone, "And why shall we not even approach Loi-wing, which is a large air base and quite close to the border?"

"Because," said the general, "the rascally Chinese Communists, those brave but childlike agrarian reformers, now number several former Nationalist pilots and even a battalion of paratroopers, though I confess"—he sounded truly wistful—"that I should love to see them in action, a mass drop, think of the number of things that might go wrong! If there's one spot down here they may leapfrog into, it's Loi-wing. Besides that, the Burma side of the border is six deep with Reds. They've got White Flag Communists and Red Flag Communists and Trotskyite Centrists and for all I know Vegetarian Mensheviks. And besides again, Pawlu is in another direction."

"Ah yes, Pawlu. Show me. That is, please."

"Well, I can't show you Pawlu. I dashed through Pawlu in nineteen forty-four and an old foreign comrade—allow me the word; why should you let them preempt it?—saved my head, and I mean that literally, the place swarms with headhunters, and at some point I crossed into China. It was a sideshow and a splendid dash, but we moved fast, so all I can tell you is that Pawlu is on one side of the border or the other, and even on these American army air corps maps the border is marked 'indefinite,' as you see. It's somewhere up there not far from Nan-san."

"Good God. No roads."

"No roads. Which is why I sent for you. I want to take the column south from Fang-shih."

Olevskoy studied the map in silence, saying finally, "That's a climb of ten thousand feet."

"Don't exaggerate. We start at two thousand. And to the man of stout heart—"

"And then the Salween."

"And then, as you say, the Salween."

"You're mad. With respect, sir, you're mad."

"Come now. That's twenty miles to the inch. Which means perhaps thirty miles to the Salween—"

"Uphill all the way, one of the steepest valleys in Asia and no road—"

"—and—"

—"excuse me," General, but it's thirty miles uphill to ten thousand feet, and then down to two thousand to cross the river and up to seven thousand again, and you're really talking about several days' march."

"I don't think I want you to interrupt me again," General Yang said.

"Sorry, sir. But up and down all the way, and half the men deserted and the rest mutinous, and how do you know we can ford the Salween? That's a prehistoric gorge in terra incognita and you mentioned headhunters."

"We shall find a way," the general orated. "An epic. History will not forget this loyal band."

"Oh stop that," Olevskoy said. "I need a drink. Can we have a drink?"

"But absolutely. We shall drink to the memory of that poor sniper. Cheers. Why did you murder the boy?"

"Because Communists sicken my nostrils," Olevskoy said calmly. "His very existence was an insult to me." He had shifted to French. "Forget him. You really intend to cross this range and find your little village. Ah, this is good stuff! I can't imagine life without alcohol."

"The exhilaration induced by liquor restores the humors and balances," Yang assured him in Mandarin. "We won't have more than fifty or

sixty men left by the time we leave Fang-shih.
They simply melt into the population. But I
thought you might like to review the survivors,
and put them on ponies, and be a colonel of
cavalry again."

"A colonel of cavalry," Olevskoy repeated
softly. And a village of my own. I shall be a prince
again, among brown-skinned peasant girls, who
bloom early in the tropics. Sobolyevo in Burma!
"Ponies!" He shed years, and laughed aloud.
"Wee little ponies!" He waved a jubilant salute.
"Yours to command, General!"

7

A Wedding
in Pawlu

At dawn a toktay croaked incessantly and Loi-
mae dreamed of her childhood. She dreamed of
herself at five or six sitting naked in the small
branch of Lower Stream while the women
pounded garments and retold ancient stories;
and then of many Wild Wa, identical of feature,
grinning in a circle; and then of Green Wood and
the golden hair and the long bone milky white. At
this she was torn by remorse, and cried out. A
voice soothed her: "Be easy, woman." Green
Wood faded, and the dark glimmered to rose-
gray. She knew that she was in her own house before sunrise, and Naung was stroking her breast
and murmuring comfort, and the toktay croaked
and croaked.

"It will wake the bridegroom too," Naung
whispered, "and he wll have a longer morning to
regret his foolishness."

"As you regret yours."

"Never," he said, "never," and his hands
flowed on her flesh. "We have never been
together too often or too long."

186

"Never," she said, "never," and hugged him close. Her breast glowed, and she pressed it to Naung's hand, and pressed her body hard against his. What a joy a man was! Even Naung, who was sullen in the bed, timid, often held back by inner demons, scarred perhaps by failures and humiliations in Indochina, now and then hasty or rank or rude, resentful perhaps of Green Wood's shadow; nevertheless, when his good times came he filled life's hollow as honey sweetly fills the hollow tree. "O, o, o," she sang. "O my Naung!"

"Once for each croak of the toktay," he teased her afterward.

"Braggart!" Her fingertips brushed his smile; she smoothed back his sparse beard. His brows were rich and handsome, and his teeth were healthy, a complete mouthful, not common in Pawlu, and bone-white; Naung took a cheroot often but did not chew betel or smoke opium, barring purely ceremonial occasions.

"An omen for Cha and Ko-yang," he said. "Let them be happy as long as the toktay croaks in these hills."

The toktay chose that moment to fall silent. Loi-mae and Naung giggled. They heard Lola stir behind the hanging straw mat, and her light barefoot patter receding through the brushy grove; and then she was back, dancing around the mat, peering excitedly at them and, once sure of her welcome, sprawling atop them.

Naung and Loi-mae pinned her down and tickled her. "O stop! O stop! Or I will laugh all through the wedding! And how will I dance?"

They subsided then, all three, and watched the light grow and their house take shape. Comfortable familiar bulks and shadows were springing into sight: bunches of watercress strung from the bamboo, the tea box on the low teak table, a string bag lumpy with potatoes hanging from an oaken post. This, Loi-mae could wish for Cha and Ko-yang: a house like her own, ruled by generous nats, a house where even the pigs and chickens, doomed to be eaten, seemed willing and cheerful. A house, man, woman, child, perhaps many children. She had not yet conceived by Naung, who was suffering some inner wound. She hugged him closer. The three bodies lay enlaced, pressing warmly with the rise and fall of breath. Naung groaned: "Well, well. To work. The sentries are all asleep, no doubt. Sunup soon, so better give me a bite to eat."

The woman and child rose and washed and built up a small cooking fire while Naung sauntered briefly out through the brush. Naung must be fed and loved. He was First Rifle. His work never ended.

Mitraillette slung, his binoculars hanging in their leather case, Naung trudged up West Slope and found the Sawbwa staring into the sunrise and chewing absently at strips of dried fish. "No news in the night," Naung told him. The Sawbwa grunted. The Sawbwa's turban was awry and his good eye rheumy. "I must make my rounds," Naung said, and waited for comment, orders, approval, a dirty joke, a prophecy. The Sawbwa grunted again and champed at his fish.

For a moment, an uncomfortable moment, once rare but less to each season, Naung squatted and scrutinized this malformed chieftain.

Too often treachery had worked its way to the
surface of Naung's mind. That his people should
be led by this abortion! The Sawbwa had altered
much since Naung's departure in the year he had
learned to call 1939; the Sawbwa had aged in
mind and body, but his authority was undimin-
ished. He was, for one thing, a rainmaker. "In the
second night I shall bring rain," he would say,
and rain would come. Naung tended to atheism
and suspected a trick; the Sawbwa perhaps
smelled clouds forming, or sensed a shriller note
in the jungle fowl's shriek. The visions were
more difficult to account for: the Sawbwa saw
distant wars, tall foreigners, railways in the
jungle.

Naung too had seen distant wars, tall foreigners and railways in the jungle, and what the
Sawbwa conveyed was logical, reasonable and
not easily verified. Yet the village believed him
always. He spoke with gods, with the Lord Buddha and the nats of the hearth and forest, the
gods of the mountain and the river, spoke to
them in the village tongue and in Chinese; and he
transmitted messages—early monsoon, much
thunder, excessive rainfall, a plague of speckled
scabs on the whiskered fish, plant now, reap
now, send no opium to Nan-san this year. Yet it
was perhaps a long series of meaningless pre-
dictions and instructions, a run of accidental
triumphs, that had elevated this outlander to the
ranks of seers and demigods.

Naung said never a word of this aloud, not
even to Wan, his Second Rifle, who was over
forty and remembered well the Sawbwa's
arrival, half dead, half blind, raving on the road.

Now and then Naung caught a dubious frown flitting across Wan's face as the Sawbwa pronounced. "Perhaps . . . These were modern times. And Naung was a traveled man, who had seen steamships and French ticklers. His sergent-chef, his sergent-instructeur, had not functioned by rolling on opaque eye and muttering in whispers; nor had the Japanese.

Gazing thoughtfully upon his Sawbwa, Naung wondered which was working within himself, ambition or reason.

Both. He would like to be sawbwa, but principally because he believed the position required intelligence and forcefulness rather than trances, mystical communications, murmured vaporings. The life of a village lay in the hands of its sawbwa; Naung's hands were not palsied.

Now, however, he had a day's work to do.

Lola's hair shone sometimes like polished teak. Loi-mae plied the Chinese brush, an elegant brush of hog's bristles and rosewood, purchased by a barter for a lump of amber the size of a hen's egg. "No, Weng-aw should not touch you there," she said.

Lola giggled.

"You have so much time," Loi-mae said gently. "A year, perhaps two, before your moon cycles begin." In the still morning the house was pleasantly redolent of pork and peppers.

"Cha says it is like hearing birdsong, with a man inside you."

"And sometimes it is like being bruised in some crazy game. Besides, Cha has room for a man. Cha has been a woman for four years. And now she will marry Ko-yang. You must try, when your time comes, to marry an unmarried man, as Cha is doing. It is always best to be first wife."

"Weng-aw is not married."

"He is not a man either. Lovely hair! The braids will shine."

"I remember my father's hair. Was it like hearing birdsong when he was within you?"

"Oh yes. His hair was sometimes the color of the plantain and sometimes the color of cutch. In one light this, in another light that."

"And I remember his skin. Ow! A knot!"

"Stand still. His skin was like anybody's where the sun had touched it, but in other places it was like milk. There! Turn now and let me see, little dancer."

The child-woman stood almost naked, and Loi-mae smiled. Truly, the hair could not be described. The color of a gyi fawn, or the glistening tawny underfeather of a falcon's wing. And the face so lovely and fresh, the brows darker than the hair but lighter than Loi-mae's. And the breasts, young fruit, barely rounded, barely budded yet surely promising.

"Turn again. Now the plaits."

"I think it is funny that we make love as the pigs do."

Loi-mae sighed. "I wish you would think of anything else. It is not only pigs, but all creatures with warm blood. All creatures that nurse the young."

Lola said positively, "Chickens do not nurse the young. Yet Weng-aw is like a young rooster."

"Then Weng-aw has not much to boast of," Loi-mae said loftily, and Lola's laughter pealed.

"My funny mother," Lola gasped. "My beautiful mother."

"Your father was like you, always joking," Loi-
mae said. "And I am not beautiful." In the lazy
midmorning warmth a mynah scolded. "I am too
tall, like a man." But braiding her daughter's
silky hair she knew her own modesty false. She
could, and often did, still recall Green Wood's
words, "In all the world, none like you," and even
if his talk was what the Shan called honeyed
grains of rice, it had been soul-stirring. She, Loi-
mae, a beauty! "You can rouge your forehead
afterward," she said. "First we cook."

"Chicken and rice?"

"And leeks." But the memory of Green Wood
persisted; she saw Green Wood on a pony, turbanned, bearded, rifle slung, teeth flashing,
laugh booming. How he had changed, her skinny
teacher! With her he had grown almost stout,
and then overnight he had become a warrior. And
she had stood clutching her daughter and
watched him ride up over West Slope to the
Burma-side trail, and her eyes had flooded, and
everyone looked politely away as she stood
weeping, and when her sobs began, Chung took
the child and they walked together to the house.

Well, that was years ago. Never mind Green
Wood. She would not see him again, or with luck
any outsider, and Naung was a man among men.

"I was just thinking of my father," Lola said.
"Will I travel one day?"

"I have spent all my life in Pawlu," Loi-mae
said firmly, "and I do not know why you should
want to travel. All we hear of the world is

trouble. What is there to see? Pagodas as tall as an oak. Carts that roll without oxen. I knew your father for five years and what did I learn?" But a wave of heat lapped through her even as she denied it. "To boil eggs, which is already silly, and to boil them just so, with the white hard and the yolk soft, so that the egg can be neither drunk nor munched but must be eaten with a spoon." And I learned to couple like a she-leopard and to make the two snakes, and I learned that I could complain to a man when the cramps came and he would be kind to me, and not even Naung will do that, but only wrinkles his nose and mutters about women. "And to beat a raw egg into a cup of hot milk and add honey. The whole village laughed. He loved it, and let them laugh. He said it deepened his sleep. Mong taught him to tap poppies and told him the yen would help him sleep, but Green Wood preferred cheroots. I re-member he was sick the first time he smoked yen."

"He was a nice man, and so tall," Lola said. "Is my hair finished? Will it hold while I dance?"

"He was a strange man," Loi-mae said. "Yes, all right, dress now. He was the gentlest man I knew, his hands were like little birds, and he seemed to love everybody, but as it turned out, he also loved to kill Japanese. There was a warrior inside the scholar, and the war woke him, and I wonder if he ever went back to sleep."

"I like my hat," Lola said, "but I will not wear it now for Naung's sake."

"Good girl. Green Wood loved to see you wear-ing it. Down over your eyes and ears. Some Jap-anese office, you were!"

"It was his nicest gift."

"He killed the man himself; it was indeed a gift. Well, now the chicken. "Loi-mae took a straight stick and stepped out into the yard. She spotted the plump red hen, made a dash and nabbed it. She held it upside down by its flanks, its head trailing in the dirt, and she laid the stick across its neck as its bright red eye blinked, and she stepped on the stick first with one foot and then with the other, to either side of the hen, and she tugged upward and the hen fluttered and muted and died.

Naung's patrol was a five-kilometer hike, and he often thought of himself as the sergent-chef. He covered his perimeter quickly enough this morning, picking up the relief and changing the guard without incident. Mong was tired and complained of age; he would enjoy the wedding feast so much less after this dull night of starting at the scurry of toktays and other small lizards. "You liar," Naung said. "You missed your Chung, that's all."

Mong admitted this merrily, and veered off the main trail toward his own hut cackling about the detrimental effects of abstinence on a man's health. Naung clambered up the slope south of East Poppy Field and glassed a few of his roadside bandit cages, proceeding then to a slower and more meticulous examination of the upper slopes far across the hazy morning, the playgrounds of the Wild Wa. He saw only a distant tendril of smoke. It was as if the Wild Wa did not exist. If only that were so! Far to the east he noticed the faintest wisp of cloud.

He rose, took a last glance about him, and

headed home at a shuffling trot. He considered Lola as he pattered along, Lola who was growing up. There was now a certain slight roundness to her breasts. She was not his daughter and—it struck him like lightning—Shan law did not forbid her to him. For one quick, sharp instant the notion thrilled him. It then sickened him, and he winced and groaned aloud.

The women's side was like a field of summer flowers, and the tinkling voices and laughter were like silver bells. Loi-mae was most notable in red silk trousers and tunic, her coolie hat trimmed in silver from the mines of Bawdwin and amber from the Kachin diggings. Lola was in a bright blue longyi, and her hat was a bamboo cone adorned by a single silver clasp. Later, when she was a woman, she would show off jewelry. Silver and amber were earned by work or won in combat, and not to be lightly sported.

Pigs and sheep were spitted, and a saing calf; the aroma was intoxicating, and Chung made rumbling complaint, smacking her lips and sniffing windily at the pungent air. She was enormous in golden-yellow trousers and tunic, the collar and sleeves trimmed with blue and green beads; her hat was the ceremonial half-man's half-woman's, a narrow yellow turbanlike circle about a bamboo cone, and the tip of the cone was silver to the width of four fingers.

All about the roasting grounds stood lidded bowls an arm's length across, brimming with abundances of chicken, rice, dried red dates, prunes and bamboo shoots; or potatoes; or mixed fruits and nuts for nibbling before the feast, peanuts, preserved pumpkin strips, dried peach flesh, breadfruit and sugarcane, figs and orange rind and mounds of pumpkin seeds. Each house had supplied its own creation, including chickens variously prepared; the larger animals were culled from the common flocks, though the saing was owed to Wan's skill: with only one of his precious cartridges he had felled the beast clean.

The spits were tended and the bowls passed by the bride's family and, Cha's family being small as village families went, such of their friends who desired merit before the Lord. These were never lacking. There were many also who served not to acquire merit but to atone for past sins, which also were never lacking.

Cha sat modestly among the women, eyes downcast, awaiting her moment. She wore light blue silk spangled with silver disks: part of her dowry, and uncomfortably heavy. When she raised a fig to her lips, her arm strained visibly against the weight of her cuff, and the sleeve dragged. The abundance of silver was ostentatious, but a bride was forgiven. Envious and delighted, Lola neglected her munching for minutes at a time. "Manglon," Chung was saying, "for pears there is only Manglon, as I have heard; but Manglon is a long way, somewhere near India, I believe."

Dwe said with assurance, "For crab apples there is only Hsipaw."

Cha's mother and sister were assembling the bride's gifts. She would bestow not only her silver but also a soapstone Buddha, a full jute sack of ginseng root, a tusk of ivory and lesser offerings like a bale of thanat, the wrapper used for green cheroots.

An emaciated older woman, Kyau, was insisting that rainbows gave off poisonous vapors. She spat a stream of betel.

Some hundred paces north of the women, at the foot of West Slope, the Sawbwa sat beneath his white canopy, smiling and nodding. Beside him sat Ko-yang, and from time to time the Sawbwa bent to whisper. This was customary. He was imparting wisdom.

Loi-mae teased Chung: "But in Yunnan you would be a queen. In some parts of Yunnan the women warm silkworn cocoons between the breasts to hasten the hatching. You would be a rich lady!"

Lola crossed her arms on her breast and pressed gently. I will be married in summer, she decided, and serve fresh fruits, the little oranges and bananas, and fresh tomatoes too.

And a hundred paces north of the Sawbwa the men squatted on the dry grass, or sprawled or lay flat, surrounded by a ring of attentive boys and exchanging views on economics and politics. "We should have run some sheep up from Kokang a long time ago," one said. "Not only is the wool finer, but the meat is thicker and tastier."

"It would depend on the feed," said another.

"Cotton and cattle," said another. "Never mind wool. In cotton and cattle is every man's need."

"They need lusher grass."

"Where sheep graze no grass remains."

"We should reactivate the salt works."

"Who wants to go down in holes?"

"Over by Mongmao there are no holes. They dig a horizontal shaft in the correct spot, and the rains run the salt right down to their pans. How much do we need for one village?"

"At least the English are gone, with their bagged salt."

That led to talk of war and to the by now obligatory request that Naung recount his adventures. They were never the same twice. "My first day off in weeks," he complained. "Let me get drunk." But these formal protestations were customary, and soon he was launched on the prelude to his Long-Haul-with-Koko. "Has everyone a cheroot?" he asked. Ko-yang was a close-fisted young man, but today the cheroots were his gift. "Ko-yang had his sisters rolling these for weeks."

"They are very good as cheroots go," Mong said. "He knows cheroots if nothing else. You take a slug's own time starting a story."

"You have all heard it before."

"As who has not? All about what Naung was doing while the rest of us were fighting a war. Still, go on. Even the dullest ritual gives shape to life."

"I will give shape to your backside," Naung said, drawing a good laugh. "Now then: when I was a boy I believed that there was much to see and much to learn. Only later did I learn that there is nothing to learn except that there is nothing to learn."

The syllables rolled out in a chant.

"Wisdom unfolds," Naung intoned, "and does not penetrate. Wisdom blossoms from the heart, and does not enter by eye and ear."

"It is so," Mong said, and Wan at the same moment.

Naung blew smoke, smacked his lips and meditated. "Well, I ran off. You boys, you listen. Unstop your ears, now. I left Pawlu and I ran off with a trading caravan, and I worked like a Tibetan slave for weeks and was hot for the fat women who lay in the wagons. Then in Muong Sing I took my pay, a silver piece with foreign script, and I bought sandals and a new shirt and fucked away the rest, and woke with a headache, so I went to the caravan master and asked to make the return journey also. They thought I was a comical fellow, a real country boy, so they were glad to take me on, but it proved an easterly journey as much as a northerly, and do you know how many days?"

There followed a traditional and appropriate silence.

"Eighty days!"

This was the first intermission. A journey of eighty days was not an experience easily grasped by the mind, even at the fourth or fifth hearing. In two days, for example, one could travel to Nan-san. But forty times that distance? One would traverse whole countries, one would acquire new languages, one would gaze upon oceans.

Some moments of smoking, yawning and sniffing the savory drift of meat smoke seemed only fitting.

"We marched through mountain passes, and valleys of paddy. We crossed the great Mekong."

Here too a pause was seemly. The Mekong!

"And finally we came to a real city. This I do not ask you to believe, though I swear to it. At night it was all bright lights without fire, like the self-lighting torches we have from the war, but much larger and down both sides of each avenue. Some of you know Lashio, and you have all heard of Lashio—well, I tell you, Lao Cai is five Lashios and maybe ten. It is owned by the French. I went into one building twenty times the size of a house and it cost me a good copper to go in, and on one wall was a whole shadow play, with voice but without people. No real people at all. In this shadow play women danced in steel shoes, clickety-click, and all the men carried cheroot lighters, not the Zippos we all know from the war, but made of silver. For dancing the men wore uniforms, black jackets and white shirts and tiny little black neckcloths right here, so—enough to choke a man. I recall a fair amount of kissing on the mouth."

The men laughed but Naung had grown pensive. "Lao Cai is not far downriver from the mines of Kochiu."

Their silence this time was troubled. The very name, Kochiu, evoked miasmas, green fogs, toiling masses of doomed, lethargic slaves.

Naung shook himself and said, "Eh, eh! Never mind Kochiu. We went south from Lao Cai, and at Bao Ha we crossed the Yuan, or the Hong they call it here, the Red River, and finally we came to Hanoi. Now I am not going to try to tell you about Hanoi. Disbelief is disrespect and I would be obliged to resent it. I will only say that Hanoi belongs to the Big Noses, and contains as many houses as Pawlu has poppies, and would extend from here to the Wild Wa ridge, and is full of spirit carts and fire carts and is lighted up all night and noisy at all times. And as many people as there are, so many are the Birds-of-One-Hundred-Intelligences, which the French call the moineau. Immediately I set about learning French."

Mong groaned. "O this world traveler! Now we must hear the French again!"

"Sacré putain de Mong!" Naung said cheerfully. "Ane bâti et triple buse! These were terms of endearment, like stupid bullock or cut tomcat, that the sergent-chef used for us poor natives. He was a great fat man but strong, with a paunch like a buffalo in calf, eyes the color of honey and curly black hair like those sheepskins the Tibetans bring down. As you see, I joined the army. Moi aller danzarmee. These French drink much wine, red wine, from grapes, and they were at war with the Germans. Also a people called the Yi-tah-li, but I never learned much about those. They ate noodles. The French used to curse them calling them eaters of noodles and species of cunt."

"It could have been the other way," Kin-tan murmured, and the prolonged guffaw caused the women to look across and shake their heads in affectionate mockery.

"Naturally, I made a good soldier," Naung went on. "You know my hand and eye work well together. This was of value in using and maintaining weapons. Often my caporal and sergent

said good things about the care and delicacy of
my work. That mitraillette, for example, is a
complicated weapon."

But he did not tell them of his year swamping
out latrines.

"So in no time I learned not only to march but
to roll a pack, fire a weapon, salute, shave my
face and perform complex manipulations. Garde
à vous! Portez armes! Croisez la baïonnette!"

But he did not tell them that if some of his
caporaux were Annamites, all of his sergents
were blancs.

"And the politics! First I thought I was joining
the French to fight beside the British against the
Japanese. Then about a year later the French
general went away and another came, and with
him the Japanese—soldiers, trucks, ships down
at Haiphong—and the Japanese were giving
orders to the French, and raiding north into
China. Then the Japanese were running all the
chemins de fer. These are the fire carts that roll
on grooved wheels over long steel tracks. I tell
you the truth, and Wan has seen such down
Lashio way."

Wan stretched his tattoos grinning. He was
wearing blue cotton trousers and a white blouse,
once Kachin. That he wore it on a day of rejoicing
and ceremony indicated that he had taken it in
combat everyone understood. His coolie hat was
an arm's length across and the central cone of
silver was a man's hand high.

"And do you know what finally happened? The
Japanese killed the French!" Naung exploded, as
if some beloved Paris had been annexed by
Tokyo. But he did not say that at the time he had

been sweeping, window washing and scrubbing modern toilets in a Japanese officers' brothel. "That was some war! Now listen," and he chanted his litany, "the English killed Japanese and Burmese, as did the Americans; as did the Chinese when they were not killing each other by mistake; also Burmese killed Burmese, Japanese, English and Americans; and the French killed a few Indochinese but not Japanese or Germans. I never once in my life saw a German. The Japanese killed as many as possible of every kind, English, Americans, Burmese, Chinese and, finally, French. Officers in my army! They killed many officers of rank and imprisoned many others. By now"—his voice fell to a modest level—"I was of some importance myself, and I saw that it was necessary to make my own plans."

The shimmering, tintinnabulating clang of a huge brass gong silenced Naung.

"By the gods," Mong said, "a wedding!"

Kwin the drummer tapped, tam-tam, tam-tam, slower than the blood's pulse and with never a break: tam-tam, tam-tam. On the women's side the field seemed iridescent, streaked and shot with grass-green, sky-blue, sun-gold; the men's side too was peacocky but more moderately so, blue shirts mainly, a touch of yellow or white, the sun glittering off silver cones and ornaments. Tam-tam, tam-tam.

The women whispered. The tinier children toddled and tumbled. Ko-yang, all in white but blue-sashed, stood beside Cha, also in white. Loi-mae dimpled toward the men's side at Naung, who tried to assume a haughty and bored air as a joke but could not repress a smile. Lola was nowhere to be seen. The Sawbwa stood in his scarlet-trimmed turban and silken gray gown, and Za-kho stood shiny bald, puny within his voluminous saffron robe. Za-kho was not truly a priest but had once been a novice. He was all they had of the Lord. The Sawbwa's head trembled, his lips twitched; he announced: "Za-kho!"

The calm was profound. Somewhere afar, a hawk whistled. Naung's heart opened to his people. He wanted to reach out and touch them all. The breeze died, as if in respect. Tam-tam, tam-tam.

"The Lesser Cold is ended," Za-kho informed them. From the grove behind the Sawbwa's canopied chair Lola glided, naked but for a white longyi. She danced toward Za-kho, long steps and short. Slowly her arms rose, like the smooth branches of the willow after the monsoon: the villagers could almost see tiny leaves burgeon. "The Greater cold is to come, yet already the heavens are prepared for spring as Ko-yang and Cha are prepared for seedtime. The gold planet blesses the evening. The fire planet hides at dawn." Tam-tam. "The wood planet is rich with sap. There will be heavy rains and rich crops and a fruitful marriage. Now as the hour of the horse, for strength, merges with the hour of the sheep, for fecundity, let these two be joined."

"Let these two be joined," repeated the Sawbwa, "in loyalty to each other, to Pawlu and to their sawbwa." There was yet majesty to this ancient wreck. Ko-yang bowed his head; so did Cha; the Sawbwa blessed them, both hands high.

Lola danced nearer, twirled, offered her body to the sun. A baby squalled; quickly its mother gave suck.

Za-kho cried, "Ko-yang!" and chanted incomprehensible verses. He cried, "Cha!" and chanted more.

He made solemn pause, and when he knew that the silent village was listening with its heart he went on in words that all could comprehend: "And Ko-yang's house is Cha's house; and his rice her rice; and his cloth her cloth; and hers his; and they shall share love and pain and good and evil; and when one's body is sick the other's heart shall be sick; and their children will be a gift of the Lord, and the spirit of the Lord will dwell with them."

From the Sawbwa he accepted a leather bag; from the bag he drew rice. He sprinkled the happy pair who stood meekly before him. Lola darted close, dipped a hand into the pouch and flung grains high; rice fell on the couple's bare heads. Lola danced away, leapt, twirled, dashed to the grove; benevolent nats would stay to glean the rice, and evil nats would scramble after her in jealous fury, grow confused in the shadowed grove, and be lost. Tam-tam, tam-tam.

Za-kho took Cha's hands and placed them between Ko-yang's. He touched their brows with his fingertips and withdrew. Ko-yang released Cha's hands and placed them on his shoulders, and he set his on her shoulders, and they leaned to press their foreheads together. For some seconds they stood brow to brow.

Ko-yang then slipped the gold sash from Cha's shoulders and placed it in her hands. And then

the blue sash and green, and, last of all, the red
sash from her waist. Patiently he unknotted the
leather thong about her neck. He knotted it about
her own neck. He slipped a hoop of silver from
his neck to hers.

The village cheered and shouted.

Cha rushed to the women's side and flung her
sashes this way and that. Lola dashed back from
the grove to scuffle for the gold; she lost, and
pouted. Cha returned to Ko-yang's side and they
embraced before all.

Then as the Sawbwa and Za-kho stood blessing
their people—tam-tam, tam-tam—the couple's
parents, all four still alive, a good omen, came
forth with bowls of meat and wine, and Ko-yang
placed a morsel in Cha's mouth, and Cha placed a
morsel in Ko-yang's mouth, and they drank from
the same silver bowl.

At that a roar went up, and the village came to
its feet, milled, cried out, smacked it lips in
hunger and thirst, and formed a line to whack
Cha's bottom or slap Ko-yang on the back of the
head, and with a flourish and a rataplan the
drumming ended the Kwin shouted, "Beer!" and
flexed his aching fingers. "Long life!" cried the
Sawbwa, and even before his voice had faded,
Lola's piping soprano echoed him: "Long life!
And many sons! And many daughters!" A little
laughing swell of plain good humor arose from
those who heard her, and even Za-kho laughed
aloud, so that Lola too had to laugh, a quick embarrassed trill, and buried her head in Loi-mae's
breast.

"Eh, white women!" Naung said. "Sharp-smelling and flabby, with no music and no art, only the rush to the pallet with the legs spread and that coarse hair!"

Naung was pleasantly drunk. They were all flying a bit, as the Shan phrase put it, on good homemade rum. Their bellies were full, their hands and faces greasy. Heaps of bones dotted the grass, and every man clutched a bowl. A few warbled old tunes softly, each addled songster oblivious of the others. Again the boys surrounded them, all eyes and ears. "They cared only for piasters," Naung said.

But he said nothing of his first European whore, Naung the great village fornicator timid, almost terrified before this huge pink creature, and spilling his seed early, so that she made a loud joke in a foreign language and there was laughter from the other cribs. Nor did he mention the second visit, payday and his pride, scorn, resolution melting even as his hand closed on the piasters; nor admit that he had requested a very young one, so that she would not make fun of him. And she did not make fun of him, but performed like a monkey, and took all his piasters, and again and again he returned to her, the little belly, the hard white bottom, the curly hair, and he dreamed of her.

"There was an officer's wife interested in me," he confessed. He did not say that he had been gardening for a capitaine and through a crevice in the louver had seen the wife washing her parts. "Is there more of this rum?"

Bowls and jugs were plied and passed. Men and boys seized the moment to drift into the woods to relieve nature. When they were reassembled, Naung said, "It was all boring. The life those people lead is inhuman. Drunk half the time—"

"Unlike us," Mong sang out. "I cannot speak for Naung, but old Mong is drunk as a lowlander."

"Well, I am flying fairly high," Naung admitted. "Anyway, to come to the point."

"Truly a day of miracles," said Wan. "Naung comes to the point!"

Naung allowed himself an obscenity of the first rank. "I had no business there. I had just spent six years of my life in slavery, and in slavery mainly to myself. True, I was a soldat de première classe and I had earned a raise in pay, which is important, and I knew weapons. How I knew weapons! If I had an ounce of silver for every stripping and reassembly I performed, I would buy Mandalay."

He swigged at his rum. "Well, I went down to Hué on furlough and I heard a man speak, a great orator and his picture on the outer walls of many houses. He was an Annamite who had traveled much and learned much. I remember he had changed his name from Nguyen Ai Quoc to Ho Chi Minh. And he made me ashamed to work for the French, so I knew it was time to leave. I considered: Of what use was my knowledge without the weapons themselves? What gift could I bring to my people? Well, this is a world in which people kill one another with persistence and for insufficient reason; self-defense is therefore no sin and no crime. I could bring arms to my people. I could make Pawlu—are you young fellows listening?—a fortress to stand forever.

"I chose carefully—my weapons, my moment and my companions. To return with one rifle and one pistol to show for six years of service was to shame myself. My companions were therefore Koko and Foch, two mules of which Foch, after honorable service, was eaten."

On the women's side Chung was saying, "This is the tedious part."

"It is quickly over," Loi-mae said, "with all of us pitching in. Lola, those bowls, scrub them out and polish them with paddy mud."

"They ate everything," Chung said with satisfaction, "and now they will drink all day and all night."

"Lucky Cha. No cleaning up."

"Lucky Cha is right. If I know Ko-yang, she'll be gone for days."

"O, men," Loi-mae sighed.

"O, Men," Lola sighed.

"You be quiet."

"A beauty," Chung said. "Listen, Loi-mae, I always wanted to ask."

"Then ask. About Green Wood, I suppose."

"Not at all. I liked Green Wood and would never pry. I only wondered . . ."

"Go on, go on."

"The foreign women. Are they as we are? Did Green Wood say? Have they breasts like ours, or little bumps, or nipples only?"

"Breasts like ours," Loi-mae said. "Some small, some large, some divine like Chung's."

"You make fun," Chung said. "But what you say is good news. Green Wood was a stout fellow—many a time I watched him bathe in the stream—so the women of his line are healthy, and if Lola grows a good pair of breasts, she will be a real goddess and worth her weight in silver."

"And if not? She will still be a good wife to a good man and worth her weight in gold."

"I never said no. But she is a rare beauty even now."

Loi-mae saw Lola's gaze slide toward them. "You're listening!" she called. "Never mind what Chung says. Or that Weng-aw either."

Chung scoffed. "Weng-aw! A jokester!"

"It is no joke. Already he caresses her. I want her to wait till her moon cycles."

"Absolutely right. Would he force her?"

"Never!" Loi-mae said. "Long before it came to that she would force him."

"O Lord," said Chung.

"I chose two husky mules," Naung was saying, "and lashed down balanced loads of ammunition, in both sizes, and two of those crates are still in the Sawbwa's house, the eight millimeter because all the old rifles use it and the seven six five for the mitraillette and the pistols. Those mules complained! I had rifles and binoculars and rations, everything but mortars and machine guns. And we all marched down the trail, and the French army turned south, and I, Naung of Pawlu, stopped to make water and then turned north."

"And well done," the men murmured. Hazily Naung glimpsed Taw-bi loping over the crest of West Slope. "Well, that eighty-day trip was as nothing. With the caravan I had women, food, even wine." Why would Taw-bi leave his post?

Naung squeezed some of the drunkenness out of his eyes. "But now I was alone, skulking through the jungle, traveling by night and hiding by day, this day in Laos and that day in China; and always seeking fodder and water for my brace of mulish companions." If Taw-bi was after beer or rum, Naung would disgrace him in public. "The hunting was poor—this was during the first Lesser Cold after the war. So I had to trade a weapon here and there. It went against the wish of my soul, but there was no choice. Then Second Mule, old Foch, died of overwork, so I sold what I could, butchered the beast, and pushed on. Before the rains, you see—Pawlu before the rains, or all was lost."

Taw-bi was not loping. He was running hard. The men stretched and some came to their feet. Belches rang out. "Always at the best part of the story," Naung complained. "Anyway, it took me three months and when Koko and I shuffled into East Poppy Field Kin-tan almost killed me. If I had not lost so much weight on the long haul, the bullet would have had me. I was skinnier than Mong."

"Never regretted it," Kin-tan said absently. The men had ceased to follow Naung's tale. No one said, "Something has happened," because it was so clearly true.

Taw-bi waved. "Strangers," he shouted. "Travelers. From the west."

"Go arm yourselves," Naung told the men. "And sober up. You boys, join the women and be of use." To Taw-bi he called, "How many?"

"Two. Mounted. Armed. Half an hour off and in no hurry."

"Oh well, two," Naung said.

"More cages to carpenter," Mong sighed.

As they dispersed Ko-yang came trotting up. "Do we muster?"

"Two strangers," Naung said, "and no you do not muster. You have other duties to discharge."

"Go fight with Cha," Wan called. A little laughter rippled across the field, a little nervous laughter.

"That can wait," Ko-yang said. "Where do we gather?"

"At the Sawbwa's house," Naung said. "Taw-bi, who is on West Trail?"

"Shwe and Tang, with the twins in support. Shall I bring everybody in from East Poppy Field?"

"And leave us open there? Think, man, think."

Taw-bi blinked sheepishly.

"Is Shwe awake, at least?"

"Shwe is all right," Taw-bi said firmly. "He dozes, but he has never shown a pale heart."

"True," Naung said. They were trotting toward Naung's house, where his beloved mitraillette lay ready. "O Lord, I drank too much."

At the Sawbwa's they assembled quickly and in good order. Naung deployed one squad south of West Trail; with another he would straddle the trail. Unless they were directly attacked, there would be no firing of weapons until Naung had opened up.

"Today we must not kill," the Sawbwa said, "for Ko-yang's sake and Cha's."

Za-kho, still in his saffron folds, said, "There will be no firing of weapons at all."

"Cure the soul," Naung said. "Leave the body to me."

"It is a wedding day," Za-kho insisted. "We have called upon the gods, and they have taken notice of us."

The men made no answer.

"On a wedding day in Pawlu the stranger must be made welcome," Za-kho said.

Naung deferred to Ko-yang.

Ko-yang said, "It is my wedding and Cha's, and I will take the bad luck on myself. Cha has agreed that I should do my part, and if we must kill, we must. The Lord has made this day, and this wedding, but he has also sent these strangers."

Naung said to Za-kho, "You and your planets. You and your favorable hours."

"The Lord is my master," Za-kho said, "and not easy to know."

The Lord is my master too, Naung decided, but the mitraillette is my servant.

8

Greenwood's Return

Since the war Greenwood had not come awake so fast. He took in the rifles, swords, daggers, pistols, turbans and jewelry. Shan, four of these were Shan, one perhaps Chinese, the little one he supposed a lowland Burman.

His hands conspicuously empty, he played the host: "Blessings and greetings." Yunnan ponies, large saddlebags, no women—that was bad—marauders living off targets of opportunity, namely Greenwood.

One of them said, "Greetings and blessings." He was a swarthy man with a droopy black mustache and cunning eyes. Greenwood was afraid now. He and fear were old acquaintances but had not met for some time; he fought to dispel it, to sharpen his wits and see through this shameful fog. "A rare thing," the man said. "Lonely travelers in these hills."

With enormous effort Greenwood rubbed his eyes and yawned casually. He saw that Jum-aw was terrified, eyes huge, mouth trembling.

The swarthy man said, "And with a tamigan." There was also a large stout man whose presence was for some reason comforting; perhaps it was the old prejudice, fat men are slow and easygoing and even-tempered. This particular slow, easy-going and even-tempered fat man carried a machine pistol, of what nationality or make Greenwood could not distinguish.

"The tommy gun is an old companion," Greenwood said. He stretched and groaned, adding suitable morning sounds, and opened his shirt to scratch his hairy chest.

Swarthy shot a glance at Fat Man. Greenwood noted this with hope, and removed the shirt altogether, flapping it as if to free it of the night's effuvia, or of any stray nats that might have taken shelter in a sleeve.

They were openly curious about his tattoo; yet good manners prevailed. "Doubtless the traveler has a destination," Swarthy said.

"Perhaps Motai. Perhaps Fang-shih. I am only seeing a bit of the world."

"And the young one?"

"My hired guide and porter."

None of these men seemed to blink. They stared like falcons. Greenwood could not sort them out, this one friendly, this one a coward, this one cruel, but he recognized their hostile solidarity. He remembered himself and a small squad of Kachin with two Japanese prisoners. Greenwood had sat even as Swarthy sat now, calm, inscrutable, God, weighing, judging, dispensing life and death. That day he had dispersed death and the memory assailed him now.

One of the Shan, a strapping fellow of about thirty, said, "Ask him what he carries."

"I will ask him when I am ready to ask him,"

Swarthy said, with another quick glance at Fat
Man. "First I will ask if there is news or gossip."

Greenwood said, "Light me a cheroot,
Jum-aw." The boy needed help, attention, a
function. This was a cool dawn in the mountains,
but sweat glistened on the smooth lip. "Come on,
boy!" To Swarthy Greenwood said, "He may
reach into his pack?"

"Slowly," Swarthy said, and smiled a perfect
villain's smile.

"Come now, Jum-aw. These are only Shan
brothers."

Jum-aw seemed to breathe for the first time; he
fumbled for a cheroot, groped for matches, lit up
and passed it to Greenwood, who was nauseated
by smoke before breakfast but said "Thank you"
in the most amiable tone possible, and to the
Shan as a group, "Who will join me?"

Strapping said, "This one thinks he is a
sawbwa."

Swarthy said, "What is the gossip?"

"Well, all is calm up around Sumprabum,
Myitkyina and Bhamo. Probably the end has
come China-side. This we had from a Tibetan
peddler, and it is all I can tell you."

"Then tell me what you carry."

"Not much. A little food, a little clothing, a few
coppers. But, of course, what a man carries is his
own business."

"Until he is dead," Strapping said. "Then it
becomes the business of someone else." The
band laughed, a nasty babble in this peaceful
sunrise.

"I had hoped to delay that event," Greenwood

said. "The long sleep should be long at the latter end only."

This occasioned more laughter, a bit cheerier.

Swarthy said, "I can tell you what I ask myself. I ask myself why this Big Nose is speaking Shan, and why he shows a Shan tattoo."

An older man with a vacant face said, "And what is so interesting in that? Everybody hereabouts speaks Shan."

"It is very interesting," Swarthy said, "and no one asked you. This is an Englishman."

"I thought we threw the Englishmen out," said the older man.

"Please shut up," said Swarthy, and to Greenwood, "You are an Englishman?"

"An American." Greenwood felt seasick, and from more than cigar smoke. His fear was shameful.

"Ha!" This was clearly the "Ha!" of a man who is not sure of the meaning of what he has just heard; a "Ha!" that might be translated, "I have noted this extremely important datum and am giving it solemn consideration in the light of my extensive knowledge and experience." Greenwood had known a colonel who said "Ha!" much in that manner and conferred immediately with a lieutenant colonel who made the serious decisions. Now Swarthy darted another glance at Fat Man.

Greenwood was a touch giddy but drew on his cheroot patiently. There seemed little else to do. He must not vomit.

"An American is a kind of English," the little brown Burman said.

"I know that," Swarthy said impatiently.

Greenwood squinted at the wee Burman and threw the dice. There were moments in life when the stakes were high enough to justify long odds. "Aha!" he said. "The turban is a Shan turban but the voice is the voice of Shwebo near the river Mu. You are some way from home, my friend."

Swarthy turned furiously to the Burman. "What is this? You know this man?"

"I never saw him! By the gods I swear it! Besides, I am not from Shwebo!"

Greenwood asked swiftly, "Then where?"

"Wet-let," the little man said.

"Which is two hours' ride from Shwebo!" Greenwood cried in a tone of triumph. All this proved nothing, which he hoped no one would notice, but control, command, confidence, had shifted very slightly from them to him.

"That is true." The little man seemed bewildered and crestfallen.

Greenwood hoped a few of the others were equally confused.

"Nevertheless," said Swarthy, "you are an American, which is a kind of Englishman, and you are wandering these hills with a fine weapon and a pony, and your destination is Motai or perhaps Fang-shih but you seem to be taking the long way around, and you speak good Shan, and it is my opinion that you fought here in the war." He paused here with a powerful nod, as if to allow time for applause. He then stroked his mustache, left and right.

"That is well considered. I fought here in the war. I hope never to kill again, but who knows what the gods will ask. I have returned one last time to visit the land I love, whose soil has drunk some drops of my blood, and that is the whole of it. Motai, Fang-shih, these are merely names along the way, like the names of railway stations, which are of no interest; what is of interest is the landscape between.''

"He talks and talks," said Strapping.

"So you fought against the Japanese," Swarthy said.

"I fought for a free Burma," Greenwood said.

"I fought beside the Japanese, to free Burma by driving the British out," said Swarthy.

"Then we may have tried to kill each other." Greenwood raised his voice. "How many here fought against the Japanese?"

Three voices muttered.

"And against the British?"

"He and I," said the tiny Burman.

Fat Man had not spoken, not stirred.

"And who is to say now which was right and which wrong? Is Burma not free?"

"Far too free," Swarthy said. "Where did you see war?"

Greenwood spat a shred of tobacco. "First at Lashio in nineteen forty-two."

"Ha! We broke you! We drove you out! The Chinese Fifty-fifth melted away overnight!"

"We did not melt away," the Chinese called. "We ran like deer."

"Then in late forty-two I was dropped in to join the Kachin up by Loi Panglon, and we raided for a year."

"I was never there," Swarthy said, again with a glance at Fat Man. "Do you tell us that you truly jumped out of an aircraft?"

"We should kill these two and move out," Strapping said. "Those are good Kachin ponies."

Again Swarthy's temper: "I decide! I decide!"

"Then I was ordered south and joined the Shan." Greenwood kept the chatter flowing. His earlier time with the Shan was none of their business, and he would not speak of Pawlu. He hoped Jum-aw would keep silence. Fortunately, the boy seemed incapable of speech.

"How far south? Namsang?"

"Never that far." Greenwood's stomach griped and heaved. He swallowed his gorge.

Swarthy seemed disappointed. "Then we never fought, you and I."

"Then why begin?"

"This is foolish," Strapping said. "Let's do it. Talk, talk, talk."

"You may be right." Swarthy brooded. "Objections?"

"I object strongly," Greenwood said.

This jest was uncommonly successful, and there followed much whacking of thighs and wiping of tears. Greenwood was physically cold. In battle he had felt fear, but there was the job to do; one did not so much overcome fear as forget about it. But now he sat on a hillside in the land of the Tai, as the Shan called themselves, as all Burmese called them, and Greenwood was a foreigner who thought of them always by their foreign name, the Shan, and he was a long way from the nearest graduate student, and this was a most unusual faculty meeting, and he had thirty-five years of life on this earth honorably completed, with a strong body, a questing mind and a compassionate heart, and—no!—this was not the way to go!

He would have a second or two, no more; and he would have no hope; and he had at twenty been a pacifist and hoped to be one again; but now if his time had come, he would do all in his power to lay one hand on that tommy gun and take one or more of these killers with him.

"Leave the boy alone," he said. "Take his pony but leave him alone. He is only my hired hand and I am responsible for him. He has no money and no goods and is of no importance to you. Do not send me to the long sleep with his death to trouble my dreams. This much I ask you. Think of it as the last wish of a dying man. And now I want to stand up because it is the best way to die." As he scrabbled up he could clutch at the weapon. The safety was on, God damn it.

"Nonsense," said Strapping. "Both of them. If their time has come, their time has come, and who can object?"

Fat Man spoke then for the first time, in a hollow bass rumble. "Well, I may have an objection, and the gods may smite me if I do not state it! You come here, and you." Swarthy and Strapping stepped to his side and stooped to hear. Fat Man murmured, and smiled pleasantly at Greenwood.

Greenwood made no move toward his weapon. The others were armed, he was surely covered, and this was a new development and therefore an improvement.

Swarthy spoke: "Tell us your name, American."

"Greenwood."

"In Shan."

"Green Wood."

Swarthy and Strapping turned to gape at Fat Man. They were thunderstruck. Greenwood was at least puzzled. Fat Man was laughing. "Ha! Ha! Did I not say so? Green Wood!"

Greenwood was wholly wrapped in gooseflesh. He felt his hairs stir and prickle. The cheroot was dead.

Ponderously Fat Man rose. "And on midwinter day of the third winter, halfway between Bhamo and Su-i on that terrible road with— Well, what is it that never disappears on that road?"

"Mud slides," Greenwood said, and his heart leapt like a lover's.

"Mud slides indeed! And that day you destroyed— Well, what did you destroy?"

"Two Japanese armored cars and a truck full of slaves."

"And what did those slaves do?"

"They vanished into the forest, as I would have in their place." Now Greenwood too stood up, and he flung away the cheroot.

"And do you remember Pwe-nin?"

A little bad luck was due, and perhaps not fatal. "Ah no. No, I do not."

"Well, it was a village nearby. It was where the Japanese stabled those armored cars."

"That little command post. With the aerial running up the old oak. We wiped it out."

Fat Man waddled across the bivouac. For some moments he and Greenwood communed. Fat Man then turned to confront the band. "Kill if you must. But you kill me too. I stand *here*." He clapped Greenwood on the shoulder, almost breaking bone.

Swarthy grumbled, "How is a man to make a living?"

And then Strapping complained, "This is play-acting. Seven years have passed! In seven years all debts are canceled."

"All but one." Fat Man's tone banished doubt; this would be a fight. On the machine pistol Greenwood saw kana, the little Japanese phonetic characters. The weapon seemed in order and gleamed in a sleek and healthy manner. Greenwood considered retrieving his tommy gun, but rejected the notion as indelicate. Jum-aw, possibly comatose, sat like a statue.

The five unconverted brigands were on their feet, and easing apart.

Fat Man continued angrily in formal North Shan. To Greenwood it was like hearing a passage from the Book of Common Prayer. "I have been a slave and am no more. Of your be-loved Japanese was I a slave," he spat at Swarthy, "and in chains, and all bones and no flesh was I and my death soon upon me. Your Japanese had sent my father on before with a bullet in the back, and my mother too was a slave, and every man and woman in Pwe-nin, and there was not a village on those slops left free, and the Japanese were working the men to death and fucking the women to death." Fat Man clutched the weapon to him as if now, at last, the time had come for revenge. Flecks of spittle flew as he raged. "And we slept chained together and woke chained together and ate chained together and shat chained together, and when one died, another was brought to wear his chains. And one of those carried news of this Green Wood, a

golden man with ice for eyes who led Kachin and
Shan alike and fought like a living god."

Greenwood was impressed, even awed.

"And we prayed to the Lord Buddha and all his
helpers that this Green Wood would come for us,
or if not he, then death. And now I ask this: Who
upholds the world if not the righteous man? And
who is a righteous man if not he who travels far
to free a slave? And this Green Wood, when his
death was upon him today, what did he ask? That
the innocent be spared. And did he grovel? No.
And did he beg? No. And did he wail? No. And did
he haggle? No. I tell you, there was less of me
seven years ago than there is of a toktay, and now
I am half an elephant, but I am the same soul,
and even if I have not remembered this Green
Wood once a year I do not forget that my life is
his."

Other words were thronging Greenwood's
memory: I have been young and now am old, yet
never have I seen the righteous man forsaken, or
his seed begging bread. He had not believed
much in God but had held greatly by courage,
loyalty and affection, and this exotic encounter
had become a sunrise service. He wanted to
embrace Fat Man, and it was far more than
simple relief.

Fat Man ended curtly: "So say. Or do."

O, by the gods," Swarthy said immediately, "if
that is what you want."

Strapping restored proportion by picking his
nose pensively, after which he shrugged, sprawled, laid his rifle on the dewy grass against all
good sense and precept, and said, "Those are
nice ponies, just the same."

The others made mumble in disgust, apology, curiosity, resignation.

Echoing Fat Man's gesture, Greenwood set a hard, grateful hand on his shoulder. Instinct told him to seal the moment with all of them. "If these minor bickerings are resolved," he said, "old Green Wood the living god would like to empty his bladder and break his fast."

To his inexpressible pleasure the bandits guffawed in chorus. It was true: in any country, in any language, the outhouse was surefire.

"Go to it!" Swarthy called. "Do you people do it just like everybody?"

"On your feet," Greenwood said to Jum-aw. All must now be normal, daily, lighthearted, he knew, with no relapse into tension or surliness.

Jum-aw's eyes were cast down.

"Come now," Greenwood said. "It is over."

"I cannot," Jum-aw whispered.

"Of course you can. Surely you too must piss."

Tears hung glistening in the boy's eyes. "I have done so despite myself. I would be ashamed to stand up."

Fat Man had overheard, and chuckled. "Poor little fellow."

"Listen to me," Greenwood said. "In my first battle I did worse than that. Now stand up and be a man." "Wet behind the ears, wet between the legs, what difference? All men are brothers. Himself, ready to retch.

"The shame will pass," Fat Man said to Jum-aw. "And it is not true shame, only embarrassment. Green Wood," he said, "now I can thank you, as I do in the name of all gods, and I can wish you, from the heart, long life and much silver and many women, and sons to keep alive a good name. A whole ten of us walked for three days in those chains until we found a free village with a smith. I can still see that truck burning. It was a gloriout moment. I wept."

"It seems to me that I should do the thanking," Greenwood said.

"A life each," Fat Man said. "And the best is yet to come. For breakfast we have fresh gyi, three days old, exactly ripe, and white ant eggs, found only yesterday."

Jum-aw later lost the way; Greenwood found it. They clopped slowly upward into the realm of the green-and-gold-backed woodpecker and the kite, leaving paddy birds and parrots behind. In the evening bats swooped and feinted, often with a whisper of wingbeats. The moon waxed, and Greenwood's sleep was less easy; his listened, dreams intruded, his hand twitched toward his weapon. One afternoon Jum-aw said, "That is Flying Dragon Pass, there to the south."

"It is indeed. I knew it well, once."

Jum-aw reined in.

"You have something to tell me."

"Yes," Jum-aw said. "Best play no tricks. Since yesterday noon I have guided you by Flying Dragon Pass, using it to extend my track as the evening star lengthens the day. But I am now un-sure."

"You do well to tell me," Greenwood said. "Keep an eye out for cops and robbers." He used an old Shan term for "brigands and execution-ers." Jum-aw was obviously relieved by the

leniency, the little joke, and grimaced in apology.
Greenwood dug into his pack for the worn,
reliable U.S. army compass that had led him
home from so many Japanese encampments. He
flipped it open, steadied it, squinted. Magnetic
variation was negligible, about one degree west,
and he had always navigated by compass rather
than chart. He had seen many modern maps on
which this region was marked DATA UNRELIABLE
or DEMARCATION APPROXIMATE or BORDER UN-
CERTAIN. Contours would help—heights, slopes—
but only if accurate; one mountain was much like
another hereabouts. "I believe we should
continue half east half north," he said. "What do
you think?"

"That way?"

"That way."

"It seems reasonable. I have failed you."

"Nonsense. I will wager a fat cheroot that we
find a landmark this afternoon. The hard part is
accomplished, and it was you who did it."

Greenwood pocketed the compass and re-
mounted. He used it again at two forks. He was
becoming Green Wood again and had caught
himself thinking in Shan, which pleased him. His
butt was comfortable on the nappy saddle blanket
and the mountain air was sharp. He felt lighter.

In midafternoon they paused by a frothy
stream to hear its music, to drink and to repose
themselves. Here the trail branched. A few yards
upstream the bank was bare, a glistering face of
gray and pink rock, and Greenwood knew where
they were: at Three-Tined-Fork-by-the-Brook.

"You may return now if you want," he said.

"There will be Wild Wa to worry about."

Jum-aw's young brows beetled. "Then you know this trail."

"I know it well."

"So. How do you come to know it?"

"It one of half a ten that lead into or out of Pawlu," Greenwood said. "Toward the end of the war my job—among others—was to glean fallen flyers. Many hours from here I found a Chinese general, and we came by this trail to Pawlu."

"And what was a Chinese general doing in these hills?"

"He was to be decorated. The Chinese gave many medals and took many photographs for the newspapers. For this to be done in the presence of their leader so that he might be in the photograph, it was necessary to fly the heroes home to Kunming or Chungking."

"Soldiers."

"Politicians. Soldiering does not require brilliance—I have myself soldiered—but does not necessarily render a man silly. A politician, however, must smile upon all people at once, and so much become, in time, a fool or a knave."

"This you have learned from your study of man."

"Well, I go too far. But I will say for sure that during the war Chinese politicians were a rare breed and worthy of study."

"This does not tell me why a general was in these hills."

"His aircraft was crippled, he believed by ground fire, but perhaps by age and hard use. Do you know about parachutes?"

"Yes."

"We never found the aircraft. We took the

general to Pawlu, where he joined us in harassing Japanese and repelling Wild Wa, and after a while we sent him on his way to Nan-san. Where he went then I cannot say. The Japanese were here and there but not everywhere."

"I hope he reached home," Jum-aw said.

"He reached home. I imagine he even won a second medal, for surviving the jump. Medals were awarded for everything but outright treason."

"You dislike wars."

"Correct. Three-handed rogues attack the wind with loud shouts, and are promoted and enriched. Meanwhile good men die. Well, will you go back or will you come along?"

"I have guided you, now you shall guide me," Jum-aw said.

"And my wages?"

For a moment Jum-aw took him seriously.

A few hours later, when he knew he was home, Greenwood halted. "Look there." Half a skeleton hung from a tree. "A bandit. Give me your rifle."

Jum-aw only scowled.

"Do as I ask, Jum-aw. Give me obedience for my wages."

Jum-aw went on scowling, but unslung his rifle and handed it over.

"A genuine antique," Greenwood said. "That is some weapon."

"It fires true."

"Your father's?" It was a Springfield .30-03, almost half a century old; but its makers and owners had respected metal.

"My father's. Since a boy."

"Now your knife."

Jum-aw protested.

Greenwood said it again.

Jum-aw yielded.

Greenwood slung the rifle and tucked the knife into his belt. "Follow close."

"And if there is fighting?"

"It would be no fighting, only the quick death of two travelers. When the thunderclap sounds, it is already too late to cover the ears. We proceed empty-handed, smiling and singing."

They did no signing, but at intervals Greenwood called out, "I will wrestle Wan and Kin-tan at one time!" or "Old Mong is a famous fornicator!" His chest was tight, as before a fire fight or with a new woman. They were rising circuitously but persistently from the valley west of West Slope. A faint haze hung above what he thought was the village. He wondered if a house was burning. More likely a plot of brush.

One moment he was riding along, composing an elegant insult, and the next he was overwhelmed by a horde of Shan who scared him half out of his tattoos. They surged and swarmed, seizing the bridles, shouting at Greenwood, dropping from trees, hemming him about. The ponies boggled at first but stood their ground. Greenwood whooped and hollered, vaulted off his steed and commenced whacking old friends. Old friends pummeled him in return. He heard Jum-aw—"My lord! My lord!"—and craned to see the boy in Kin-tan's embrace, pedaling vainly a yard in the air.

By now there were tears in Greenwood's eyes. "By the gods," he said, "what a reception! I never heard a sound."

"We saw you half an hour ago," Wan assured him. "Old Green Wood! Never did I think to see you more."

"Nor I you, you old killer. Kin-tan, put down that boy. Or have you taken to monkish love?"

Kin-tan released Jum-aw and embraced Greenwood. "I never thought of that. He is a pretty boy. And how goes the old rifle?"

"Well. The gods have been kind."

The others were subsiding. A flight of forest crows, blue-shouldered, flapped above them.

Greenwood wiped his eyes with his bandanna. The others glanced at the crows, or fiddled with their weapons. Greenwood said, "Is Loi-mae well? And Lola?"

"Well and happy," Kin-tan said.

"The gods be thanked. And who is dead?"

"Phe-win. Dropped one noon like an old oak."

"Let him rest. The best of fighting men."

"My father Yau," said Wan.

"Let him rest. A good man and kind to me."

"Gyan died only a couple of months ago," Kin-tan said, "in a fight by the wide road."

"Let him rest. You took revenge?"

"Many times over. A couple of the old women died, old Pham, and Hu-mei of the thin lips and big teeth. Do you recall them?"

"I recall everyone," Greenwood said. They were walking toward the crest now, leading the ponies, strolling and chatting like a club or a team. "And the Sawbwa?"

Wan said. "He is the same."

Greenwood caught the dry tone. "Before I forget: treat this boy well. His name is Jum-aw and he guided me up from Kunlong."

"A city boy," Kin-tan scoffed, but he made Jum-aw the gift of one curt nod.

Greenwood returned the boy's rifle and knife. Jum-aw worked at a smile, and then a swagger.

Kin-tan went on, "Did he guide you well?"

"He let me smoke a cheroot one night and we woke up with half the bandits in Burma pissing on our fire."

A shout of laughter rewarded him. "So you surrounded them," Wan said.

"I was lucky. One was an old friend from up Bhamo way. I tell you, they scared me white." He used the Shan phrase without thinking and no one noticed; but he noticed.

"And here you are," Wan said. "This is a good thing. Ko-yang and Cha were married today and you come to bring them luck."

"Luck! I came for the feast. Tell me, who is First Rifle? You, Wan?"

"No. A good soldier called Naung. You never knew him. Where is he anyway?"

"He was with us," Kin-tan said.

Their shadows were long upon the path; the sun rode low behind them.

Wan said, "Ai-ya."

No one spoke for a bit. Greenwood understood.

The Sawbwa jittered and jigged. "Green Wood! Green Wood!"

Greenwood bowed, then patted the old man's shoulder. The Sawbwa had his name right, which was sufficient unto the day. The Sawbwa gurgled happily. "An omen! Did I not say?"

"Indeed," Wan agreed, with the look of one trying to remember.

Za-kho made syllables.

Mong whacked him on the back of the head. "Eh, Chung will be happy! Many a time she smacked her lips over you!"

"What! I never knew!" Greenwood played the fierce thwarted lover. They were encircled by half the village, all chattering and chirping laughter on the festive field. "Ko-yang, what have you done?"

"What many a better man did before me," Ko-yang called cheerily, pleased by Greenwood's notice. He had been only a boy. He laid a husband's hand on Cha's shoulder.

"My friend and guide Jum-aw," Greenwood announced. "Will you treat him as your own?" Where was Loi-mae? Where was Lola?

"And why not!" It was Chung, elbowing irrepressibly through the crowd. She burst toward him and they embraced, and she too whacked away at him, the top of his head, his shoulders.

"So, mother of us all, I see you well."

"You see me well." Chung drew back for a more leisurely inspection. She turned her head and spat betel juice. "Pale," she said, "but still strong. I remember how skinny you were ten years ago."

"Chung, come closer."

They spoke aside, quietly, beneath the crowd's chatter.

"Loi-mae," Greenwood said, "and Lola. Instruct me."

Chung's pause conveyed a judicious melancholy. "They are well. Lola is a little goddess. Now listen: Loi-mae is the woman of Naung, who is—"

"First Rifle."

"Yes. It is my feeling that you must not try to cook on ashes."

"I will do no harm," Greenwood said, remembering Horse-master's definition of wisdom.

"Who can ask more? But can it be? There was much love."

"There was."

"And when one loves another, one loves even the dogs and cats."

"I remember the saying."

"And to love without due regard to what is right is to anger the nats of the hearth."

"I will do no harm," Greenwood said. "Can we go to them now?"

He followed Chung up the trail to Loi-mae's house. He supposed it was Naung's house now. Naung's absence was understandable but awkward; better to meet, let Greenwood indicate acceptance, even submission, and have done with it.

In his left hand he carried a slender gift for Lola. She was nine now, nine and a half, and what did girls desire at nine and a half? Greenwood had been altogether uncertain. He was not yet sure what they wanted at nineteen and a half or twenty-nine and a half. He had passed a disgusted half-hour in a toy shop, examining dollhouses, tricycles, board games, tinny sets of tableware, scooters; he had decided that East was East and West was West and it was better that they not meet, not on this level, at any rate. Lola might have appreciated a small inlaid bow and half a dozen arrows—archery was now obsolete and fashionable among the Shan, like hunting in England or horse-drawn sleighs in America. But he had recalled that at the age of ten the women of Pawlu were presented with ceremonial daggers, which they were thenceforth entitled to wear at the waist, and he had found a genuine dagger of Lapland, of Swedish steel with a haft of reindeer antler and a sheath of hardened reindeer leather lined with lamb's wool.

And now this path, and the flash of a hoopoe; the last stand of bamboo. The last turn.

The house was shockingly small. In his memory it was spacious and sprawling, love's mansion; in life it was no more than twenty feet by twenty. Would Loi-mae too be small, squat, weathered? The memory of Eden. How many hundred nights of young love, all ideal, the age, the body, the climate, the rules there to be broken one by one, all life a dazzlement and an exploration, and in spring the night breeze suffused with wild rose and honeysuckle.

He stood aside, the stranger, the guest, to let Chung pass before. "Here he is!" She padded inside, and Greenwood followed. "He looks well enough," Chung went on. "Neither starving nor diseased."

Loi-mae was not small, squat, weathered. She was the same Loi-mae, rangy for a Shan, oval brownish face, eyes and lips to drown in. Greenwood took one step and halted; went blank and then shy; swallowed; felt love's surge and swell, and the hint of an ebb. Loi-mae shut her eyes in joy and held forth both hands. "O Loi-mae!" he said, and kissed the hands. She sighed then, a long-drawn musical breath, hugged him tight, and averted her lips when he kissed her face. "Ah no," he said, held her chin, kissed her again, a lingering kiss and a molten kiss, lips melting, tongue soft, body straining. He groaned aloud. Would you stay? Would you fight for her? Take her back?

There came a tug at his jacket.

Lola stared up at him, moon-eyed, sweet, timid, awed, hoping to smile. Loi-mae had gone limp in his embrace, only the clutch of her arms still tight.

"Lola!" he cried. Do no harm. Loi-mae released him, and a look passed between them of almost inhuman intensity—a look of grief, of joy, of fear, of understanding. We have stolen our years of glory, this look said, of perfection, of bliss; we have been like gods; and now it is for the gods to do what they will with us; what they cannot do is annul those years.

He stooped like any father to take Lola by the waist and hoist her high. Like any child, she squealed and shrieked. "O Green Wood! O Father!" He smothered her, nuzzled, held her off for a stern scrutiny. "Why, you are almost a woman!" he said. "And a beauty like your mother!" Loi-mae's perfume was still in his nostrils, and the memory of her embrace still warm. A faint spicy odor: the ginger on her breath. The house too: aromas of pepper and grease. He remembered faint latrine smells when the wind shifted.

Chung had slipped away. Loi-mae stood smiling bravely, eyes bright; she blinked, the smile dissolved. "You are hungry," she said. She raised a startled hand to her lips: "Yet what is that to me?"

"How could I think of food?" he asked. "You too, you are a beauty; there is none so beautiful anywhere."

For another hot moment there seemed nothing to say.

Greenwood made an effort. "Have you been well? And Lola?"

"She had chicken skin two years ago. No scars, as you see."

Lola asked, "Have you come to take me away?"

"O poor Lola!" Loi-mae cried, and hugged her. "No, no, no, would we let him do that?"

Lola teased: "And if I want to go?"

"And leave Weng-aw?"

"Who is Weng-aw?" Greenwood asked.

"A boy who flirts and paws."

"By the gods," Greenwood said huffily.

Lola asked, "Have you a child in your own country?"

"Of course he has," Loi-mae answered swiftly, as if forestalling pain. "Enough pestering."

"No wife and no child," Greenwood said, and saw pleasure suffuse Loi-mae's face.

"But women," she murmured.

"Well, a few, but none like Loi-mae, with the tall swaying beauty of rushes and the melting eyes of the gyi."

Her pleasure deepened, her smooth tan cheeks mantled, but she rebuked him: "You must not say so. Have you met Naung?"

"No."

"He is a good man. He has been loving with Lola."

"Good indeed, as all say. And he is First Rifle."

She meditated for some moments, saying then,
"I never spoke of him, but he wanted me before
you came, and I sent him away. He was a soldier
in Laos and Tonkin."

"A traveled man and surely a good soldier.
Lola"—he shifted ground—"I have brought you a
gift; not much, but from the heart."

"Green Wood!"

"Loi-mae," he said more quietly, "I bring no
gift, only myself. I could not know if I had the
right."

"It will do," Loi-mae assured him. "As well you
brought nothing; but for Lola, yes."

"Naung is . . . a difficult man?"

"No more so than any man. But you were wise
to refrain."

He saw again the stacked wooden bowls, the
larger pot, the quern to grind grain or pepper.
The hanging straw mat was rolled away now. At
night it would hang where it had always hung,
and Loi-mae and Naung would enjoy privacy.

"What, then? What have you brought me?"
Lola cried. "Do you tell and not give?"

"Some daughter," Greenwood grumbled.
"Who has taught this one manners? Or omitted
to?" He held forth the package. "For my
beautiful Lola."

Lola tore at the thick brown paper. As the scab-
bard came into view she exclaimed, ecstatic. "O!
It is *mine*?"

"And you must care for it as a warrior would."

"Where is it from? Who made it?" She drew
the knife and danced a few ceremonial steps,
slashing.

"It is from a land in the far north," he said,

"with snow and ice the whole year, and it was made by men who wear furs and hides the whole year. The haft is carved from the antler of a northern gyi, and the sheath is of his hide."

"Green Wood!" She rushed to fling her arms about him.

"Ow! Put that thing away! Fine thanks! You pricked me."

"I love it," she said again. "I will wear it always."

Wear it when that Weng-aw comes around." But Loi-mae was waiting, Loi-mae had more to say, or perhaps did not, and expected more of him, or pehaps not. He felt once more gangling and young.

"I am glad with all my heart that life has been good to you," he said, and the simple speech rang awkward and insufficient.

"I am glad with all my heart that you remained solid and did not shrink away," Loi-mae said lightly. "You were skin and bones when I first set eyes on you."

"I was still growing up. Without you I would not have become a man. Even now I am not fully a man without you."

"Do not talk so. It is not seemly now. Besides, it was fighting and killing that made a man of you."

There was justice in that. It was a pleasantly neutral and gossipy statement. Greenwood had, over the previous month, steeled himself to a variety of possible emotions at this reunion, a resurgence of love, sudden revulsion, remorse, dismay, mellow friendship, chatty indifference. He was perturbed now to feel embarrassment, like a man taken in adultery, or an impostor.

Loi-mae and Lola were prosperous and happy, and he could think of nothing original to say.

Yang. His mind leapt to General Yang and his old bones. Where was the smiler now? If Yang was dead, if Greenwood lingered here too long . . . Do no harm.

"Can he not sit down?" Lola asked. "He is my father and this is my house. Who will sleep here tonight? Green Wood or Naung?"

Greenwood and Loi-mae burst into relieved laughter.

At sunset—early, as West Slope cheated them of an hour—Greenwood and a ten of leaders sat upon the grass outside the Sawbwa's house. The Sawbwa was jubilant, strutting about in an old, genuine Arikara headband from North Dakota, of buffalo hide. Greenwood had considered bringing him a full-feathered war bonnet of the kind sold in souvenir shops, but was now sufficiently mature to dismiss condescending frivolities. Trouble enough when some future savant found a Pawnee headband in a Shan village. For the people of Pawlu he had brought five hundred rounds of ammunition, 7.65 millimeter and .30 caliber. This was a gift of importance, and the council had assembled in a relaxed and jollified mood. Za-kho instructed Ang-ang the Woman-in-Common to serve them. There was Wan; there was Kin-tan; there was Mong; there were half a ten more; and there was Naung. Jum-aw was off lying to Chung's daughters about the big town.

No one had said, "Green Wood, this is Naung,"

or "Naung, this is Green Wood." No one had to.
The American sat cross-legged and Ang-ang set
before him hot pork, glutinous balls of rice, a
bowl of chicken and spices. He sniffed, and his
soul was replete. His teabowl was replenished.
He waited until all were served and Za-kho had
pronounced a blessing.

As they fell to then, his eyes met Naung's. Both
took the moment calmly, neither speaking nor
nodding. The conversation remained general—
crops, weather, the war in China. Greenwood
told them that all was quiet over by Sumprabum,
Myitkyina and Bhamo. The sun set, but light
lingered long in the clear sky. "This afternoon I
saw a cloud," Za-kho reported.

"I saw it too," Naung said. "A little rain would
not go amiss."

Greenwood had disliked Naung's face at first
glance, a tough, suspicious face with an
aggressive jaw and theatrically rich black brows;
now he noted the fine teeth and sympathized
with the sparse but ambitious beard.

"There will be no rain yet," the Sawbwa said.

On this matter he was never wrong, Greenwood remembered.

Later Greenwood asked easily, "Naung, how is
that French submachine gun?"

Naung could not suppress a smile. "My mitraillette. A good weapon within fifty paces; after
that, wild as a frightened hare. Also, there is no
provision for the single shot. But one feels safe."

"As with mine. How many rounds do you
hold?"

"Thirty-two. Of the seven six five long."

"Eh. I have only thirty, but more like eleven millimeters."

"I remember the power of it," Wan said.

"I have three or four more catties to carry around," Greenwood said.

"Yes, much heavier, it would stop a leopard," Kin-tan said, "but Naung's is more accurate beyond twenty paces, which is sufficient for defense."

"I have the single shot," Greenwood said. "You have a higher muzzle velocity, I think."

"That seems of little importance," Naung said. "The bullets fly fast enough, and who will measure the difference?"

At this they laughed, and Greenwood acknowledged the jest with a lift of the teabowl. He asked Za-kho, "May I drink to the bride and groom?"

"How not, how not!" Za-kho called out, "Ang-ang! Wine for all!"

"Well, and how about rum?"

"A good idea," said Mong.

"Mong, you bag of sticks. My heart is full."

"It is a day Pawlu will remember," Kin-tan said.

Still later, boozy, they asked and Greenwood told the tale. "You remember the smiling Chinese general."

Wan slapped thigh. "Do I remember! Phe-win loved the man! He left a gold piece. We have it still. And he was an honest smiler. He knew a joke when he heard one and he smiled only for reason."

"A general?" Naung asked. "I have heard the story, but I allowed for natural exaggeration. Perhaps a colonel, I thought."

"No, a general," Greenwood said. "A major general then; you remember the shoulder board with one star? And he has three stars now, a full general and a man of some importance."

"To whom?" Wan asked.

"Always a plain blunt man, Wan." Greenwood mulled the question. "Well then: to me."

"That is sufficient," said Kin-tan.

"Thank you."

"And what has he to do with us? Will you proceed into China?" Naung seemed hopeful.

"No." Greenwood delayed; drank; wiped his mouth on his sleeve. Flames danced, shadows danced, across the dark field voices rose and fell, the black sky was spangled white. In the end Greenwood said, "He is fleeing China."

"May the gods speed him," Wan said. "May he flee all the way to Siam, or Tonkin. Mind you, I liked him. But generals."

"Well," Greenwood said, and plunged, "he is coming here."

In the silence Greenwood prickled, as if he would soon sweat.

"That is not for you to say," Naung told him.

"Well then, he is on his way. There was no time for other plans and no one to trust with a message. And the truth is, I do not know if he is dead or alive."

"It is unreasonable," Naung said testily. "Why can he not flee to the Chinese islands like the others? Or to Tonkin? Or out along the Burma Road?"

Greenwood said, "First: he was trapped by war, and cut off, and so moved west and south. Second: he would risk capture at frontier stations, as along the Burma Road, capture by the Chinese Communists or by the Burmese authorities. Third: he has something I want."

Wan said, "Ah."

Naung's eye was steady and knowing.

Kin-tan sipped pensively.

By God, here was a falling-off! Greenwood sat perplexed, vaguely ashamed and not sure why. The prodigal son! These simple valiant souls, the lovely compliant woman. The adopted Shan. Well, had he or had he not saved their skins? Our little brown brothers.

He called for more rum. Damn! He had expected ebullience, bustle, the excitement and approval of warriors with work to do.

Naung said, "He will not enter Pawlu."

"Pawlu owes Green Wood much," Kin-tan said slowly. "During the war not one Japanese set foot in Pawlu and not one Englishman either, and the Wild Wa never crossed the road. Yang too killed his Wa."

Naung made no reply. Naung had fought the war elsewhere.

"And the weapons," Wan said. "Rifles and ammunition and those pistols. Green Wood never came home empty-handed. American weapons and English and Japanese. And with Naung's loot from the French after the Long-Haul-with-Koko," he added tactfully, placatingly, generously, "Pawlu is armed for our lifetime."

"You could meet him in Nan-san," Kin-tan said.

"I do not know that he will come by Nan-san;
or on foot or mounted or by air. It must be here."

"Perhaps nearby," Wan suggested.

"He will not enter Pawlu," Naung repeated.
"You will go to Nan-san and we shall bring him
to you there."

If it is the woman, Greenwood wanted to say, if
it is Loi-mae, I will do no harm. You need not
send me away.

The others were silent, until Wan spoke. "His
bodyguard. Who comes with him?"

"A guide, perhaps, and a few armed men,
surely, to defend against bandits."

"It is true," Naung said, "that the hills are full
of Kachin."

"They fought well," Greenwood said.

"So did we all," said Naung.

"The Kachin fought on my side," Greenwood
said.

Naung drank deep.

"Not all of them," Wan said. "Some Kachin,
like some Shan, hated the English."

"I meant no slight," Greenwood said.

"I liked the general," Wan continued. "He
displayed a sense of propriety. He was old and
wise but not officious."

"When he smiled in starlight," Kin-tan said, "it
made noon."

At that the Sawbwa chuckled moistly. "He
bowed to me always."

"He bowed to the Sawbwa," Wan said solemnly.

Naung drew lines in the earth with his short
dagger. Za-kho's fire flared. Greenwood stared
into it until his eyes ached.

Naung said, "One hesitates to pry. Nevertheless, it is our village. What does this general carry that is so important?"

Still gazing blindly into the fire, Greenwood said, "The true bones of his ancestors."

"That is very Chinese and commendable," Naung said. "And why do you want them?"

Greenwood peered up unseeing at the night, and waited; slowly a blizzard of stars pricked out the velvet black sky. How explain these old bones? How count off half a million years?

"Five lakhs of years," he began.

"Now, that is a long time," Naung agreed.

"So long ago were those bones laid down. So long ago did those first men and women live and die."

"Yes, and there are some who say we have been here for ten lakhs of years and more. Yet are five lakhs venerable. Your general is a deeply religious man. Still we do not know why these bones are of interest to you."

Let me tell you all about world capitals, universities, learned societies, international conferences, man's endless struggle to identify himself. As well tell of ice in the south. "No earlier Chinese bones are known. So these are holy bones to all priests and scholars."

"Ah well, now we have it," Wan said. "Green Wood is a scholar, with his writings and his making pictures, and he will achieve eminence with these bones."

"That is making much trouble for eminence," Naung said.

"It is much eminence," Greenwood told him.

Kin-tan said, "Green Wood. A well-laid

ambush. And we will spare your general or not, as you wish."

"The man is my friend," Greenwood said. "By the gods, Kin-tan! Yours too! He fought beside you and shared your rice and your wine and your jokes. And now you would set his life at hazard?"

"Naturally, you cannot set his life at hazard," Naung said. "Yet you set Pawlu at hazard."

"I see no risk."

"An unknown number of unknown men are to descend upon Pawlu so that you and this general may pay old debts."

"I see no danger."

"It seems to me," Wan said, "that the question is, how much does Pawlu owe Green Wood?"

"That is well stated," said Kin-tan.

"I cannot know what Pawlu owes Green Wood," Naung said, "so I will shut up. My advice is to let no outlander into Pawlu." He slipped the dagger into its sheath and rose swiftly. "I rose at first light and am tired. Kin-tan, will you visit the sentries?"

"I will. Sleep well."

"Sleep well, all." Naung stood immobile and impassive; he gazed first at Greenwood, then at the Sawbwa, then at Wan and Kin-tan; and he padded into the darkness.

Za-kho said, "The planets are in favorable position."

The Sawbwa said, "Green Wood has come back to us."

Wan said, "They must not cross the road. We can fetch Yang from there, but his men may not cross."

"That is the way to do it," Kin-tan said. "When

will Yang arrive?"

Greenwood showed palm. "Perhaps a day, perhaps a month."

"Perhaps he is dead," Wan said.

Greenwood was to sleep in the House of the Dead, a clean, bare, two-walled hut where corpses were washed and laid out, and later that evening, pack stowed, belly full, heart sore, he stood out back in the brush pissing manfully.

He heard no footstep, only felt the hard hand on his shoulder and heard the hostile voice. "Green Wood."

"Naung," he said. "Let me piss."

He tucked in and turned. Naung's dagger flicked out like a toktay's tongue. Its sharp tip pricked Greenwood's chin. "This is for you," Naung said, "what harm soever comes to Pawlu." Naung's meaty, rummy breath stank.

"If harm comes, it will come to me first. I have stood before between Pawlu and harm."

"I fear that the harm has already come."

"Put up the dagger."

"I should kill you now. I know this as the Sawbwa knows the rain."

"Would I bring harm to Lola? Or to Loi-mae?" When Naung's gaze shifted at the mention of his woman, Greenwood made a move, half in earnest, nimbly whacking Naung's wrist back, reaching swiftly under the arm to grasp the hand, haft and all, and wrench down and back, not far enough to do harm or cause great pain but far enough to say, I am not a beginner. He released Naung immediately. "You must do better than that."

Naung said, "When the time comes I will. Now listen: whatever the Sawbwa says, you will not leave the village unless for good; and if your general comes at all he will enter the village alone."

"If he comes, I will take him away within three days."

"Three days I give you," Naung said, and backed away, and seemed to vanish.

Greenwood slept badly. Too much rum. He woke several times, once from a dream of Loimae, and he considered simply retreating; but he knew that he would not. Perhaps he had not yet exhausted his luck.

They owed him this much. He had once been First Rifle, and that was no small thing. He had once held Pawlu in the hollow of his hand. He had once been a Shan.

Lying in the dark, he ransacked his heart, and he found greed, and selfishness, and impatience, and dread, and he wished he were half a world away.

9

Across
the Salween

General Yang's tatterdemalion company rattled and backfired into Fang-shih at sunrise of a frosty winter morn just after the turn of the year 1950. The general drove point, he and Major Wei and the two footlockers wedged into the one operational jeep. Colonel Olevskoy and his lady brought up the rear. The army of fifty-six men rode in four ill-assorted trucks and one weapons carrier. The general and the colonel, mollified by adversity, had learned to be cordial.

In a small square the vehicles drew into a column of twos and halted. Olevskoy vaulted his tailgate and marched briskly to his general. "Good morning, sir."

"Good morning, Colonel. You seem jaunty."

"I'm filthy and hungry. Is there a hotel? A barracks? Are there public baths?"

"I hope so. I am none too savory myself. The sawbwa here is a modern soul."

"Ah. We shall call upon him."

Yang could not restrain a feeble grin. "He will not see us, you know. He'll be out of town."

The sawbwa was indeed out of town. His prime

minister, or grand vizier, received General Yang. While the sawbwa here was a cosmopolitan gentleman, noted gourmet and keen judge of women without regard to provenance or ancestry, his factotum was dapper, bald and faintly feminine, a classic mandarin in his gray gown and black hat with red button. This statesman affirmed that the sawbwa enjoyed electricity, foreign journals, indoor water closets and spectacles from Hong Kong, actually made to prescription. To meet General Yang would have afforded him unforgettable pleasure. It was nothing short of calamitous that he should be at this moment visiting his outlying parishioners and constituents.

General Yang was jolly: "We're lepers now." The sawbwa's house seemed to be humming, vibrating; this was somehow a comfort.

The secretary, fifyish, barbered, showed palm. "Surely not lepers. Only an embarrassment."

Yang had bathed and shaved, though his uniform was scruffy. He sighed. He did not mind wars so much, or famine or even pestilence. But an accumulation of small evils, balks, frustrations, annoyances dissipated the energies. A man, even an army, could be annihilated by hordes of mocking, invulnerable evil spirits. "On est bien dans la merde," he murmured.

In sibilant French, like a Moroccan or Tunisian, the plumpish secretary said, "Ce n'est pas si grave que ça."

"Mon Dieu," Yang said. "I suppose you speak English too."

"American. They came through here like some Hunnish migration. Though I cannot," he added quickly, "deny China's debt to them."

"Indeed not," Yang said, losing his reserve, abruptly churlish. "About one percent of the Chinese army fought at all, and it had to compete with the other ninety-nine percent for supplies and trained men. I seem to recall that as long as the Burma Road was open, your sawbwa imported Havana cigars and French brandy. One shudders to imagine his privations when the Japanese cut the Road. If not for the Americans, China would still be absorbing the invader, and in a century or so the new Sino-Japanese race would spill into Siberia, Persia, Malaya, goose-stepping and shouting a bastard language."

"You have eaten much bitterness," the secretary said in Chinese.

"Yes, forgive me, forgive me." Yang rubbed his eyes with both hands. "I must say there is little patriotism left in my own heart. I have just spent thirteen years taking orders from scoundrels and blackguards, watching my men die by the thousands, losing a wife and son, losing a mistress, losing a whole war, for the sake of feudalism and foreign bank accounts. Your sawbwa is no hero."

The secretary reproached him lightly: "But he is remaining."

"Ah yes." Yang's good cheer was restored. "While I, being a man of the world, shall transcend narrow nationalism and confer upon a crude materialistic world the benefits of Chinese charm and sensibility."

"With that sort of talk," the secretary allowed, "you cannot fail."

"Kind of you to say so. My problem at the moment is transport. Shall I speak plainly?"

"Speak plainly."

"I have four trucks, a weapons carrier and a jeep, all aged and weary but functioning. I am prepared to barter them for forty ponies, mules or donkeys. I lose by the deal; but I have my reasons."

The secretary sat back in his armchair, making a traditional steeple of his fingers. "Shall I speak plainly?"

"Speak plainly."

"The Communists will be here shortly. They will simply commandeer those vehicles."

"How if the sawbwa prepared them as a gift? A peace offering?"

"Then he would lose the price of forty ponies, mules and donkeys."

Yang grunted. "I could take the city, you know, with my fifty men."

The secretary was shocked.

"I could destroy the power plant," Yang pursued, "fire Fang-shih, level your compound. War, after all, is war. Permit me to threaten you directly. If your sawbwa sees fit to treat us like pye-dogs, we are justified in razing his little principality."

"Not pye-dogs," the secretary protested. "It is awkward only."

"I could kill a few," Yang offered, "which, when your new masters arrive, will witness to your resistance and our inhuman ferocity. Perhaps the sawbwa's secretary's head on a tall stake, high above the fabled Burma Road."

"My dear general," said the secretary, "what a distasteful notion. You argue persuasively if without subtlety. Is there petrol?"

"What fuels your power plant?"

"Coal."

That puzzled Yang: whence this hum, this vibration? "The sawbwa has his own electricity?"

The secretary nodded.

"A generator? Running on diesel oil?"

The secretary nodded.

"Then he bought, stole and commandeered all through the war. He must have thousands of gallons stored. Two of my trucks are diesels. I have also about a hundred gallons of gasoline left and will be glad to see the last of it. I was sure I'd be blown to bits by now."

The secretary mulled all this.

"Well?"

"Done."

"And the noble steeds?"

"I shall introduce you to our Donkey Woman."

"A local beauty," Yang said.

"She has a large nose and is illiterate," said the secretary, "and looks rather like a donkey—"

"Long silky ears?" Yang murmured. "A bony rump?"

"—but she knows more about domestic animals than any man in Fang-shih. She converses with them."

"I am already in love," Yang said.

Olevskoy had proceeded directly to the public baths, men's side, bearing a bundle, dragging Hsiao-chi after him and overriding the feeble protests of the attendant, a wizened old man with hairy ears who shrilled his objections in a kind of pidgin Chinese—"No female! Male side! No inside!"—until Olevskoy said "Shut up" and pushed him away.

The baths were sunken basins of stone. Olevskoy shouted for hot water and soap. When there was no response, he shouted promises of castration, broken bones and merciful hanging. Shortly the attendant, assisted by a goggling boy, padded swiftly in with buckets, poured, vanished, returned; the basin filled. Rough towels were stacked on a wooden bench.

Olevskoy had already stripped Hsiao-chi. The old man lingered to salivate; Olevskoy kicked him. "Go away. If you come back before I call you, I shall strike you slightly above both thighs and then strangle you with my bare hands. Do you understand?" Old Hairy Ears absented himself willingly.

Olevskoy stripped himself as well and led Hsiao-chi into the bath. She giggled. "Allez, glousse," he said. "Giggle away. You are about to be transformed, rendered immaculate body and soul."

"It is hot," she said.

"How perceptive. It is indeed hot. No purification without agony. If you want to live in a stinking crib for the rest of your life, all right; but if you listen to me you can be the sawbwa's mistress. Or some commissar's. Sit still, now." He soaked her down. He scrubbed her first with soap and then with the stiff brush. She cried out. "In the name of God," he said, "the dirt is peeling off like orange rind. You're three shades lighter already." He soaped her again, and in detail, paying happy attention to her nipples, her crotch and her navel. "Sit there in your lather," he ordered. He then soaped himself, rinsed, soaped again, rinsed. "Bath man!" he roared. Clogs clattered. "Four buckets more, tepid, and hurry it up!" The old fellow stared at Hsiao-chi, who sat like a doll, hair lank, body streaked white; he darted away, and returned with four buckets. "Be off," Olevskoy said. He washed Hsiao-chi's hair. He washed his own hair. He rinsed them both. He handed her gallantly out of the tub and dried her vigorously. "There!" he said. "By God, that's better! You're almost human."

She was that. She was, he acknowledged, rather pretty. She was sniffing at her own fresh skin, running her fingers along her lustrous breasts and belly with little cries of pleasure. To Olevskoy's joy, he found his penis erect and peremptory. "Let us make the fish with two backs," he said.

"This one will surely do," Yang said. "A good round barrel."

"But a sore on one ear," said Major Wei.

"For a few days only it won't matter." They were in the sawbwa's corral, of thirty-odd mou, the general judged; or two hectares or five acres; I am a citizen of the world now.

Donkey Woman said, "Two years old. Look at those quarters."

Major Wei said, "How odd. Her teeth are seven or eight years old."

"A vastly accomplished little girl," Olevskoy said. He sat at ease in the secretary's office, one leg crossed over the other, boots gleaming. He drew happily on a Russian cigarette—this sawbwa must be quite a fellow—and sipped at good green tea.

"She's pretty," the secretary conceded. "How old?"

"Fifteen." Olevskoy was firm.

The secretary allowed dubiety to fleet across his glossy face, but made no protest.

"Nothing like a mule," Donkey Woman said. "Strong, reliable and uncomplaining."

"Independent and obstinate," Yang said.

"This one will load two hundred catties."

"She's right," Wei said. "The sawbwa's hay is good stuff."

The secretary asked, "Truly talented? The full range?"

"I guarantee it."

Hsiao-chi stood shyly against the wall, eyes cast down.

"You understand," the secretary said easily, "our sawbwa is something of a connoissuer. A lifetime of lore, also practical knowledge. He is no dilettante."

"I can tell that by his tea," Olevskoy said. "Fit for the gods."

The secretary bowed acknowledgment.

"I myself," Olevskoy went on, "am not without experience. An exile, you understand. Thirty-five years of international service, so to speak."

"I regret more than ever that the sawbwa cannot make your acquaintance," said the secretary.

"How many is that now?" Yang asked.

"Four mules, eighteen ponies, twenty-one donkeys."

"Every one as good as a horse," Donkey Woman said. She was a homely little thing but had, to Yang's surprise, short silky hair.

"How many will we need?" Yang wondered aloud.

"We are down to the hard core," Wei said. "Who has endured until now should be loyal."

"Or curious, or opportunistic, or imaginative; but some will not want to leave Chinese soil. Think, Major Wei, it has come to this: thirty-eight years of the Republic of China have left to the world one general, one colonel, two majors, two lieutenants and fifty-two exhausted, underpaid soldiers."

"And when we cross the border—"

"The end. Some must hold out in the north-west, but not for long."

"Then we shall make a new world," Wei said lightly. "How good to be single, without obligations, and trained in the military arts."

"Just so," said Yang, and to Donkey Woman, "now, little lady, choose the best of the ponies for the officers. And which are the two sturdiest pack mules?"

Major Wei said, "Ah yes. The footlockers. One day you will tell us, I hope."

"When the time is right," General Yang promised. "Until then, only remember: they are worth all the tea in China."

"You do have a sense of humor," said Major Wei, "sir."

"An ounce of gold!" The secretary was outraged.

"Think," Olevskoy said. "The sawbwa can have what he wants, agreed, but here is a filly all broken in, docile, four-gaited and genuinely affectionate. How many of the sawbwa's women actually love it? And some are foreign, some querulous and demanding, some will desert him in time of trouble. Not little Hsiao-chi."

"You argue well." The secretary sipped. "Show the goods."

Olevskoy gestured to Hsiao-chi, who unbuttoned her gown and let it slip to the floor; she stood in her cloth shoes only. And now sadness veiled her face, and loneliness shaded her moist eyes.

"Yes, yes, yes," the secretary conceded. "A bird of paradise indeed. The breasts are very much what the sawbwa likes, round and high and with those large brown nipples. He kept a Khmer woman for a time whose nipples were three inches broad. And I like the long pale thighs; and the hair between seems quite feathery."

Olevskoy gestured again.

Hsiao-chi shied. "Must I?"

"Do as I say."

Reluctantly she glided forward, and the secretary stroked her mons. "Good girl. Turn about, please." He stroked her buttocks. Olevskoy almost laughed aloud at this dispassionate connoisseur. Perhaps the fellow was a capon. "Splendid. Very well, Colonel. I see no need to haggle. Our new masters will surely confiscate specie."

Olevskoy said, "They may also confiscate the sawbwa. He had best enjoy his last days of sin and glory."

"She even has good teeth," said the secretary.

Hsiao-chi spoke again, imploring; her voice trembled. "You will not take me with you?"

"You understand," said General Yang, "the sawbwa will pay."

Donkey Woman stood sullen.

Yang understood and sympathized. It was an old story. He dug into his watch pocket. "Take this, now, for your good counsel; and take some advice too. When the Communists come, go to an officer of the highest rank possible, and go as soon as possible, and tell him of the evils that have been done to you here."

"They will put me to slavery in the tin mines," Donkey Woman muttered.

"They will not," Yang said. "Not the army. Later when the politicians come, all will be at sevens and eights. But the army pays for what it takes, and respects women who labor. They are my enemy, yet I tell you this. Also, they will be looking for grievances to avenge; they will be pleased with you. Do you understand? Donkey Woman will be a heroine."

Donkey Woman laughed a harsh, mannish laugh. "I understand. And by the gods I hope you are not wrong." She glanced at the tiny coin. "But this is gold!"

"Chin yü chih yen!" he said cheerily. "Your advice was worth gold and jade!"

She did not know the classics, and stood confused. Then, because she was a blunt woman who spoke mainly with animals, she looked him in the eye and said, "I hope yours is as good."

Major Wei sat later like a giant of old in Fang-shih's Emerald Tavern, arguing soberly with Major Ho, Lieutenant An and Lieutenant Chi. Ordinarily Major Wei did not argue but commanded. Ordinarily he carried—showing off, and he knew it—a Browning automatic rifle rather than the light carbine that now stood propped against the wall beside him. Ordinarily he drank beer and not gassy foreign soda waters, but there seemed to be no beer in Fang-shih. Extraordinary times indeed!

"I would not mind knowing what is in those footlockers," Lieutenant Chi said. "If we are merely an armed guard for a million in gold . . ."

"Not gold," said Wei. "Too light. Gems, perhaps."

Lieutenant An looked more like a slim provincial teacher than a warrior. "I have never set foot outside China. It feels like treason."

"I have a large family in Shansi," Lieutenant Chi said. "Mother and father and *their* mothers and fathers, and innumerable brothers, sisters, uncles, aunts and cousins."

Wei said, "I stay. This is the only fighting general I ever knew, and so far the only truthful general. He pays his men and goes hungry when they do. As far as I know, he has not one copper in any bank anywhere, and no gold ingots in foreign lands. Do you know another general of whom that can be said? And what will you do when the Communists come to hang you?"

Chi made a frog's mouth and shook his head

emphatically. "They *must* forgive. They cannot hang half the country."

"They welcomed generals," Major Ho said.

Wei said, "Pah! Generals brought them whole cities, whole armies. What can majors and lieutenants offer?"

"Love of country," Chi said. "Soldiers' skills."

"It is so," An said. "You go ahead, wander the face of the earth and end your days buying and selling in Rangoon or New Delhi. Not me."

"And where would he take us?" Chi asked. "Into those cursed mountains, across those devilish rivers, and through headhunter country."

Major Wei said, "That's for me. You do what you like, wear numbers on your back or study Marxism for the rest of your life. I have yet dragons to slay." He glanced about him at the lazy, chatty, unconcerned drinkers and snorted. "Look at them! Civilians! Sheep!"

That night Yang's gang, war-weary but once more spruce, sat, stood, sprawled and smoked cigarettes in the dingy barracks of the Fang-shih constabulary, vacated by the local police at the first approach of these killers and pariahs, the Nationalist army. Olevskoy sat beside the general. Yang counted the house: only forty-one.

"Lao-tzu says, 'The way that can be traversed is not the way.' But we have had no choice; we have traveled our road and I believe with honor. We now come to a fork in the trail. Like all generals, I tell the truth only with reluctance, but you have earned it." The men emitted a nervous rill of laughter. Yang smiled moderately.

"The old China will make its history and its

presence felt in various ways henceforth, and in odd places, and by odd refugees like us. It was my obligation to lead you out, but in a few days my mandate will not run: our China is gone, and outside its borders I am only an elderly civilian." A ripple of protest greeted this, and many chuckles.

"We shall leave the Road tomorrow and take to the hills, and eventually enter Burma. We cannot say precisely where because to this day the frontier has never been mapped. I do not lead you to some heroic old soldiers' utopia; I only take you to neutral territory and let you start a new life.

"Some of you even now, on this last evening, will decide to stay in China. I must counsel you to vanish discreetly overnight.

"Those who join me will make a short but difficult journey to a border village called Pawlu. Its people are friendly enough and its poppies ripple like lakes of blood. Pawlu means freedom, a new life, riches. The crude opium is traded down to Hsenwi and then out; it is cheap now, but Chinese opium is about to come under tight control and foreign markets are opening. Revenge at last: for a century the foreigners made fortunes addicting the Chinese people, and now you may return the favor.

"I expect some of you will pass through Pawlu as I did in nineteen forty-four, maintaining the courtesies and paying for what you need. Some will scatter by ones and twos and threes to the great cities of Burma, India, Thailand, Indochina, Malaya. Some will even, in time, go back to China to be forgiven and humbled.

"Whatever you decide, you have my thanks. You have been more than good soldiers, you have been good men; you have endured privation, pain and the loneliness of forlorn hopes. If there are questions, you must ask them now."

There were rarely questions, but tonight a current of unease excited the roomful. China was the Middle Kingdom; the rest of the world was Outside.

Major Ho stood at stiff military rest. "Sir."

"Major."

A rustle of exhalations, an air of expectancy.

"I have fought beside the general since before Taierhchuang."

"You were a sergeant then."

"And the general a colonel." In his gruffest tone Ho said, "Sir. The men have talked much among themselves, and have asked me to be one voice from ten mouths."

General Yang's calm interest invited further revelations.

Ho hesitated. "Many would feel better knowing . . ." Ho's glance darted about, seeking help; none came.

"Proceed, Major. You have full immunity if you speak for the men."

"Well, sir," Ho said, "they would march on with lighter hearts if they knew what was in those footlockers. With permission, sir."

"Of course," said Yang, taking a moment to smile understandingly at Olevskoy. "But will you believe me?"

The silence was embarrassing, until finally Major Wei spoke up. "You have a home." It was the ancient way to say that a man was reliable, that his word could be trusted, and in the circumstances it was an epic joke. The tension vanished in an explosion of laughter. Even Olevskoy whinnied.

"Well then," said Yang, "as I have a home, and as generals love truth, here it is: in those foot-lockers are the bones of my ancestors. Nothing more and nothing less."

An ill-timed jest, for all that it was true; Yang could almost hear the esprit de corps shattering. He could show them the bones. No! One was a general or one was not. If they all left him he would strike out for Pawlu alone.

Firmly he said, "I have told you the truth," and then more crisply, "We rendezvous tomorrow morning at eight in the square before the sawbwa's corral. That is all for now. Dismissed."

Men and benches creaked and scuffed; his soldiers avoided his eye. This was a bad moment, but he could not resist an afterthought: "To those who remain with me, one last consideration." For a summery instant his smile warmed them all. "I offer you more than freedom. I offer you anarchy." A few, he thought, might understand.

"The neighborhood is run-down," Yang complained. "Here they once served fried bees. I have no idea how to cook them, but they were fat and delicious. One could tuck away hundreds."

"Be grateful for fresh beef," Olevskoy said. "With luck we shall never again eat as badly as we have this past year." They were in Fang-shih's Burma Road Wine Shop gobbling diced beef with leeks and ginger. Business was bad. A couple of customers sat morosely nursing cups of tea.

Yang's rice was delicious, fresh meat a joy, hot wine a luxury. The restaurant was dim and shabby, lit by oil lamps, to the rear a cook-fire flickering, casting restless shadows.

"As far as the ford," Yang said, "which is perhaps thirty miles as the crow flies but will more like eighty on the trail, we shall be a caravan in single file, following narrow trails across the face of steep slopes. From the next ridge each man will be nicely outlined against the mountain. Like the ducks in the booth at the fête foraine. What do you call them?"

"Jeux de tir. Shooting galleries. Are there Communists in those hills?"

"Not to my knowledge. There is, however, a surfeit of free enterprise."

"Ah. Bandits. Many many, I suppose."

"Eastern Burma is not oppressed by rules and regulations," Yang said. "Now: bandits travel in small packs. . . . I wonder if anyone has ever written about that?" Yang shoveled rice into his mouth and ruminated.

"Written?"

"The natural laws that govern banditry. If there are more than ten or so, stresses destroy the way of life: a permanent woman seems necessary, a servant class is established, large and reliable supplies of food became desirable—in short, a tendency to bourgeoisify makes itself felt. I should think the ideal pack would be four to seven."

Olevskoy grunted.

"Quite right; I digress. It is not the trail that worries me; there is little purpose to killing men at long range and watching them tumble a thousand feet into an inaccessible valley. I worry about the ford, and about the hostile territory beyond it."

"Scouts on the flanks," Olevskoy said. "A beachhead assault at the ford."

"We shall be lieutenants again."

"Life improves." Olevskoy returned the smile. "I could scarcely ask for more. Had a fine little girl and am rid of her with no fuss and no clap. Now eating a good dinner for the first time in days. And an old-fashioned military exercise coming up. Dry cup!"

"Dry cup!"

"What is in the footlockers?"

"I told the truth, Nicky."

"Bizarre."

"Let us trust each for yet a week or so," Yang said carefully. "A genuine armistice during a difficult troop movement. When you can no longer trust me, I shall tell you so."

"But will I be able to trust you to do so?"

Yang's smile was at full stretch.

The platoon set out under blue skies, striking southeast and rising rapidly into the foothills. Bobbing along behind his footlockers, General Yang found time hanging heavy, a cumbersome load, his kidneys twinging. His mind drifted back to old resentments, the pretty wife dead of cancer in Peking while he was on campaign; the air-cadet son wasted in a useless training accident that was, however delicately phrased the formal report, his own foolish fault; grafting generals promoted over his head; grafting civilians who fattened indirectly on dead soldiers; even those same dead soldiers, barely alive at any time, ignorant, underfed, purposeless, terrified, disregarding orders, misunderstanding orders, contradicting orders.

Well, he could remember heroes too. Whole companies that stood fast, died in their tracks, sacrificing themselves for regiments, divisions, passes, towns.

He dozed in the saddle. He wondered whether Greenwood had reached Pawlu, whether even one of the half-dozen letters had ever found its way to that honorable, engaging and naive American.

. . . I shall be leaving China for good, with luck by way of Kunming and through Pawlu sometime around the New Year. I prefer not to leave Asia at once, or to deal directly with any government; governments, even yours, have a way of appropriating the goods and clapping the merchant into jail. Meet me. There will be rewards for you beyond simple academic distinction or publicity, and I cannot do this alone; I need you, for verification and to lend a bit more integrity to the enterprise than a Nationalist Chinese general can inspire alone.

Remember the world we share, the world of men who *do*. If you cannot meet me I shall proceed warily toward some understanding with the British, who may consider it a coup. Not, God knows, the Burmese or Indians or Pakistanis.

Dear old Greenwood: I owe you much. Allow me the opportunity to balance the books, as we Chinese traditionally do (or did) at the New

Year. I have thought of you often during the recent descent into Hell.

> Your friend and debtor,
> Yang Yu-lin

Now on the trail Yang dreamed of Switzerland. A small chalet overlooking a lake. Red shutters. Time to read, and to paint. An honorable retirement, earned, God knows.

There was also a place called Riverdale, near New York City. Many of his friends recommended it: stretches of lawn, trees, parks and views of a broad river, with the metropolis only minutes away, museums and galleries.

He remembered the Louvre, and a funny old painting of two patrician women naked to the waist, one tweaking the other's nipple. Odd people, foreigners. Paris, Paris.

He was a foreigner himself now, forever.

If Olevskoy's past life was more present to him than his present life, he was nonetheless aware of, and grateful for, a future. His considerations were at first encyclopedic, a new climate, language, cuisine, and then geopolitical: how would an out-of-practice prince govern a small province? He recalled Semenov out by Irkutsk, ruling his ephemeral quicksilver state by cruelty alone, shooting, flogging, raping, burning, yet surviving. An image resurged: raped Red women tied to the tracks to derail a Red train. Another: Reds burned alive in a church and Semenov growling, "They deserve worse! That's sacrilege!" Men, women and children, screaming and bellowing, and the stench afterward sickening. Semenov! A monster, really. And then to let himself be taken, just like that, as if weary of it all, by Russian troops dashing through Manchuria in 1945! After persisting so long! Even the devil grows old. He had been executed almost on the spot.

And the reoccupation of Peking, ah what a city! And this crazy General Yang with his footlockers. Three years' worth of footlockers, and the general wriggling his way in and out of battles, ambushes, disguises, provinces, now the motherland itself. "Shall we turn coat, Nicky?" But always with that broad grin; Yang would never join them.

Nor would Olevskoy, to be shot at dawn or strangled in a cell. No, far better this jaunt to the tropics, to a broad-leafed new world of slim and acquiescent women, half-naked, a sparkle in the eye, betel juice all over your—

With a despairing laugh at himself he settled into his reverie. Here in the south girls would mature more rapidly, so he had heard, more rapidly than Varya and Katya. He daydreamed a tropical variation of the theme with which he habitually beguiled tedious hours on horseback: at what age a young paramour's pupilage might commence.

"Smoke," said General Yang, peering off to the south.

"Wild Wa?" It was a single faint tendril.

"Too soon. Push on."

"Yessir." Major Wei inhaled vast quantities of mountain air.

General Yang rallied him: "I believe you're enjoying yourself."

"I am, General, I am. New places, new ways!
How many travel to the ends of the earth to
achieve their heart's desire?"

"Few indeed. And what is this heart's desire?"

"How can I know until I arrive?" Wei laughed,
a deep boom.

General Yang awaited an echo; none came. He
was blue, gloomy. Not because his army had now
been pared to thirty-three; they were superfluous
in any case. Not because he had, when all was
said and done, been chased ignominiously from
the homeland he had spent his life defending; it
was no longer his China. He was not hungry or
cold or lonely; just blue.

Reminiscing does it, he reflected. The memory
of Taierhchuang obsessed him like an erotic
fantasy, and Taierhchuang would never come
again. Hand to hand, they had fought! Chinese
troops, trained to withdraw, retreat, flee, desert,
had stood their ground with bayonets. Not
Colonel Yang himself; he was commanding a
regiment of the old 31st Division—ah, by the
gods, the 31st! General Chih, furious with these
monkeys, and three-fourths of the rural Shan-
tung town in Japanese hands, and Yang's regiment holding the rest, inspired or resigned,
awaiting—hoping for—the "flanking and en-
circling movement of high-speed motorized battalions"; incredulous when these units did move
at high speed, did flank, did encircle; dizzy,
almost hysterical, when the Japanese 5th
Division, diverted from another action, was

driven back and dispersed; and all but insane
with pride when the whole Chinese force merged,
obeying orders, and cut the invaders to pieces.

Sergeant Chang and Corporal Pao were by now
good friends; the matter of the corporal's medal
had become a joke, and as the story made the
rounds—a chestful of Orders of the Tripod—Pao
even admitted sheepish embarrassment. Like
their fellows—privates first, second and third
class; corporals; sergeants; master sergeants—
they now viewed life with wide eyes, happy to be
alive, appalled to be leaving China, jittery about
the Communist flying columns, fearing the
future yet excited by the adventure of it. Their
stride was brisker, their eye sharper. As their
number dwindled, they seemed to become
General Yang's intimate friends. "I think I like
this," the sergeant confided. "It is better than
war," the corporal agreed. "How do you suppose
it will end?" the sergeant asked. "Well, I am a
farm boy," the corporal said, "and may find myself a nice piece of land somewhere."

"A fine idea in this climate," Sergeant Chang
approved. "I am a Manchurian, you know, and I
can remember fields too hard to plow as late as
May."

The corporal shivered theatrically. "I am a
Cantonese myself, and accustomed to sunny
skies."

"That is why you talk so oddly."

"No, no: it is *you* who talk oddly."

They shared a cigarette, and agreed that they
would be learning a new language shortly. They
also agreed that there had never, at least in

modern times, been as good a general as Yang
Yu-lin; that the colonel was a martinet but
trustworthy in combat; and that the general
would never desert them in time of danger but
the colonel just might.

His back pains alarmed the general. He recalled a kidney stone, excruciating, and here he
was at the back of beyond. A long day's ride.
Winding into the hills they had traveled some
thirty miles, by his guess, and covered half that or
less as the crow flew. They seemed to be at four
thousand feet or so. Would his old lungs wheeze,
his old heart pump painfully at nine thousand?

The pack mule had plodded its steady way. The
general held it in affection. Now at night the footlockers were off-loaded and flanked his head as
he lay in aching repose. The stars were innumerable, a thick white carpet.

Major Wei approached, bearing rice, chicken,
dried plums and hot tea. Groaning, the general
sat up.

"How awful to make this journey in monsoon
time," the major observed.

Up, and up. Yang's heart did not labor; it leapt
at vista after gorgeous vista. He had traveled
these hills in 1944, but under distracting
pressure; their majesty had escaped him. Now he
was awed. Range upon range of black, purple,
pink, green hillsides and crests. Nothing over ten
thousand feet, he knew that from his maps; yet
this was surely enough, and the fetch of them,
the infinity, stopped his breath. Could the Alps
surpass them? He imagined them clad in snow.

The downward prospect also stopped his breath. The trail was for the most part a good two paces wide, and wound undemandingly through shallower slopes; but now and then he found himself at the edge of a true declivity, peering down into the abyss of a deep valley and suppressing a shiver.

Late one afternoon they reached the crest, some ninety-five hundred feet, and General Yang Yu-lin was rewarded by a sixty-mile panorama. South of him rolled range after range again, gorge after gorge. Through one of those gorges wound the great Salween. He judged that he was still in China, but it would not be long now. Exile. All downhill hereafter to the Salween. Twenty miles more? Southwest, then west.

He instructed Major Wei to make camp here, on the crest, that the men might contemplate the world's grandeur. Do not forget, however, fodder for beast and soldier alike. Tell the men to bundle up. This night will be frosty.

To the south, another tendril of smoke.

Olevskoy's pedagogical speculations had been supplanted by a sudden nostalgia for blond women. The trouble with being a lord in the Orient was the eternal sameness: black hair, probably bangs, high cheekbones, epicanthic fold, unvarying submission. The demands of survival: do as the foreign lord wishes. In retrospect blond women seemed to him fiery, rebellious, self-assertive and delightfully cruel. European. They drove autos and bore arms and voted; they smoked cigarettes and drank cocktails; some were aggressive in bed. Faint after-images of his

youth fleeted across his memory—Katya,
Varya—a third of a century and more.

He tried to recapture the imagined face of his
fledgling Burmese mistress, but her features had
blurred.

The winding descent, the dizzying spiral to the
river, was horrific, a nightmare. Yang thanked
his gods that the weather held fair and dry; one
good rain and they must all have perished
ignobly, cart-wheeling off slick trails down soggy
slopes, piling together in the valley; bones indeed, in great heaps. The animals pawed
cautiously, halted to sniff and whicker, proceeded with resigned deliberation, or so it
seemed. Yang watched his footlockers bob and
sway before him and tried to calculate how many
miles they had traveled, and wondered what he
would do if they were suddenly cast off, if the
mule stumbled.

Well, he would surely proceed to the floor of
the valley and retrieve what he could. Imagine a
paleontologist, next century, finding those bones
in a gorge near the Salween! History's tricks.
Two fiercely contending schools, one (the
Patriots) contending that these bones represented an early southwest China civilization; the
other (the Cosmopolites) insisting that because
these were identical to the bones of Peking Man,
to the measurements, the plaster casts, the
photographs, and were indeed and indubitably
the bones of Peking Man, either they had arrived
at the Salween by some process of deep mystery
and teleportation or Peking Man had *walked* the
whole way.

Yang laughed aloud. Suppose, he speculated, suppose these bones were carried to Peking by some holy man a thousand years ago. From Africa, from South America, from anywhere. Suppose Peking Man was Japanese!

"Many a time I have carried them," Olevskoy told Major Ho. "You know what the old man has been through—dressing as a woman, passing across the lines, wearing tatters and claiming to be my coolie. More than once I have helped him shift a load, and those chests are extremely light. He has carried them both himself, many times, slung fore and aft, or on a yoke, or one in either hand."

"Diamonds, it must be diamonds."

Olevskoy shook his head certainly. "Of course not. So many gems would weigh a hundred catties. A fortune in diamonds covers the palm of a hand; a sockful of diamonds is uncountable wealth. Well, surely not gold, and if objets d'art—"

"What is that?"

"What did I say?" Olevskoy was amused; he would no longer be sure what language he spoke.

"Ob-zay da."

"Valuable pieces of ancient art. But the lockers have been dropped and flung; swaying from the yoke, they have banged walls and wagons. Let me tell you, there is a streak of the elf in our general. When he spoke of the bones of his ancestors, he was telling the truth, in some obscure way."

"Bones?" Ho was stunned.

"In some obscure way," Olevskoy repeated.

Wei came racing back up the trail, overwhelming his mount, a huge mule. "What a moment! I want to ride with you around this bend." He backed his mule, swung downhill again.

Yang said, "Ah," and was too moved even to smile. They were rounding a bluff, the trail comfortable, a few old washouts but always room to skirt danger. He followed Wei. Four o'clock, and the sun westering fast in these mountains. Yang was hungry. A good sign. Sick men lost appetite. He rounded the last outcropping.

The Salween was majestic. Even from a thousand feet up, its white fury challenged the heart: it leapt and boiled, frothed and raced, deep in its purple gorge. It defied the wanderer: you are only man, I am river.

After a time Wei said dubiously, "I suppose it can be forded."

"That is what trails are for," Yang confirmed. "There will be a bowl, a little floodplain, a flattening, and the stream will slow." Yang twisted in the saddle. Behind him the mule stood, cloudy of intellect, unbowed by its easy burden.

"You must remember," Olevskoy said to Ho, "he is an old man now. Not even a general; we are all refugees."

"Then you are not a colonel."

"No. I am once more a prince."

"He keeps them always in sight," Ho said, "or leaves Wei to stand guard. Never me. And there are ropes and locks."

"An occasion will present itself." Olevskoy squinted, scanning hillsides. "Do you know what I might want if I were General Yang?"

Major Ho waited.

"I might want to arrive in this Pawlu with my footlockers and a small, easily disposable bodyguard."

Major Ho exhaled in noisy dismay. Such perfidy from his General Yang?

Olevskoy said, "So you like the women, do you?"

It was as Yang had predicted. The riverbed broadened, perhaps deepening too, and the rush and roll of the angry water fell to an even flow. Its banks amazed the men, brilliant sand, scattered boulders, monolithic slabs.

The trail resumed a quarter-mile or more downstream. A long sandy spit jutted from the far shore almost to midstream. On this side the trail ran for another half-mile; crossing to this shore one would be borne downstream from the spit. The general seemed to remember this ford, yet with puzzlement, the geography askew, perhaps a trick of the memory, perhaps a shift of the sands.

There were violent eddies off the point, but the sharp bend in the river assured that anyone even halfway across would be swept—perhaps drowning but not lost—ashore on that beckoning strand. "Imagine this in monsoon time," he said. Perhaps that was it: a different season. "Even here at this wide stretch—eight or ten feet higher, and all this under water."

"I always heard that the air of the Salween's valleys was poisonous," Major Wei said.

"Rivers breed legends. Dragons. Plagues. Spells and curses."

"With permission, sir, we ought to drive a donkey into the river and see what becomes of him."

"Not a bad notion," Yang said, "but surely not before lunch. We have more than that to do. We shall rest today and cross tomorrow."

They did drive a donkey into the stream. He, naturally, made every effort to turn back, and had to be pelted with stones, and the water behind him made frothy by rifle fire and finally a grenade; frantically the beast struck out then, swimming, braying, choking and blowing, aimless and terrified; the current rammed him ashore near the tip of the strand; he scrambled to dry land and stood indignant.

Yang, Olevskoy, Wei and Ho spent the rest of that afternoon planning a tactical exercise of much beauty, considering the resources and techniques at hand. "No air cover," said Yang. The exercise was minutely detailed. The majors instructed the sergeants. The sergeants instructed the common soldiers. They all gobbled a noisy dinner, turned in early, left small fires to burn down. Before the midnight moonrise, by starshine and in silence, a fire team crossed, swimming, led by Major Wei. Their orders were to dig in on the beach, with scouts to melt into the screen of oaks and evergreens.

Before dawn the second wave, under Colonel Olevskoy, followed. This was risky beneath a waning gibbous moon, but every man and every weapon on both banks covered the move. Olevskoy's men landed, fanned out, and set up machine guns.

At first light Yang and the main body crossed. Yang sat his pony insouciantly, the footlockers ingeniously hitched to his own shoulders, high and dry fore and aft. His insouciance was slightly demented: if he was killed, if he should lose the footlockers . . .

Major Wei, exultant, waved his automatic rifle. He was a large handsome man in rude health crossing borders, and dawn was as good a time as any to be a soldier.

"Not bad," Olevskoy conceded. "Our last maneuver."

He was proved wrong within the day. Alert now to signs of Wild Wa, Yang sent scout teams flanking wide, and when the southerly team stumbled on a gang of well-armed bandits and opened fire immediately, the ruffians—some said four, some seven, some ten—fled firing and galloped directly toward the main body, which, ready and waiting, wrought destruction. The brigands wheeled and flew, leaving two dead behind. Olevskoy suggested taking their heads as an offering to the Wild Wa: one was swarthy and mustached, a striking specimen, and the other fat and bald. Yang opined that parading through these mountains with heads on pikes was less refined, and more bellicose, than he cared to appear.

Sergeant Chang approached then, diffidently, with the day's bad news: one of the scouts had taken a bandit's lucky snap shot full in the chest, and was dead.

They bore the body to General Yang, the body of a corporal from Honan, a scrawny farm boy conscripted to fight Communists. The men

gathered in soldiers' silence, and Yang said a few
words, and they buried him there, just off the
trail, in a glade ten miles from the majestic Salween, a long way from home, but what dead man
is not?

They rode on, wearied. Olevskoy napped,
nodding in time to his pony's steps. In the main
Yang was honest; he had not lied about his intentions, merely been smoky. Too smoky?
Shifty? An honest man and a fine general mais
tout de même que'qu'chose de louche ici. This
Pawlu: were they Wild Wa, perhaps? Was Yang
leading the column into a lion's den? Most
logically Yang would attach himself to an opium
run and push on to Lashio and Mandalay. But
what then? What was in those footlockers? His
future.

Olevskoy reverted to his sexual reveries.
Would it be possible, he wondered, to create a
young woman who literally could not sleep
without it? Two of them, perhaps, each renewing
the other's ardor. No, no. Perverse.

General Yang's pony ambled along as if retired
from a mail route, and the general let himself be
lulled. He had begun to recognize the country-
side, mainly by looking back, as he had seen it
first while entering China; stretches of trail now
seemed familiar, and oddly contoured hilltops.
Within half a day they should strike a green
valley running south, perhaps brown at this
season, but fringed by stately mountain oaks.

At need he could set the footlockers one atop
the other on his knees. Even the smallest aircraft

would suffice. He spun visions: a landing field, a car purring, a warm hotel with a cocktail bar, no, not a bar, what did they call it? A lounge, a cocktail lounge. A tailor then. A small house, eventually, with a view of mountains or river, perhaps both, classically Chinese, all those scrolls of mountains and rivers, the single gnarled tree, the single fishing boat. A salon facing south and a studio facing north. Perhaps he would marry again, perhaps a housekeeper would do. The promptings of the flesh were feeble now and intermittent, to say the least; was he only tired, or truly aging?

Well, much to do still. Wild Wa, Pawlu, Olevskoy, thirty-three—no, thirty-two now—men learning freedom and perhaps rebellion. His control more tenuous, less satisfying each day. Only let Greenwood be there! He could handle Greenwood. Major Wei: he must do something generous for Major Wei.

They were strung out along a slope, shambling westward and scanning ridges and valleys to the south, when they saw, high on the next ridge, half a mile from them and a bit below, three short, dark men—presumably men—surely men, as the glasses focused, with straight black hair and wide, flat noses. Yang lowered the glasses. "One rifle. A crossbow, I think. The village higher on the ridge: you can see smoke."

"I saw." Olevskoy emitted a scornful, sickened grunt. "Wild Wa! Wild animals!"

"With a religion," Yang said, "and a strict moral code."

"That's about eight hundred meters," Olevskoy

said. He called to a corporal. "Your rifle."

"A vain and foolish cruelty," Yang said.

Olevskoy sighted and fired; donkeys bucked.

"High," Yang said, "and see them scatter! They disppeared into the brush like rabbits." The glasses fell to his chest. "Possibly a good idea. The warning shot across the bow."

"Animals," Olevskoy said.

And that was all: two days more, six meals, two nights' deep sleep in the nippy mountain air. Yang suffered fresh pangs at each landmark. He had been five years younger. It seemed an infinity of time, as if he had aged by a generation in those five years. He led them down and down, to a grassy plateau that seemed a valley and that gave way to accommodating foothills, rolling and green even in winter, and then along shadowed, verdant trails by a whispering brook. He halted the column, turned to encourage his men with a wave and a smile, and led them up onto a road. A serious, broad road, suitable for civilian horsemen, for merchants' carts. The men exclaimed. He led them south.

Between the lines of cage they halted. In silence they contemplated the grotesque human heads in their tiny barred bamboo cells, like counters in some grisly game. The afternoon light fell clear on the living, and sharpened each wrinkle in flesh or cloth, polished each glitter of metal, blanched the skin's pallor. General Yang realized that they were all exhausted, physically and morally. Not sleepless; not diseased; not starved; in Fang-shih most had found food, women, liquor, beds. A deeper exhaustion, an exhaustion of years and not of weeks. They were strong, healthy men, yet a company of ghosts, exiled and empty. A chill fell upon his heart.

So this was the end of the odyssey, the epic journey: Peking, Paris, thirty years of army life, innumerable wars that constituted in truth one long war: Shanghai and Taierhchuang, Burma and again Peking, Manchuria and Huai-Hai and Kunming and the Salween, barracks and tents and hotels and hovels, and now this road lined with miniatory gibbets and gory bandits' heads. Welcome, General Yang. Welcome to the future.

"We shall bivouac east of the road," he told Olevskoy, "and we shall not cross the road without permission."

Olevskoy was startled. "Pawlu?"

"Pawlu," said General Yang.

10

Rendezvous in Pawlu

The Sawbwa was inclined to give great weight to Green Wood's opinions, this because his own, though tenaciously held, were few; and because he was grateful, Green Wood being American and the Sawbwa clearly remembering that Americans were good; and because he was still ashamed that when, at Green Wood's advent years before, a natural indifference to fine foreign distinctions had led Wan to refer to "this Englishman," the Sawbwa had stubbornly detested the foreigner for three months.

Later the gods had offered unmistakable signs that the Sawbwa was forgiven his sins of snobbery and prejudice: Green Wood had left Pawlu upon a rumor of war and had then, miraculously, returned with a trove of arms, in the guise of a warrior, roaming the Shan States, doing good works and coming home always to Pawlu. The arrival of the general and his enthusiastic participation in actions against the Japanese, the Wild Wa and stray bandits had also gratified the Sawbwa. He had noted that it pleased old Phewin, Huchot's successor, Wan and Kin-tan as well, though he was never certain why. (It was because General Yang had cheerfully placed himself under Green Wood's command. This eminent humility, not to mention good sense, was a rarity at any level, and won the general not merely respect but outright affection.)

So now four years and more after the war, in a cold month and the poppies ripe, the Sawbwa sent for Green Wood, and once more the council sat about a fire before the Sawbwa's house. He was delighted with this gathering, like a grandfather, and rejoicing in Green Wood's return he forgot Naung's news, and was disconcerted to hear Naung say, "Well, Green Wood. Your general has arrived."

"No!" Greenwood's arms rose in ritual gratitude. "By the gods! Is this true?" So the old man had won through! Lost countless battles, crossed countless bridges, slugged his way through provinces and clawed his way over mountains, and here he was! Greenwood's luck! If it had held this far, it would hold to the end; suddenly and certainly he knew that. "Is he here in the village?"

From the north Lola twinkled toward them.

"He is across the road from East Poppy Field."

Wan and Kin-tan did not appear suitably joyful.

Greenwood asked, "What is it? There is trouble. Is he wounded? Sick?"

'He enjoys good health," Naung said regretfully. "He is not alone."

Za-kho joined them and set a jug of rum before Naung, who plied it and passed it along.

"Of course not," Greenwood said. Rum at sunset; Shan; mountains; Loi-mae and Lola; Yang and the bones! "His bodyguard."

Naung waited until Greenwood was in the act of drinking, and said, "A bodyguard of thirty-two fully armed soldiers, one of whom is a Big Nose and a colonel."

Greenwood lowered the jug.

Lola scampered into the circle, hugged Naung and came to cuddle Greenwood. Playfully she grasped the jug.

"Wait, Lola," Greenwood said softly. "Not now."

"Thirty-two," Naung said. "Four light machine guns, automatic rifles, a full range of rifles, carbines, side arms and grenades, and a sufficiency of ammunition."

Lamely Greenwood said, "Gifts for Pawlu?"

"You speak foolishness."

"And an American colonel?"

"American or Englishman or Frenchman, who can tell?"

"The general is a man of good bones," Wan said.

"All the same," Naung said, "no one enters or leaves Pawlu without my permission."

Within the crook of Greenwood's arm, Lola too was subdued.

The Sawbwa cleared his throat, croaked, and sat taller. "As to that, the Sawbwa has a word to say." He had quickened; it was as if his blood had begun to flow again after many years. "Naung is my First Rifle," the Sawbwa began.

"Pawlu's," Naung interrupted.

"But Yang is my friend and may call Pawlu home. To turn away friends is to offend the gods and nats, and would bring wrath and shame to our village."

"It is not the general," Kin-tan said. "The general may share my house and my cook-pot. He is a friend, as you say. But thirty-two armed men!"

"Where are they camped?" Greenwood asked.

"In the clearing by the white-pebbled stretch of stream, just across the road," Naung said. "I have tripled the guard and postponed the harvesting of yen. Maybe"—he brightened visibly—"the Wild Wa will wipe them out."

Greenwood made a sick mouth. "Thirty-two!"

The Sawbwa said, "With Green Wood he beat off the Wild Wa, in the last year of the Japanese, before the monsoon."

"Thirty-two," Naung echoed, ignoring the Sawbwa, "and they have come bumbling through the forest like a herd of elephants and brought a war party of Wild Wa behind them."

"They seem unaware of this," Wan said.

"Out of season," Kin-tan said. "The Wild Wa are even now preparing niches in their cursed oak trees."

Greenwood sat cold and empty. He tightened his embrace; Lola snuggled. "May I go to him?"

"No."

"May he—"

"Not yet. It must be thought on."

"It is the Sawbwa who must decide," Za-kho rebuked Naung.

Naung said bluntly, "I think not."

The Sawbwa frothed only slightly. "To deny order in the morning is to invite chaos in the evening."

"It is I who must fight, and Wan and Kin-tan and the men, and it is we who will say." Naung's voice trembled; his anger pressed upon them all.

"Yet we owe the general much," Wan said, "and it is true that Pawlu must pay it debts or face future afflictions."

"We must learn his plans," Kin-tan said, "and his men's, and we must discover the nature of this foreigner."

"So much I concede," Naung said.

"That is well," said the Sawbwa. "To rage at a small flame is to fan a great fire. As lustful desire clouds the brain, so heedless hatred fogs the judgment."

Naung said, "Bugger."

"Let Pawlu betray its benefactors and we shall drink the wind," the Sawbwa went on. "In a dissolute age the honest beggar is the gods' favorite."

Naung said, "Bugger again."

"The general may come here. And the foreigner if he is not an Englishman or a Frenchman."

Naung pondered. "That too I concede. But I do not concede that these outlanders may call Pawlu home. Green Wood, I want the truth. Every man here and your own daughter will listen, so tell me the truth or make your peace with your gods. You came here to find your general and take him out?"

"No more and no less," Greenwood said promptly. "With no evil intent. This I swear by the life of my daughter." He rubbed Lola's head. "But thirty-two men! My heart shrinks."

"So does mine," said Naung, "but my guard triples. Well then. This I propose, o Sawbwa!"

The mockery was lost; the Sawbwa thawed.
Naung's glance was for Wan and Kin-tan. "Green
Wood will not leave the village; this, as a bar to
evil communications. He may send a message,
and we can bring his general and his colonel
under escort. They will concert plans immediately to leave Pawlu and take their rabble with
them. These soldiers are not to cross the road
and will be shot down like pye-dogs if they do
so."

"That is what I recommend," the Sawbwa said.
Wan and Kin-tan agreed.
"Three days," Naung said to Greenwood.

Greenwood kept his peace and contented himself with visits to old friends, Na-yuan the blind
woman, Kung the one-armed veteran, Chung's
daughters, whom he praised appropriately and
warned of Jum-aw's citified wiles. He chatted
with Chung, he chatted with Loi-mae and Lola.
He slept badly, stimulated by Yang's arrival,
tense at Naung's hostility, depressed by insistent
forebodings, odd spurts and pricks of shame and
guilt. All that night, it seemed, dusky Wild Wa
slipped into his nightmare like personal demons
to mock and menace.
Next morning he tramped heavy-eyed to
Naung's house, where he drank tea and ate twice-
cooked fish. His manner with Loi-mae, and hers
with him, were the easy ways of old friends, and
Greenwood felt that it would be possible after all
to do no harm. Lola chattered, wore the Japanese
officer's hat at a perky tilt, showed Greenwood
how her breasts wer budding. When he left for
the Sawbwa's house, Loi-mae hugged him tight.

Always, he felt at that moment, there would be
love and trust, and the rest, the panting and
gymnastics, was perhaps not as important as he
had once believed.

"I attend council with my father," Lola announced. Her tone was peremptory. "And I wear
my Japanese cap."

Loi-mae pursed her lips, but said, "Why not?"

"She will be safe with me," Greenwood said,
scowling. "Just let that Weng-aw even smile at
her!"

Lola pranced and preened.

The morning drifted by. Tension hung like
mist. On the slopes and in the common field, men
went armed, and some of the women carried
daggers, or a dah slung through a waist sash. The
high command—Naung, Wan, Kin-tan—was nowhere to be seen.

The Sawbwa sat before his house in ceremonial dress, his Pawnee headband natural and
appropriate. Za-kho attended him like a body
servant. Greenwood and Lola strolled not far
from them, pausing once for a game of jack-
straws with dry reed stems. All along the slopes,
and in clumps or couples on the field, villagers
consulted and smoked. The sun inched higher in
a bright, wintry sky: January in the mountains,
yet warm enough to strip away the blouse.

It was not a cry or a stir that warned them but
an eddy in the tension, a ripple, hoofbeats sensed
but not yet heard. Heads turned, and groups
drew together. Greenwood said, "They come."

Lola clutched his hand beside the Sawbwa and
Za-kho. Far across the grass, just this side of Red

Bullock Pass, a a procession emerged, a squad of horsemen, Naung leading, Wan and Kin-tan on the wings, and in the center, side by side, the general, oddly bulky, and a foreigner. The Shan wore blue, the guests—prisoners?—khaki. The ponies proceeded at a walk. Excitement grew among the villagers, and cries rose. Someone shouted, "Hey, Smiler! Welcome back!" and then they were all shouting, waving, crowding close to the line of march as if to fling blossoms. Yang did smile then, his best effort, and a cheer erupted.

Greenwood saw that the general had contrived a sling and was wearing footlockers. One jounced against the paunch, another hung behind. The hoofbeats were firm and sharp now on the winter turf.

Za-kho said, "General Yang is carrying chests."

"Ah! Ah! Gifts!" The Sawbwa clapped hands.

Gifts indeed, Greenwood thought, and then the cavalcade was upon them and he was meeting Yang's lively gaze. Naung rode proudly and formally. Behind him the foreign colonel sat tall on a Yunnan pony. All dismounted at one time, General Yang sliding to the ground, steadying his footlockers. He reminded Greenwood of a street vendor, display case up front, spare stock hanging behind.

All observed the proprieties. General Yang stepped first to the Sawbwa, bowed and exchanged with him fraternal pats on the shoulder. The Sawbwa uttered chirps of joy, as did Za-kho. Naung and the Shan warriors, neutral, sat their ponies and waited. The other foreigner was a colonel in Chinese uniform, a cold man and pale. His presence enraged

Greenwood. Another Occidental here! Greenwood was also alarmed. A capable colonel leading thirty-odd survivors . . .

General Yang came before Greenwood, ex-
tricated himself from looped ropes and let the
footlockers slide gently to earth, an offering at
Greenwood's feet. For a long moment the village
was still while the two friends rejoiced in silence.
Far away a peacock shrilled. For that moment all
under a bright heaven stood well.

"By God, you did it," Greenwood said.

"Hot dog," said the general, and it set them off,
broke the spell; they guffawed like schoolboys,
shaking hands, embracing.

Yang broke away and glared down at Lola.
"And who is this woman?" he asked fiercely in
his primitive Shan. "Who is this beauty?"

Greenwood said, "It is no woman. It is merely
my daughter, Lola."

Yang said, "Nonsense! Your daughter, Lola, is
a child. This is a lovely woman!" And he swept
her up, tossing her high while she laughed and
cried out, "O Yang! Welcome, old Smiler! What
have you brought me?"

Even Naung laughed.

Warily Greenwood took stock of the bizarre
foreigner, who was observing all this with a fixed
smile and a flare of the nostrils, as if viewing a
mirage, or a vision.

When everyone had said "Blessings and greetings!" a dozen times and all backs save he
colonel's had been slapped, and Lola was riding
on Yang's shoulders, and it had just struck
Greenwood as ridiculous but also possibly sub-

lime that his best friends in the world should be Yang, Wan, Kin-tan, Mong—at that instant Yang said quietly in English, "These footlockers must not leave the village. Find a way to ensure that I too remain. House arrest, hostage, honored guest, anything."

Greenwood said, "Yes." He was observing Mong, who had decided to cast an inquisitive glance upon the colonel.

The colonel's chin rose; distaste warped his features, as if Mong smelled bad.

Mong's chin rose; he mimicked the colonel perfectly.

"You must present me to your colonel," Greenwood said quickly.

The colonel, a head taller than most, the officers' kepi lending him a rigid, posed appearance, snubbed Mong and said to Greenwood, "Colonel Prince Nikolai Andreevich Olevskoy. Your servant." "Colonel," he said, and he was obviously, icily, nobody's servant. He was taller than Greenwood and fairer, his hair almost platinum, his eyes blue-gray.

"I'm Greenwood." Neither offered to shake hands.

Behind Greenwood the Sawbwa asked, "Is this an Englishman?"

Greenwood said, "No, a Russian."

For another startled instant no one spoke. Then, even more startling, the Sawbwa burst into a flood of some language not Shan.

"What says the Sawbwa?"

Yang spoke: "That Russians are good, according to a certain Shang, who revealed this to him long ago. Odd that he should suddenly break into Yunnan Chinese. He is positively vehement at this grand conjunction—Green Wood! The Smiler! And a Russian!"

Greenwood asked, "Who is Shang?"

"His nat," Naung said, "his demon and familiar spirit."

Greenwood explained this to the visitors.

Meanwhile the Sawbwa made his way to Olevskoy, placed a trembling hand on his shoulder and spoke in Shan.

Naung snarled. They all heard it.

Olevskoy seemed to find the hand repellent, soiled or diseased. "What was all that?"

Greenwood answered. "He says that Pawlu is your home."

"Good God," said Olevskoy. "Thank him for me."

Greenwood did so, with ceremony, and then said, "Let us sit upon the ground. Za-kho, will you will see to a fire and beer, and some pineapple? Mong, will you ask Jum-aw to tend the ponies?"

After the beer and pineapple Ang-ang the Woman-in-Common served sizzling strips of gingered goat, bowls of boiled rice, tea and rum. A ring of spectators gathered: half the village. Greenwood saw with amusement that the Russian prince was fretting.

"They're a friendly people. Only curious."

"I am unarmed," Olevskoy brooded, "on new ground."

"You won't need arms. You have no enemies here."

"On a frontier there is always an enemy." The

Russian sucked at his rum. "Even among the salt of the earth."

"They are folk of good bones," Yang said, "and much honor among them."

"Savages. Tattoos."

Greenwood let his jacket fall open.

"Good God," Olevskoy said again. "A man of the people."

"Exactly right. They call themselves 'the people' and they have made me one of them."

"How democratic. You Americans, treating all the world's ills with your clammy liberal poultices."

Leebral pawltices. Probably this prince heard his own voice as that of an English gentleman. "Not quite," Greenwood said. Hating America was an international pastime; he had learned that since the war. If you want a man to hate you, save his life. "We do tend to meddle, but we pass along a little science and art and home rule. Not to mention money."

"All commerce and gasconade," Olevskoy said. "There is only fucking and dying."

The shock of it, the searing flash of profound, appalling truth, stopped Greenwood's breath. He recovered: "The rest is so everybody can do both well."

The Shan listened intently. The ring of them was denser. Greenwood stroked Lola's hair.

"Look at them!" Olevskoy was enraged. "Regardez-moi ces sauvages. Et ce sawbwa qui n'est pas sawbwa. C'est un *starosta*, un petit chef de village, et de plus imbecile."

Naung was puffing at a cheroot, his face blank.

"English, Colonel. No secrets from Greenwood."

"No French?"

"Sorry." Greenwood was curt. "What was all that?"

"This sawbwa is no sawbwa, only a half-witted village headman."

"The conversation has taken a low turn," Yang complained. He smiled at the Sawbwa, who dithered happily.

"Avec mes trente hommes je vais prendre ce village," Olevskoy muttered.

Yang said, "No more war, Colonel."

The field was sunny and warm; children scampered and shouted. To the Sawbwa Greenwood said, "Yang and I would share a house. Can that be?"

Naung said, "The Russian does not sleep in Pawlu," and the warriors stiffened at this rude disregard of the Sawbwa.

Olevskoy asked, "What was all that?"

"I asked if you could sleep here," Greenwood lied. "I'm afraid they won't have it."

"I sleep with my men," Olevskoy said. "I don't require the company of savages."

Yang said, "Poor Nicky. What a foul mood. How grumpy and unTolstoyan."

"That one!" Olevskoy spat.

Greenwood, ever the diplomat, said, "One of the glories of Russia, isn't he?"

For an instant Olevskoy left them, and traveled far; melancholy crossed his face, and unmistakable anguish. Then he said, "A fool. In the greatest novel ever written about a woman he had Venus rising in the west!"

From the edge of the field Loi-mae called: "Lola! Lola!"

Lola glanced casually in other directions and settled back against Greenwood's shoulder.

Naung said, "Lola. Go to your mother."

Lola pouted.

"Do as Naung says," Greenwood told her.

Naung scowled.

Lola hopped up and made tiger faces, growling and clawing the air before Greenwood.

"There is no doing anything with the children these days," Wan said. "Shall I beat her?"

Lola dashed at Wan, fell upon him with a hug and knocked him backward. She then sprang up, bowed to the Sawbwa and danced three romping steps, arms outflung, braids spinning and glinting rusty gold in the sunshine, eyes alight with youthful excitement, moist lips parting over perfect white teeth unstained by betel. She danced back to the crowd of warriors and, as they parted, down the lane they made to Loi-mae. The Shan warriors chuckled and murmured, "Good! Good!"

Olevskoy shook a long cigarette from a cardboard box, dropped it, retrieved it, thumbed his wooden match. It flared. His lips were dry on the paper mouthpiece.

"Thirty-two men!" Greenwood, Yang and the footlockers were alone at last, at sunset in the House of the Dead.

"How could I know what lay before me?" Yang demanded. "Communists. Bandits. Ambitious police. How many letters reached you?"

"Three. Hong Kong, Macao, Tokyo."

"I sent six. It was the only way, you know. We were well and truly cut off. January now; my last chance of air transport was Shanghai in May. To Formosa, where the high command would have abused me for a common criminal and whisked those footlockers away. Je suis mal vu à l'archêveché, tu sais."

"Oh, stop the French. What was that?"

"The brass hats have always hated me."

Greenwood said, "You're grayer. White-haired, even."

"Venerable! You're softer, laddie."

"The academic life. This Russian."

"What of him?"

"I dislike him. Dog and cat. Also he looked at my daughter in a man's way. Is he insane?"

"No, only a prince," Yang said. "I too dislike him. I have never met a Russian that I liked. They are either bullies or bores. I trust they will not let him cross the road again."

"Does he know?" Greenwood indicated the footlockers.

"No one knows."

"Incredible. Shall I ask how you found them?"

"A Japanese. He wanted his freedom."

"You freed him?"

"Forever."

Greenwood sighed at the world's rude ways. "The padlocks?"

"My own. I sawed through the old ones. As I understand it, these bones were dug out of a hill called Chou Kou Tien near Peking, delivered to your marines in nineteen forty-one and run down to Tientsin for shipment to the States from Chinwangtao."

"Somewhere they vanished," Greenwood said. "They were to be loaded aboard a liner, the *President Harrison*, on the eighth of December."

"Of all days. Remember Pearl Harbor."

"Of all days. The Japanese fleet chased the *Harrison* and ran her aground down around Shanghai somewhere. As far as we know, these little boxes sat in a warehouse—"

"In Tientsin," Yang said, "behind several tons of civilian furniture, beds, cupboards, armoires, Western stuff that no Japanese would have in his house. My own Japanese was a colonel, but he was one of those fellows who *keep track*, the sort of man who likes to go through his own garbage for the thrill of finding a bent spoon or half a comb."

Greenwood's finger traced the letters, USMC. "Do you know what a benefactor you are? Do you know what you've done? What it means?"

"All in a day's work," Yang said. "Any boy scout would have done the same. All I ask is half a million dollars."

"I don't see how you managed."

"Nor do I. Two small children could not have been more trouble."

"Well," Greenwood said, "shall we?"

"You have photos?"

"Better." Greenwood unstrapped his pack.

Yang drew a metal necklace over his head. Keys clinked. He squatted. He opened one chest, then the second. He tossed aside paper wadding

and uncovered cardboard boxes. He opened
cardboard boxes and plucked out wads of cotton.
He held up a bone. He sniffed at it.

Greenwood passed him a sheaf of photos and
two plaster casts, and set aside a thick manila
envelope.

"A skull," Yang said, raising it into a shaft of
dying sunlight, "and this long one. A thighbone?"

"Yes." Greenwood took the skull with
reverence. Side by side, skull and cast were
identical, a small dent precisely where it should
be. "My God," Greenwood said. "My God, my
God."

"Switzerland," Yang said, as his smile
bloomed.

Greenwood said again, "My God."

Yang seated himself, leaning back against the
north wall. "A long journey we've had, he and I.
Tell me about him."

"Them. Little bits of about forty people." Carefully Greenwood rewrapped the skull. "Half a
million years old next month."

Yang said, "They don't look a day over three
hundred thousand."

"Sinanthropus pekinensis," Greenwood said.
"Chinese man from Peking. Not Homo sapiens,
but well on the way. I know a professor who has
a reconstruction hanging behind his desk, like a
skeleton in a doctor's office. He calls it Sin."

"Because it's Chinese."

"And because it's what everything is as old as."

Yang liked that.

"They were little fellows," Greenwood said.
"About five feet. Not deep thinkers but had a

fair-sized brain for the times. They knew how to make fire. We have reason to believe they experienced love."

"Poor fellows. And look at the result: half a billion Chinese."

"Not just sex," Greenwood said. "Bonds. Emotions. Let me catch my breath."

It was a moment beyond speech. Greenwood and Yang and these old friends; old bones. In the mortuary hut: fitting.

The two living men communed in silence. The bones slept on.

Yang asked, "How do you know they loved?"

"Inference," Greenwood said. "Riddles within riddles. They used fire. Lived in groups. Gathered and hunted and cooked, cooperated and crowded into caves, overcame a bad climate somehow, and survived. There must have been likes and dislikes, attachments, protective feelings. Maybe there were other tribes, another species even, that were the enemy and reinforced the bonds."

"On the frontier there is always an enemy," the general murmured. "Now what?"

Still dazed, Greenwood said, "Yang's luck. At noon tomorrow a plane will make its first run over Pawlu. I think tomorrow anyway. Is today Wednesday the eleventh?"

"I believe so," Yang said. "Dates don't seem to mean much in the presence of these bones. Will there be trouble with the Shan? That Naung is a tough soldier."

"All they want is to be rid of us. But there is plenty of trouble. Mine, not yours."

"Nonsense. One for all and all for one. We're

veterans of the old Fifty-fifth."

Greenwood handed him the manila envelope. "Letters, from the State Department and the university. If we're separated . . ."

"You have more to say."

"I can't leave my people with soldiers outside Pawlu and the Wild Wa prowling the woods. My daughter, my little woman, my brothers, even if that sounds foolish. I can't leave Pawlu under two dangers. Your troops: will they follow orders?"

"Not for long. Until today there was . . . mutual need. More: loyalty. They came here expecting to resupply, move out and when practicable go their own ways."

"With you or without you?"

"Without me. I was mysterious but not deceptive. I have now abdicated and they know it. Although . . ."

"Well?"

"They probably expect me to *do* something for them. Make these Wild Wa go away, provide an escort into Burma, something."

"Failing which, they'll turn to the colonel."

"That or disperse."

"They can't disperse," Greenwood said. "The Wild Wa would take thirty-two heads. And Naung won't let them into Pawlu."

General Yang bowed his head.

Naung said, "We should have killed all three in silence and attacked the Chinese immediately."

"You talk like a barbarian," the Sawbwa said, lucid tonight and even stern.

Wan spat betel juice. The fire hissed. Half a ten

of grim captains, cold sober now, were trying to
recall past lessons and forestall present dangers.
Kin-tan and Shwe had seen a bearded vulture
coast across the red sunset.

Kin-tan said, "We must narrow the heart here,
and slip between two fires. The Wild Wa never
edged so close; and these cursed Chinese are real
soldiers."

"Survivors, they are," Wan said. "The boys
fled; the men stood."

"It is the Chinese who will be scorched,"
Naung said. "They want Pawlu, I tell you. We
shall pin them down and let the Wild Wa play
among them."

This lightened the council's spirits.

"You would violate the laws of your
ancestors," said the Sawbwa. "Would you cease
to be Shan?"

"Bugger!" Naung said. "Never again admit a
foreigner. Shoot them on sight."

"Green Wood and Yang want only to leave,"
Kin-tan said.

"Now that they have brought these plagues
upon us!" Naung flared. "Running out! Well, let
who will, leave Pawlu; let none enter."

"That is sound," Wan said. "How painful is
life. Green Wood is one of us."

"Green Wood is not one of us," Naung said.
"Green Wood's is a world of machines and paper
money and women for sale. It is a world I know.
He is a buggering sightseer and no more."

"He has his tattoo."

"And his general and his footlockers—and
what are those to us? Worse than nothing:

danger. Green Woods come and go like the black flies in the tiger heat."

"They destroyed a whole Japanese village with one bomb."

"A town."

"Bigger than Kunlong."

"This one is no black fly," said Kin-tan, "and no destroyer of towns. After the war I rode with him to Kunlong and he grieved for that Japanese village. He wept for his own woman and child, and cried out for the Japanese women and children."

"That is long past and of no importance," Mong said. "It is time now to speak of seeds and not rind."

"Naung was a long time away," said Wan.

"Green Wood has a claim on Pawlu."

"Green Wood was more Sawbwa than the Sawbwa," said the Sawbwa.

"Green Wood has killed his Wild Wa."

"Green Wood, Green Wood, Green Wood!" Naung exploded. "Perhaps I should restore Loi-mae to this god!"

They smoked in silence.

"It is not for any other man to say," the Sawbwa declared. "But it is not contrary to custom or law, and generosity is in order and would please the gods."

"He could be useful tomorrow," Kin-tan said.

"He fights like a tiger."

"He did five years ago. Now he is a school-master and seeks eminence."

"For eminence what would a man not do?" asked Mong.

They pondered this foolishness.

"He will run out," Naung repeated.

"We had better talk to them."

"Yes," Naung said bitterly, "and I must fetch them myself. One does not *send for* a former First Rifle."

At the Chinese camp Olevskoy too had summoned a council, every man of his command. In the gathering dusk he had traced upon the ground what his soldier's eye had seen of Pawlu, the valley, the slopes, the upper stream and the lower, the great field, the Sawbwa's house. He sat between Majors Wei and Ho, and the men made a half-moon before them. "I warn you all," he said, "we have been abandoned. The general and the American have plans of their own. We will not see Yang Yu-lin again."

"Forgive me, Colonel," said Wei. "After so many years with the general I cannot immediately believe in this casual defection."

"It is not casual," Olevskoy said. "It was planned. And it is no defection because there is no China. There is consequently no Chinese army. He is not a general and I am not a colonel and you are not majors and sergeants and corporals. We are a band of homeless men who have done our job with some honor and are fighting our way across a border; and who is not our friend is our enemy." Matthew. An aged priest rose before him, and an ikon of Saint Matthew—he who is not with me is against me—an aged priest at Sobolyevo. An image of the girl blotted him out: Lola, budding. He drew in a deliberate, therapeutic breath of mountain air.

"We have posted no sentries," Major Ho observed.

"We are better off by the fire," Olevskoy said. "Sentries would be gutted one by one. Whatever is out there moves like the night itself. Do not wander. Even for the relief of nature, go two by two at least." Into the ark, two and two of all flesh, that is the breath of life, and why these echoes, why these warnings? Should he begin again to cross himself?

"I propose one day's delay before judgment," said Major Wei.

Olevskoy hardly heard him. The girl had distracted him again. "Yes, yes, one day, all right. Night watches close in, by the eight points of the wind. But remember this. We must act together. We cannot survive in ones and twos. We can fight our way down this road to God knows where, living on God knows what; or we can rule Pawlu."

"By force," said Major Wei.

"Of course."

"Villages are better ruled by consent."

Olevskoy emitted a vomitous gutteral. "Another Communist."

"Hardly," said Major Wei. "But you have seen what happens: the women and children grow sad and hostile, the men disappear, the police are picked off one by one, there are shots in the night, stabbings, accidents—"

"You have not seen what rules them now," Olevskoy said. "I have. A dim-witted old man and a religious moron with a shaven head. But you *have* seen that poppy field, and I tell you there is a richness in Pawlu: opium and paddy, livestock and tobacco, silver and jade, even a good fat woman for Major Ho."

The men made manly laughter; Major Ho smiled modestly.

Major Wei did not smile. "Twelve years have I been a soldier," he said. "Not for this."

Olevskoy soothed him. "We shall see what tomorrow brings." Her legs, beneath the longyi, would be slim, childish, barely downy. Taut, smooth thighs, and the long hair wrapped about her budding breasts and narrow waist, floating and fringing to her knees. The others vanished, thirty-five years of them. So it always proved; to princely hot blood each woman was the first woman and the rest had never existed; fat peasants; voracious army whores; Red women raped unyielding, biting and shouting, bludgeoned; European sluts in cities like Harbin, European courtesans in cities like Shanghai; thousands of nameless Oriental cunts; the wife of a British attaché; Siberian animals little more than Stone Age tribeswomen; past, vanished, annihilated by an imp.

Olevskoy was neither subhuman nor insane. He now mocked himself. But his eye glittered and his blood simmered.

"I suppose you had no choice," Greenwood was saying, "but it's a whole damn army."

Yang spoke wearily. "What can that matter? Think, laddie, think what we have here. What can you matter or I or even Pawlu?"

"You're wrong. These bones and this village—"

"Half a million years, you said. The oldest *group*, you said. Chou Kou Tien was a village too, you said, a village like Pawlu in its own way, five hundred thousand years ago. What does Pawlu give the world but opium? Mankind has just fought two long wars and killed some hundred million people in half a century, to very little effect; and you boggle at this risk? These bones are like a piece of the beginning of the universe.''

Greenwood's mind dwelt on Loi-mae and Lola, on the bonds of flesh, on Lola's leap to womanhood; on the Little River Mon and the seeded fish and the rum and tobacco and yen at nightfall. "I boggle," he said.

"Then back off," Yang said, "and stay here, but for God's sake help me first. Only help me aboard that plane. Greenwood! I am a retired general, a permanently defeated field marshal of lost causes. I have wasted a life! I am a human sacrifice to fools and knaves! I have nothing to show for decades of work, pain, wounds, idiot honor in a world of thugs—"

They started like thieves when Naung emerged from the night. "Blessings and greetings," said the Shan.

"Greetings and blessings."

"All is well? Do you require rum? tobacco? yen?"

"All is well," Greenwood said, "but these new dangers are my fault, or so it seems to me."

"The sentries are three-deep and the village stands safe," Naung said politely.

"Then sit," Greenwood invited him. "Be at home."

"In the House of the Dead?" Naung allowed a quick smile.

"Then command me."

"I cannot command you, and you know it."

"Then ask."

"I ask in the name of all: join our council."

When Greenwood had translated, the general said, "I will not leave these boxes."

Naung shrugged. "Bring them. And your weapons."

"Always," said the general.

So Naung and Greenwood and General Yang walked beneath the stars, each outlander bearing a footlocker. "So many stars," Greenwood said. "Like snow, like all the grains of sand on all the shores of all the seas."

"Or all the words in all the languages," Naung said.

Greenwood laughed, well rebuked, and shut up.

"Any one of us would give his life for Pawlu," Kin-tan said reasonably, "so we are prepared to give yours at need."

Greenwood found this inarguable, so did not protest.

"How simple was the war," said Mong.

"Now we must fight on two fronts," Wan said.

"And one of them is no front at all," Kin-tan said, "but a myriad of shadows. Green Wood: can we hire these Chinese?"

"Hire, perhaps. Not trust. Who rides the tiger . . ."

"Come to the point," said Mong. "What are your own plans? Tell me the truth, now."

"Remind me of one lie I have ever told you." Greenwood laid a firm hand on Mong's forearm.

"This quest for eminence," Mong muttered.

Mong was not often glum.

"I hope to put the general aboard an aircraft, with luck tomorrow, and to remain with you until these dangers are past."

"And the eminence?"

"And my tattoos? And my daughter? And my blood that sank into Shan soil?"

A rumble of approval cleared the air. This was oratory.

"Then to work," Kin-tan said briskly. "An order of battle."

"Let Green Wood speak," the Sawbwa said.

"Naung is First Rifle," Greenwood said.

"Green Wood fought the harder war," Naung said.

Greenwood, vigilant at this excessive courtesy, said, "Naung too has fought his wars, and here and now he is the better man. I wish that he and I had fought side by side in the big one."

"As to that"—briefly Naung's face lit up, elfin, v's and creases—"I am not sure to this day who was my friend and who my enemy."

General Yang sat between his footlockers. He obviously understood little of this, and seemed a weary intruder, a traveler tired of his journey, an old man in danger of flab and ennui.

"The boy Jum-aw could be useful," Wan said.

"He has been useful to my daughters," Mong said lugubriously, and the tension vanished in a rattle of laughter.

"No help for it," Kin-tan said. "We must sacrifice these Chinese."

"We cannot," said the Sawbwa.

"I stand with the Sawbwa," said Ko-yang. "He has invited the Russian."

"The Russian will not again enter Pawlu," Naung said.

It was in the open now, but this was no time for faction; Mong spoke quickly. "Say our lines hold. Say the Wild Wa drive the Chinese across the road. Then one question alone must be answered tonight, and the rest can wait until this war ends: Do we exterminate the Chinese at the road and fight the Wild Wa alone; or do we admit the beleaguered Chinese as allies?"

"Now that is clearly stated," Kin-tan said.

"We admit the Chinese, with the Russian," said the Sawbwa.

"We admit the Chinese, with the Russian," said the Sawbwa.

"We admit no foreigner whatever," said Naung. "The Russian said he would take this village. With my own ears I heard him say this, in the language of the French."

Ko-yang scowled. "If we are plucking all the feathers, then I will pluck this one: I think you say that because Green Wood's return has made you uneasy, and you see all foreigners as one foreigner."

"This is strong speech for a young warrior," Mong said.

"Ko-yang has a duty to speak plainly," Naung said. "Life and death are at stake."

"But to doubt your words is to pass the bounds," Wan said.

Ko-yang said, "True. I do not give Naung the lie. I only believe that he look a jest for a threat, and I stand by my Sawbwa."

"And I say we must welcome our Chinese brothers."

"There speaks a Chinese Sawbwa," said Naung.

"A sawbwa has no nation but only his people," said the Sawbwa, "and I am a Shan as was the sawbwa before me, and the Shan of Pawlu are vowed to the Way." He dabbed at the white froth in the corners of his mouth. His marbled eye rolled fiercely. "To kill an enemy is not the Way, but we accept imperfection. To kill a friend is not the Way and would be not imperfection but sin."

"To die is surely more virtuous," Naung said.

"All saints have believed that," Greenwood said.

"But you and I are not saints," Naung said.

"It seems to me," Wan began with dignity, "that perhaps the question is less elevated. We do not know the number of Wild Wa. If it is a raid of impulse they will content themselves with a few Chinese heads and return to Ranga. But if it is a war, if every able-bodied Wild Wa is under arms—"

Oppressed, they sat quietly until Kin-tan said, "It is surely sinful, but there is only the one strategy: the Chinese are intruders, and must bear the brunt."

"Well then, the remnant must be taken in," said the Sawbwa.

"I will not object to that," said Mong.

"I will," said Naung.

"I am with the Sawbwa," said Ko-yang again, and Wan and Kin-tan joined him.

"The remnant will be expelled or shot dead," Naung said. "There will be no armed foreigners in Pawlu while I am First Rifle."

Only the low crackling of the fire and the Sawbwa's asthmatic indignation relieved a grim silence.

"In war," Wan said, "the First Rifle commands."

"So say I," Kin-tan told them.

"Well and good," Mong agreed.

"The Sawbwa blessed my marriage," Ko-yang said. "If the Sawbwa is no Sawbwa, can a Rifle be a Rifle? Will a father be a father, a son a son?"

The silence resumed. Greenwood knew what they were waiting for, and experienced great vexation of spirit. He had earned the right to speak, but only to speak as a Shan. As Yang's comrade-in-arms, he was an intruder; as a foreigner, with an obscure kinship to the Russian, he was seditious; as an American social scientist, he was irrelevant, as superfluous as the Sawbwa and Za-kho, who sat here unarmed. There was Naung with the mitraillette to hand; next Wan and Kin-tan, rifles within reach, pistols at the belt, daggers; Mong with a carbine, a baby Nambu pistol, a Shan dagger; the general's nine-millimeter Canadian Browning a permanent appendage like a goiter, a deformity banal and disregarded; Greenwood himself, the humanist, with a tommy gun and a .45; more weapons in Pawlu than men, women and children. What were a few lives? Chinese lives at that. Nevertheless.

"No," he said.

General Yang drew a packet of Chinese cigarettes from the pocket of his tunic. He passed the packet. It was declined with grunted thanks. Yang lit up and exhaled gusts of smoke.

It was evident that he had grasped little, and was exhausted.

"There is another loyalty," Greenwood began, and could not go on; his mind balked; even the Shan language fled. Good Christ! Loyalty! To the race of man? All men are brothers? He felt a great fool, an interplanetary tourist, but gathered scraps of moral courage for a last attempt. "Naung: now above all I would wish to be your friend, but now above all I must be a Rifle. When my own country made its revolution against the British—"

"Good, good!" cried the Sawbwa.

"—one of us said," and he paused to frame the translation, which flowed smoothly enough, " 'We must all hang together or assuredly we shall all hang separately.' "

"Poetry," Naung said.

"Tactics," Greenwood corrected him, and felt the first faint beat of guerrilla's blood. "The Wild Wa can annihilate small units. With the Chinese we are twice the force. Let them in. Let them ring us about. Let us man the inner ring behind them. In a day or two or three, with Pawlu's weapons and the Chinese machine guns, the Wild Wa will be halved and will slink home."

"And when the Wild Wa slink home, and the Chinese reverse their guns and command the poor surrounded villagers of Pawlu?" Naung hawked contemptuously and spat a fat gob into the flames.

Greenwood wanted to say, "Never," and call upon the general to witness, to swear a solemn oath; he remembered Yang's praise of the Chinese fighting man at Taierhchuang. But he also remembered the famous Fifty-fifth. And he remembered other Russian Whites, other Olevskoys, Denikin, Kolchak, Semenov, massacres, betrayals, savage and fiendish atrocities. He could not answer.

Naung harried him. "Say we let them in. Say they ring us about. Say the Wild Wa slink home. Will you help us then to wipe them out?"

And if not, hold your peace.

"What is all this?" asked General Yang. He yawned prodigiously.

"We're trying to extricate your troops," Greenwood said.

"Very good. Let me know if I can be of help."

"The boy must make contact with the Wild Wa," said Wan.

"Foolishness," said Mong. "They will gobble him alive. I told you once."

"He's a Tame Wa," Greenwood said. "They'll take his head like any foreigner's."

Gloomy, reluctant, conciliatory, the Sawbwa spoke: "We must use all foreigners first. Even my Russian friend. Even Green Wood's Tame Wa."

With that, Greenwood experienced a curious sense of release, as if he were no longer in this house, no longer a Shan—and further stirrings of anger and pugnacity, warlike impatience, his breath shallow and tight, his skin crawling; in his nostrils a cruel reminiscent whiff of gunpowder, in his heart a cruel nostalgic wrench. By God! How long had it been since he killed a man? Or wanted to? Ah, holy simplicity!

Wan pursued his idea: "He will tell them that they may have all the Chinese heads they want but must not cross the road."

"He'll be dead before he sees them," Greenwood said.

"We must keep those Chinese confined," Naung said, "not only east of the road but blocked north and south. Here is what must be done."

They hunched attentively, Greenwood along with the rest. "How is your stock of grenades?" Greenwood asked.

Olevskoy lay beneath the stars amused by Greenwood's moment of speechless shock. They all wanted it, didn't they! And damn little else! They pretended, they lied, they squirmed, but they all burned for it. Some were open, like the Muslims with their four wives and obliging boys. Americans liked to show indignation. The British —British well, there were so many kinds of British, the English gentleman, the Antipodean roughneck, the Cockney. Perhaps the Australians were not British. A strange race. One day there would be one race only, everywhere, a world of mutts.

Or would we all be like that girl? Devoutly to be wished. That glossy hair, floating, the color of alfalfa honey at Sobolyevo. Obviously the American's daughter. And at home he is doubtless impotent. He was here for those footlockers, and not for glory, women or rule. As if this whole rotten civil war had been a conspiracy to transport those silly wooden boxes from one corner of China to another. If Yang should be killed . . . so light, so light, what the devil—the bones of his ancestors! Some joke there but some truth also. By God, that girl!

And those animals in the forest. Poisoned darts, possibly. Witchcraft, their women at home, crooked, gnarled, drinking blood.

Down the road with her, toward Siam. Not a bad little country. Temples and dancing women.

Or take Pawlu. To rule here! Sobolyevo in Burma!

But the victor never sleeps easy; Major Wei was right.

Siam. Yes.

"He will not stay," Naung said flatly. The American and the general had returned to the House of the Dead. The fire burned low, the order of battle was clear, cheroot smoke perfumed the night.

Kin-tan was equally positive. "He will stay."

"He will run out." Naung shrugged. "If he does stay, and if we live through tomorrow, I will give him a night with his daughter."

They understood and were pleased.

"Generosity is what makes us what we are," Mong said, "Shan, and not avaricious Indians."

"A friend is a friend in all things," Wan said.

"As to that," Naung said, "I am not sure to this day who is my friend and who my enemy."

General Yang, worn out, lay wizened and mummified in the dying flicker of the tiny fire. "We couldn't decide," Greenwood told him, "whether to let them operate as a unit under Olevskoy or integrate them with the Shan."

"A unit, absolutely," Yang said, and closed his eyes.

Greenwood let him be. The general would fly

out tomorrow, that had been agreed; let him leave without this burden. He had faced the truth all his life; let him rest now.

Greenwood lay awake and recalled what he had done that was good, and what he had done that was evil. He recalled family and friends: women he had loved; country matters; Loi-mae and Lola. All for these bones, for old carvings and cave paintings, for new stars and ideas: so many lives lived, so many deaths died, in the one ceaseless human quest: Know thyself! Seek, seek, seek! And suppose it was all deathful, all the delving and learning, like the saber-toothed tiger's saber teeth or the Irish elk's fatally top-heavy antlers? Like Oedipus' blind, proud insistence? Suppose this unquenchable thirst for insight and enlightenment, this feverish cerebral evolution, out of the Dark Ages and into the Light!—suppose all that was irresistible, inevitable, suicidal self-indulgence, deadly to biological evolution and so to the survival of the human race? Ignorance was bliss; all religion taught that.

He prayed to the God he did not believe in that he was wrong, and that his luck would hold for one more while.

11

The War
of the Bones

The Wild Wa are small and dark, and in their own villages they welcome the sun like all mountain people, but when raiding they use the night. In Ranga were forty warriors above the age of twelve, and though the season was winter, with the monsoon yet weeks off, they had spoken as one, saying, "Let us make our raid, let us take alien heads."

They oiled the crossbows, cleaned their few rifles, polished their scarce ammunition with superstitious fervor and sharpened their long knives. Their women wove string bags for fetching home prizes. Only then did they forgather for divination with chicken bones. They had made plain to the gods their intentions; now the gods would comment.

The chicken bones fell crazily into the flames, and one split with a loud pop, which was unusual. One writhed. One was scorched black. One had burned away to a sharp point. The headman was emphatic: they would make a saga for later generations. This was not a raid: it was a war. Unlike most of the Wild Wa, the headman was tattooed, and one of his tattoos was of a viper: they saw now that the bent and twisted bone had cooled to the form of a serpent, and they made hearty acclaim.

When the intruders were a day's march from Ranga, and closely tracked, a feast of roast dog was prepared. All shared in this feast—men and women and children—and the scouts and sentries were recalled in turn to come and share. More than twenty dogs were eaten, and each warrior ate one dog testicle, each warrior ate one eye; the teeth would be pierced for necklaces, with the large eye-teeth awarded to heroes. That night was much coupling. That night a man with one wife—this was usual—would share her, and a man with more than one wife—this was less common—would share them all.

Next day they dozed. Until dusk they lay napping, ears pricked and skin tingling, waking only for water, or for an obeisance to the household god, the gem, the skull, the petrified root. All performed a last, and again a last, ritual inspection of their weapons. At dusk they blackened themselves with kohl and earth, and donned black loincloths and dark leather sandals. They reviewed the tactical plan and the forest calls to serve as signals; and then they disappeared.

They melted into the night. They stepped soundlessly; they did not speak; they flew through the forest as shadows fly; and at night what shadow can be seen? The fat of the moon was past, and by the time she rose they had surrounded the Chinese. Thuan-yi lay among boughs and needles a man's length from a Chinese sentry, and was unseen. By sunrise every Wild

Wa had found a burrow. They were not to attack until Thuan-yi himself passed the direct order. They would pluck a few pears before shaking the tree.

They saw the Shan emissaries come to the road, and take away a Chinese and an albino. They saw the Shan return, restoring the albino. They understood: the Shan was warning these Chinese, and keeping a hostage.

The Wild Wa waited. Perhaps there would be Shan heads also.

On the day following General Yang's arrival and Colonel Olevskoy's visit, Greenwood woke with a headache and made a feeble joke about aspirin or a Wild Wa. Yang was stiff and sore, and looked forward wistfully to his chalet, a thick soft mattress and an eiderdown. In the frank light of sunrise Greenwood saw that the general was old, fatigue wrinkling his features and bowing his shoulders, his movements uncertain, as if he must now think through the simplest procedure.

The two men visited the latrines, returned to the House of the Dead and spruced up with a bucket of water apiece. They were to breakfast with the Sawbwa, a command performance. Greenwood was an early starter, headache or no, but Yang confided that with the years he had found himself taciturn, even morose, until later and later in the day. "Cheer up," Greenwood instructed him. "A hot bath tonight, servants, a room of your own in Maymyo or even Mandalay."

"The eternal American optimist." But Yang managed half a smile.

Naung had hardly slept, roaming his perimeter, he too flitting like a shadow, angrily certain that whatever dispositions had been made were insufficient: there would be a gap in the line, Shwe would smoke himself to sleep, old ammunition would misfire. He had spent an hour of the middle watch with Loi-mae and Lola, the child trustfully asleep, the man and wife gently entwined, affectionate and melancholy.

At first light Naung loped off again. All lay calm before him; peace blessed Pawlu. From the ridges he saw crops, the stream, poppies. From Red Bullock Pass he saw the haze above the Chinese bivouac, and he ate bitterness.

Olevskoy's troops found a sentry dead and headless. It was scrawny Corporal Pao, who had proudly worn the Order of the Tripod, third class. The men rushed to gawk until Major Wei cursed them and tongue-lashed them back to full alert. Olevskoy was furious. Projecting from the corporal's chest was a queer tufted missile: a crossbow bolt. "In the open," Olevskoy snapped at his majors. "As close to the road as possible and as far from cover and ambushes. These bolts can carry a hundred meters. Our machine guns will annihilate anything that moves within that range. Understood? Wide field of fire. This entire side of the road."

"If the Shan decide to attack," Major Wei said, "we'll be like Singapore in nineteen forty-one, with all the guns bearing the wrong way."

"The Shan won't attack," Olevskoy said. "They'll want us to do their work for them. Have your men dig in, Major."

The Wild Wa hugged the earth. One chirred like a grasshopper. One squeaked like a swallow. One chittered like a squirrel. They lay embedded on the forest floor, immobile, endlessly patient, like dark desires whose moment has not yet come, but surely will. From one slope to another, raucous peacocks greeted the day.

"My heart is full," the Sawbwa declaimed. "You have come to Pawlu in our time of need."

Neither the American nor the general was courageous enough to say the obvious.

"Green Wood," the Sawbwa went on, "will you return to the house of Loi-mae?"

"It is now the house of Naung also."

"Well, but ancient custom," the Sawbwa said.

The infinite morning sky soared above them, clear and blue; far to the east Greenwood could discern the jagged lines of range upon range. It would be a day for gliding hawks, vultures, kites. Owls would shelter in the lower boughs, and hares would forage in short, cautious dashes.

"I shall do no harm," Greenwood said.

Za-kho approved.

The Sawbwa said, "I have known that since the beginning. I hope you will remain here all your lives."

In English Yang asked, "Surely he knows our plans?"

Greenwood said, "I believe he knew them yesterday but has forgotten."

"Really the First Rifle should take command."

"I am very sure," Greenwood said, "that he will."

Naung said, "The roadside is secure and our men well hidden, though thin. Our little squad must not show itself until the aircraft approaches. The Wild Wa will be frightened and confused. They are barbarous and superstitious and will wait for a further sign or interpretation. Nevertheless, we must be quick."

"And quick back up too, or into East Poppy Field," Kin-tan reminded him.

"Yes. With or without Green Wood."

"With," said Wan.

"Without," said Mong.

This took them off guard. Mong? Green Wood's great friend? "You?"

"Eminence," Mong exclaimed sadly.

"I bet a half-slice of silver he stays," Kin-yan offered.

"Done," said Mong.

"Ah, bugger!" said an exasperated Naung. "It is a morning for the gods, and we should be tapping the poppies."

To Greenwood the wait was interminable, yet not sufficiently so. With Lola he played mumbledy-peg; her shiny blade of northern steel flashed in the sunlight. Loi-mae looked on, and brewed tea; her eyes and Greenwood's made shy love. She too was harking back. Memory closed his throat. His tommy gun stood against the shaded wall. The sun rose, and rose. A distant woodpecker hammered. Greenwood recalled his resolve, so many years ago, never to leave. He drowsed. The morning's peace was perfect.

At the first sound of firing, all women and children were to rush to the Common Field and mass before the Sawbwa's slope. At need, the warriors would fall back in a shrinking circle with the children at its center. Against a broad, open field of fire the Wild Wa would be powerless. Only to the west was there no guard. The Wild Wa came always from the east. They had never since the beginning of time crossed to the west of the Little River Mon.

General Yang had indeed grown old at last, overnight it seemed, as if the loss of China were the end of purpose and function. He felt slack all over: cheeks, shoulders, buttocks. His knees ached. Wearily in the House of the Dead he entertained dignitaries. The Sawbwa chattered on about the gods, and Pawlu as a favored spot, a foretaste of heaven. From time to time Za-kho interjected an elegant hum of pious approval.

Eventually all sat upon the ground, Yang again between his footlockers. Ironies depressed him: he would accomplish this last mission and succumb immediately to a kidney ailment. Or the American authorities, in the name of civilization, would take the bones by force and call upon world opinion to justify the larceny. Or this little aircraft would crash in the hills and his own bones and Sin's would lie mingled for decades, centuries: another puzzle for the great minds of the future. "One," they would say, "was significantly taller with significantly larger cranial capacity. His maxillaries were hypertrophied, presumably from excessive smiling in the face of defeat."

The Sawbwa was reminiscing, something about green men and red men. The Sawbwa had asked him a question.

"Forgive me, Sawbwa," said the general. "You asked . . .?"

"If the Frenchmen and the Englishmen were now gone from China."

"Oh yes," said Yang, "and all their servants too."

Some of the Wild Wa nibbled at dried meat. Some sucked at sugarcane. At dawn they had licked water from leaves and blades of grass. There was an hour for every thing, and it would make itself known: the cry of a parrot, a bolt of lightning, a breath of hot wind, a ululating whoop from Thuan-yi. Until the gods spoke through Thuan-yi, they would kill for mischief, and for practice.

"I know it is not easy," Olevskoy said, "but this is a time for patience. Even the fox sniffs the wind twice before racing down a new trail, and we are no foxes. Badgers, more like, dug in and hanging on."

"We can't cross the road without negotiating," Major Wei said.

"And we can't march down it without being picked off. Or even withdraw to the Salween. And the American said these savages were even thicker to the north. So we defend."

"Should there come an attack," Major Wei said, "we must try to slip out, retreat—"

"Withdraw," Olevskoy said.

"Withdraw in such a way that the attackers will fall upon the village, which will then welcome us."

"With permission, sir."

"Sergeant Chang."

"Is there no way around this village, sir? To the west?"

"I'll lead the way, Sergeant, if there is. Perhaps the general is even now working out our salvation. Meantime, hug the earth and keep your heads."

Lola sat on Greenwood's lap with her flossy hair tickling his neck; they basked in the sun's benevolence while Loi-mae selected utensils, provender, clothing, and stowed them in reed baskets. Greenwood was cursing himself for an inhuman fool, more vehemently every hour. "If I send for you, come!" The old romantic East!" "Never mind why, *do it!*" And Pawlu?"

Naung emerged from the shady lane. Greenwood set Lola gently on her feet and rose at once.

Naung said, "To the ridge now. Kin-tan is fetching the general and his chests."

Greenwood wiped his mouth needlessly with the back of his hand. As always when a brawl loomed he felt large and vulnerable. He hefted the submachine gun, his hand clenching hard; he slung the weapon and said, "All ready. Loi-mae, Lola: we shall take the midday meal together. All four of us."

Naung smiled a thin acknowledgment of this bravado. "No pack?"

"Only this." Greenwood slapped the Thompson.

"All the same," Naung suggested, "make a kind of farewell."

This was no threat, only a warrior's precaution. Greenwood took Loi-mae by the shoulders, hesitated while Naung turned away, and then set his forehead to his woman's. "Only an hour or so."

"You will come back," she said softly.

Greenwood released her; decorum mattered. He embraced Lola. The rustle and twitter of the forest seemed sharp and close. The air was piny, aromatic. "Lola, remember all that I have told you. And when some silly Weng-aw carries you off, think of me now and then."

"I shall think of you always, my father," Lola said, willing herself brave. "Naung has told me that it would be unnatural to forget you, and he is right."

"Then try not to forget me for an hour or so," Greenwood said, tickling her, "and cook me some chicken for the midday meal, and I shall be your young man and smuggle the best bits into your bowl."

"You always did!" Lola cried, and hugged him tight.

"Come," Naung said.

Both men shaded their eyes and saw by the remorseless sun that it was indeed time. Naung stepped to Loi-mae for a quick embrace, and they made a queer family of four in the sun-dappled yard of the little bamboo house; and the two men marched down the leafy trail.

The Sawbwa, in his Pawnee gaungbaung, wished them Godspeed. Za-kho had uttered platitudes. Benedictions were intoned. Naung glanced nervously at the sun. So did Greenwood. Some of the women watched; at their belts hung the dah, or a dagger.

Greenwood toted one footlocker, Yang the other. They set off for Red Bullock Pass with Naung leading at a fast pace. Taw-bi the runner met them halfway and reported all quiet. Shwe thought that a Chinese soldier had been killed before dawn but was not certain. "One less," Naung grunted.

Near a lookout called the Roost on South Slope, a broad ledge of rhododendrons above East Poppy Field, they joined Wan and Kin-tan. General Yang puffed, and mopped his face, and sat on a footlocker in the noonday sun, buttons and buckles winking gold. "Not before we hear the airplane," Naung said. "You will not so much as show your heads against the ridge until we hear the airplane."

"And then we dash," Greenwood said. Wind: not much wind, light air, and that was lucky. Gordon-Cumming could save himself a long taxi—just set down, pick up his passenger, turn and take off. The Chinese would not fire. Greenwood was morally certain that the Chinese would not open fire. "He'll come from the south. We cut straight for the road."

"Yes, yes," Wan said. "The men are in place, the orders have been passed. Only let him come, by the gods."

Above them a kite mewed. They watched it circle.

"We can only wait," Kin-tan said.

"Where is Mong?"

"Commanding the North Slope."

"A cheroot?"

"Not now, you fool." ·

General Yang asked, "Everything all right?"

"Perfect," Greenwood said. "As planned. No time for sentimental farewells, my general, but you're one of a kind and I'll see you in Mandalay."

"Come out with me."

"Get thee behind me, Satan."

Abruptly and unaccountably fear assailed Greenwood. The Sawbwa was a silly, sick old man. Za-kho was a bumpkin preacher. Naung might or might not be competent. Greenwood was not sure where error had first crept in, but error mocked him now, bloated and belching, the uninvited guest. The Shan proverb: Events have their ancestors and their progeny. If the past was a mistake, if the future was an idiot child?

He imagined himself on the plane. He imagined fame and fortune.

He had promised to take the midday meal with Loi-mae and Lola. The promise steadied him now. He had so far kept his promises.

Gordon-Cumming homed in on the right stretch of the right road. He had worn sandals, which was a mistake; his big feet were icy on the rudder pedals. He wiggled his toes and began an exploratory descent. His memory had been true. The road was straight enough and long enough.

He saw the Chinese bivouac. Now who the hell are these? Bloody Wa? Drag the strip, old boy.

He barreled in fast, leveled off, saw the uniforms, the faces blooming upward. Chinese!

Then he saw something else, and cursed, and stood the damned ship on its tail.

"Hold your fire," Olevskoy said. What was wrong here?

"He has come for General Yang," Major Ho said. "General Yang did not mention an aircraft."

Major Wei, much saddened, did not speak. They gazed wistfully at the approaching aircraft. It was the color of old pewter. It zoomed sharply.

"God in heaven!" Olevskoy cried, understanding at once. "The fools never knew!"

Thuan-yi lay rigid and asked himself what this sign meant. The thing itself was a foreign thing and known to exist. It was mysterious, like a rifle, and not supernatural like the voice of the storm. But the meaning of its appearance at this moment required priestly explanation, and Thuan-yi contracted in dread. He wondered if a crossbow could kill this thing. They were known to be metallic, and Thuan-yi wondered how thick their hides were.

Naung cried, "Now!"

Greenwood gripped General Yang's hand and tugged him up. "Time, old friend. You're on your way."

The general stood like a stump, disbelieving. He and Greenwood hoisted the footlockers. The engine droned, and as they topped the ridge the roar swelled. Greenwood paused to salute the Argus, good old Gordon-Cumming, good old RAF, never have so many owed so much to so few; then he scanned the foilage for Wild Wa; then he checked the Chinese camp, approving their tight semicircle, doing justice to Olevskoy even as something nagged, something odd, wrong, even as an altered landscape warned him.

The others were lurching downhill now in a clumsy bullish gallop. Greenwood shot one more outraged look at the road and bellowed, "No! No! Back! Naung, bugger you, back!"

They skidded, halted, crouched and stared wildly up the hill at this madman; far below, the Chinese faces turned like sunflowers.

"The poles!" he shouted. "Those buggering cages! He cannot land! Do you hear me? Come back! Come back!"

He watched the Argus zoom, climb steeply, bank and diminish.

"You saw," Olevskoy said. He and his majors were drinking local tea within their ring of ready ordnance and placid donkeys. The Wild Wa had not molested the animals, perhaps because they wished these foreigners to depart, perhaps because asses' heads did not satisfy their gods' demands.

"I saw," said Major Wei, much subdued.

"We are in a peck of trouble," said Major Ho.

"I cannot believe it," Major Wei said. "He led us out. He could have had himself flown out months ago, but he led us out. He was loyal to us as we were loyal to him."

"And what more can we ask?" Major Ho was matter-of-fact. "He led us out. That is all he promised."

"They were carrying those accursed foot-lockers," Olevskoy said. "Do you know, I think our position has improved."

The majors waited. Major Wei was no longer toting his Browning automatic rifle; it was set up in their front and only line, manned by two nervous corporals.

"They'll need us," the colonel said.

General Yang sat bewildered. What were those poles, those cages? No one had explained. They had raced pell-mell back over the ridge, then trotted cursing to council. Fate lay heavy upon the general. He was a baffled immigrant with two footlockers. "Those poles could be chopped down and cleared away," he said.

"Not now," Greenwood said. "The Wild Wa would cut us to pieces from the woods."

"I could return to my troops," the general suggested, "and establish a defense. Even attack. We could coordinate."

"Attack what?" And would they have you? Greenwood was busy, translating aloud, assessing, sifting quick ideas. "You go out on foot tomorrow, to the west, with Jum-aw."

Wan said, "We must send this Jum-aw to parley with his cousins the Wild Wa."

Mong said, "We could send a piglet to parley with a leopard."

"Let us have the Russian officer," said the Sawbwa.

Naung spat. They were in council before the Sawbwa's house, but this time they were not seated gravely in a circle. They were standing, kneeling, pacing and cursing. Below them women and children were drifting onto the Common Field, burdened with foodstuffs, trailing livestock. Each isolated house was a trap; a massed village was blood and bone, brothers and sisters, companions in life or death.

"We need them" Greenwood said. "Thirty-some trained fighting men. That's about as many as there are Wild Wa."

"Then let them stand and fight," Naung said. "Let them each kill one Wild Wa."

"Well, curse it, Naung," Kin-tan said, "today I think you may be wrong."

Naung dipped deep into his rum; the bowl hid his eyes.

"Bugger it, Naung," Greenwood said, "no rum now!"

"I shall send an emissary," the Sawbwa said. "Perhaps Ko-yang." The Sawbwa was impelled by powerful memories, by impressions that had become certanties: Shang, a soothing American voice that eased his blindness, his early injustice to Green Wood. And now the gods had sent a Russian in the hour of need; to the Sawbwa, events were proceeding harmoniously.

"Well, we have the mule by the wrong end this time," Mong said, "but here is what I believe. I believe that if we invite the Chinese to enter, the Wild Wa will flow in behind them."

"So I believe," said Naung, "and then you will have an occupied Pawlu."

"That need not follow," said Wan. "What if, as the Wild Wa flow in, we attack from both flanks?"

They mulled this.

"And further suppose," Kin-tan said, "that upon a signal the Chinese turned and made a stand. There is a tale of Hu-chot proceeding in that manner."

"So that we squeeze those flowing Wild Wa from north, west and south," Greenwood said, "and slice them up and fling them back across the road."

"One does not squeeze shadows," Naung said. "One does not slice shadows. One does not fling shadows."

"Then why have the Wild Wa never taken Pawlu? Has Naung surrendered before the battle? Is Naung already beaten?" Greenwood chose the soft voice and the sorrowful gaze.

Naung chose thunder. "By the gods, you know better!" His hand leapt to the hilt of his knife. "Rather I would die! You speak so to *me*?"

"That's better," Greenwood said coldly. "We need anger and not rum. Wan and Kin-tan are right. We cannot fight the Wild Wa at night; we need to see. If the Chinese cross the road at sunrise, the Wild Wa must move, attack, infiltrate or go home; and even the Wild Wa cannot move in daylight without some stir. How many can there be? Thirty, forty? If we pick off ten, the battle is won."

"So it must be," said the Sawbwa. No one even looked at him.

"But it cannot be done without Naung," Greenwood said. "I am older now and bookish, and unused to command. My weapon fits my hand still, but Naung must give the word."

Naung dried his bowl, tossed it aside and said, "Complete the assembly in the Common Field. Order latrines dug. Bring livestock; rice; pots and bowls. Meanwhile there is only murder in my heart, so I leave you for a while."

"Come back," Greenwood asked. "I am going to the road. I shall be the Sawbwa's emissary."

"Curse you," Naung said, but returned. "Was there no other way but by Pawlu?"

Olevskoy too felt the fever rising. He was a general at last, and he coped with all problems: stores, munitions, discontent, deployment, grand strategy. And with all possibilities: weather, disease, attack, withdrawal, allies. The men muttered against General Yang and he did not upbraid them; this shift in loyalty was to his own advantage. Major Wei was unhappy, Major Ho bovine. Olevskoy kept close watch on the obvious approaches to Pawlu, the gaps in vegetation, the ditches and depressions. On the Shan slopes he had spotted observation posts, great clumps of Alpenrose, the Chinese called it sheep-stagger-bush, on flats or shelving rock.

He hoped for a message. Corporal Pao's death had taken him. The colonel had stood, sometimes alone, against a variety of enemies, but never against lethal shadows. He supposed that this was like jungle fighting. He had read of jungle fighting. It made good reading.

He knew what ought to be done, what he wanted to do, and he smoked half a packet of Russian cigarettes from Fang-shih reviewing the problem and refining his solution. At first light tomorrow he would enter Pawlu. The Wild Wa would harass him. If the Shan were alert, they could annihilate these little beasts from both flanks. Meanwhile he and his men would drive for the center of Pawlu. After that, some arrangement: provisions, a guide, a laissez-passer. Or a dash south toward Siam. But first these pestilential trolls.

He was all soldier now and wasted no energy in lamentations. If he was not invited, he would crash the gate. There was, of course, a flaw. There was always a flaw. Everyone had agreed upon this, from Clausewitz to some American called Murphy, and General Yang had told him that it was the rule even in mathematics, even in physics: there was always a flaw. The flaw here was that if the Shan could annihilate the Wild Wa from both flanks, they could annihilate the Chinese from those same flanks.

"Major Ho," he called. "Major Wei. To me, please."

Thuan-yi now lay on South Slope sheltered by masses of sheep-stagger-bush. He had seized his moment, daring all alone for the good of his people: when the flying metallic thing thundered past the cages and every man's eyes followed, Thuan-yi had sprinted across the road like a hare and dived into deep foliage, breathless at his own courage and wit. He was well and truly cut off for now; he could call his men only by risking his life and theirs; but he lay between the Chinese and the Shan. Once this side of the great road he had made his way up the slope at a slug's pace;

and now he was a clod, or a rock, or the shadow of a bush. His gods had smiled, and would again.

"You'll do as I say," Greenwood told Yang. "You'll go out tomorrow with the boy."

"And leave others to fight."

"You've done your fighting. The last thing we need is a general." They were back in the House of the Dead, and Greenwood, prowling and taut, felt larger every moment. He could not fill his lungs. He inhaled enormous quantities but could not still his soul. With the bandits in the hills he had been shamefully frightened, and now he was resolute and almost exhilarated. It was the comfort of compulsion, the absence of choice.

"I am here only because my men stood by me," Yang muttered, "and now you ask me to run out. I did not foresee these complications."

"Stop that," Greenwood said. "I didn't foresee them either, and it's my territory, not yours. I'll save Pawlu and you save those bones. Jum-aw knows the trail, and owes me a life. If I don't show up later, you tell everybody Greenwood deserves a footnote somewhere, and write to my folks. Tell them I did right."

"I think you're a damn fool," Yang said. "Death wish."

"Not at all. Plenty to live for. We'll put your colonel to work and clean up this here town."

"You won't cross?"

"No! We holler from our side of the road, he hollers from his."

"The telephones in Shanghai," Yang murmured.

"What?"

" 'Czarist fascist!' 'Crypto-Communist!' "

"You all right?"

"I have never been older," Yang said. "I am exhausted, deeply depressed and in no humor to seek the bubble reputation in the cannon's mouth. Furthermore, every time I come to Pawlu you start ordering me around."

"I see down," Naung said. He hunkered at his own hearth.

Loi-mae touched his lips. "It is your voice that commands."

"It is the web of events. No man truly commands. And I must bow to the Sawbwa and clap your Green Wood on the shoulder."

"He is not my Green Wood."

"I want to hear his funny stories and see the hair on his chest," Lola said.

"You be quiet."

"He is Lola's father. As the Sawbwa says, it would not have displeased the gods had Green Wood paid a visit to his family."

Loi-mae did not speak.

"I would not have barred the gate to him," Naung said, "nor reminded you, ever."

"I would never hurt you," Loi-mae said.

"Well, it would have done no harm," Naung said, but his eyes were cold. "You must look into your heart now, and take strength from what you find. He may be killed. He may leave, never to return. I believe he would have left had that aircraft landed."

Lola crouched, her eyes enormous. "No."

"What does Green Wood matter?" Loi-mae asked. The question was a lie; she knew that

Naung sensed that. "With all Pawlu at the edge of life."

"He is said to be a fighter, at any rate. How inscrutable is destiny! Without him, no Lola; with him . . ."

Solemnly Lola hitched the sheath of the northern dagger to her leather waistband.

The Shan gathered in the Common Field. By families they came, by couples. Old ones trudged, bowed by the weight of food and hoarded silver. On the field, neighborhoods sprang up. Loi-mae and Chung made common household, attended by the boy Jum-aw, abashed to be out of the fighting yet with his rifle to hand. In the center, the Sawbwa and Za-kho held court. Goats and bullocks grazed outside the circle. Fires flickered and leapt, faces loomed and faded. Sadness fell upon the Shan like slow rain: for the lives that might be lost, the houses that might be burned, the animals that might stampede, the children who would learn terror. Beneath, there lay a deeper sadness: that the gods had permitted this. Soon there rose the aroma of roasting saing, and that lightened their hearts, but not much.

Thuan-yi turned on his side and urinated quietly. He ran a thumb along the blade of his long knife. The thumb bled. He ate a strip of dried dog, and then a cricket.

_In midafternoon Greenwood and Kin-tan set out. A chain of silent, invisible Shan flanked them as they trotted through Red Bullock Pass. Wan had pronounced the road secure, the ridges and East Poppy Field clear. Greenwood, Kin-tan and a shifting, shuttling guard of armed runners made their way to South Slope, where the Shan was thickest, perhaps two hundred paces above the road and the Chinese. Greenwood's excitement was intense—fervor and not jitters; he still felt large, was sweating copiously and hardly noticed the weight of his weapon.

No one hindered their progress. Not even a toktay crossed their path. Greenwood dismounted, tethered his pony to an evergreen, dashed the last hundred paces and flung himself flat on the spongy, resinous earth. He crawled then, Kin-tan behind him, to the Roost. Snaking forward he saw the road and the Chinese camp.

Thuan-yi had contracted, and curled himself about the trunk of his sheep-stagger-bush like the hard-worm about the melon vine. With the sun westering he lay in shadow. He saw Shan, and he saw the albino. This was magic. The albino was with his soldiers below.

There were two albinos!

This one trod within a pace of him. Thuan-yi saw the fair skin, the bony nose, the wrinkled corners of the light eyes, the curly golden hair. He also saw the weapon.

Greenwood cupped his hands and shouted, "Olevskoy! Olevskoy!"

There was motion among the Chinese. Kin-tan adjusted the binoculars.

"Oleveskoy!"

"Who . . . are . . . you . . . and . . . what . . . do . . . you . . . want?"

"Greenwood! The American!"

"It was the Russian who called, "Kin-tan said. "His officers now seek us with their field glasses."

"They won't fire," Greenwood said. He hollered again, "Olevskoy!" and outlined the tactical problem.

"Now they are conferring," Kin-tan said. "They are taking their time about it. The Russian has started a cigarette."

At this season there were no blossoms on the rhododendrons, and their odor was earthy and cool, even moist. Perhaps Greenwood did not want a reply from the Russian. This was a recess, a truce; he was lying on a hillside sniffing at shrubbery and the Wild Wa did not exist.

Olevskoy shouted, "No! Absolutely not! I will not risk an ambush!"

"I swear to you," Greenwood shouted, "that there will be no ambush, and that you will have the freedom of the village afterward." Distant echoes, then calm again.

Olevskoy shouted, "Do you believe in God?"

Greenwood was flabbergasted. After a moment he shouted, "No!"

"Then who are you to swear to anything?"

Greenwood laughed aloud. His spirits soared at this sudden metaphysical turn. "Do you believe in democracy?" he shouted.

The answer was immediate. "No!"

"Then why do you confer with your officers?"

"That's what officers are for!" Olevskoy called.

"He just smiled," Kin-tan said. "I see machine guns and two of those heavy automatic rifles."

"And they'll have grenades and small arms. We

can use it all."

Olevskoy shouted. "You must send us a hostage!"

Greenwood now translated for the Shan. Contempt crossed their faces, but they considered the demand. Jum-aw. They could offer a hostage and a guide in one person, showing good faith and common sense.

Greenwood shouted this to Olevskoy.

Olevskoy shouted, "No. No outsider. Maybe . . . the little girl."

Greenwood remembered what was at stake and bit back savage obscenities, but could not disguise the anger in his voice. "We do not make war with children, Colonel. But you may take me."

"You!" Olevskoy's acid laughter carried up the slope. "They would sacrifice you without thinking twice!"

"He tossed his head back as if in contempt," Kin-tan reported. "The sunlight is full on them."

Greenwood told Kin-tan what Olevskoy had said.

Kin-tan fiddled with the binoculars. Then he met Greenwood's eye and said, "For Pawlu, yes. You or any other hostage."

"Lola? He will take Lola."

Kin-tan's dark Oriental features twisted, altering swiftly to incomprehension, incredulity, anger; the stained teeth gritted in disdain. "Men do not think such things! By the gods! That you could even ask me!"

"I do not want to talk more to him," Greenwood said. "The seed is planted. If we have time, we'll come back. He may change his mind."

"He is not worth having, this Russian. But he may indeed change his mind, given time. They have no water. That one is *rude*."

"Then I too shall be rude."

"Please!"

"No hostage!" Greenwood shouted. "But the offer stands, and the plan is simple and strong. Afterward, you and I will fight. Do you hear me? I do not want my daughter's name in your foul mouth!"

"Then send your wife!" Olevskoy called. "American son of a bitch!"

Again they passed within reach of Thuan-yi; again he lay immobile. If he killed one? Nothing. He was within their lines, and a weasel was here more useful than a tiger. Already he had learned much. That there was hatred between the two albinos. That there was hatred between the Chinese and the Shan. That his enemy was divided by more than a road or a field, and would never be united. They might, if left properly alone, or if skillfully tricked, make corpses without help from the Wild Wa.

A choke of laughter escaped him.

"They'll be back," Olevskoy told his majors. "They need us."

"But I *must* go," the Sawbwa said. His confidence was sublime and he spoke perkily, as if to children who must be humored. "Who better? All my life I have prepared for this; in my youth my fate was linked to the Russians."

"This is courage," Naung said.

"It is a shock," Greenwood said, "but it makes sense."

"There is no precedent for it," Mong said. "I have never heard of a sawbwa leaving his village, much less as a hostage, and I do not believe that good can come of it."

"New times, new remedies," Wan said, "but I confess this violates my sense of the proprieties."

"The idea makes me nervous," said Kin-tan.

"Kin-tan nervous? *That* is without precedent." The Sawbwa's good eye stared down at his people and their village-within-a-village, at smoke rising from a dozen campfires. "I shall go, and I shall bring them here tomorrow to exterminate these Wild Wa. After all, who else speaks Chinese? We shall suppress the Wild Wa for a generation to come."

"The general speaks Chinese," said Naung.

Greenwood was firm: "The general goes west with Jum-aw. Sawbwa: if this is to be done, *how* is it to be done?"

In the end it was done simply. The Sawbwa decked himself in his ceremonial gray and scarlet. Around his neck he draped strings of prayer beads, at Za-kho's instance. On his head he wore the Pawnee headband. He was placed aboard a pony.

Wan assured them once more that this side of the road was clear of Wild Wa. Eight horsemen, appropriately armed, surrounded the Sawbwa, four close, four ranging. They proceeded by the most direct route, straight through Red Bullock Pass and along the southern edge of East Poppy Field.

At the roadside they formed a defensive cluster. A curt Greenwood parleyed with Olevskoy. The Sawbwa added a word or two in creaking Yunnan Chinese. They waited, the Shan squirming in vague humiliation, while the Chinese soldiers conferred. Greenwood could not understand their talk. Probably Olevskoy was saying, "Well, they're serious," and the majors were agreeing. Perhaps they were also discussing the shortage of water. Perhaps too the joys of village life.

Finally Olevskoy agreed. To Greenwood he said, "A truce for now."

"For now."

"At sunrise tomorrow we move. These hills: will your sun rise at the same hour?"

"We'll be watching," Greenwood said. "At this end of the pass, dig in."

Olevskoy said, "If you lay an ambush, we'll kill the lot of you. We'll roast you alive."

"If this were an ambush we'd want you *within* the pass."

"I've never trusted anyone," Olevskoy said. "Not for years and years. It is not easy to start now."

And in high state the Sawbwa, sitting his pony like a trained gibbon, crossed the road into the Chinese camp, where he became immediately the object of vulgar curiosity, and was offered whisky and cigarettes, which he declined with dignity.

In the lowering dusk Thuan-yi watched the Shan ride back into Pawlu. Here was a mystery! Strange ways indeed! These people had bound

over their headman to the Chinese and one
albino; and the other albino rode merrily back to
Pawlu like a true Shan! This conduct was not
meet. By such unseemly behavior the Shan had
surely lost favor with the gods. The Shan were no
longer righteous!

Exultant, Thuan-yi ghosted through the
evening to rejoin his men, and to tell them what
the gods had ordained.

"Try not to blame me," Greenwood said.

"There is no blame," Loi-mae said. "Who can
say when this war began, and why, or how it will
end, and why?"

"It is all one war, perhaps, with longer or
shorter truces."

Lola slept. About them in the Common Field
the hum and stir of a jittery village filled the
night; low talk, a snore, a cough, the drifting
smoke of fires and cheroots.

"It is better not to touch," Loi-mae said.

"Naung hates me."

"What did he say?"

" 'Go to your daughter.' I cannot make him out.
He is hot and cold."

"Happy and sad. He has been hurt."

"Then we shall not hurt him more."

"We shall be virtuous, and the gods will be
kind."

Greenwood did not believe this but said, "Yes."

Once this had been all he desired: Loi-mae,
Lola, Pawlu. Now it was a place he had spoiled,
on the eve of battle.

True, events have many ancestors, and there is

never one that may be singled out. Yet if not for
Major Wei, all might have ended otherwise, and
order prevailed. Hulking, reliable Major Wei. A
man of honor, a soldier of valor. With nightfall
Major Wei agonized. General Yang had not lied;
yet the major had expected more honorable
behavior. He allowed professional latitude;
superior officers were constantly issuing cryptic
orders and conducting maneuvers incomprehensible to lower grades because part of a greater,
unknowable whole. Major Wei needed a confi-
dant, and time to think. But he was alone,
possibly assisting a mutiny, and the decision
must be his. First: he could disappear into the
night and slog his way to some town. Impossible.
Second: he could accept the situation and shift
his allegiance to the Russian. Difficult. Third: he
could follow along, and bide his time. Unworthy.
Fourth: he could make his way to General Yang,
confront him, warn him and judge him.

But how to enter the village, with pickets
three-deep? He had considered offering himself
in exchange for the Sawbwa, but his men needed
him. He shrugged into his jacket and inspected
his weapon. A white flag? Useless at night; nevertheless, once clear of the bivouac he would knot a
white kerchief to the muzzle of his weapon. He
did not fear the Wild Wa; he was a man of some
sophistication and knew that no human eye
could see in true darkness. Besides, the Sawbwa
had crossed without incident. He would be
exposed for a few seconds only. He imagined
himself crossing the road, entering the Shan
lines. He heard himself challenged, calling
"Friend!"

His heart somewhat eased, he lay back. The foundations were indeed trembling; no longer was up up, down down.

"You will ride out tomorrow with the general," Mong told Jum-aw, "so make the most of tonight."

Chung smacked the boy's shoulder. The daughters cooed.

"I want someone awake at all times," Mong went on. "We are at war."

"I should stay," Jum-aw said, "and fight beside you."

"Suckling babes do not decide these matters," Mong scoffed. "Listen, boy: you have a long life yet to live. Ride away from here and live it." He threw an arm around Chung. "A bad day coming, old woman."

"Unless the gods relent," she said.

"The gods may be busy elsewhere," Mong said.

"Hu-chot is with them, and Phe-win," Chung said, "and many old friends."

"Not bad company," Mong said, "old friends and gods; but I prefer my good woman."

Chung grasped his hand.

General Yang sat alone, in the dark, between his footlockers.

Thuan-yi hovered at the edge of sleep.

Lola dozed. Cookery proceeded. At the boundaries of Pawlu, sentries lay immobile. Livestock ruminated placidly, whuffling and blatting. Greenwood himself was gloomy. His belligerence had subsided, he was no longer in love, he took

joy in his daughter but had brought peril in his
train. He was older, sadder and wiser, as philoso-
phers had told him he would be. He had crossed
his peak at twenty-seven, and his imperceptible
slide downhill had brought him—and Pawlu—to
this mournful pass.

Major Wei inspected his positions. Now before
moonrise the night glowed faintly; sentries'
whispers floated like mist.

At the northern end of his line, ten meters from
the road, he melted into the night. He must cross
now, keep low, burrow in on the far side, and
make his way with infinite patience toward this
famous poppy field. Once clear of the Wild Wa he
could risk a friendly call.

He knelt beside the road for several minutes.
The silence impressed him: he was worlds away
from man and all his works.

He saw the road clearly, a lighter black—was
that possible?—than the forest. He half rose, and
in the rapid bent-legged lope that had carried
him across so many frozen fields of millet
stubble, he glided onto the road.

At first he thought that he had collided with a
post or been buffeted by a cudgel. Then he recalled the whir. Then he realized that his knees
were not supporting him. This was annoying. His
weapon seemed oily, slipping from his grasp. He
could see the surface of the road, swirls in the
dust; he saw his weapon falling, spinning slowly,
settling endlessly; and then he saw the bolt in the
center of his chest. It was as if some stupid
soaring sharp-beaked bird had blundered, diving
to its own death in the heart of him. Against his

cheek the dust of the road was cool, and then cold.

Only Major Wei slept well that night. Green-wood woke to Loi-mae's embrace, and drifted off again. Loi-mae was oppressed by fears, and clung to Greenwood as she had in the old days, when he was invulnerable. He returned her embrace but asked no more of her. He would not transgress. Perhaps she was right and the gods would, in return, spare them all. Lola tossed and whimpered.

The captains napped briefly, in turn.

General Yang struggled to the surface of swampy dreams: his legs failed, his arms were bound, ooze sucked at his feet; his own men accused him.

Olevskoy muttered, started awake, sat up puzzled: Siberia? No, China. No, Burma. That Burmese child! Perhaps he was monstrous and not princely at all. A lifetime of self-disgust, disguised as pride. Tomorrow he would lose himself in his work.

Thuan-yi prayed to his gods and heeded the voices of the night. He recalled strategies and deceptions from the time of the wider war, when also an albino had been among them, perhaps one of these very same. He recalled the Wild Wa tricked into reckless advances and cut down from both flanks. Not this time. This time they would lurk awhile, like the wild dogs that follow leopards.

These leopards would snarl and claw in the field of poppies or at the pass.

A dazzling vision kindled the night: he saw himself crossing the Little River Mon. He thanked his gods. When the storytellers recited this war, one name would be spoken again and again.

Major Ho raised the alarm. A false dawn had roused him; obedient to his colonel, he had tried to nudge Major Wei, so that they might proceed together to the latrine and the ring of sentries; he had nudged thin air. "Wei!" he called. Men stirred. "Major Wei!"

"What is it?" Olevskoy's voice was slurred.

"Major Wei, sir. Not present."

"Up, up, up," Olevskoy called. "Major Wei? Major Wei?"

Men commenced cursing, blundering into one another, damning the dark and the cold. Louder, Olevskoy called, "Major Wei! Who has seen Major Wei?"

The men fell silent.

"Major Ho: check your perimeter. Sergeant Chang: check the road. All of you: ready alert!"

Olevskoy peered into the uncertain dawn. All his life he had been a soldier, and never more, never better, than when alone against the world. "I want silence," he said. "I shall be giving orders and I shall not shout."

In the murk nothing stirred: so the world had begun, before there were men. In how many dawns had he stood prickling, straining for a sign?

"Ai yah! The major!" Sergeant Chang was audible for half a mile. Olevskoy swore.

"What is it, then?"

Sergeant Chang lumbered to his colonel. "Dead! Dead! In the road! And . . ." He loomed misshapen in the half-light.

"And?"

"Beheaded!"

A rumble rose, of fear. Men whined and moved aimlessly. Olevskoy knew he must hold them now or lose them forever. "Form squads!" he called out. "Bring this Sawbwa to me!"

Dazed with sleep, the Sawbwa was bundled out of his sleeping-cloth and into Olevskoy's presence. "The Wild Wa have killed a man," Olevskoy said. "They are all about us. We shall enter the village now. Do you understand me?"

"The sun is not yet risen; but I understand you."

"We shall move quickly. You shall ride at my side."

"That too I understand."

"You must hang on and not fall off. There will be no coming back for you."

"I shall grasp the mane," the Sawbwa said.

For the first time, peering through the gray dawn, Olevskoy examined the Sawbwa's headband. Woven into it were small five- and six-pointed stars. Curious.

"All prepare to mount!" he shouted. Too late now for the commanding dignity of soft-spoken orders. "Lash down machine guns! Flankers at the ready!" After a half minute he continued, "No! Leave all bedding, all food, everything but weapons!" They set to, and readied themselves. "At my word we cross: three ranks of ten, flankers close, not wide, a pony's length apart, all of you; keep low, keep your heads on the mane; and ride like the wind through that field of poppies.

"You know that they expect us to face about, and slaughter the savages coming in behind us—after which, they may slaughter us."

"Not so!" cried the Sawbwa.

"Perhaps they speak truly; perhaps they lie. Remember our alternate plans, discussed last night! Remember all that we have done together!" Olevskoy swung onto his pony. "Form on the march! Forward!" He added in Russian, "And you, you summer fool, behave yourself or I shall squash you with one thumb."

The Sawbwa nodded thoughtful agreement.

Naung heard the commotion. Kin-tan lay beside him on South Slope. "Taw-bi: fetch Green Wood, quick! Warn the village!"

"Something has frightened them."

Olevskoy's voice carried in the dry, lifeless dawn.

"That northern dialect," Naung said. "Jabber and babble."

"Ponies blowing," Kin-tan said.

"He's giving orders. I can tell that much."

"If they come?"

"Why so early? Ah, these foreign bastards! These sons of turtles! Well, we're ready for them. Blessings."

"Blessings," said Kin-tan, and slipped away. Naung raced west, and raised the alarm.

Thuan-yi bubbled laughter and made squirrel talk. He slipped from his hollow, fleeting southward. Thuan-yi was a creature of the forest. He had hunted all other creatures of the forest, man

among them, and he knew their ways as the owl
knew the mouse's ways. Not merely Thuan-yi's
youthful strength but his shrewdness as well had
raised him to this command. It told him now that
these Chinese had panicked, and were following
the albino to attack the village, rather than
darting and doubling like the mountain fox.
Thuan-yi guessed that the villagers would lie in
wait for these strangers, and at the proper time
close the jaws of their trap. This would occupy
them for some while; they would surely require
all their forces; they would perhaps fire at one
another; any reinforcements would be drawn
from— Ah! From where the Wild Wa had never
set foot!

Thuan-yi gave orders in many voices, and the
Wild Wa flowed into the shallow valley south of
South Slope, and surged west parallel to the
Chinese north of South Slope. The Wild Wa were
skimming the earth now, sprinting and scurrying
toward the Little River Mon and unknown lands
beyond it. Thuan-yi's excitement was feverish,
and he knew that his forty warriors were also
ablaze.

Like Olevskoy and Thuan-yi, Naung was doing
what he did best. His strategy—Green Wood's,
Wan's, Kin-tan's, he admitted, but one that he
himself might have framed—was workable and
even elegant as far as it went. It depended on the
brute stupidity of the Wild Wa, but they were a
reliably base people, were they not? "Bring those
men up here from the Little River Mon," he told
Taw-bi.

Olevskoy and his crew charged into Pawlu like the desperate refugees they were. The Sawbwa bobbed along, clutching his pony's mane. They swept through East Poppy Field, trampling a rich crop, hundreds of catties of crude opium ground to chaff. They charged toward Red Bullock Pass. Major Ho, with the rear guard, saw Shan movement on the slopes; he fired in the air, slowing the column. Olevskoy saw Greenwood, mounted, both arms raised, and his own right arm shot up, slowing the Chinese.

By God! If this was honest and succeeded! It was possible: General Yang was their friend. The old Smiler. Olevskoy was shouting orders. His machine gunners and infantry tumbled into place. "Fireteam Blue—cover the village!" The Shan was now behind us. And before us is a classic enfilade, a ninety-degree field of fire and slopes at either hand. Why did I obey this American? Olevskoy readied his carbine. His lungs pumped, and the old sweat broke out, the sweet ache. His horse handlers had rounded up the ponies. The Shan were darting down both slopes. Where were the Wild Wa?

Thuan-yi halted at the river. His men gathered, crouching, jittering in place, overcome by their own daring. Among them were crossbows, ancient rifles, swords and daggers. Before them lay countless heads; behind them, their own women, who would jeer at failure. Thuan-yi spoke: "All across! To the north! For the gods!" No Shan remained to oppose them.

In the Common Field, as dawn flared over the

pass, the women and children chewed on cane and formed a watchful, loosely packed mass. Some prayed aloud. Loi-mae and Chung stood together, and Lola with them. Za-kho invoked the gods. They heard voices toward Red Bullock Pass, and then shots. Near them Jum-aw, shaking with fear yet also with the need to perform well before Mong's and Chung's daughters, scanned the screen of forest to the south and sighted along the barrel of his father's rifle.

Olevskoy watched the Shan sweep down both slopes and close behind his platoon; he saw no Wild Wa; and knew bitterly that he had once more been deceived by peasants. And by the American. He cursed himself for a fool. "Form up!" he bawled. "Mount up! Major Ho! Into the village! The village! Cut your way to the village!"

"Yes, yes!" cried the Sawbwa. "To the village!"

"Ah, you again," said Olevskoy. He drew his .45 and shot the Sawbwa between the eyes, or just above, through the Pawnee headband. The Sawbwa slid off the pony with his customary glassy smile, and his mottled white eye shut forever.

Naung, like Olevskoy, cursed himself; he also cursed Green Wood and the Sawbwa. The Russian and his Chinese scum were turning on the village, on the women and children. And where were the Wild Wa? "Wan! Wan!"

"I hear!"

"The Wild Wa!"

"None!"

"Then rally all," Naung shouted. "Come after

these Chinese and come firing! To the Common Field!"

Greenwood was sweeping down North Slope in a long S-curve when he saw the Chinese lines dissolve and re-form. He was panting, and not with effort alone. He did not know where the Wild Wa were. His pony scrabbled downhill to East Poppy Field, and here came Ko-yang from the south. "Nothing! No one!"

Mounted men galloped to them, gathered and milled.

They heard firing to the west, and they raced for the pass.

A machine gun opened fire. Ko-yang's pony tumbled, and Ko-yang flew; he landed like a rock and lay still. Greenwood shouted, "Cease firing! Cease firing!" but the clatter of gunfire drowned him out. So he shouted instead, "Oh Christ!" and swung up toward the ridge.

Some of Thuan-yi's men struck north toward the village as soon as they had crossed the Little River Mon. A few kept by Thuan-yi's side and ran even farther west, veering toward the village then from the southwest. They streaked toward the House of the Dead, which seemed deserted and might provide treasure or cover. They were moving swiftly, committed to the assault, when the first shot dropped one of them. Thuan-yi crouched lower, dodged, pivoted, zigzagged. His men yipped and whooped. One more fell as they stormed the House of the Dead.

General Yang was not doing what he did best.

He was miserable in the knowledge that he had failed them all, friend and foe alike, and principally himself. Some miscalculation years ago. He stood between his footlockers in the House of the Dead and could not decide which path to take. He heard commotion, shots and shouts. Was he to wait here for the boy Jum-aw? Should he abandon the bones and seek out his own men? Look for Greenwood? Join the women and children? Why was he here?

He discovered why he was there when the first Wild Wa erupted from the forest and darted up toward the Common Field. Others veered toward him; dimly he recognized them, dwarfish specters; they scampered closer. He heard a wail go up from the Common Field, and rifle fire. He heard the boom of a hand grenade.

He took up his carbine, snapped the safety off and knelt in his wall that was no wall, knelt in the unshelter of the House of the Dead, and pumped shots into the crowd of small charging tribesmen. Some ran past him. Some fell. One slipped toward him from the side. They were all but naked, smeared with grime, and when General Yang's clip was empty and he paused to ram home another, these savages gave meaning to his life. He stood almost exultant. It is easier to die hard.

Fifty years. Fifty years of Latin and socialism, tactics and romance, Confucious and Darwin. Fifty years of short rations, mud, insults, carnage, and now these pygmies, these cannibals, these horrors from the center of the earth—Yang stood squarely before his footlockers and swung his carbine by the barrel. There was no time for a fresh clip, but there was, really, all the time in

the world, the whole rest of his life, time to meet
the flat alien gaze of one dark stunted man, time
to puzzle at the operation of the curious crossbow and to admire the man's courage, time to remember another crossbow clutched by the
bloody mutilated corpse of a Boxer on the ramparts half a century before in Peking, time to
wonder that he had not learned the truth earlier
—the truth that his enemy, his barbarian enemy,
was not the Japanese or the Communist or the
Other but the primitive, the mindless, the
fanatic, the slaver without equitable law, even-
handed justice, conscientious science and pain-
staking art, without decency and mutuality and,
yes, fraternity, liberté egalité fraternité—

All that neatly summarized in the unspoken
words "On est bien dans la merde" while this
warlock from a nightmare leveled the crossbow
and, eyes flashing, teeth happily bared, sent a
bolt through his heart. Yang Yu-lin felt a
smashing blow, a minor pain, saw his enemy
through a pink haze, glimpsed a chalet; the red
shutters flew open and Florence beckoned to him
as his heart broke a second time.

Jum-aw owned four clips of five shots each and
a leather bag of individual cartridges. He was a
hunter, so shot sparingly; even so, in the first
minutes he enjoyed himself and wiped out the
shame of his and Green Wood's encounter with
the bandits. He was sure that he had killed two of
the Wild Wa and he began to feel heroic. This was
a holding action; he was waiting for the Shan to
return and help him. He heard firing to the east
and decided that the Shan had joined battle with

another force of Wild Wa. He rammed home another clip, aimed and fired. Chung's daughters, behind him, exclaimed.

Olevskoy and his men had spent two or three wars perfecting rearguard actions. As they struggled into Red Bullock Pass they kept the Shan at bay, leapfrogging men and machine guns along the trail and sweeping both flanks with heavy fire. The hillsides above were fatal, and they took losses. They killed but took more losses. They abandoned a machine gun. They could not disengage. Behind them were some Shan and then possibly the Wild Wa. There was no going back. But there was no going forward either.

Major Ho was almost merry. He had no choice! There was nothing to decide!

He fired, and bellowed like a bull, still alive, still alive, and fired again.

Naung made one irresolute effort to break through the Chinese lines from the east, but quickly disengaged. No Wild Wa had been flushed, and the Chinese were firing in all directions. The machine guns were murderous. "We cannot force the pass," he shouted. "Over the ridge and be quick!" He left a squad to seal off the pass, sent Taw-bi alone to the Roost to watch the road, and then he ran, ran until his chest hurt, toward the Common Field and Loi-mae and Lola.

The Wild Wa kept up a steady slow fire, advancing from the House of the Dead toward the Common Field. Their bolts were fashioned of hard metals smelted from crude ore or acquired

by barter; there was not always time to recover
them; and as they were heavy, ammunition was
limited. They had scarcely more old cartridges
than old rifles. At hand-to-hand work their
curved knives—the long ones, almost swords—
were deadly, sharper than blades of tiger grass,
and sharp on both edges.

They darted toward the Common Field in
relays, a line to fire while another line advanced,
the second line then pausing to fire while the
first line advanced.

The women and children of Pawlu, with the
boy Jum-aw and the toothless home guard of
ancients, stood their ground. The livestock were
out of control and plunging against their tethers.
Half the beasts had fled. Cha and Ang-ang were
releasing the others; this would be no siege,
requiring supplies, but a sharp battle quickly
over. Loi-mae prayed for Lola. Chung prayed for
Mong. Jum-aw took his time, a veteran now, and
dealt death to his cousins the Wild Wa. "We shall
survive," Za-kho chanted to his people. "It is the
last lakh of years and we Shan shall endure to the
end." The old men flashed out the first rank, and
seemed to lose their years; if die they must, the
would die like Shan, and not like flies in autumn.

Once more the Wild Wa paused, knelt, and
loosed a volley of bolts and bullets. A random
bolt tore through Loi-mae's cheek, ripping away
half her mouth and breaking the opposite cheekbone; she shrieked and choked on her blood, and
Chung ministered to her. Lola screamed and
clutched at her dagger. Where were the men?
Where was Green Wood, where was Naung? Per-

haps Naung had been killed! Perhaps they were all to be killed! Her tears gushed, but she turned to face the onslaught. She drew her dagger. Why, these savages were hardly taller than she!

Olevskoy raced in from the pass, spurring his pony ruthlessly, flying along the fringes of the massed villagers, who could not know whether he was friend or enemy. His men were dying. He had not seen Major Ho for some time; how much time, he could not tell; in a battle time sped, slowed, lost meaning. "The general!" he cried. "Where is the general?" One of these dolts must speak Chinese. He reined in hard before an old man with an older rifle. The man shrank away. With two fingers Olevskoy gave himself slanted eyes, and parodied a clown's grin. The Shan understood, and for an insane moment cackled laughter; he gestured. The insanity was contagious; Olevskoy said, "Thank you," as he wheeled to gallop off.

He saw small naked savages at the far end of the Common Field. So these were the Wild Wa! He ignored them. He skirted the Common Field and dashed south to the House of the Dead. He hauled his pony to a racking halt, sprang to earth and strode through the open wall. He did not see General Yang immediately. He saw two footlockers. He then saw a body lying between them. He recognized Yang's uniform and knelt. Yang was dead; the famous grin was frozen. "So he had time to smile," Olevskoy said. "I liked him after all." A stab of grief perplexed him.

He saw the keys on the necklace. He set down his carbine and tugged the necklace over the

general's head. The bloody keys were slick, and
the locks opened obligingly. Olevskoy tore open
boxes, tore away wrappings.

He saw a few bones. One was a skull. One was
an obvious leg bone.

His grief soured, and became confused dismay.
"In the name of God the Father," he cried in
Russian, "ancestor worship!"

He fled. He sprang back upon his pony and
headed for the people of Pawlu.

The Wild Wa were at their last gasp now, least
effective in an open field, their supply of bolts
dwindling, their dead warning them. They had
approached the edge of the stubborn mass and
made random carnage, chiefly maiming women,
but their momentum was spent and it was time
to melt away. When the Shan were distracted by
a Chinese irruption across the field, Thuan-yi
gave the leopard's cry, and paused to see his men
disengage, and escape southward. It was then
that a girl, not yet a woman, picked up a dah
almost as long as she was tall and hurled herself
toward him.

Thuan-yi took time for a laugh, admiring this
little one, and darted toward her, drawing his
long knife from his breechclout. He saw her eyes
grow huge with fear, yet she raised the dah.
Again he admired her. With his long knife he
chopped at the dah, and sent it spinning. Still
laughing, he rushed at her, grasped her by the
waist and slung her over his shoulder. He
whirled to dash for the cover of the little open
house where the Chinese lay dead; and when he
saw the albino racing toward him, the albino who

was not a Shan, he too felt a flash of terror.

Olevskoy scorned these animals; if they could kill him, then life was of little value. But he saw one of them disarm the girl, and recognized her, that very face, saw him disarm her and fling her high. He had no choice, and said in Russian, "Even the devil grows old. Imagine doing something *good*."

Thuan-yi let the girl fall and scuttled away, string bag swishing against his thigh. The albino thundered past, toward the girl, and Thuan-yi offered thanks. Many of his friends had died today; he had seen them die. But he would not die. He was happy. He sprinted toward the little open house. There were rites to be observed; there was a purpose to this day.

Olevskoy let the Wild Wa scoot away, and swooped down on the girl, plucking her from the turf with the zest of a circus Cossack snatching a kerchief from the grass. He dumped her across the pony's withers. A hand tugged hard at his sleeve, a hand not hers. He saw that a spent bolt had torn the khaki and still dangled. Olevskoy's luck: not a scratch. These little buggers were still firing, were they! He reined in, momentarily uncertain. The crackle of gunfire decided him, and he wasted no more time, but bore off to the south. When he was away from the village he angled sharply east, toward the avenue to freedom, Siam, the luxuries that life had always owed him, cities, servants, polo, champagne—all at the end of that dusty road on the China-Burma border. The girl was in shock, or unconscious.

Naung and his men came down from the north inside the pass, Kin-tan and his men came up from the south, all scrambling down the hillsides like goats, and caught the Chinese well in time, from both flanks. The Chinese, who had believed since the first shot that they were the victims of a ruse, a betrayal, expected no quarter and fought back hard and snarling. Beside Wan a running Kin-tan fell as old Phe-win had fallen; the earth seemed to tremble. Wan cried out in bitter sorrow. Sergeant Chang died at his machine gun, struck by half a ten of slugs in half a ten of seconds. No one cried out in bitter sorrow. Chinese lay strewn from Red Bullock Pass to the Common Field. Shan too. No one ever knew whether a Chinese or two had escaped, fleeing into the forest, crawling north, holing up and moving on.

The Shan forced the main body of Chinese back into the pass, where more Shan waited. A few Chinese actually reached the Common Field and were killed by the women and the old men. Za-kho had steeled himself but was not required to kill; women and children did it for him. Jum-aw killed anyone not a Shan, toward the end; he lost count, but when it was over, had four cartridges left for some thirty-five.

Greenwood too had killed Chinese soldiers. He had not wanted to do that. One of his best friends was a Chinese soldier. He was now seeing double. He was not soldiering properly. His left arm gave him great pain. He was staggering

through the forest and his submachine gun
would present problems. It could not be con-
trolled with one hand. The muzzle bucked immediately and higher throughout the burst. He
recalled with joyous nostalgia the old British
drum magazines. With those the gun bucked not
only upward but sharply to the right. The box
magazine was a distinct improvement.

He heard a drum roll of gunfire. The British
Sten gun bucked so high so quickly that a soldier
had to lay the left hand on the barrel and push
down hard while firing. This technical information made him happier. It was specific. The
mind could grasp it.

He halted, and concentrated. He had been
injured. He had banged his head, or something
had gouged it; his fingers came away bloody. He
was confused but not so confused that he did not
know that he was confused. That struck him
funny.

An abrupt flood of good cheer eased his pain.
He had been wounded. And some residual illusion, some soldier's false optimism, told him that
in battle men were wounded or killed but not
both.

Thaun-yi had retreated from Olevskoy and
called two of his lingering men to join him. They
had converged on the deserted House of the Dead
and briskly detached Yang Yu-lin's head, which
they dropped into Thuan-yi's string bag. They
then inspected the footlockers.

At the sight of the bones they paused, and knew
awe. Thuan-yi poked at the skull with one finger.
The heavens did not fall. Working quickly, they

made a heap of the larger bones. Thuan-yi unknotted his black loincloth and stood naked.
They wrapped these larger bones in the
loincloth. The oldest of them, tired after this
day's work, then gathered up the cloth and loped
off toward the forest and home. In a string bag
slung over his shoulder, two heads bobbed
against his haunch. Thuan-yi saw that one of
them seemed to be smiling broadly, and impishly
he returned the grin.

The battle ebbed and ended. Corpses lay like
fallen game; there were dead men in the brush,
paddy, tobacco and leafy lanes. Most wore
Chinese uniforms. Just west of Red Bullock Pass,
Naung found a heap of sticks that had been
Mong. He bore the body back to the Common
Field. Among the wailing villagers, among the
milling survivors, stupefied children, groaning
old women, now placid livestock, Chung had
been tending Loi-mae. The bolt had torn away
several teeth and propelled the cheekbone upward, so that Loi-mae's left eye protruded.
Chung had been stanching the flow of blood from
the torn cheek and teasing the cheekbone down;
slowly the eye resumed its proper place. Chung
asked, "Can you see?" but Loi-mae was unconscious. Chung's eldest daughter wailed. "Be
quiet," Chung told her, but then all her
daughters wailed, and she knew.
Naung set Mong's body at her feet and knelt as
if to beg forgiveness. He saw Loi-mae then, and
screamed in anguish. His tears fell on the beloved face. He laid his head between her breasts
and tenderly embraced her inert body. Chung

pulled him away and returned to her healing. Naung squatted and wept. When Wan came to see, Naung glared through the tears, and his eyes spoke. Reluctantly, Wan nodded.

All about the Common Field, old men were dispatching wounded beasts. The wounded Chinese had already been dispatched.

Greenwood was once more under arms against the Wild Wa. This was now clear to him. He was perturbed also by the certainty that he had, after all, done harm. For moments on end he enjoyed unusual lucidity, and then waves of guilt drowned him and he was not sure of anything. He was now on North Slope, traveling eastward toward the road. He did not know why. The firing had ceased. He decided to face about and return to the village.

He scanned the slopes with care. He detected motion, and concentrated.

It was that fellow. That damned Russian. He had forgotten the Russian. The Russian was low on South Slope and seemed to be lugging a Wild Wa. Imagine! The Russian was bound for the road and was carrying with him a Wild Wa! Well, that was odd. With lively good humor Greenwood now recalled his binoculars, and extracted them from their leather case.

Thuan-yi had sent the others back with his crossbow and a good harvest, and now lay alone at the Roost, where he could look westward to the faint smoky drift above the Shan's great field, or eastward to the road, or downward to the field of poppies. He was still excited. His eyes glistened and his fingers twitched. He was famished. His maleness swelled rudely against the leafy earth.

Naked, he carried only his long knife. It would suffice. Often he had hunted with the knife alone, and neither crossbow nor firearm.

It was, as all forest creatures knew, motion and not shape that caught the eye. He bided his time, and did not stir. After some while—the sun was clear of all hills now, warmed him, married him to the earth he lay on—he was rewarded.

He saw one of the albinos, and his heart beat faster.

"She will do now," Chung said, and sank back onto the bloody ground. Her daughters ringed her; the boys sat apart, mute and stolid. Loi-mae was unconscious but stirred and groaned. A foul-smelling compress of ginseng and papaya meat lacquered half her face. Chung's dull grief broke; tears streaked her cheeks, and she sobbed wildly.

Naung said, "The Sawbwa is dead."

"My Mong is dead."

"Let me stay," Jum-aw asked, and folded Chung in his arms.

"If you like."

Lamentations rose and fell all across the field, repeatedly, as if here were many hundreds and not only a few score. The sun was not halfway to noon, but survivors were huddled or wandering as at dusk.

"We killed two tens of the Wild Wa," Wan said, "and perhaps more. Some must have slunk home to die."

"We would give them all for Mong, or Kin-tan

or Ko-yang. Who is with Cha?"

"Her old mother."

Loi-mae whimpered. Naung knelt. Fearing to touch her mutilated face, he took her hand. "Bring Lola," he said. "Let her see what her father has done."

"You were right," Wan said. "No more outsiders."

"Where is he?" Chung asked.

They looked about them. It was a field of families, each with its dead and wounded, none ready yet for the fearful isolation of a house. Smoke was rising, and that was a comfort, a familiar and homey tang, rich and friendly in the nostrils.

"There will be much cremation," Naung said. "Green Wood too, perhaps. Has no one seen him?"

Jum-aw asked, "Shall I seek him out?"

"Look a little at the House of the Dead," Wan told the young man, "where those cursed bones are." To Naung he said, "I saw him at Red Bullock Pass. He was fighting hard."

"He may be with the general," Naung said. "Where is Lola?"

Wan asked, "Chung, where is Lola?"

"She was with us. And then she was not."

All stood now and peered about. "Shwe! Have you seen Lola?"

Shwe was holding a clout to a wound in his side. "No. Lola!"

From family to family the question sped.

Naung cried out again.

"A squad, quickly," Wan said.

Chung stooped. "Yes. Here. Do what you

must." She tossed the mitraillette to Naung.

Za-kho called out, and approached in his mincing trot. "The one with yellow hair! On a pony!"

"Green Wood?"

Naung said, "No one here calls Green Wood 'the one with yellow hair' "

"The Russian," Za-kho gasped. "The Sawbwa's Russian friend." He clutched at Naung's arm as if for support. "He saved her! She ran forth to meet the Wild Wa and he galloped up from the House of the Dead and he plunged into the mass and he carried her to safety!"

Now Jum-aw was running toward them. "The general! The Chinese general!"

"What of him?"

The villagers were gathering and making an effort to comprehend. A child laughed.

"Dead!" Jum-aw cried. "Headless! And the boxes open!"

"By the gods!" Naung roared. "Green Wood and that Russian between them! The old bones and Lola!"

"But why?" Chung stood bewildered. "And where?"

"East," Za-kho said. "With my own eyes I saw this. The Russian rode south and then east."

"To the road? To the Wild Wa? Ponies! Round up half a ten, and quickly. More: two squads. One east to the road, one south and then east. Taw-bi, run to my house. Perhaps she fled there. Hurry, man!"

Naung sprang to his pony. At the gallop he unslung his mitraillette and inserted a fresh clip.

Greenwood lumbered through the forest, his heart laboring and his arm swinging erratically. He would intercept them in East Poppy Field. He wanted not to think, only to run, but a persistent, mild delirium animated his mind. He would kill the Russian and restore Lola to Loi-mae. He tried hard to think only of Loi-mae and Lola, to picture their glad reunion, but his memory and imagination were racing. If he had time to set himself prone, then the tommy gun. He who lives by the tamigan dies by the tamigan. He who lives, dies. Otherwise it must be the pistol. The winner calls upon his last reserves. War is the continuation of personal foolishness by other means. Von Greenwood.

He reeled and lurched, but pushed on. The battle must be over, the village safe; he heard a hoopoe, he heard a toktay. A huge black bee buzzed him and shot away. The morning was sunny and peaceful. Naung: he would have to deal with Naung. He would not make an offering of Lola, but somehow he must win forgiveness. Christ, it was a long way to East Poppy Field!

Thuan-yi was beside himself. Here was *both* these grotesque outlanders, *and* the brave little girl! They would meet at the field of poppies. Clutching his knife, he flowed down the slope.

Naung lashed at his pony and galloped into the pass. Wan and the others would come shortly, but they did not matter. The road: only let him reach the road alive. Let the Wild Wa be once more at home, he prayed. Let it be me and these Big Noses.

To his surprise, he found that he was still weeping.

Olevskoy had plunged into the forest and made the best time he could on a weary, nervous pony. He was unsure of his way, and the trail meandered. He was not certain that these little people had dispersed. But he was unhurt and, in truth, not even tired. Before him the little girl strained to rise. "Ça va," he said. French was the language of love. His fingertips smoothed her hair, the color of rich amber, the texture of soft silk. "Probably a charming little girl," he said. He might release her. Even the devil grows old.

His pony was walking through a little swale, barely more than a gully. As they came into the open he saw by the sun that they were traveling northeast, and then he knew where they were—they had cut through the southern slopes and back into Pawlu's valley; they were somewhere near the south slope of the poppy field, traveling toward the trampled poppy blooms. The little girl spoke. She said something in her own language and then—so odd on her lips, in this setting!—"Greenwood." As her father might have said it. "Yes, yes," he replied. "Greenwood. Did he teach you English?"

"Greenwood," she said, and wriggled her way to a sitting position on the withers. They were face-to-face, knee-to-knee. "Oh my God," he said in Russian, amazed by a feathery touch of lust. "You *are* a beauty." Her lips were full and moist; she was apparently unafraid.

They were on the fringes of the poppy field. Crushed white blossoms were strewn in their path, as if for a king and a queen. The girl spoke again. Their eyes met and held. He looked deeply and with true curiosity into hers. He liked her. Her breath was spicy. "Lust is a form of love," he said, still in Russian, "and perhaps the highest form. Dying for love is recommended by romantics but seems to defeat the purpose of the exercise."

"Greenwood," she said. "Greenwood." They were advancing among the trodden poppies; brave survivors stood tall; some swayed and seemed to bow at their passage. He heard birdcalls. The sun shone full on his face, the day promised fair. He glanced up at the clear blue sky. Birds of prey circled, or carrion birds, local vultures.

Thuan-yi too had reached the field of poppies. He too was truly curious, almost overwhelmed. Clutching his long knife, he scurried from tree to tree just within the forest. He had even forgotten that he was hungry.

Greenwood emerged at the foot of North Slope, breathing hard, a stitch in his side now and his sweaty shirt itching, apart from his other woes. The sun was high and dazzling. Above him kites wheeled. He saw Olevskoy and Lola, a hundred paces from him, almost hidden by the slope of the field; they were in a little dell, and he could not see the pony's legs. On his best day he could hit nothing at that range, not with a submachine gun. He sucked air greedily.

Olevskoy had brought the pony to a halt.

Greenwood thought he could hear the Russian's voice.

Naung burst out of the pass and saw Green Wood immediately. The foreigner was alone and winded. No Lola. Naung slipped off his pony, dodged into the brush at the foot of North Slope, and worked his way rapidly into the forest to a point uphill from Green Wood and behind him. He kept before him the vision of Loi-mae's ruined face. He padded quickly but with care through the woods. At a tiny gap he saw Green Wood again. Green Wood was slinging the tamigan and preparing to flee. In Naung's heart fury renewed itself, and doubly; his eyes stung with rage, his mouth trembled, he could not swallow. He knew his enemy. Since the year they had taught him to call 1939 he had known his enemy; and now the enemy stood before him like a panting old gyi after a long chase. Green Wood! Everybody's hero!

Olevskoy had paused for good reasons. The road now seemed a danger. Who knew where these little brutes lurked, or whether they had in truth withdrawn to their fastnesses? What lay down that road—another tribe of little brutes? Would the Shan forgive him if he returned the girl safe and sound? So much for lust. It seemed there was more to life than lust. His pony shifted restlessly, and shuffled forward.

Greenwood saw Olevskoy start off again, toward the road, and knew he must prevent them. He drew a deep breath, started forward, and shouted, "Olevskoy!"

Olevskoy slewed about on his pony's bare back, flipping open the holster and drawing the .45 in a swift, practiced motion. Lola gritted her teeth, drew her dagger, grasped the haft in both fists and stabbed him underhand, the blade slicing into his stomach from the side and rising. She ripped upward, as when gutting hares. Breathless, she waited.

Astonished, Olevskoy turned back to her. He knew precisely what had happened but did not mind. What an extraordinary child! The pistol fell from his hand, and his vision dimmed. He went on by instinct—Russian's? prince's? soldier's? man's? His instinct instructed him to bestow life if he must yield his own; to bless if he was damned. A faltering hand made the sign of the cross over her, and dropped nerveless to her hair. His cap fell; his lank flaxen hair swung. Love, he thought, I missed it, always.

It is not easy to die well when you have lived badly. He swayed toward her mouth, one last kiss; but only spewed blood.

Greenwood's shout was still echoing when he heard Naung's voice. "Green Wood!"

He turned gratefully, here was help, and he had just begun to speak, to say "Naung," when he saw the set lines of Naung's square face in the gloom of the forest, and the rising mitraillette. He raised a hand and cried desperately, "No!" It is not easy to die badly when you have lived well. And then sheer shock stilled him. He had time to

believe that he would be wounded but in the end
all would be well; he would wake tomorrow with
Loi-mae bathing his brow and Naung apologetic.
He thought he could see the bullets. He heard
nothing.

Lola heard the gunfire, and saw Greenwood
fall. She stifled a shriek—More Chinese! She slid
off the pony and scampered into forest.

For a moment she thought it was Weng-aw, he
was so small.

Naung and his men abandoned caution. With
Pawlu's survivors they beat the forest, slopes,
fields; they searched every house; they rode
every pace of Pawlu's perimeter and even pushed
beyond, firing and shouting, "Lola! Lola!" They
squinted upward into the trees, they walked the
stream, they sounded the paddy, they ferreted in
stands of poppy. In the end they abandoned
speech too, and would not look at one another.

In late afternoon Naung, his heart still swollen
and raw, raced back to East Poppy Field for one
more sweep, dismounting then, parting the denser clumps. He mopped his scalding eyes to peer
for sign. He paused to empty a full clip into
Greenwood. The taste of revenge was vinegar
now. He continued along the edge of East Poppy
Field and in time he spotted the other pony,
peacefully cropping poppies, and beside it the
Russian's body. He emptied his fresh clip into
the Russian's back. By then Wan and Shwe and
Taw-bi had come into the field. No one spoke.
They rode on, well apart, each covering a sector,
and they emerged at the roadside. Boldly, as if it

could not matter now what became of them, they sought sign again in the dusty road. They saw only what they had known they would see: the imprint of many little Wild Wa feet crossing and recrossing.

Naung led them back to the Russian. They took his head cleanly. He led them then to Green Wood. They took his head cleanly. They rode to the nearest cages, undid the hempen knots, released the balance beams and set each head in a separate cage, tossing the old heads into the brush at the side of the road.

Next day, when they came to loot the Chinese camp, the heads had vanished.

12

Ranga

And then the headman of Ranga turns to another precious relic. This too is the head of a wise man, who came from a far place. Its hair and eyes are also light. Old Thuan-yi the warrior took his head also, in fierce combat as he tells the tale; each head with one stroke.

And when the headman turns to the bones. For the bones a platform has been built of oak; and a stout tanned hide shelters the bones from wind and rain. The bones are of several small people, perhaps children, perhaps the smaller forefathers that figure in ceremonial tales of the ancient hot green land to the south. Thirty years ago, when these bones were taken, the headman declared that they were old indeed, older than any bones yet seen by him, older than any head yet taken by the Wild Wa; perhaps even older than the headman's grandfather's grandfather. In those days men and gods roamed the earth together, and copulated freely; these bones are surely the relics of living gods.

Thuan-yi's woman will not walk the avenue between the double line of trees. She will pause before the platform of bones at the northern end, and often she prays there, or meditates. She will not look upon the two heads or even pass near them. She is a somber woman of some forty monsoons, taken in the War of the Bones, a stranger to the Wild Wa and of unknown family, too golden for a Shan. She was owned by each man of Ranga in turn, and Thuan-yi then took her to wife. She has borne him five sons and three daughters, and among them there is an occasional lock of wavy hair the color of tobacco. Because of her mysterious birth, her tawny complexion and her habitual silence, Ranga deems her holy, and no man spoke against it when she called her first son Green Wood.

ABOUT THE AUTHOR

Stephen Becker was educated at Harvard, in Peking after the war, and in Paris, where he lived for four years. Among his ten novels are *A Convenant with Death* and *The Chinese Bandit*; among his translations, *The Last of the Just* and Malraux's *The Conquerors*. He has also published biography, history, short stories, magazine articles, reviews and columns; has lectured in China, France, Alaska and Mexico, and taught at various universities. Since 1979 he has lived in the West Indies.